Mark Furness is an award-nominated writer of thrillers, mysteries and black comedy crime.

A former journalist and foreign correspondent who lived and worked in the USA, the UK, Australia, and East Asia, Furness's stories often feature journalists. He has also been a corporate spin doctor and political lobbyist. He claims his novel, *Under Eden*, is a work of fiction. The good characters are based on real people. The black hats are purely fictional. Truly.

Mark is an Australian who is based in Sydney where he lives with his wife and two young adult children.

UNDER EDEN

Complete Edition
Parts 1-3

Mark Furness

First published by Liquorice Light Publishing in 2018
This edition published in 2019 by Liquorice Light Publishing

Under Eden

POD: 9780648529903

Cover design by Red Tally Studios

Publishing services provided by Critical Mass
www.critmassconsulting.com

UNDER EDEN

Part 1

I

BLACK CIRCLES

I'VE DONE a nice job of wrapping Mr Browning in cling-film, but it's not workmanship I intend to show off. I do a three-sixty-degree turn, scanning the forest that surrounds the paddock. The only witness I can see is a red-bellied black snake which slides out of sight over the far edge of the dam beside me. I get the feeling the snake sensed things coming, but it clearly wasn't a talker.

When I stab the blade of my shovel into the earth to bury Mr Browning, the toots of an old-style police whistle send my heart clattering like a boxer's speed bag.

I dig my phone from my jeans pocket, vowing to get rid of my son's ringtone gift before it kills me, and spit out the smouldering tail of a pretty good joint of cannabis. It's my boss on the line.

"What's up?" I try to sound sharp.

"Where are you?" says Jack Darling.

"Moon Hill."

"You alone?"

I know he's angling at workplace health and safety issues, but he reminds me I'm missing my kids. And Claire.

"I needed peace and quiet to work on the yarn. I'm nearly finished."

"Listen to me, Gar, you …"

"Jack? … Jack?"

Reception is as patchy as a granny quilt at the southern end of the Blue Mountains, west of Sydney. My signal is lost. Jack is in China. I guess he wants me back in the city office of *The Citizen* to co-ordinate the exposé we are writing about a network of thieves we've code-named Ebola. My laptop and boxes of research are in my four-wheel-drive at camp on top of the hill. But I have to finish the job with Mr Browning first. He doesn't need a big hole. He's a handgun I had the brainwave of naming after its maker when my father left it to me, along with a note. After seeing that slithering red-belly, my old man's words are blazing upon my retinas like neon lights: '*Dear Gar - I still sometimes wonder if a bullet in the head might be in order, but whose head would I choose? Why stop at one? Only kidding. I'd rather shove a snake in your bed. Metaphorically speaking. So you'll know what I'm dealing with.*'

I try to switch off my father's brilliance and place Mr Browning in a cake tin which I drop in the hole and backfill, topping it with a divot of grass that could double as a toupee for a bald man with a sense of humour, or mental health issues. I resist the urge to try it on and trudge uphill towards my camp.

After crossing a gravel road, I walk the shadow of an overhead wire attached to a timber pole behind me. The wire stretches uphill to the centre of my camp, where it's tied to a giant pine tree. I'm impressed the flying fox I built for Hugo is still intact. We laughed ourselves to tears the last time we rode it, until he threw me a question that stirs inside me now like a restless sleeper.

"Remember when Mum flew down hanging by one hand like a monkey?"

"Yeah. She was strong," I said, smiling, thinking I had the quizmaster covered.

"Then why did she die?"

Responses had collided inside my skull like crazed atoms: an unlucky roll of the dice; predisposed genetics; the chemotherapy was too late.

"She's still in here," I said eventually, placing my palm upon his skinny, trembling chest, trying to absorb his agony.

"I hate life," he said, pushing me away. He grabbed the handlebar of the fox and leapt from the tree before I could catch him.

*

I take a breather leaning on the handle of my shovel next to a handful of steel pegs banged into a pentagon shape around a patch of grass. The pegs are linked by blue-and-white-checked police tape, marking the spot where a man fell dead a few weeks ago. I was in London at the time. His passing put me in a relieved state of mind, given he was a psychopath who was on the payroll of Ebola. But right now I'm as relaxed as a drunk without a drink because the homicide squad wants to have another poke around on site, with me in tow. They're due in the morning. The deceased took a rifle bullet in the head from long range, not a shot from the unlicensed, nine-millimetre semi-automatic I'd just buried. But I'm due in court next week on charges of threats to kill the psycho's employer, so burying Mr Browning is a no-brainer as far as my defence strategy is concerned.

On the clearing atop the hill, I suck hard to extract oxygen from the thin air and climb a handful of steps to a timber deck

I've built around the old pine's trunk. A black-painted ring on the deck marks the spot where I get the best of the mostly rotten phone reception. Right now it's as rotten as it gets.

I pocket my phone and stroke the pine's bark, which is dark as chocolate and rutted like croc skin. The tree's like me, the offspring of seed transported from Great Britain with convict settlers who felled the native forest and the local people who'd been caretakers here for over fifty thousand years. The new landscapers grew grass to feed sheep, but their children retreated to towns and cities a few decades ago, leaving the place to tree huggers and star gazers.

The pine's limbs cradle a timber-clad room inside which I've installed a couple of single beds. The sheets need changing. A window faces east to the mountains via an opening I've chain-sawed through the branches. They need a trim. I tug on a rope and drag down to the deck a folding ladder that connects to a trapdoor in the cabin floor. But I'm called by hunger and thirst, and cross to the opposite side of the deck into a ground-level cabin clad with corrugated iron. Through an open window of my kitchen-cum-sitting room, I hear an engine revving in the forest, followed by a faint squeal that sounds like a child in pain. It's probably pig hunters cornering a terrified animal, but it makes me feel for Mr Browning like an amputated limb. I strap my hunting knife to my belt and decide to drive to town and phone Jack after I've eaten here. Our unfinished call gnaws at me. I need to call Hugo and Alice too, to check that they're still safe. I decide to fry a steak in a pan on the gas cooker. When it's sizzling, I open a bottle of red and quaff a glass.

In twilight, I light a fire inside a ring of rocks beside the deck and settle into a camp chair, eating and drinking by a crackling orange blaze. Above me, a slit-eyed moon floats beside the Milky Way. Faces form in the flames of my *bush telly* ... white lights interrupt the show, criss-crossing my body from inside the forest.

"Hughie?" I call, squinting, hoping it's my neighbour from the next hilltop south. The torch bearers approach under the cover of smoke windswept from my fire. They don't run, so nor do I. Three dark figures close me inside a triangle.

Black stocking masks over their heads are holed at the eyes and mouths. One points a shotgun at me. Single barrel, lever action. The smallest probes my camp with a flashlight. The third figure, more gorilla-shaped than man, tugs a chain and drags someone into the firelight.

It's a lean woman with a big ball of dark hair, dressed in a white tee-shirt and body-hugging black pants. Her face is scratched and filthy and her arms are buckled behind her back. A band of silver tape is wrapped around her head, covering her ears and mouth. Mucous bubbles under her nostrils. I recognise Sandy Wallace.

The last time I clapped eyes on her she'd knocked on my front door at home in the city, smiling like she meant it, wearing most of a black cocktail dress, droplets running down her angular cheeks from a dash through the rain. Now, the droplets are tears, or look like them. Her eyes lock on mine, their whites glistening, almost popping from their sockets. The shotgun spits a fireball into the sky. The percussion hurts my ears and draws my full attention. The gorilla-man sticks a finger inside the tape near Sandy's mouth and rips it down. I wait for the theatrics.

"Gar," Sandy blurts, gulping in air, "they want ... want your stuff on Baker. Just give them ... tell them what you have. Then we'll be okay. All okay."

If she's acting, it's A-grade. I eye a run-line into the forest.

"What stuff?" I say.

"Do you think we are here for a pantomime, Mr Hart?" The smallest figure has a female voice with an Afrikaans twang. She turns her light on Sandy, whose handler takes his cue and pushes Sandy to her knees. She yelps as he straddles her and squeezes his knees into her ribs. He grabs a fistful of her frizzy hair, jerks her head back, and puts the point of his knife to her windpipe. A hideous squeal rips from inside the forest.

A black pig staggers out into the mongrel light of the fire and flashlights. It is as tall as a man's thighs with pale tusks curling either side of its snotty snout. Gone mad from a poison bait, I guess. It stumbles forward, like a drunk looking for a fight. The man trapping Sandy roars a strange warrior cry, dropping her chain as he points his knife at the pig. *Click-clack. Bam!* The shotgun strike sends the pig shrieking and dragging its shredded hind towards the trees. Another click-clack. *Bam!*

If the second blast was meant for the pig, the shooter was a shithouse shot. Not even close. I hear the tinkling of chain and turn towards the sound. Sandy is running towards the trees. *Click-clack!*

Ms Afrikaans seems to yawn. Moving like a shadow, she gives the shooter a thumbs-down ...

The blast hits Sandy's back, somewhere around the neck. She glides, briefly airborne, arms swinging, her body tumbling to earth near the edge of the forest. I'm frozen. Sandy murmurs.

The shooter steps coolly towards her, levering another cartridge into the chamber as he goes. Arriving at her side, he pulls a flashlight from a pouch on his belt and examines his work. It doesn't take long. He slots the light back in its pouch and gives Ms Afrikaans a thumbs-up as he strolls back to us. I choke on some lumps that rise in my gullet. I feel like I've dropped LSD. Fuck the consequences: I pick my line into the forest, trying to hide the thoughts from my face. *Whack*! Yellow and blue flashes blur my vision. The shotgun carrier lifts the barrel, ready to crack me again.

"We have your family, Mr Hart. We will trade," says the woman.

I picture Alice and Hugo. Does she know where I've put them into hiding? Does she really have them? I hear my old psychologist: 'You've just got fear of fear, Gar. Think your way out.'

"What … what do you want … about Baker?"

"All you have," she says.

I have no idea of the current whereabouts of John K. Baker. But I know what they want from me: my knowledge. He owns real estate, cash, gold bullion, shares, boats, businesses. Football teams, for god's sake. Baker holds the keys to an international network of stolen wealth which *The Citizen* has discovered - but not yet exposed.

"I have a laptop. In my treehouse. Everything's in there." I point to the ladder to the treetop cabin.

"Kojo," the woman says to gorilla-man. "Get it."

"It's in the ceiling," I say. "A hidden panel."

"Follow him," she orders Kojo.

Climbing the ladder gives me seconds to think. Inside the cabin, the trapdoor is leaning on its hinges against a wall. It's dark. I ignore the flashlight on the bedside table.

"I need a torch," I tell Kojo, who is standing on the ladder below me.

"Light," Kojo yells down. Only his head and shoulders are inside the room. When he reaches for the torch, I snatch the pick handle I keep under the bed - the one I thought I'd never need because my world would never get this crazy - and smash it on his stockinged skull with a double-handed grip. His head falls forward, his nose cracking on the rim of the hatch, but he catches the rim's perimeter with his hands. His head starts rising. I smash his skull, again and again. It's like hitting a rock that won't break. I work on his hands. He crashes to the deck. I'm shaking, slow to move. The nose of the shotgun rises through the hatch hole, then the pale fingers of an unbroken hand fold over the rim. I slam the trapdoor down. A severed fingertip twitches on the floor. I hear shrieking. I bolt the trapdoor.

I fling the cabin window open, climb through the frame, and haul myself on to the corrugated iron roof by grasping a branch. *Vroom*! Shotgun pellets wallop the cabin's walls.

The woman yells: "Don't be a fool, Gar. You'll kill your children this way."

My phone is in my pocket. I'm close to the black-painted ring on the deck. I speed dial Ireland. Four rings.

"Hi, Dad," says Alice.

"You okay?" I hiss.

"Yeah – why?"

"Get Hugo. Get Nanna. Go to a police station. Now!"

"What's wrong?"

"Killers at Moon Hill. A woman's dead."

Flashlight beams strafe the space around me. My signal is lost.

I use the moonlight to walk a thin line of floorboards joined end-to-end through the tree. It takes me to the platform of the flying fox. The handlebar is hooked to a branch by the wire's tie-point to the tree. I release the bar and launch. Light beams cross my path. I brace for flak. A shotgun thunders. Nothing hits me. I'm riding fast, a few body lengths above the ground ... the wire whistles and whips. It snaps. I fall. A wet summer has made the open pasture thick, but there are sharp, man-sized boulders in the mix. I hit the grass feet first, let my body roll, find myself standing. No pain; nothing broken, nothing big enough to notice. A dog barks. I run. I see my feet thumping grass, arms flashing. I hear my breathing. My body is working by itself, letting my mind think ahead. I need to get to Mr Browning.

I cross a white-gravel road and roll under a barbed-wire fence. I sprint through a paddock of knee-high grass. *Pop*! A flare casts me in violet light. Near the lip of the dam, I fall low and slither over gravel and grass to where I think I buried the pistol.

On the hill above me, two white eyes, side by side, are moving. The car rolls down the road. A third white eye pops on. A dark figure stands on the back tray of the ute, probing the paddock with a spotlight. A dog bounces on the tray, barking, furious.

The flare drifts into the treetops and its light dies. I dig for Mr Browning with my hands. My fingernails scrape the metal box. I flip it open and rip Mr Browning from the wrap, slam the loaded magazine into the hand grip and release the safety. The spotlight sweeps the paddock. I wade into the dam, staying low, backing into tall reeds at the far edge. The spotlight catches my face. I shuffle left, then right, slowed by the muddy bottom, holding Mr Browning out of the water. The spotlight sticks to me.

A figure appears at the edge of the dam, side-lit by the spot beam from the ute, aiming a crossbow at me with one hand. His other, cloth-wrapped, restrains the snarling white dog on a rope. The animal leaps at me, swinging its arse in mid-air before thumping back to earth, desperate to break its tie. The dog's body is as thick as a tree stump, with bandy legs for speed and power.

"Get out of the water," calls the woman from the back of the ute, holding me in the spotlight, "or we let the dog go."

The dog doesn't wait. It breaks the man's weakened grip. The manic hunk of meat and teeth and electricity goes airborne, belly-flops, sinks, surfaces, churns towards me. I stand tall, grip Mr Browning with both hands and fire. The bullet smashes the dog's mouth. It keeps coming. I fire into the top of its head. It floats into me. I knee it away. Three bullets left by my count.

The woman is calling from the ute in a new language I don't understand. Instructions for the crossbow phantom, I guess. I aim at him, part-blinded by the spotlight. I think about his head and then focus on his chest because it's bigger. I squeeze: a burst of gold and white. The arrow and the bullet cross each other inside the flash. Searing cold flares inside my thigh, like I've been shot with ice.

My bullet should have hit him square in the breastplate. I can't see more than his outline. He staggers, drops on one knee. I fire again into his chest. He falls on his side, not backwards as I expect. I hope Mr Browning is powerful enough. The spotlight stays on me. I move from its glare. It doesn't follow me. A shadow jumps from the back of the ute.

I limp fast from the dam and push into trees beside the paddock, falling on my side behind a trunk. The ripped nerves in my thigh scream. I finger the arrow shaft: the tip is protruding from the back of my leg, the feather fletching in front.

"We will never stop coming for you, Gar," she calls, spraying light from her hand-held torch, scanning the edges of the paddock. "Come out now and save your children. Or be a coward."

I check my phone; the dam water has killed it. I lift my jumper at the neckline and bite it to help me do the job in silence. Using the heel of my hand, I punch the feather-end of the shaft into my leg and pull the arrowhead from behind.

It slides through, burning like yanked rope as I wrench the whole shaft out. I rub my fingers over the wounds and hold the fingers up to a shard of moonlight. There's not enough blood to suggest an artery is split. I take off my jacket and jumper and tie the jumper against my wounds using the sleeves, then limp into the forest, following the groove of a kangaroo track, careful not to tread on fallen branches and break the silence. I glance behind me, looking for pursuing light.

II

93 days earlier ...

ACCORDING to the café clock, I had an hour to wait for courtroom 7C to open in the building next door. I sipped a latte and returned to a newspaper story titled *Snow White and the Seven Dunces,* a moralising tale about some teenage boys and a girl who got rat-faced on one of their father's yachts and flashed their naked bums at ferry passengers on Sydney Harbour. One of the cleverest boys posted photos of the outing on Facebook, adding to evidence discovered by police upon the yacht that nostrils full of cocaine cut with laundry powder, and bellies full of vodka, are sure-fire sources of A-grade ideas.

What kept me reading was the fact that the boys attended the same illustrious school that had educated Henry East, who was due to appear shortly in 7C. Accompanying the ferry tale was a story noting that Henry, 26, was about to be sentenced for his guilty plea to using 'inside information' that he stole from his employer, a global investment bank, to profit from buying and selling shares in companies listed on the public stock market. He pocketed just over one million dollars – and faced up to ten years in prison.

What the newspaper didn't say was that Henry had more than his freedom and fine young body on the line. He had a few hundred million dollars waiting for him if he could survive this day and outlive his father. I wasn't putting my money on him achieving either when I read his body language as he walked into the café. After listening to his trial for days on end, I still didn't get why he'd risked so much for what amounted to pocket money for a human being born with his ancestral gifts. Simple greed didn't cut it for me.

Henry, who was on bail pending sentencing, towered over his lawyer, a squat man with a pimply, pink forehead framed by wispy fair hair. The man o' law sported a red necktie with its tongue swept back over the shoulder of his dark suit. I cupped a hand to my brow to make a visor as Henry and his swashbuckler passed me. They sat at my back, so absorbed in their tête-à-tête I doubt they'd have noticed if I was starkers. I looked in a wall mirror. Henry's face was in it.

He had a thick, dark mane framing a perfectly symmetrical face that was as pale as candle wax, inset with large brown eyes and offset by a long but not-protruding nose. He was cleverly dressed in an unfashionably roomy, single-breasted navy blue suit, white shirt and dull blue tie; it maintained the sensibly conservative image he'd aimed at the judge through-out his trial. I wondered if his wan complexion this morning was a ruse, a bit of make-up applied in the law chambers on legal advice before the walk to court, to squeeze any last juices of sympathy from the judge. But it seemed a bit late for that. Justice Tobias Tanner, who now waited for him next door, looked like he sucked lemons prior to every courtroom curtain rise that I had witnessed.

In the café, Henry's lawyer was perky as he ordered an espresso, and why wouldn't he be? Unlike his client, he knew that whatever happened in court, he would be sleeping at home this night on his king-sized mattress and fancy sheets.

"What if I go to prison?" hissed Henry.

Now in my game as a journalist, I only have a couple of rules when it comes to speaking the truth you'd rather hide. Rule number one: never do it within earshot of strangers. Rule number two: capitalise on people breaking rule one. I slipped my notepad and pen from my jacket pocket, kept my head down, and casually scribbled.

"You won't go to jail," said the lawyer. "You'll be fined at most."

"You can't guarantee that. They can come after me in there."

I circled 'they' in my notebook. Henry shuffled in his seat like a racehorse trapped in a barrier gate, like he could smell the testosterone-rich sweat of the men waiting for him inside the razor-wire fences of Silverwater Prison.

The lawyer's volume lifted: "Listen. We've agreed the strategy with your father. Whatever happens today, this ends it, Henry. Right?"

The lawyer, who was facing the café entrance, looked up past my right shoulder and went wide-eyed.

"Hello, Edgar," I heard behind my back. I turned around. Charles East was grinning like he'd found something nasty stuck to his shoe. He was more obviously horse-faced than his son, but then Charles's skin and bones had spent nearly seventy years succumbing to gravity and the waning reproductive capacity of his body cells.

"Good morning, Charles," I said, closing my notebook. I returned his grin with equal sincerity.

He had gone for a grey pinstripe suit, white shirt and royal blue tie. The grey leftovers of his hair were clipped tight against his narrow head and his irises were smoke-coloured and barely visible inside the watery whites of his pink-rimmed eyes. He had the mouldy air of a funeral director. I guessed that spectating the fruit of your loins being battered in court for days on end would do that.

The three of them wandered away whispering, Henry in the middle of the huddle. Charles glanced back at me and then poked his lawyer in the chest with a stiff finger. Henry's head and shoulders slumped. He looked like an overgrown toddler who'd been smacked. I felt sorry for him. I followed them.

As Henry waited on the footpath for the building's revolving door to meet him, he glanced at me. I got the feeling he wanted *my* help. I sensed a young man who had botched an escape plan. What he was running from, and where he had wanted to go, intrigued me. They entered the building, passed through a security checkpoint, and opened a door to a private room reserved for lawyers and their clients.

On my way up to 7C in the lift, a couple of male television reporters who were wearing corsets – their flesh-coloured, spandex belly-flatteners were visible through their white shirts when their jackets weren't buttoned up – explained to each other, and therefore the rest of the passengers in the lift, with great eloquence why Henry, the son of a man worth just south of a billion dollars according to the latest published rich list, would steal a million dollars through insider trading and ruin his young life. They didn't buy the defence team's submission about Henry succumbing to gambling addiction and depression. In the reporters' summation: "He's a greedy fuckwit."

I found a seat near the front of the courtroom in the row behind Charles and skimmed background notes I'd made so I could file my report quickly after the outcome was known. Charles had groomed his only male offspring for great things, sending him to Sydney's prestigious Cranbrook School, then to Oxford University in England where he studied international law and politics, and met the right people. But I'd found a brighter jewel. Henry's late grandfather, Sir Arthur Allan East, had been fond of parroting the even longer dead American President, Theodore Roosevelt, on the subject of eugenics: *The great problem of civilization is to secure a relative increase of the valuable as compared with the less valuable or noxious elements in the population ... Criminals should be sterilized ... Society has no business to permit degenerates to reproduce their kind ...*

Room 7C was a soundproof, windowless theatre illuminated by hard, white ceiling lights and occupied by about thirty, mostly sober-looking men and women wearing dark suits. They were the usual mix: friends, enemies pretending to be friends, hired legal help licking their lips at the minutes they were billing their client, and yawning reporters. I looked for Henry's mother, the Family Court Judge Victoria East, but couldn't spot her in the settling crowd.

A wiry man wearing a pinstripe suit squeezed past several people in my aisle and sat beside me, so close our hips touched. I moved out of contact but I needed to have a look at him. He had silvery, Caesar-cut hair and stared at my notes. When I closed my pad, he grinned at me with a face that reminded me of a saw-toothed greyhound in need of a muzzle. Charles turned, staying seated, and shook the man's hand. They said nothing.

"Very theatrical, Charles," I said.

"All rise," interrupted the court officer.

Henry stood, chin up, buttoned his jacket and crossed his hands over his crotch like a choir boy about to sing solo.

Justice Tanner strode, white-wigged and black-robed, into the room through his private back door, spittle glistening on his lips. He sat and the rest of us followed, except the defendant, who saved the court officer the trouble of ordering him to stand.

Tanner knew his words this morning would echo through corporate boardrooms, airport Chairman's Club lounges, and the plushest homes in the land for days on end, even rippling overseas. So he spoke from notes.

"Insider trading," the judge said, "is a cancer eating the flesh and bone of our society. It amounts to the privileged acquiring secret knowledge and using it to cheat others. The defendant, because of his position, had a crystal ball to future events in our financial markets. The law prohibited him – not from having that crystal ball – but from using it for personal gain."

Tanner paused for effect. Charles tilted his head down and pressed his temples with his middle fingers. His pet greyhound polished some of his own teeth with the pad of a middle finger.

"When a young person enters the workforce, do we want to teach that person to value honesty and fair play, or do we want to encourage them to develop skills of deception and manipulation for personal gain at the expense of others? I have taken the defendant's background into account. I have also taken account of his guilty plea. Justice knows no favour. I do not believe a simple fine is appropriate in this case."

I turned to Henry. It looked as if his neck snapped; his head fell and he faced his feet, keeping his body stiff and straight.

The judge swung his axe: "I therefore sentence the defendant to two years' imprisonment, with a minimum of twelve months to be served before eligibility for parole. Additionally, I impose a fine equal to two times his illegal benefit."

Henry grasped the railing in front of him, looking at his father. I turned an ear to them and prepared to scribble their conversation into my notepad.

"You've got to move forward now," Charles called, not bothering to stand. "Be strong. This time will pass."

Charles's version of that 'be a man' codswallop rang a bell; I saw myself at the age of six. My father and I were fishing from a dinghy with rods. He cast his line with one hand, the other locked, as usual, on a can of beer. A glint of steel whizzed near my eye and I threw up a hand in self-defence. His hook embedded itself deep inside my middle finger. "There's only one way out of this, Garsy," he said. "If we go backwards, the barb will rip your finger to shreds." So he grabbed my hand, cut the line with a knife, and nipped the tie-end off the hook with a pair of pliers. Then he pushed the body of the hook out, barb first. "Sometimes in life," he said, as he knotted his hanky around my bleeding wound, "the only way out of the shit is to forward ho!" My mother took me to the doctor for a tetanus shot and stitches. Bert went to the horse races.

When Henry was led through a side door to begin his term, the chatter started like thickening rain. I too had expected Henry to get mates' rates - community service or a suspended sentence.

"For God's sake," someone chirped in the hallway outside the courtroom, "the judge lives just a few doors down from the Easts."

I got the chirper's point: The judge's family and the Easts were birds of similar feathers. But I reckoned Tobias had a smaller house without the harbour frontage of the East's 100-year-old family home, Tamerlane. And maybe he'd never been invited to the East's parties, or not the right ones. Their big charity events attracted the chauffer-driven: government ministers, foreign ambassadors, corporate chairmen, Hollywood actors. That sort of herd.

Charles's greyhound joined me in the crowded courtroom lift. He followed me into the street. I walked for almost a block and saw reflected in shopfront windows that he was keeping just a few steps behind me. I didn't fancy being tailgated all the way to my office. At a red pedestrian light, I turned to face him. He looked about forty: fit, tanned, clean-shaven. The outdoors type. As we went eye-to-eye, I worked out why he had made me feel so uneasy in the courtroom, and it wasn't his fondness for rubbing hips with strangers. The pupils inside his grey irises were big, far too big and black for the amount of midday light, and his mouth had white spittle stuck in the corners. Anti-depressants, I guessed: maybe anti-psychotics. I gambled he was still taking them, or wasn't long off the last dose.

"I already have a dog," I said.

"I know," he said.

I did have a real dog.

"Are you the East's new errand boy?" I countered.

Shaping the fingers of his right hand into what looked like a gun, he smiled, pointed at me from his hip and said, "Ka-Pow!" He grinned and walked away.

He turned a corner into a shopping arcade and disappeared before I had the brilliant idea of taking his photo with my mobile phone. I wished I could draw as well as my daughter, Alice. My hands were sweaty when I massaged my neck, and it was a cool day. I figured Charles was in severe pain right now, but he was employing some strange tactics to share it around and try to keep my reporting on his son's imprisonment inside the rails.

I hailed a taxi to go to my office, pondering on exactly how I'd report Henry's imprisonment to the global readers of *The Citizen*. Charles East was a corporate marriage broker.

He had business tentacles across the world, but he was best known among a clique of the internationally wealthy for plugging Western businesses into China, and helping the richest Chinese plant their money and children overseas as insurance, in case they fell afoul of the revolving rulers of the Peoples' Republic.

For publication, my editors chipped out my side-commentary about Henry's grandfather wanting to sterilise criminals. They also removed my speculation that Henry may not have acted alone, and my open question: did he really just stumble across his inside information in his workplace? *The Citizen*'s editorial hierarchy – supported by jelly-backed defamation lawyers – stuck with the facts accepted by the court: Henry was a rogue, a one-man-band. On the upside, I guessed my editors' approach would keep Charles and his new dog feeling relaxed and cocky while I sniffed around their affairs in private.

*

Months passed. I kept my eyes open for a legal appeal by the Easts against Henry's jail sentence, but it didn't come. That wasn't the Charles East I knew, letting his only son go down for the count. I took a punt that after this long in a prison, Henry's mind might be a pressure cooker full of fear. I decided to offer him an outlet valve.

The New South Wales prison system is delightfully quaint. To contact a prisoner you need to use snail mail. No emailing or cold calling, either in person or by phone. So I wrote Henry a letter asking if we could have a chat. In case someone unpleasant intercepted my correspondence, I thought it wise to hire myself a post office box to help filter any reply. The post office was next door to my local pub, so it was easy to check it every evening. I wasn't sure if it was common sense or paranoia, but I purchased a pocket mirror so I could look behind my back whenever I opened the box.

III

A NAKED, wiry-limbed man relaxed against a built-in bench seat in a baking hot sauna room, barely a bead of sweat visible upon his cashew-nut-coloured skin. He spread his arms across the top of the wooden-slat seat and eyed the younger man sitting opposite him. "Are you sure about this? Absolutely sure?"

The man to whom the question was aimed shaped his long fingers into a make-shift comb and swept straw-coloured hair from his glistening forehead. "One hundred per cent."

The wiry man smiled and browsed his companion's sun-tanned skin which was streaked with rivulets of sweat and reminded him of crackling emerging on a side of roast pork. Wiry-man licked his lips and said, "You look good enough to eat."

The young man grimaced: "Do we have to meet like this, every time?"

"I need to know you are playing straight with me, my lawyer friend. From the look on your face, you may have a transmitter stuffed up your arse. Maybe I should check."

The lawyer shifted uncomfortably on the bench. "How do I know *you* are being straight with me?"

"What *the fuck* did you just say?"

"No offence. Jesus, I've told you what Henry is threatening to do. If we don't get him out of Silverwater, he is going to make a fresh statement to the Crown prosecutor and drop us all in the shit."

The wiry man leaned forward and scooped a ladle of water from a wooden bucket that was sitting on the floor. He tossed the water over a tray-table of hot rocks, triggering an angry hiss of steam. He felt like a wizard setting up a magic trick.

"I can't take any more of this," said the lawyer, sweat dripping into his eyes, the salt of it turning the whites pinker. He stood, the crown of his head scraping the wooden-slat-lined ceiling. "I'm out."

The wiry man threw another ladle of water on the rocks, using the resultant mist to obscure his face as he spoke. "I'm sensing you mean, *out*. As in, you don't want to work for me anymore."

"Correct," said the lawyer, trying to see his companion's eyes through the mist. It cleared. The lawyer's heart banged harder and faster. He eyed the sauna door. His penis retreated even further.

The wiry man wiped a strand of spittle from the corner of his mouth. "That's a shame, my friend, because if you do leave me, I am going to have to take something from you."

"You mean a refund? Sure. You can have all the money back."

"You misunderstand me."

Staying seated, the wiry man rolled onto his left buttock and kicked his right leg in a fierce, sweeping motion, slapping his foot and shin into the standing lawyer's lower calves. The lawyer's feet flew up and he fell onto his back, the rear of his skull whiplashing the wooden floor. The lawyer groaned. Seconds later, he began screaming: "Help! Help me!"

"Go for your life," the wiry man said. "Squeal away." He didn't expect anyone would hear the cries from the sauna room in the garden of Tamerlane. It was a weekday mid-afternoon. The property's owners - Charles East, his wife, and their daughter - were at their various workplaces.

The wiry man stood, plucked a towel from a wall hook, dunked a corner of the towel in the water bucket, withdrew it and swizzled the cloth around itself. He flick-whipped the lawyer's rump. The lawyer yelped and curled into a ball.

"Lay on your guts," the wiry man ordered, "legs and arms straight. Imagine you are diving into a pool."

The lawyer stayed balled. He was whipped harder. The lawyer rolled onto his stomach, stretched his arms and legs, and whimpered: "Please. Don't." The lawyer couldn't help himself: he covered his anus with a hand.

"You are joking, kaffir," said the wiry man, who unfurled the towel and laid it like a blanket over the lawyer's lower back. Leading with his knees and shins, the wiry man dropped at a right angle upon the towel and the lawyer. The lawyer huffed. The wiry man reached with his right hand between his squirming victim's legs and grabbed. The lawyer groaned.

"Easy, boy. Easy," said the wiry man, as if he was calming a spooked horse. "Now, do you feel that?" He rolled the twin fibrous knots that he held in his hand against each other. "This is the nature of our relationship for the rest of time, literally and metaphorically. *Comprende*?"

The lawyer groaned.

The wiry man yanked his greasy captives to punctuate each sentence. "You live in a nice house. You have a nice job. You sleep safe in your bed at night. Don't mess that up."

The wiry man rolled the knots again. But as he tormented the lawyer, the wiry man had to fight the flickering of his own arousal. He slowed his breathing and said, "Now, I'm going to let go of these little baby-makers. But if you disappoint me, I will cut them out, dry them like walnuts, and wear them as a necklace."

When his manhood had relaxed into what he regarded as a dignified posture, the wiry man stood and looked down at the lawyer, who curled up on his side and pulled the towel over his buttocks, tears dripping from his eyes.

"You can find your own way out." The wiry man bent his neck like a bird of prey until he had eye contact with the lawyer, whereupon he smiled and pretended to roll something in his right hand: "This is our little secret, darling. Okay?"

*

Henry East slept poorly, as usual, on the top bunk in his two-man cell. He rolled on to his right side, then back on to his left.

"For fuck's sake," said his cellmate, "will you settle down?"

"Sorry."

"Here," said his cellmate, "take one of these. In fact, take two."

"What are they?"

"Sleeping pills."

"Thanks," said Henry, who sucked saliva from his tongue and used the fluid to wash the pills down his throat.

Henry had a dream. He felt like he was leaking: into his pillow, into his sheets, down the sides of his bunk bed. He woke in the gloom with a terrible pain in his face, gurgling, coughing, drowning in warm fluid that had the taste and texture of tomato juice. He spat it out, but it kept coming. His wrists burned.

His cellmate was screaming through the bars into the corridor: "Help! Help! Medical Emergency. Help!"

IV

I WOKE sitting on the floor, back to the wall inside my home office, first room off the hallway from the front door of our two-level, Victorian-era terrace house. My trilling phone was the waker. *Tom Steele*, the screen said.

"He's cut his wrists," said the Crime Editor of *The Sydney Daily News*.

"What?" My headache from last night's bar-crawling with Steele returned for a second bout as I stood and almost knocked over an open tin of house paint that I'd been smothering the walls with before the urge for a nap sent me sliding to the floor.

"Henry East. He's an innovative young man. Used the peel-off lid of a tuna can."

Steele added that Henry was flat-backed in the Silverwater Prison hospital's psychiatric wing, sedated and strapped into a bed that was anchored to the floor.

"You sure he did it to himself?"

"You're a cynical character. Wait 'til you hear the rest."

"I'm all ears."

"Where are you?"

"Darlinghurst."

"Good. I'll home deliver the next exciting episode of The Strange Life of Henry East. I've also got something tasty in my pocket for afternoon tea."

I smiled at the idea of *home*. At the time of our purchase, ours was advertised as a renovator's delight in the inner-Sydney suburb of Darlinghurst. Now the agents might say *once beautiful old lady in need of a facelift*. To the man or woman in the street, it was a century old building made out of decent bricks, handy to schools and public transport. And at night, I could throw a stone from my front porch across the street through the front window of the nearest pub if I felt like it.

Steele was chirpy for a bloke with whom I parted company at around 4am on a footpath up the street outside the Pickled Pig.

"Are you with me?" said Steele. He seemed to detect that a fair-sized lump of my brain was astral travelling. He's got extra sensory perception, I've always thought, but he just calls it awareness. He's been my psychological counsellor since primary school when we nicked our thumbs with his mum's veggie knife and shook hands under his bed on a Friday night sleepover. Our secret club was just that, until a burning candle set fire to the mattress, and the hair that once crowned Steele's skull.

While I was revisiting old flames and smoke, Steele hung up. I time travelled to the now and leaned on a stack of cardboard boxes, sending the top one toppling. It spewed stuff I'd just stripped off the walls: photos of the Easts, newspaper clippings about Henry's case and its lead-up, and glow-pen-highlighted pages of court transcripts. I intended to cremate the past in a bonfire in the back garden and celebrate my East-free future. The tins of Summer Mint paint were going to refresh my mind as well as my walls.

I scooped a photo from the floor and sat on a sofa against a wall. It showed Henry towering over the Australian Prime Minister. Charles wedged the PM from the other side. The three of them were parading in tuxedos in the winner's circle at a political fundraiser held about a year ago, smiling at the camera with effortless insincerity. Henry had the sharpest suit, the TV newsreader's smile. That's when newspaper gossip writers started saying he was set for a career in politics, and that he had the savvy and connections to make PM one day, given his smarts, his pedigree, and his grandfather being a former foreign minister. My theory was that Charles's PR people leaked the idea to a toadying scribe, sweetening it with a box of real French champagne sent to the toad's home address.

I found a red marker pen and scrawled 'why?' on Henry's photo, putting the word in a thought bubble and connecting it to his lips. Then I had a cleverer idea; I reviewed the notes that I'd made of the café conversation outside court the day Henry was sentenced. A line from his lawyer stuck out like a fractured bone: *We've agreed the strategy with your father. Whatever happens today, this ends it, Henry.*

It had taken Henry about three months to disagree. I almost cheered for him. The brass ship's bell with a clapper on a rope attached to our front door donged with a mellow tone for which my senses were grateful.

A bald-headed Steele clutching a six-pack of beer grinned at me when I opened the door. His body strained the seams of a slim-fit powder-blue suit. A tee-shirt and board shorts were his natural second skin. But he was a professional man, being a journalist, and always dressed up-to-the-minute, even though his body hated the idea. His white business shirt had unbuttoned itself at the neck, making his black tie look strangely tight.

In my office, Steele passed me the beers and sat on the sofa where he worked his mobile phone with big, fast thumbs. I opened a bottle, took a decent slug, turned my office chair to face him and sat down. My headache began dissolving.

"You know," I said, "why do we bother with this stuff?"

"You mean throwing light into society's darkest corners?"

"What's the point?"

"That's too deep for a daylight discussion." He shook his head in frustration at my high-mindedness. "Just read, will you." He handed me his phone. "Go to page two, the stuff highlighted in red. I'm holding it as draft copy for now."

"Shit. He cut his lips?"

"Slashed them back to the teeth and gums in the shape of an X. I can't publish yet because the coppers won't confirm, but they won't deny either. Can you imagine what a mess that makes?"

"I thought he was under special protection."

"They moved him out three weeks ago."

"Why would you slice your lips?"

"Makes you pretty unattractive to other inmates."

"You reckon that stuff was happening to him?"

"Maybe."

"Or someone was trying to shut him up?"

"That's a very poetic interpretation," said Steele, glancing at my office door. "Anyone home?"

"Hugo and Fish are upstairs."

"Lock the door."

I obeyed. Steele pulled a small plastic bag from his jacket pocket, tapped some white crystals onto the coffee table and started chopping them with his credit card.

"Not good timing," I said. "It's Hugo's farewell dinner tonight."

"Small," he said. He put his card at one end of my line and compressed it, making it shorter but fatter. He took a banknote from his shirt pocket, rolled it into a tube and hoovered his. He handed me the note and I followed suit. High quality cocaine: that cleared my head, though my heart went for a gallop which prompted me to open a fresh beer to calm things down.

"You want to stay for dinner?"

"Naa, thanks. Time for some repair work at home. And you guys should have your private time. Give the nipper my best for his travels."

He tapped another pile of crystals onto the coffee table, patted me on the shoulder and said, "For Ron." He left.

I scraped the coke onto a piece of paper, folded it and tucked it in my wallet. *For Ron*, my father used to say; for later on. It was like having a spare tyre in case of a flat.

I looked at a photo of Charles and Henry East, but I thought about a different father and son. And about that son standing alone in a hostile, alien world inside which the father could not protect him. The longest time Hugo and I had been apart was his week at high school camp. In just over twenty-four hours, fate willing, Hugo would be on the other side of the planet for a year on a student program. Uninvited chemicals worked my insides; I wiped my eyes. My phone pinged. Steele: *Update. A third party might have done the job on Henry East. Keep you posted.*

Steele sparked an idea. I went back through my notes of the café conversation between Henry and his lawyer.

Lawyer: *You won't go to jail. You'll be fined at most.*

Henry: *You can't guarantee that. They can come after me in there.*

It's funny how people over the years change their friends and spouses more often than their mobile phone numbers. I had one of Charles East's numbers from a time when he offered me a job. I chanced it and dialled. Someone picked up; I heard classical music far away in the background.

"Charles, it's Gar Hart here. I want to talk to you about Henry."

Whoever had picked up didn't utter a thing. They waited a few seconds and hung up. So I fired off a text message: *Who was Henry afraid would come after him in jail?*

Maybe it was the cocaine and beer doing my thinking, but firing a shot into Charles seemed like a cracking idea: poke the beast, see what happens. I leaned back in my chair, grinning with admiration for my slick tactical manoeuvre, and glanced out my window in time to see my daughter climbing out of a car I didn't recognise. Alice had a red and white beach towel over a shoulder. I hid the beer bottles in an empty box by the sofa, stepped from my office into the hallway and opened the front door for her.

"What's that around your nose?" she said.

I scraped the rim of my nostrils with a thumb. "I must have missed some shaving cream."

"Come on, Dad. It's Hugo's last night."

She walked along the hallway to the bathroom and calmly closed the door. I stood outside, clenched a fist and poised to knock. I heard the shower start. I went to the kitchen and rinsed my nose under the tap in the sink.

It was Hugo's idea to go to his mother Charlotte's birthplace in seaside Brighton, England, to stay with his grandparents on a student exchange for a year. Another boy from Sydney was joining him at the same school. Clancy was a bit shifty, I thought, but a companion made of flesh and bone instead of digital bits was a good thing for Hugo. They were flying out the next morning. I trudged upstairs to Hugo's bedroom and knocked on his door.

"I'm packing, okay," he grizzled from behind the locked door. I heard Fish scratching at the door and Hugo let him out, then he shut his door again. Fish had been a rolling ball of grey wool when he crawled over his sleepy rivals in a puppy box to lick the kids' hands and join our pack, not long after Charlotte died.

Fish followed me as I walked back to the stairwell, moving as elegantly as a dog with three legs can. He lost his left back prop in a steel-jawed hunting trap at our place in the bush a few years ago.

Alice was still in the bathroom as we passed it, so I went back to my office, sat on the sofa and pulled a faded newspaper clipping out my East box.

The headline read: *China Behind* 'Made in Australia' *Media Bid - by Business Editor, Gar Hart*. It was dated about ten years ago. Charles East was heading a syndicate of local businessmen who'd launched what they dubbed a patriotic 'Made in Australia' takeover bid for the Mirror News Group that owned the collection of television stations and newspapers that employed me. I'd been trying to prove anonymous tips from other businessmen claiming Charles and his mates were a front for Chinese industrialists backed by the Communist Party in Beijing who wanted to use their money and our media to exert power and influence over Australian business, politics and foreign policy. The problem that Charles appeared to be fixing for the Chinese was that foreigners were not allowed to own and control Australian media companies. The Poms and Yanks would have been bad enough in the public eye, but China was a bogeyman like no other. In the midst of my investigations, I had received a call from Charles, who invited me to dinner, over which he offered me a job as a public relations man for his family company at twice my reporter's salary. We had a big home mortgage, so the bribe to stop me stuffing up his bid and damaging his reputation was tempting. A few days after rejecting his offer, another businessman gave me a document, following which I phoned Charles.

"Mr East," I remember saying a tad too gleefully, "I have a letter that says you are being retained by China's Golden Bell Corporation to buy the Mirror News Group on their behalf. It is signed by GBC's chairman. If this is true, you would be in breach of our foreign media ownership laws, as well as faking your patriotism. Are you a Trojan horse for the Chinese?"

East said: "That letter's a fake, Edgar; you're being had. Forget about it. Listen. What you should be focusing on is your long-term career and your family's future."

"Why would you care about my family?"

"Don't be paranoid. I've been pondering our dinner conversation. I really do want someone on my PR team with fire in their belly. So why don't you come on board with us on a consultancy basis? We can pay you a very decent monthly retainer and you can help us with our press releases, strategy, that sort of thing. And you get to keep your journalism job as well. It's a win-win."

"Do you think that is ethical?" I said, holding a straight face, even though he couldn't see it. Secretly tape recording our conversation would have been illegal if I had done so without telling him. Inconveniently my recorder had jammed when I commenced the call.

"It's simply an employment offer," he said. "It's up to you."

"Can you answer my question about GBC?"

East said: "On the record? The letter is a fake. Off the record? Remember what happened to Humpty Dumpty."

I paused for a second or two. "Thank you for taking my call, Mr Dumpty."

After my story was published, Charles and his PR team publicly denounced the letter as a fraud, and I did not have the original to prove otherwise, but he did not sue us for defamation. A few weeks later his 'Made in Australia' syndicate withdrew from the bidding for Mirror News Group, saying the price had gone too high. I empathised with Charles in a way; his wasn't the only house perched upon the nob hills of the city inside which ethics were as popular as bottled water from a Mumbai sewer.

In a lowlands street, I had purchased a new tape recorder with a cord to link it to my phone.

*

I tucked the news clipping back in the box to the sound of fierce chopping coming from the kitchen. Fish led me down the hallway. Alice was stony-faced, slicing tomato and cucumber salad. Fish nudged her leg and licked her hand when she patted him. She smiled. That was his job in our house. Dr Fix-it.

I turned the oven on, got ready-made pizza bases out of the fridge, along with a block of cheese, and started grating. Alice went to her room with Fish.

The smell of cooking pizza drew Hugo from his room. He shuffled into the kitchen roughing up the mop of dark hair on top of his lanky body. His skin rarely saw sunlight. I made him take vitamin D tablets. He was barefoot, wearing skinny black jeans and an old white tee-shirt of mine which made me a little dizzy: its front was printed with a red hypnotic wheel. The words *Look into your Morning Sun* were printed in an arc above the wheel. The tee-shirt was a gift from my wife's father, Malcolm Halliday, who had owned *The Morning Sun* newspaper in Brighton for decades.

I called Alice and Fish down for dinner. My phone rang as we sat at the long kitchen table. The handset was face-up beside my plate. Alice saw the Shanghai phone code and the caller's name on the screen: *Jack Darling.*

"I'll be five minutes," I said.

Alice shook her head in silence, staring at her plate. Hugo fed Fish his pizza crust. I walked down the hall towards my office.

Jack said: "I just read about Henry East's suicide attempt on the wires. What do you know?"

"He might be a victim, not suicide. You remember what I overheard in that café near the courtroom? The kid was shitting himself about people coming after him if he went to prison."

"Go back at it hard," said Jack. "Charles East has just partnered in China with a former British Prime Minister, Tim Winter. They announced it today in Beijing. There's a smell about Winter in London, suggestions he took bribes to get the kids of Communist Party bigwigs into top UK schools and flash finance jobs in the city."

"While he was PM?"

"He's not quite that stupid. It was when he knew he was on his way out. Talk is that the Chinese bought his wife a holiday house in the Bahamas, and then good old Timmy returned ball by pressing the puffy flesh of his chums in the city for old favours to be repaid."

"Hard evidence of this?"

"Not a cracker."

"Excellent start."

"I tell you what," said Jack. "Get Claire to help you. You need to give her more to do. We'll have another nose around East's businesses here at the China end."

Claire Styler was a recent arrival at *The Citizen*'s Sydney office from our London headquarters. She came with a freshly minted Master of Business Administration in her briefcase and a husband-come-public-relations-flak on her arm. I didn't like that combination, a journalist and a PR. I'd seen it before, with the PR feeding his spouse spin about his high-paying clients. It was especially shifty when they went by different names in public like Claire Styler and Carl Cousins did. I reckoned their type did the dual-name thing so casual observers wouldn't connect them. They had the potential to be what Charles East tried to turn me into: an *independent* journalist on one hand, a corporate spin doctor on the other. I knew reporters who were in on this racket, taking back-handers of cash or kind from people they wrote nicely about. Jack reckoned I was reading too much into the Styler-Cousins name thing. So I'd decided to let Claire's work do the talking. It had spoken in monosyllables so far.

I phoned Claire at home and briefed her about Henry East. I asked her to gather some background on the former British PM and to review the transcripts and news clippings of Henry's court case to bring her up to speed. As we were talking, Alice appeared in my office doorway and waved. She had a bulging bag over her shoulder. I watched through the front window as she climbed into a taxi. I guessed she was going to her boyfriend's.

After ending the call with Claire, Hugo and I finished packing his bags in readiness for his early morning take-off.

Then he sat on his bed and fired up his laptop. I saw he now had three bolts on his door.

"Wasn't one bolt enough?" I said. "What if there's a fire?"

"I've got a window."

"I'll miss you."

"I'll call you when I land."

I went to bed. Fish whimpered until I lifted him up. He put his head on the pillow beside me and was snoring within minutes. I closed my eyes but there were too many weird shapes moving in there. I slid out of bed. Fish is great at unaided descent and followed me down to my office. I kept the light off. The streetlamps shining through the part-closed window shutters covered us in zebra prints. I fired up my laptop and sent Steele a text by phone: "You awake?"

My laptop clock said 2:17am. In the nearby streets, night clubs were spewing out their customers. Sirens howled. I can never tell the difference between police, firemen, ambulances. Not from the sounds alone. They just remind me of the myriads of shit humans get into. Fish has a beautiful voice and howled in tune with the sirens, like he was singing in a choir with his mates. That bucked me up.

My phone rang. Steele.

"So was he attacked?" I said.

"Everyone's clammed up again. Coppers are sticking with the attempted suicide line."

"How about the sources who tipped you off. Can I talk to one of them?"

"Now?"

"Sure."

"You're obsessed."

"How about downgrading that charge to tenacious? Anyway, what else am I going to do at this hour?"

"Have a drink, abuse yourself, or nip around the corner to the Scarlet Garter if your memory of the female form is impaired."

"And in the morning?"

"Get a proper job, something useful like a golfer. In the meantime, I'll come back to you if one of my snouts is prepared to break cover."

I dozed off sitting at my office table. Fish's furious yapping woke me; he was front paws-up on the edge of the table, balancing on his back leg, barking at the window. The leafy branches of a tree backlit by streetlights were moving shadows around the room. Wind rattled the window glass. I looked outside into a haze of rain and could see neither human nor animal. Fish relaxed; whatever had unsettled him, he had chased away.

I checked that the front and back doors were locked, and climbed the stairs to bed. It was almost 3:30am when I put my head down. Fish was unusually restless.

V

THE WIRY man sat alone in the front seat of a parked four-wheel drive, working under the dull glow of streetlights through the car's rain-spotted windows. Using a small towel, he wiped fresh blood off the blade of a hunting knife.

He glanced in the rear view mirror, then the wings. He checked the car's clock. *Why hadn't she returned his calls?*

He inserted the blade of his knife into a leather sheath that was strapped to his chest, over which he wore a business shirt and jacket. He sniffed his fingers, enjoying the salty, ammonia smell of what he had just killed. He wiped his fingers with the towel and tapped the screen on an encrypted phone that sat in a cradle on the dashboard. The handset speed dialled.

Leave a message, said a computer-generated voice - again.

He admired the girl's craftiness, but it infuriated him too. "When I call, I expect you to answer," he barked. "I've made my delivery. Call me. Now!"

He hit the ignition button and motored away, fighting the urge to drive past the scene of his very funny crime.

The girl had recognised the incoming caller's number. Six times. He could wait. She was busy. Her assignment may take hours to complete.

She looked around the sitting room of the Hong Kong high-rise apartment. Coloured lights blinked outside in the towering Kowloon cityscape. She crossed to a glass screen that was fixed to the wall near the entrance door. With her hands protected by wafer-thin, white leather designer gloves, she used an e-stick to tap the screen: floor-to-ceiling curtains began closing across all of the room's windows. She turned up the luminosity of the ceiling lights so she could get a better look at a dozing, plump, grey-haired Englishman sitting slouched on a three-seat sofa in the middle of the room. A red tie was loose around the unbuttoned collar of his white shirt; his hairy belly was exposed, and his trousers and underpants were piled around his calves.

The stench of his breath and his searching, scum-coated tongue had made her want to vomit when he had tried to kiss her. She went to the sink in the open plan kitchen-living room and knocked the arm of a mixer tap with a gloved hand. She put her mouth into the stream of cool water and lapped it up, careful not to touch the stainless steel with her lips. She knocked the tap off and checked her black-haired wig in a kitchen wall-mirror. Her real hair was tucked inside it as carefully as a surgeons' in an operating cap.

The man murmured. She grimaced, hoping she had stuffed enough pink grains of heroin into the tip of the cigarette that sat smouldering in the ashtray beside a glass of Scotch whisky on the coffee table alongside the sofa. After two thirds of a bottle and a few tokes on the secretly loaded cigarette, he had now fallen upon his side with his face turned into the back of the sofa. He snorted and snored. She looked at the rectangular glass tank on a stand behind the sofa. The creatures inside it were as still and dozy as the man.

She wiped her lips dry on the hairless skin of her foreman, huffed on it and sniffed, enjoying her odourless breath. That's how she saw herself: as traceless as clean air, when she wanted to be. And tonight she wanted to be.

She stepped to the sofa and pulled up the man's trousers and underpants by rolling his bulky frame. She stuffed his shirt tails into his trousers, buttoned the waist with difficulty, tightened his belt and zipped up his fly. She considered removing his diamond-studded, gold cufflinks and rolling up his shirtsleeves, but decided to simply tug the cuff up a little on his left wrist to expose the puffy white flesh of his palm.

The man's liquid-sounding belch interrupted her. She chuckled. *Porky might drown in his own vomit and save me a lot of time and effort.* But that would not do, not really. This job must be performed with symbolism and ritualism; her employer liked that sort of thing. Moreover, she liked it.

The fat man had bragged to her earlier in the Kowloon bar tonight about his snake collection. The Indian Cobra, a North American diamond-backed Rattler, and an Australian inland Taipan lived side-by-side in separate compartments of the display tank in his home for all his visitors to see. She guessed it was his superego speaking to those who might take him on in a fight. I'm a tough guy, the man was saying, a strange guy, so don't fuck with me.

This type of guy proved easy prey for the girl, playing the pretty young stranger in the bar where she said she had a soft spot for trouser snakes in fancy apartments, and a thousand US dollars in cash. She did not tell him that she had learned to handle venomous snakes at a paramilitary training camp in South Africa. Nor did she tell him that *his* employer was also *her* employer.

She lifted his metal snake-handling hook from a shelf under the tank and flipped open the lid of a compartment. The choice was obvious; a few drops of Taipan venom were enough to kill a hundred men. Its body felt heavy on the hook, but the animal was dozy and she soon had it gripped by the tail, its body dangling, its head swinging to and fro beside her calves

"Wakey, wakey," she said to the snake, the beast becoming angrier with each of her shakes and gentle knocks of its head against the legs of the coffee table.

She turned her attention to the snoring blackmailer and said to him, "When you bite the hand that feeds you, you might get a dose of your own medicine in return."

She grinned at her mangled metaphors and tapped the snake's head against the man's bulbous, blue-veined thumb muscle. The snake bared its fangs and struck: once, twice, three times. At the third strike, the snake's mouth stayed fixed upon the muscle. She wanted several strikes because the creatures are not fools. Often, they won't waste venom on a first strike, using it as a warning shot for a foe to leave it alone or face the consequences. And the girl had to be sure of the consequences.

When the man's hand was dotted with weeping red spots, she laid the exhausted creature on the tiled floor and watched it muster enough energy to slither slowly under the skirt of a curtain that flanked the room's main windows.

The girl looked at her phone for the time. It could take hours to be sure this exercise had worked, or it may only take thirty minutes or so for the venom to shut down the man's nervous system, for his muscles, including his heart, to become paralysed, and for internal bleeding to start.

Ninety-three minutes passed before he stopped grumbling and writhing, and his breathing ceased. His obesity, the girl calculated, had probably hastened a cardiac arrest. Blood trickled from his nose; pink foam bubbled from his lips. She speed-dialled the wiry man.

"What if the shit had really hit the fan?" he yelled at her. "I've been in the dark here for over two hours. Not good enough."

"Take a pill," she said. "I've got to clean up and get out of here before the hired help arrives with orange juice and the morning papers."

"What's the headline going to read like in a day or two?"

"Lone drunk smokes heroin and plays with killer snake. Something like that."

"I need you here."

"When?"

"Yesterday."

"So the lawyer and that journalist are not for turning?"

"I want to be set, in case we need to drop a bomb on the pricks."

VI

MY RADIO alarm went off with the 5am news bulletin. I banged on Hugo's bedroom door until he unbolted it, and let Fish in to finish the job of rousing him while I carried his bags downstairs and put them in the hallway, ready to pack in the car for the drive to the airport. When I opened the front door, the sight hit me first - the blood and guts - followed by the ammonia stink.

An orange-and-white speckled carp as big as my forearm stared at me. The fish had a single steel hook through both its eyes. The hook was tied with green twine to the black-painted, steel frame of our security door. The carp's gut had been slashed and its entrails dangled like glistening purple streamers, its blood pooled on the doorstep.

I thought about calling the police, but then remembered my call to Charles East last night. Had we just been visited by the *they* Henry East feared, or by Mr Greyhound from courtroom 7C? That would take some explaining, and possibly inside a cop shop. Get Hugo out of here was my overriding thought. Get Hugo to the airport. And don't frighten him. We were already behind schedule.

I managed to cut the fish down and use a bucket of soapy water and a rag to clean away the evidence before a sleepy Hugo clumped down the internal stairs into the hallway, stuffing his earmuff-sized headset into a shoulder bag, Fish hopping alongside him.

Fish could smell the carnage and snuffled madly around the door. I put him on his lead and knocked on our neighbour's door. I apologised for the hour. Retired Sue Sinclair owned Fish's four-legged brother, who bounced beside her. She took Fish in without question, as she often did.

My old Land Rover Defender was parked in the street a few doors down. Hugo and I threw his bags on the back seat and we jumped in the front. I phoned Alice. She didn't answer. Why would she? It was 5.45am. My insides churned. I lifted my hand to press the car's ignition button.

"Mate," I said to Hugo. "I think I left your passport on the kitchen bench. Can you get it?"

He grumbled. I gave him the house key and he went inside. I looked in the rear view mirror and checked the rest of the street was clear. Surely these lunatics wouldn't put a Baghdad Surprise under my bonnet? There were lots of ways for me to find out, but given my schedule, and a quick calculation of the odds, I chose the fastest.

VII

THE ENGINE coughed, then growled into life, but they'd got what they wanted: me thinking about the possibility of things.

Hugo opened the passenger door. "There's nothing on the kitchen bench."

I tapped my jacket pockets and pulled out his passport. "My mistake."

He shook his head like I was the village idiot, if further proof was needed.

An hour later, we waved to each other and he disappeared behind the barriers into the passport checking hall of Sydney International Airport, en route to London Heathrow via Dubai.

Standing in the airport hall, in a line of vacant-eyed people waiting for their take-away coffee, I phoned Steele.

"Someone left a calling card on my door overnight. A dead fish."

"Serious?"

"Incoming missile." I forwarded him a photo I'd taken on my phone of the gutted carp and confessed to Steele that I'd tried to contact Charles East about Henry's mutilation.

"Mm," said Steele, "making good use of your vast intellect as usual. My guess is that the carp is a note, telling you to keep your nose out of their business. Quite crudely written, though."

"Genius deduction," I said, collecting my latte off the café counter and taking that glorious first sip, my taste buds telling me I'd been dudded with just a single shot of beans for a double-shot price.

"What are you going to do?" said Steele.

"Take it back."

"What?"

"Sorry." I binned the coffee. "The coppers will laugh at me, won't they?"

"Nice photo, but you pulled the fucking thing down. If I was a copper, I'd put you in the nutcase file under Kamikaze Carp: oddball claims Jap fish attacked his door."

"I want to know what happened in Henry's cell. Can you put me on to one of your prison sources?"

"I'll twist some fins and get back to you."

I phoned Jack in Shanghai. It took a while to clarify with him that it wasn't our dog I found gutted and hanging off the front door. He reminded me it was 4.30am where he was.

"You want to back off?"

"Are you serious?"

"Watch your back," he said, "and keep your head screwed on. Don't let East provoke you into doing anything stupid."

I phoned Claire. It was just after 8am. She was at *The Citizen*'s office at Circular Quay, overlooking the main ferry wharf in the city. She liked to walk to work early and watch the sun rising over the harbour and ferry docks we can see from our tower on the northern edge of the central business district.

Claire hadn't attended the East trial, nor had she been in Sydney to read the publicity or hear the rabid speculation before it. She was fresh eyes and ears on an old landscape.

"How'd you go running your eyes over the court transcripts?" I said.

"That takeover bid by the Double Happiness Trading Company that Henry made one of his inside share trades on. Remember it?"

"Vaguely. Tiny, wasn't it? Barely worth his trouble."

"What did you tell me when I started here? Stand back, close my eyes, open them, look for the odd man out."

"And?"

"Double Happiness was the only trade he did that involved a totally foreign company."

"Okay," I said. "Find out who's behind them. I'll be in the office a bit later. Doctor's appointment."

As I walked to my car, I tried to make sense of the dead fish. Charles East's speciality was terrorising people with his lawyers and his PR people. He attacked people's money and their reputations, and he did so in public to maximise the impact. Nothing physical, no direct violence, so apart from Henry, did he have unusual problems? Or new advisers? Mr Greyhound's spittle-mouthed antics outside the courthouse were a twist on East's psychological tactics.

Hugo would be okay on the far side of the world with his nana, I told myself, but maybe I should move Fish next door long-term - and persuade Alice to move to her boyfriend's house for a while.

My head ached with possibilities, so I put my mind to work on the tangible lunacy of the freeway traffic and drove into the city. I couldn't find a car space near our house, or anywhere else on the nearby streets, so I rolled into an underground carpark a couple of blocks from home. I parked and walked towards the stairwell that led up to the street. The route took me past bay B9. It was empty, so I couldn't miss a stain on the concrete floor that looked like an old oil spill. Nor could I stop the flooding recall of an image of my father sitting on his arse, with his back leaning against the front wheel of my parked Defender in that bay, his head hanging sideways and his brain matter splattered against my driver's side door, his right hand holding the gun. That's when I found the letter in his pocket about wanting to put a snake in my bed, metaphorically speaking, along with instructions about where to find the twin Browning 9mm he'd left for me and buried in my garden at home beside the frangipani tree.

I walked quickly up the stairs and out to the street. My phoned pinged. A text from Steele: *Got someone. Where RU?*

I replied: *About to hit The Pig.*

VIII

THE PICKLED PIG'S owner locked his horse-sized black eyes on me. Mick O'Hara was grinning inside his permanent five o'clock shadow, hands on his narrow hips, dressed in a long-sleeved black shirt, sleeves rolled up past his elbows, button-down pockets sporting mother-of-pearl buttons. He wore grey woollen britches held up by braces and ankle-high riding boots in matte black. A grey homburg cocked at a slight angle topped him off.

"Looks like you need a drink," he observed.

"And coffee," I said, studying him back. "Let me guess. Gold miner, not cattle hand."

"Correct," he replied.

I like that subtlety about Mick, who's a regular theme dresser and does great German lederhosen on Mondays. He headed to his glistening coffee machine, gave it a couple of pats and milked its hissing pipes. I looked around the *Pig's* dozen worn booths. The old leather suitcases stacked on high shelves around the walls reminded me of a steam-era railway carriage. The occupants were just me and three lean young women in matching orange spray-on tans with bleached teeth sucking juice from straws in jam-jar glasses.

I opened my iPad and browsed the newspapers online. Mick plonked a latte on the table, a shot glass of bourbon by its side. I sipped the coffee and pondered the shot. Steele walked in.

He had a red welt on the bridge of his nose. I said nothing. He may have stumbled, or told a bad joke to another reveller somewhere last night. But I knew things were getting crazier between him and his wife, and she wasn't the shy type.

"It'll cost you," Steele said.

"For what?"

"I can hook you up with a prison psych nurse who's looking after Henry East, but he wants $500 for the privilege."

"When?"

"This afternoon. You take the cash with you. I'll text you time and place."

"What do I get for my investment?"

"My man's at the kid's bedside most nights."

"You coming with me?"

"Sorry: got other work. Someone's wonderful son has just hurled his girlfriend off the 25th floor. Apparently he didn't like the way she did the dishes."

Steele took a few steps to leave and turned. He picked up my bourbon and threw the contents down his throat. "You want us to take the dog?"

"I think he'll be okay next door for now."

"Alice?"

"I have a plan."

Steele winked and walked.

Mick plonked another shot of bourbon, a cup of iced water, and a plate of thick, hand-cut raisin toast, butter on the side, on my table. He insists that I eat breakfast. I applied a smear of butter.

"You'll die with a fine heart one day," he said before looking at my iPad and shaking his head. "You know, Gar, the human mind creates some sad things."

"Such as?"

"Take that fancy electric mat you have there."

"They're called tablets."

"Magic mats to me. You can fly on 'em all over the world without leavin' home and peep into people's windows twenty-four-seven. It's just that you miss the bloody point."

"What point's that?"

Mick shook his head again, slowly: "Human contact. Smellin', touchin', tastin'. You're married to that fuckin' thing."

"It works for us." The truth was I got his point. I stood up and headed for the toilet.

When I pushed the door open, one of the young women with the orange-stained skin was standing over the bowl, panties mid-thigh, using one hand to hold her dress up. A stream of urine was arcing into the toilet. She turned sideways and smiled.

"Sorry," I said. She was holding a substantial penis with a silver ring through its hole. I closed the door and walked back to my table.

A few minutes later, Mick came over. He pulled a business card from behind my ear like he used to pull magic coins from behind my kids' ears, and out of their noses.

"The girls over there asked me to give this to you. If you need some R and R," he said with a mighty grin. The card read: *Seahorse Club. Saddle up for the most exciting rides in town.*

He couldn't know I'd found one of Charlotte's old dresses in Hugo's wardrobe last week when I was looking for a travel case. Hugo had black eyeliner pencils and jacaranda-coloured lipstick in a drawer. And a magazine article about a male super model who walked the world's most famous catwalks in women's clothes.

I drained my coffee, walked home, had a nap to make up for last night, showered and headed to *The Citizen*'s office wearing a suit and tie to tell the world, and myself, that I was a serious man.

In the taxi, I checked my wallet for the paper packet of cocaine I was saving for Ron. I put the Seahorse Club card in beside it.

IX

MY PHONE pinged in the taxi as we closed in on *The Citizen*'s office building clustered with other towers along the harbour-front stretch of the central business district, or CBD as the occupiers called it to save a bit of breath and sound hip. A text from Steele read: "*Fly Half Hotel, East Sydney. 4pm. He will be wearing a Sydney Swans cap.*" I had over an hour to burn.

Our news bureau was perched about halfway up a sixty storey, white-marble-entranced monument called Gunnaroo Tower. It was smack bang in the middle of a postcard cliché, flanked by the Sydney Harbour Bridge and the Opera House. If strutting was an Olympic sport, the occupants of Gunnaroo would win medals every time they crossed the lobby.

The tower wasn't my choice of local HQ. Most of the new-media HQs were located in cheaper low-rise on the other side of the CBD in the inner urban grime around Central Railway Station and Surry Hills. But a German pension fund owned Gunnaroo and Jack Darling assured me we had got a good leasing deal through Ailsa Dusseldorf, a half-owner of *The Citizen*. The family of the Frankfurt-born industrial heiress made its fortune crafting engine cogs for luxury cars, before the Chinese and Indians worked out how to copy them at lower cost. She had partnered with a Californian named Zac Werner eighteen months ago to fund our start-up global media operation. Zac made his pile by creating computer security software.

Online-only media, like *The Citizen*, was cheap on technical infrastructure – there was no paper, no printing presses and no costly physical distribution. Journalists didn't cost much either, not these days, but managing them was like herding monkeys and consumers didn't want to pay for news, not much anyway. Advertising was thin too, so *The Citizen* ran at a loss. Some of our competitors called it a vanity project for the owners. I didn't give a shit about that – ninety-nine percent of media workers are mirror gazers, the bigger mirrors, the better. I was gambling that the tax benefits to our founders, enabled by global money shuffling by smart accountants - legitimate, of course - would keep Dusseldorf and Werner pouring money into the hopper for a while yet. My mortgage repayments depended on it, Alice was in art school, and Hugo in high school. Moreover, job offers were thin on the ground for a man with my reputation.

Claire was sitting at her desk, one of four butted together in our mostly open-plan space, talking on the phone. There was one desk for another reporter we were yet to hire. The other two were for our subscription-come-advertising-sales person, and the office administrator who worked two days a week. Neither of them were in. As the bureau chief, I got a glass-walled private office with a harbour view through a window the size of a modest wardrobe.

I glanced at a TV screen fixed to a wall in the main room. It was turned to a twenty-four-hour news channel where half a dozen journalists and politicians were spread along a desk in a studio, clucking at each other like over-coiffed roosters and lip-sticked hens.

Claire brushed the liquorice strands of her Cleopatra haircut away from a milk-coloured cheek. I glimpsed a purple mark on her throat next to her white shirt collar. She always wore long sleeves and trousers and I'd begun to wonder why.

"Tell me about Double Happiness," I said.

"It's a Shanghai stock exchange listed company that made a takeover bid for an Australian mining company named Austar Gold. Henry made about $25,000 by buying Austar shares before the bid was announced and selling them afterwards when the price almost doubled."

"And?"

"Double Happiness is 30 per cent owned by a group of Hong Kong investors, but none of them own more than 5 per cent. Another 20 per cent is owned by a Chinese steel mill boss from Guangdong Province. The biggest shareholder is a London-based firm named Cavalcade Investment Group with 38 per cent. Rats and mice own the rest out of Singapore and South-East Asia."

"So," I said, "pursuing the odd-man-out idea, why would one Western investor be sitting among all those Chinese?"

Claire tapped her keyboard. I pulled a chair next to hers and we looked at her screen.

The Cavalcade Investment Group is a privately owned, UK-based asset management and financial services company. We work with individuals and financial institutions to invest internationally in growth industries including banking, telecommunications, property development and travel.

Cavalcade is headquartered in London, with offices in New York, Los Angeles, Paris, Sydney, Tokyo, Hong Kong, Shanghai, Mumbai and Dubai.

"Let me see that logo," I said.

Claire zoomed in. The Cavalcade logo on the company's home page was the shape of a heraldic shield.

"Very *Game of Thrones*," she concluded. "House of Lannister, don't you think?"

I had to agree. "Memory test," I said. "Mine."

Claire followed me into my office. I sat at my desk and opened the photos file on my laptop. I clicked on a picture of Henry East swinging a polo mallet atop a pony. Hooray Henry was wearing a black peaked cap, cream jodhpurs, and a short-sleeved black shirt with the collar turned up. I magnified the left breast of Henry's shirt, focussing on the place where the sponsors put their mark, and there sat the Cavalcade shield logo, slightly distorted in the folds of the cloth, but there nonetheless. The photo caption said Henry was playing at the Ascot Park Polo Club in Surrey outside London.

"Find out who Cavalcade's key people are," I said, "and any other links between them and the Easts."

"Henry East," said Claire. "Do you think maybe someone was trying to extort money from him?"

"Why extortion?"

"He knew how to play the financial markets, didn't he? Maybe someone in the prison wanted him to do the same for them - to make him their puppet - and so he cut himself to get away."

"That's possible. Maybe they wanted to terrorise some cash out his father too. But let's just probe Cavalcade for now. I have a meeting with a man in a hat."

"An interesting hat?"

"I hope so."

Claire's mobile phone rang as I passed her desk on the way to the main door. Her husband's name was on the screen. She stroked her throat and let it ring out.

X

THE MAN in the hat was late.

So I perched on a stool at the front bar of the rundown Fly Half Hotel. Happy Hour ran from 4-6pm and building workers in fluoro vests rubbed shoulders with office workers. I recognised the solo types in suits who drift around the CBD hoping that if they change pubs every drink or two and keep their neckties done up, their dependency will stay secret.

"What are you having, love?" said the barmaid, whose appearance was worthy of a long look. She was in her late twenties, I guessed, and handsome with a red crew-cut. She had cat-like, green eyes and what appeared to be black-painted champagne corks stuffed in her drooping ear lobes. That was the least interesting part of her. Her nipples stood proud from her chest, which looked more hard muscle than soft breast, over which she was wearing a tight white singlet with the words 'wife beater' stencilled on it in black.

I ordered a Happy Hour beer which tasted like cooking oil and soda water. I was thinking about how you get what you pay for when the Swans cap arrived on the head of a large man. He wore a red-and-white-checked shirt tucked into blue jeans with a crease ironed down the middle of each leg. I figured he lived with his mum, or he had done so for too long. He had white running shoes on his feet: new ones. I waved and he came over. His face was so freshly shaven there was soap and whiskers stuck to the rims of his ears. This man was dressed for business.

"Gar Hart," I said, extending my hand. His hand was big enough to hold a man's head comfortably, which I concluded was an asset for a psych nurse in a prison hospital.

"Bruce Tyson," he said. "Tom says you're okay - most days."

I let him have that one without a fight. He dug his fingers into a bowl of free Happy Hour crisps that was sitting on the bar and ordered a craft beer not on the Happy Hour menu. The barmaid winked at him as she pulled the beer, flexing biceps that were magnificent, being tattooed with red and blue veins that made it look like her skin had been stripped away for anatomy study.

"Drink here often?" I said to Tyson.

"My local."

That was good information. I knew where to find him if he worked out. I pointed at a table next to a wall and we sat down.

"Mind if I take notes?" I pulled a pad and pen from my jacket pocket.

"Tom said you'd pay."

I gave Tyson the envelope with the cash. He didn't count it. He stood up and stuffed the envelope into the back of his jeans. That was weird because he had two perfectly good back pockets, though this was a rough part of the city at night, and I guessed it would be late by the time he headed home, or somewhere else. If I was a mugger, I wouldn't look inside Tyson's bum crack either.

"So you are looking after Henry East at Silverwater?" I said.

"He's a fucking mess. Not much looking after I can do."

"Badly cut?"

"His head. Inside his head."

"Tom says Henry might have been attacked, not self-inflicted. Is that true?"

"That's what I'm hearing. But the prison plods are going for the suicide line."

"Why would they do that?"

"I don't know. Suits someone up top."

"What does Henry say?"

"Fuck all. He won't talk."

"Because of his mouth? The wounds. Can't talk?"

"His lips are full of stitches, but he does all right in his sleep."

"So what are you hearing?"

"From Henry? Gibberish. Goes on and on about Christ. Asking for help."

"What's the talk around Silverwater?"

"The kid's cellmate did it."

"Why would Henry's cellmate want to cut him up?"

"No idea. You're the journalist."

"Who's visiting him?"

"His sister and mother. Not many others," Tyson sneered. "Great friends he's got."

"Not his father?"

"Not that I know of, but I'm mostly not there during the day. I'm doing four to midnight. Day off today."

"Anything else catching your attention?"

"There's a book he's got next to his bed. About a kid who turns into a cockroach. A fucking weird read."

"*Metamorphosis*? Franz Kafka?"

"That sounds like it."

"Do you know who gave it to him?"

"Naa. But there's some words written inside the cover: *Stay cool, buddy. I'm with you, Bart.*

"Bart?"

"That's it."

I gave Tyson a $20 bill and he went to the bar for another round. I checked my notebook.

Tyson came back. "Carol likes your eyes," he said, handing me a schooner, but no change.

"Is that a good thing?"

"She's an eye reader: character analysis."

"So can I have your mobile phone number then?"

"Early days," he said. "Go through Tom. He said you won't quote me. No prison sources or any of that crap either. I could lose my job."

I gave Tyson my business card. It just had my mobile number, email, and the office address.

"Ed-gar Hart," he said, studying my card. "Why don't people call you Ed?"

I told him the truth. "Apparently I was born arse-about, so my father started calling me by the arse-end of my name and it stuck."

As I walked home, I figured I knew who "Bart" was. But to be certain, I needed to check a file. That could wait until morning. I picked Fish up from our next door neighbour. Sue was a godsend. All that the regular doggy day-care cost me was a box of mid-priced chardonnay now and then, the occasional box of cigars, a not-too-long chat at the door, and filling an extra shopping list at the supermarket once in a while. This night, I agreed to pay her later with a marijuana joint to smoke on the occasion of her 73rd birthday in three weeks' time.

I scanned the street for shifty strangers before putting the key in my front door. A girl holding a lead attached to a black cat dressed in a pink waistcoat counted as strange, but not shifty. The hallway was as lively as a morgue at night, and the wall-light failed when I flicked the switch. Fish charged fearlessly into the gloomy kitchen. I started to wonder if someone had been fiddling with the fuse box, but the kitchen lights worked. On the bench, there was a note from Alice. She was staying the night at her boyfriend Fred's. I calculated that Hugo should be wandering around Dubai Airport on his stopover to London. I tried his phone but it went to voice mail.

I opened a beer and sat on a bench in the courtyard under the frangipani tree, enjoying the honey-salt scent of its flowers, and tossed around ideas about how to persuade Alice to move in with Fred without causing alarm. My ideas were unconvincing, whatever way I shaped them, so I took them to bed with a glass of red and turned them to mist.

XI

I TRACKED Hugo down the next morning from my taxi on the way to the office. He'd arrived at his grandparent's home in Brighton without incident, or so he said, and answered every question with 'good'.

"I have to go. Nanna's waiting to take me to hospital."

"What for?"

"To visit grandad."

"Of course, mate. Sorry. Give him my love." Hugo's words had activated fast-moving chemistry that I wiped from my eyes, but I couldn't wipe away my imagining of little Malcolm, hooked up to a morphine drip, his skin the colour of egg yolk. We'd known for months that the chemo for his liver cancer had failed and it was too late for a transplant because the tumours had spread. I'd dubbed it the *Halliday Curse* because of the melanoma that took his daughter, Charlotte, but I was keeping that piece of wit to myself.

I hung up on Hugo and swam gladly into the shallows of my frontal lobe. My first task this morning was to find the Bart who had given Henry East the copy of Kafka's

Metamorphosis to read in prison. If he was a friend, Bart had a weird sense of humour, because the ending was not happy for the protagonist.

At my desk, I typed 'Bartholomew Edmund Hills' into the search bar for the East files I kept on my laptop. His name was mentioned several times in the court transcripts. He was a childhood friend of Henry's who provided the court with a written testimonial about Henry's fight against gambling addiction and teenage-onset depression. The testimonial was legal *haute cuisine*: a delicate *carpaccio* of logic lightly peppered with pathos. No doubt written by lawyers, and Hills was one of them.

When I phoned Hills' firm, Greenhill Partners, the receptionist put me through to a chirpy young man. I guess he sniffed a potential client.

"Oh, you're that Hart," he sneered when I revealed I was a journalist, and that I wanted to talk about Henry East.

"I'm hearing that someone attacked your friend - maybe his cellmate - that it wasn't a suicide attempt."

"You know nothing, Mr Hart."

"What is there to know?"

Hills went silent.

"I think he's in danger," I said.

Hills hung up, but I had him thinking, seed planted. My next attempt at contact might be more fruitful.

Claire was standing in my open doorway, listening.

"That's an interesting twist," she said. "If Henry wasn't a self-harmer, what would drive his cellmate to do it?"

"A motive."

Claire smiled. I felt mean.

"Our friends at Cavalcade," she said, stepping into my office. "I found a photo of their co-founder and chairman, a Mr John K. Baker."

She grinned as she put the large photo on my desk. When I looked at the picture, I saw why. Baker had wavy, shoulder-length hair parted down the middle, set off with a goatee beard and long moustache with upward curls at either end. The business-suited musketeer, whom I guessed was aged in his fifties, was standing between a smiling Henry East wearing his polo kit, and Charles East sporting a brass-buttoned navy blazer with a polka-dot cravat tucked into his white shirt. What was it about the Easts sandwiching powerful people? And a fucking cravat?

"I found this too," she said, handing me a printed copy of a newspaper story from *The London Business Examiner*. It was dated more than five years ago.

Cavalcade Founder Lost at Sea

Jean-Paul Marais, 52, the co-founder of the global private equity pioneer, Cavalcade Investment Group, is lost at sea, presumed dead.

He fell from the company's ocean yacht, Electra, during a leg of the MarcoP Classic race between Newport, Rhode Island in the US and Portsmouth, UK.

Mr Marais disappeared during the night in calm weather about 200 nautical miles west of Portsmouth. The crew on board included Cavalcade's other co-founder, John K. Baker.

Cavalcade recently denied reports it is under financial stress."

"Talk to the London office and copy Jack in Shanghai," I said. "See what they know about Baker and Cavalcade."

Claire left my office. I phoned Alice and arranged to meet her at a nearby pub. I was still tossing up whether to mention the mutilated fish, but I had become sure of one thing: I didn't want her staying at home in Darlinghurst until I had solved the mystery of the speckled carp.

*

"Dad," Alice said, looking me in the eye across a table at the Ship Inn Hotel opposite Circular Quay, gripping a beer glass with both her hands. "I want to tell you something."

"Fire away." I feared she was pregnant.

"I want to move out and live with Fred. His parents have gone overseas for a year and we can have their house."

I looked down at my beer to hide my face.

"I trust your judgement," I said, swirling the dregs. "I like Fred. I think it's a good idea. When?"

"As soon as we like."

"I'll drive your stuff over when you're ready."

Alice seemed offended that I didn't put up more of a fight, but she was already spending most nights of the week at Fred's. I just hoped she wasn't already being tracked by the fish butchers. I told myself not to be paranoid as she left the bar. I used my phone to look up Bart Hills on the Greenhill Partners' website. I found his portrait photo and made a screenshot. It was odd, I thought as I studied his features; I couldn't recall seeing his face in the courtroom during Henry's trial.

Later, back at the office, as the sun was approaching the horizon, I approached Claire, who was at her desk tapping on her keyboard. I invited her for a drink at the recently opened Babel Bar. I figured I would be less conspicuous with a partner. She agreed to meet me after she'd filed a story to the London office.

After walking a few blocks from Gunnaroo, I ascended white marble steps towards a towering sandstone building fronted by a Gothic arch over glass doors big enough to swallow a bus. The Babel Bar was housed inside a heritage-listed cathedral owned by a multi-national corporation called the Catholic Church. With their old customers dying and new recruits rarer than *bleu* steaks, the local cardinal and his advisers had come up with an inspired money spinner: leasing church buildings to private enterprise. As I stepped under the arch into the roaring booze hall, I wondered how much of the cash being poured into the place each night ended up in the coffers of the lawyers and PR people the church had hired to shade it from the light of a Royal Commission into institutional child abuse.

God should have been impressed by the cheerful assembly inside his old digs, though he would have found it hard to get a word in, or find a seat. I recognised many of the preening stockbrokers and lawyers, political hacks, investment bankers and sports stars, journalists, PR flunkies and other hangers on paying $20 for drinks worth $2. Most of them were paying with corporate credit cards, passing the cost on to their shareholders, taxpayers or clients, so this mob showed no sign of pain as Babel's owners milked them.

I leaned against the long island bar in the middle of the room, browsing for my prey, sipping slowly on a tall glass of obscure Belgian beer. I was grateful when Claire arrived and lifted my tone. I bought her a glass of wine.

"On the house," I said, handing her the glass before putting the drink receipt in my wallet so I could charge it later against *The Citizen*'s research budget. "I'm looking for this guy."

I showed her the screenshot of Hills on my phone. It was a long-odds gamble coming here, but I was thirsty and figured we might kill two birds with one stone.

"I'll take a stroll," said Claire.

I was an owl on a branch. She was a hawk on the wing. I started to think we might make a team. She returned a few minutes later.

"Up there," she said, pointing at a babbling group of men and women on the mezzanine floor above. They were standing against a giant mural of Adam and Eve sans fig leaves. Eve was wet-nursing a golden baby with a strangely adult head. Adam had the serpent knotted around his neck like a business tie. What looked, from my distance, like a stack of French fries, encrusted with rubies and diamonds, was sitting on Adam's shoulder.

I arrived on the mezzanine level and leaned against a wall to study my photo. Bart Hills, in the flesh, was tall and athletic, with a lightly freckled face and plenty of straw-coloured hair. He could have been Henry East's fair-skinned doppelganger. I tucked my phone in my jacket and stepped a few metres into the vocal range of my man.

"Bart Hills?" I asked.

Hills examined me quickly from feet to forehead and gave me that should-I-know-you look that important people learn at.

"Gar Hart," I said, extending my hand. "We spoke earlier on the phone."

Hills ignored my paw. He was holding a glass of white wine by its lower stem. He ran the fingers of his free hand through his hair and nodded for me to follow him to an empty spot beside a wall.

"Jesus," he said. "I told you. I have nothing to say. Leave me alone. Okay?"

"I don't want to quote you. We're off the record. But if someone has hurt your friend, it does him no good to hide it."

"The police are handling it."

"Do you trust the police? They're saying it was a suicide attempt, but that's not what I'm hearing."

Hills's face drained of colour. "Fuck off," he hissed, glancing over my shoulder.

I felt a gentle tap on my arm and turned.

Sandy Wallace had the same frizzy Afro hair, bee-stung lips, honey-coloured skin, and athletic build that had dazzled both sexes at high school. She was a fine fit for Babel in her three-piece business suit and dagger heels. A thick-knotted necktie, patterned with silver fishhooks on blue water, hung loose around the unbuttoned neck of her steep-collared, white shirt, its tongue tucked into her waistcoat.

Hills used the interruption to put his drink on a table and pluck an un-ringing phone from his jacket pocket. He held it against an ear and exited Babel.

"Sorry," said Sandy, placing her hand on my arm. "Was that important?"

"Just saying hello to someone."

"Do you know Bart Hills?" she said.

"Not really. Seems you do, though." She was standing so close I could smell she'd been drinking for a while.

"Our firm does a bit of work with his."

Her brown eyes gleamed. She took hold of my free hand. "It's been too long." Her touch reminded me of Saturday nights, the rush of riding with her drunk and groping in the boot of an over-crowded car to a party with even madder teenagers at the wheel.

Sandy resumed course. "Sorry, Gar, I have big ears. I heard you asking Hills about Henry East. That poor boy. What's your angle?"

I tugged my hand away from hers and pretended to zip my lips, as in no comment, then tried not to blink at my clumsy Freudian slip. There was no way I wanted to divulge Steele's unpublished info about Henry mutilating his mouth, as opposed to simply cutting his wrists.

I hadn't seen Sandy for several years, but I had no doubt she remained a serial leaker who banked favours with journalists by giving them anonymous tips about business deals, as well as gossip she picked up about the private lives of the titans of industry. I didn't want her spilling our lines of inquiry on the Easts to our media competitors. Claire arrived at my side, by chance or intuition, and helped me duck Sandy's question. I introduced them.

"Let's find a seat," said Sandy, hooking her arm around mine, leading us to a big sofa against a wall near the Adam and Eve mural. I manoeuvred Claire in between us as we sat. Sandy flagged a waiter and focussed her attention on acquiring a bottle of champagne, so I glanced at Claire and placed an index finger over my lips for a moment. Sandy could be a useful source of information, but only if carefully managed.

While we waited for the champagne, Claire answered Sandy's questions. I discovered Claire's parents were divorced, that she had a younger sister with autism, and she and Carl were still on their learner plates as a married couple.

Claire reversed the tables as the waiter filled three flutes with Dom Perignon. Sandy revealed she and I had gone to the same university, and after graduation, she had worked as a journalist in the US, Europe and Asia. To the crunching sound of the waiter tucking the bottle into an ice bucket on the table in front of us, Sandy talked as modestly as she could about her stint as press secretary to an Australian Treasurer.

Claire dragged us all into the moment: "So what are you doing now?"

"Investment banking."

"You must be a wizard on the share markets then."

"It's more algorithms than magic."

"Can you explain something to me?"

"If I like the question."

"What was Henry East's big mistake?"

Sandy's response was PR text book. "Breaking the law."

Claire furrowed her brow, apparently troubled. "How could he have got away with it?"

"Are you trying to trap me?"

"Just curious."

"Well, he traded in his own name and he did it onshore. A rookie's error." Sandy's eyes showed more than a hint of growing irritation.

"So how would a pro do it?"

"If I told you, I'd have to kill you."

Claire smiled. It was a nice smile, at least from my point of view.

"Claire, please don't think I'm rude, but could I have a private word with Gar?"

"Of course." She took her glass and walked to the mezzanine railing to look down on the main room.

Sandy shuffled along until we were thigh-to-thigh and whispered in my ear, "She's a saucy little thing."

"She's married," I said.

"So?" said Sandy, raising her eyebrows at me.

I sipped champagne and thought about Sandy, the taste of her. She seemed to sense she'd flicked my switch. We looked into each other's eyes; Sandy was shuffling her large pack of characters behind hers.

"Gar," she said, without warmth or humour, "be careful with Charles East. His son made a mistake. That's it. Don't forget what happened the last time you went after the old guy."

"Thank you for your concern."

I tried not to show it, but she had pierced me with a tiny but un-ignorable splinter.

"Anyway," she said, reverting to kind-and-sensitive-Sandy, patting my hand. "Do you still have that delightful terrace in Darlinghurst?"

"Yes."

"And what about that place in the Blue Mountains? That old farm?"

"That too."

"You must take me back there sometime."

"Sure."

"And your children? How old are they now?"

"Alice is twenty. Hugo is sixteen. And you?"

She smiled and waved her ring-less fingers at me. If she had a ring, it was probably in her pocket. Her phone pinged; she looked at the screen.

"Must go. Lovely seeing you again, Gar."

Sandy kissed me on the cheek, stood and walked over to Claire. They exchanged business cards and shook hands. Sandy walked down the curling staircase towards the main bar, chatting on her phone, hurling a hand about with fury in her eyes. It looked like one of her business deals had gone sour.

Claire returned and sat beside me. "A bit of history there?"

"Ancient," I said.

Claire topped our flutes from the waiting bottle. "It's on Dankebank," she said, showing me Sandy's business card. Her job title was *Vice President – Strategy – Asia-Pacific*. I knew a little of Dankebank; it was a giant German-based investment bank and pension fund manager.

"She has an unusual handshake," said Claire.

"How so?"

"She stroked her fingers on the inside of my wrist."

"She must like you."

Claire smiled that great smile again. I wanted to bottle it. I wondered if I should tell her that I had lived with Sandy before I married Charlotte, and that a few weeks after we moved into a flat, Sandy started staying out all night with other men - and women. She thought it was a perfectly acceptable lifestyle; after all, she came home eventually. When I objected, she said I could take it or leave it. I tried it for a couple of weeks before I left it. The last twenty minutes with Sandy in Babel reminded me I'd never properly unpacked after leaving.

Claire's phone beeped.

"Carl's getting cross," she said. "We're having dinner with some of his firm's clients. I have to pretend I care about shopping malls. Oh, and the Catholic Church; his firm's doing their PR for the Royal Commission. Do you want to come?"

"Thanks, but I'm already booked." I wasn't, and despite the delicious prospect of knocking a flaming Sambuca over a bishop's cassock, I didn't intend to become another tick on Carl Cousins' journalist scorecard so he could fatten his next invoice to his clients.

"Have a good night," she said.

She reminded me of someone who was about to fall backwards without confidence that anyone would catch her. I nearly called her back to say I'd come, but the police whistle on my phone trilled, startling some nearby drinkers, a couple of whom bolted for the toilets. I chuckled at the thought that Hugo's ringtone was sending some decent drugs down the Babel's drain, but it wasn't him calling.

"Gar, it's Bruce Tyson here, the psych nurse. I might have something for you."

"Shoot."

"Not over the phone. Can we meet in the morning?"

"Why not now?"

"I'm trying to shake a tail."

"Seriously?"

"Dance lessons, mate!"

"You know the Pickled Pig in Darlinghurst?" I said.

"I can find it."

"See you there at 8am."

When Tyson hung up, I realised I still didn't have his phone number. His call showed on my handset register as *No caller ID*.

He didn't have the body-shape for boogying. Whatever he was up to, I hoped he'd survive the night.

XII

"YOU LEAD a charmed life," the girl called behind her. She leaned upon a stainless steel railing atop a glass-walled balcony overlooking Bondi Beach, drawing air through her nostrils, searching for salt. But the line of cocaine she had just consumed with her new-found friend had numbed her sense of smell. Her sense of light, however, had sharpened. Sunset had come and gone, but the white caps of breaking waves were visible in the dark. She liked nights, the cool of them - the shadows. She closed her eyes; the cracking surf reminded her of artillery fire. It excited her.

Bart Hills opened his fridge and extracted another bottle of Vintage Krug champagne. This girl was worth it. He could have sworn she was an English actress he had seen on the Game of Thrones TV series, the blond mother of dragons, when she had tapped on the window of his Uber outside the Babel bar and asked the driver if he was in fact her ride. When she said her destination was Bondi, and smiled at him in his back seat, Hills didn't hesitate to offer to share his car. During the drive, the girl had tried to phone her flatmate, telling Hills she had lost her house key, but the friend did not answer. "Would you like to come to my place while you wait for your friend to call you?" Hills had asked.

Inside his apartment, mid-way through their first bottle of Krug, after she broke out a packet of what turned out to be A-grade cocaine, well, Hill's figured his stars were aligning. He wanted to forget about that sneaky bitch, Sandy Wallace, and that sleazy journalist, Gar Hart. And most of all, he wanted to forget about the breaking mind of his friend, Henry East. Good drugs and fine alcohol, and the chance company of a beautiful stranger who knew nothing about him, and expected nothing of him but a good time – yes, that would do the trick.

Hills filled two flutes and joined the best piece of luck he'd had all day on the balcony.

"You haven't told me your name," he said, handing her a glass.

She reached up and put a hand around his neck, drawing his ear towards her mouth. "I … am the white witch," she whispered with warm breath.

Her lips brushed his ear. Hills stiffened inside his trousers.

The girl stroked his cheek and turned his face gently towards hers. She put her lips upon his and opened her mouth, letting his searching tongue inside her, using her eyes to search the insides of the apartment for more clues about his home life. The only items that held her interest were two things she'd already noticed on the coffee table: an antique-looking book titled *The Occult World,* and a Ouija board, the items which had inspired her hastily constructed line about the white witch.

"Is that a wand?" she said, smiling, letting her hand fall upon his hardness. He was a proper stallion, this one, the girl thought. What a shame.

The apartment's entrance door opened and a young man, shorter and stumpier than Hills, and wearing a suit and tie, stepped inside.

"Shi … ," she hissed.

"I beg your pardon?" said Hills.

"Sorry. I think my phone is ringing." She stepped from the balcony into the sitting room and retrieved it from her handbag on the sofa. Looking at her screen, she said, "My flatmate is having a relationship breakdown. I need to go. But can we have dinner?"

"When?" said Hills.

"Tomorrow night. By candlelight."

"Where?"

"Here. Alone."

XIII

I FOUND Bruce Tyson waiting for me inside a booth at the *Pig*, feeding his alleged dancer's body with bacon and fried eggs, sausages, mushrooms, fried tomatoes and toast coated with finger-thick butter. I was pleased that he'd lived through the night, but surviving breakfast looked a fifty-fifty bet.

"So what's your oil?" I said, sitting opposite Tyson, waving my hand at Mick for a latte.

"There was a bloke visiting Henry East yesterday. Tall feller, Henry's age. Didn't hear his name."

"Freckled? Sun-bleached hair?"

"Sounds about right."

It had to be Bart Hills.

"Hear what they talked about?"

Tyson dabbed a finger on some egg yolk that had escaped from his lower lip and was dripping down his chin. He eyed it, licked it off. "What's it worth?"

"You're costing me a fortune, mate."

"Same as last time?"

"Let me hear it first."

"I heard your name mentioned. And they talked about some bloke called Jeff, or Zeff. I'm pretty sure it was Zeff."

"And?"

"They're shitting themselves about this Zeff."

"Okay. Get Henry to talk to me and I'll double your salary."

"Fat chance, but I'll try. By the way, I'd watch your back. It's the way that blond kid was talking about you today."

"How?"

"This Zeff is on to you."

"Okay, what else have you got?"

Tyson reached into his shirt pocket and extracted a scrap of paper. He handed it to me. It contained a mobile phone number. "It's mine"

I keyed it into the contact list on my phone. Tyson mopped up the scraps on his plate with toast and dabbed the corners of his mouth with a napkin. The plate looked like it had just stepped out of the dishwasher.

"I know what you are thinking," said Tyson, who drained his coffee.

"What's that?"

He winked and tapped the plate. "That I'm the sort of guy who doesn't like to leave a trail of evidence"

I started to like him. As he walked away, I wondered: was *Zeff* Mr Greyhound? Did he deliver the dead fish to our home? How might he escalate, now he knows that I've been chasing Bart Hills?

*

That evening, I picked up takeaway sushi on my way home from *The Citizen* and collected Fish from next door. We shared the food and watched TV in the lounge room. On our way up to bed, I stopped at Alice's bedroom and peered inside. There was a pencil sketch in a frame hanging on the wall behind her bed. The single red poppy had delicate folds of petals, upon which were intricately-drawn, rainbow-coloured ladybirds having a tea party. It was drawn by my father. This was the man who walked out on my mother when I was Alice's age and phoned me at work to say I should go home because Mum needed me. I walked into the house and found her drunk to vomiting, slumped against a hallway wall, hysterical, smeared in her own shit, spilled pills by her side. I called an ambulance and cleaned her up. Bert had packed his bags that afternoon and moved in with 30-year-old twin sisters. House sharing, he called it. "You've only got one life," he explained to me later over the phone, "and I've wasted enough of it."

I looked into Hugo's room and studied his three door bolts. My resistance was broken. I went back downstairs to my office.

I used some specialist software provided to me by the IT expert who set up *The Citizen*'s network at Gunnaroo Tower to browse the websites that had been visited from our home internet in the last few days. It had to be Hugo's trail to a porn video showing simultaneous penetration of a tiny, pubescent girl by three heavy men with eastern European accents. What the hell did Hugo make of that? What was it with Hugo and his dead mother's dress and the eye make-up? What was I going to do about it? Anything? I closed my eyelids and massaged my eyeballs. Inside that dark space, I saw Charlotte, like a mime artist behind a glass wall, pleading with me, but I couldn't understand her sign language. I just felt her frustration.

I pulled from my wallet the packet with Steele's cocaine inside, prepared it and sniffed the lot. I went to the kitchen, poured a large glass of red wine and sat beside the frangipani in the garden. It had been Charlotte's favourite tree when in flower. A few sips in, the police whistle trilled. It was a call from the Tangleton Hotel on the southern fringe of the Blue Mountains, west of Sydney.

"Garsy, it's Hughie Jones here, mate."

"Good to hear from you, Hughie. What's up?"

"You haven't forgotten, have you? The council officer is coming tomorrow to inspect the factory site at the Hill. We're booked for 2pm."

"Of course not," I lied.

My Moon Hill neighbour, Hughie, and I were seeking a permit from the local council to build a factory shed for our joint venture business: Black Snake Organic Bush Foods. It was my plan to escape from journalism. A long shot, I knew. Hughie and I had already planted Bunya Nut and Quandong fruit tree saplings on the sunny slopes to produce native herbal flavouring for our meat range. Our first recipe for wild suckling pig and yabby sausages, spiced with native lemon myrtle, had tested well with customers in a city restaurant. We had the little freshwater crayfish growing in our dams, and the baby pigs were roaming in the forest, free for the picking. All we needed was the council OK to build our food processing shed so we could hit commercial scale for the gourmet market.

I agreed to meet Hughie and the man from the Canterwell Shire Council tomorrow at mid-afternoon as planned.

Fish and I went to bed. The doorbell woke us. It was just after 12am. Mr Browning was in my bedside dresser. I clipped the magazine into the handgrip, flipped the safety catch off and tip-toed downstairs dressed in my shorts. Fish broke the peace by yapping at the door. I kept the lights off and looked through the security lens at a lone figure standing on the porch.

XIV

SANDY WALLACE'S meerkat eyes peered back at me through the security lens.

She said nothing when I opened the door. The air was damp and her hair and skin were glistening from a rain shower. Her clingy, sleeveless black cocktail dress was slit from the collar to just above her navel, revealing a ribbon of flesh. She carried a pair of black dagger-heels in one hand and a glittering clutch bag.

"What do you want?" I said.

"I'm locked out."

She looked at the gun in my hand.

"Since when have you had one of those?"

"Family heirloom."

"Alice and Hugo at home?"

"Why?"

"Can I come in? I'm wet."

Fish knew what was happening before I did. He disappeared into my office.

I closed the front door. When I turned around, Sandy put her damp palm on my naked stomach in the shadowy hallway. Her hand slid down and she led me upstairs like she was tugging a bull by a nose ring.

*

I lay soft and spent inside her, keeping my weight on my elbows and knees.

"Stay still," she whispered. "Dead still, or I'll stop."

I guessed right about what was coming. She began squeezing me from her inside, rolling her vaginal muscles in waves upon the quickly expanding length of me. Neither of us moved our outer bodies; I fought the urge to thrust and buck. With her fingers she fondled my scrotum, pressing my hardness into her to the hilt, where she held me tight and rolled her waves over me, and in time she milked me.

I woke to sunlight through the dormer window, rolled to face the inside of the bed, and was disappointed for a moment. I licked the tip of a middle finger and mopped crumbs of cocaine off a small china plate on my bedside table. All that was left of Sandy was a trace of salt-caramel scent and a smear of cherry-coloured lipstick on my pillow. The bitter taste on my finger helped get me out of bed. Sandy had left her business card on the table, next to my phone and Mr Browning.

Fish followed me about as I packed clothes for the drive to Moon Hill to meet the council inspector and Hughie.

I made two phone calls while I had tea and toast in the kitchen. Alice and Fred were flying to Melbourne for the weekend. Hugo had finished his first day at school in Brighton; he was going to bed when I called. I told him to beware of who he talked to on the internet, to be careful what he looked at, and reminded him that everywhere you go, you leave a digital trail. If Hugo understood what I was getting at, he didn't let on. He passed the phone to his nana and after talking with her I began mentally preparing for an earlier visit to England than I had anticipated only days ago. Malcolm's final deadline was approaching fast.

I walked to the local supermarket, tugging a shopping bag on little wheels that Alice bought me for Father's Day, and purchased fresh fish, fruit and vegetables for my trip to the Hill. I had plenty of beer and wine at home that I could plunder. It was a Friday so I would spend the weekend there. Fish had never liked the bush after he lost his leg in that trap, so I delivered him next door to Sue, along with a box of Cuban cigars I'd been saving since my last overseas trip.

Claire was at her desk when I arrived at *The Citizen*'s office. She cocked a green eye and put a long index finger to her chin. "Can I ask where you're off to?"

I was wearing a black tee-shirt and jeans and hiking boots.

"Bush business: just overnight, maybe two."

"Branch office, is it?"

"I do have a treehouse, as a matter of fact."

"You contactable?"

"Sure. Phone and email, but reception's patchy. The atmosphere can be strange."

"Sounds like another planet."

"Feels like it at times."

I packed some files on the East case in my briefcase and downloaded some related documents onto my laptop, then checked my emails at my desk. Jack had copied me and Claire a new press clipping from the latest English edition of *The Shanghai Business Journal*:

Former Australian Ambassador to China, Ms Kathy Throsby, has joined the Shanghai office of the Trust8 investment advisory firm, the company's chairman, Mr Charles East, announced today.

Trust8 provides advice to overseas companies seeking to invest in China. The firm's clients include some of the world's largest pension funds, as well as individual investors.

Claire appeared in my doorway, excited, waving a sheet of paper.

"You need to see this," she said, handing me the document. It was a copy of Trust8's client list. "Cavalcade isn't just sponsoring Henry's polo ponies. They have East working for them in China. *And* there's another client of East's that might interest you."

I scanned the list. The name DankeBank, Sandy Wallace's DankeBank, made my eyes open wide. I put my phone on open speaker, so Claire could hear, and hand-signalled her to stay a silent witness. I pulled Sandy's card from my wallet and dialled her private line.

"Why didn't you tell me that you are a client of Charles East?"

"What?"

"DankeBank. You are one of East's clients in China."

"You are paranoid, Gar. You need to take a cold shower. I've got nothing to do with the bank's China business. I didn't even know the bank was employing him, if that's even a fact. For god's sake, we have over a hundred offices worldwide and five thousand staff. I don't keep track of every movement."

"You know Bart Hills," I said, "and he's Henry East's best buddy. Hills shit himself when he saw you at Babel last night."

"Gar, watch your imagination. I met Hills once through work. I don't know the Easts beyond chatting at a charity ball; you know what happens when you leave the ground. You're sounding mentally unhinged. I've got to go. Call me when you want to be sensible." She hung up.

Claire looked baffled.

"Stay away from her," I said.

I collected my briefcase and laptop and left the building.

I've always thought Sylvia Plath nailed electrocution of the brain in her poem 'The Hanging Man'. I can only ever recall the first couple of lines: *By the roots of my hair some god got hold of me. I sizzled in his blue volts like a desert prophet.*

I don't remember agreeing to my electroconvulsive therapy. I refused to see Sandy when I was in the psychiatric unit. The LSD we took together triggered my psychosis, so the doctors speculated. It was more than twenty years ago. My BC period: Before Charlotte.

As I got behind the wheel of the Land Rover to drive to Moon Hill, a sick-making thought flashed inside my skull like one of Plath's blue volts. Had Sandy been poking around at home last night inside my office while I, the dopey bull, slumbered?

XV

IT WAS late-morning when I hit the Hume Highway, heading south-west under clear sky towards the Blue Mountains. Claire phoned me and I put her on speaker.

"I did those background checks on Henry East and Bart Hills that you asked for," she said.

"Impressions?"

"Henry's parents must be very cold."

"Why?"

"They sent him to boarding school, all through junior and high."

"It's pretty standard in their world."

"When you live a stone's throw across the street from your school?"

"You have a problem with boarding schools?"

"I went to one for a while, when my parents split."

"Didn't like it?"

"Better than home at the time."

I left the ball in her court. She hit it. "I had a friend at boarding school. She could see her home behind the sports field. Her parents only took her out on school holidays, when they had no other choice. It broke her heart."

"What's she like now?"

Claire paused, then served with confidence.

"A mother hen: happily married, five children."

"I went to boarding school," I said. "I was seven and eight years old. I got to sleep with a nun."

"Lucky you; at least it wasn't a priest. Oh, one other thing. There was a fire at Redleaf Pool next to Tamerlane when Henry was a teenager. Vandals set fire to the boardwalk with petrol. The local paper reported Henry and Bart tried to put it out with another boy. One of them burnt his hand. There were suspicions they'd actually started it. Nothing proved, but Charles East paid for the pool repairs."

"Okay. Let's reconvene on Monday."

About an hour later, I rolled off the bitumen onto a pale grit track inside a tall forest and wound down the windows. Overnight rain had drawn out the sharp scent of eucalyptus leaves and earthy aroma of humus-rich soil. The track narrowed and sliced into the midriff of a mountain, sending me into a concertina of relentless hairpin bends. A feral goat scurried up a slope, sending stones tumbling, forcing me to swerve to the edge of the track where I eyeballed a sheer rock-face drop of a few hundred metres to the valley floor. On the cliffs above, rivers of stones were frozen between the trees. Somehow it all held together, as it had done for thousands of years, as I hoped it would for a few seconds more while I passed by.

Several thousand seconds later, I opened the wire-mesh gate to Moon Hill and drove the dirt road to my camp, stopping near a timber deck under the branches of a giant pine.

I stepped out of the car and looked into a massive canyon, its sides carpeted by eucalypt forests, its middle split by a tannin-brown river. Mountains either side of the canyon stretched the entire width of the horizon. The place I called Moon Hill was cleared of forest a century ago, planted with pasture for raising sheep, then abandoned. The old bush was fighting back which was fine by me. I just wanted a patch to play in.

I carried my food bags from the car up a handful of steps onto the deck and looked up at the cabin of my treehouse in the lower branches. The drop-down ladder that tucks into the floor of the sleeping cabin was secured. I turned around to face the ground level cabin which functioned as a kitchen-living room, with a fridge, a stove, and a sink fed by a rainwater tank. It also housed a wooden dining table and chairs, an armchair, and a wood-burning heater for the freezing winters. The door was intact.

There was no sign of Hughie Jones and the council man for our meeting. I carried my food bags over to the kitchen cabin. On inspection, a piece of folded brown paper was tucked under the door. Hughie Jones had left me a yarn written in pencil on a gravy-stained pie bag: *Accident! Councillor Sims did his fetlock. I've took him to Canterwell Hospital. My fault. I shouted him early lunch at the pub. The big man went in hard. Cost me plenty. You wouldn't believe it. Soon as we get here, he jumps out of my truck and sticks his hoof in a wombat hole and tips over. Nasty. Bones sticking out. I'll be back in the morning. H"*

Hughie lived with two dogs on the next property to the south.

As I walked back across the deck to collect my laptop and briefcase from the car, I crossed through the black painted circle on the deck. The phone gods were working; my handset bleeped as emails and text messages dropped from space. Steele's message alarmed me more than Claire's.

XVI

STEELE: *Have you heard from Bruce Tyson? I got a garbled voice message from him. He's gone AWOL from the psych hospital. No-one at his home. Phone not answering.*

Claire: *Feedback from London on Cavalcade and John Baker. Cavalcade was on the financial brink a few years ago, but now in rude health. No evidence of more connections with East beyond polo ponies and Trust8. Sandy Wallace has asked me out to dinner. Just 'us two girls'. What should I do?*

I sent Claire a quick reply: *Postpone.*

I phoned Steele's number; I wanted a live voice call to flesh that one out. It started ringing but the signal bars disappeared. I looked around. I could have been isolated in worse places.

A handful of sulphur-crested white cockatoos spun across the sky at twelve o'clock high. They wrestled and shrieked like schoolkids after the home-time bell. A wedge-tailed eagle landed on top of a dead tree on a far hill to survey the valley. Kangaroos scratched their backs and nibbled the sweet tips of grass downhill by the dam.

It was sunny, so I stripped to my shorts and dragged the armchair from the ground cabin onto the deck. The chair had handy wooden drink rests on the tips of its arms, so I opened a cold beer and placed it on one. The chair was an old art deco thing that had seen some life, heard a lot of stories. It had been my mum's.

I felt a presence near the deck and turned slowly in order not to spook it. The male kangaroo I call Buck was nearly as tall as my car. I recognised him from a scar on the white fur of his chest, maybe ripped by barbed wire, the teeth of a dog, or a bullet. The Eastern Grey had arrived quietly with his mob of half a dozen females and joeys for a late afternoon picnic. He got my attention with his big brown eyes and long lashes, leaned back on his huge tail and put his little front paws up, rotating them like a boxer at a speed bag. I got the message about who the boss was.

"It's going to be a cracking night," I called to him. "Milky Way as far as you can see."

The big feller winked at me, scratched his bum with a paw, then set back to eating grass like I was boring him. Moments later, he bounded down an old path pounded out by his ancestors, followed by his mob.

I opened a bottle of red and poured a glass. A burst of wind whistled around the rusty wire of the flying fox in the pine tree. I had hoped it might entice Hugo to spend more time here with me, and it did for a while. But with Hugo, I have a knack of arriving in a place just as he is leaving it behind. I closed my eyes, tired from the drive and the night with Sandy, and its aftermath.

I woke shivering in the dark. A white light was strobing behind the trees in the forest. I leaped to my feet, trying to remember where I'd put Mr Browning. Bruce Tyson's voice echoed inside my skull: Watch your back...there's a bloke called Zeff.

XVII

I DARTED into the kitchen cabin and pulled the pistol from its holster on the table. I backed against the cabin wall as the torchlight scanned my car and the treehouse. The flashlight wouldn't be Hughie's – his dogs would have been upon the deck by now. My other neighbours, the Watsons, were travelling overseas. They had given me a set of house keys and asked me to check on their place if I was visiting.

"Gar?! You here?"

I lowered my gun and stepped outside into the gloom.

"Jesus," said Tania Watson as she climbed up to the deck carrying a flashlight and a shoulder bag. "You alright?"

"Fell asleep," I said, hugging my arms around my naked chest, clutching Mr Browning.

Tania and I embraced, kissing each other on the cheek. Her skin was a shock, rough and dry like I was kissing bark. I saw in the moonlight that her skin was indeed rutted, cracked. I reached inside the cabin and turned on a deck light. It took me a few seconds to grasp. Her cheeks, temples, nose, and neck were streaked with red, blue, green and yellow. Her long hair was pulled into a top knot speared with white feathers. Her face was covered with thick layers of paint; acrylics or artist's oils of some sort, I guessed.

"Bird of paradise?" I asked.

"If that's what you see."

Tania was an uncertified nutcase, but also a fine illustrator of animals and a decent landscape painter. She had a strong following in Japan and China, getting stronger from what I read in the media. On a wall at home, I had her painting of five hundred galahs coiffed with thinning chestnut-coloured hair, dressed in blue suits, white shirts and red ties, seated soberly in straight lines in the Great Hall of the People in Beijing.

She explained to me that she and her husband, Steve, had returned early from their overseas trip.

While Tania built a campfire, I dressed in warm clothes in the ground cabin. Steve, she called to me, had gone to the south coast to do his carpenter's job.

I collected folding chairs from my car and we sat by the fire with glasses of wine. Tania rummaged in her big bag.

"Got something for you." She pulled out a thin, hand-made cigarette, lit it with a stick from the fire and released the sweet smoke of hashish. She passed it to me. Then she pulled another object from her bag. A kangaroo's head!

"Relax," said Tania.

It was a mask. Just to cover the wearer's forehead, eyes and nose, with an elastic strap at the back. It had large eyeholes with great dark eyelashes lining the rims, and large ears pointing up and alert. I saw the face of Buck.

"You can join the mob," she said, handing it to me.

The mask's base was made of papier-mache so it was lightweight, she explained, then it was covered with fake fur and its nose painted black. I put it on and wondered what the real Buck would make of the weird bird and kangaroo sitting around the fire.

"Steve did a great job," I said, nodding at the treehouse. I had handed him the tools, banged in a few nails, made the tea, chilled the beers, cooked the BBQ.

"Can I have a look? I've not been up since you painted and put the beds in."

I followed her up the ladder. Inside, she lit a candle in a glass lantern on the windowsill, sending light prancing around the walls and ceiling, adding shadows to her face.

"How does it go in a storm?" she said as a gust rocked the branches. The cabin swayed and then steadied, like a boat bouncing over a wave into clear water.

"You know you're alive up here."

I was sitting on one of the two single beds. She stepped across the floor, gently lifted my mask away, and put her arm around my shoulder. We both looked at the candle inside the lantern. Tania and Charlotte had been close.

"I still miss mine too," she said. "I walk with him in the forest sometimes. Like tonight."

The Watson's six-year old boy, Dizzy, slipped off his father's sunscreen-oiled back at the beach into a freak wave that pounded the boy's head into a sand bar and snapped his neck.

Tania and I climbed down. We sat around the fire, saying little, staring at the flames, then looking at the stars, Tania telling me a little about Aboriginal dreaming in the sky. Her veins flowed with the blood of the local Gandangara people, though I couldn't tell to look at her. I wondered how she felt purchasing her rural plot from a white farmer whose family took it from her ancestors with a gun. She never mentioned it, so nor did I.

An hour or two later, she walked back into the trees and home. I cleaned up around the fire. I found a flat bottle of tequila under Tania's chair where her shoulder bag had been. *Angels Tears* was a typically exotic Tania item, a brand I'd never heard of. The night was cold and the fire was almost out. I took a few hefty swigs and carried the bottle and my rubbish bag up the steps. I passed back through the black circle on my way to the kitchen. My phone beeped. I pulled it from my pocket. An email from Steele had downloaded.

Subject: "Celebrity Doctor's Son Dead from Heroin" by Tom Steele, Crime Editor.

"The son of a prominent Sydney cosmetician has died from a heroin overdose in his luxury Bondi Beach flat. Bart Hills was 26.

"Hills' flatmate called an ambulance when he discovered Hills unconscious in bed. Hills, a corporate lawyer, was pronounced dead on arrival at St Vincent's Hospital in Darlinghurst.

"His father, Maximilian Hills, is known as the 'Father of Famous Faces' after re-birthing the visages of some of Australia's most prominent families and celebrities. He has his own cable TV show...."

I dialled Steele's number; the screen went black. Dead battery. I realised the phone had exhausted itself by constantly searching for a non-existent network connection, trying to find something that wasn't there. I chuckled; it was a bit like journalism at times - a lot of times.

I took another swig of Tania's tequila against the cold and searched my car and the cabins for my phone charger. After about half-an-hour of fruitless endeavour, I concluded that I'd left the charger in Sydney. I stood on the deck tossing up whether or not to drive back to the city in the night to talk to Steele about Hills.

The wind whistled like panpipes through the needle-leaves of the pine. I made out the silhouette of a roosting crow on a branch. Moonlight shimmered on the painted ring of the black circle on the deck. The black ring uncoiled into a snake.

XVIII

I STAGGERED backwards. Hideous shrieking burst from the canopy of the pine. A black blotch shot out and was sucked into the sky and torn apart. The branches began writhing, squirming. Snakes: a tree full of black snakes.

I jumped off the deck, bouncing as if landing on a trampoline by the campfire. I threw dry leaves and twigs on the dwindling flames and kick-started the blaze. The fire surged. Flaming dogs jumped up at me. I stumbled back. The frenzied animals tried to bite me.

Squealing, terrible squealing from the forest; I turned. A line of bedraggled figures had gathered at the forest's edge. The blackened shapes of deformed people swayed drunkenly, edging towards me. I bounded up the steps and found Mr Browning on the kitchen table. I heard my father's voice as I picked it up: "That's it. Do the world a favour, you fucking waste of space. Put it in. Go on. Put it in, you weak cunt!"

I put Mr Browning's muzzle inside my mouth. It would get me out of this place. I'd been here before. Plath's blue volts flickered around the cabin.

"Get the angle right, you moron. Ah, I get it. Half a job by half a man. That's you, Gar. End up in hospital. A fucking veggie. People blubbering over you. That'd be right. A fucking burden."

I turned to the door. Outside, someone was sitting in my mother's armchair; they beckoned me with a hand. The deck rose and fell like an ocean swell as I traversed it, stumbling. I saw that I held Mr Browning in one hand and a flashlight in the other. My mother pointed at the hillside by the deck. I followed her line with my light to the opening of a cave. I stepped downstairs from the deck, across grass, up to the mouth of the hole. I lay on my stomach and crawled in, pushing my torch on the dirt in front of me. It was tight upon my chest. The earth was breathing, expanding and contracting, suffocating me. I pushed past its sphincter into a massive, glistening chamber. In a corner, Charlotte, Alice, and Hugo squatted naked and filthy around a fire. I tapped Charlotte on the shoulder. My fingers travelled through her flesh, but I felt her bones and took comfort that she had substance of some sort. She scratched the spot where I had touched her like it was an itch.

"His mind is shot," said Alice.

"I'm here!" I screamed. None of them noticed me.

Alice was missing an arm and a leg. There was a red hole in her face where an eyeball should have been. Hugo's ears and nose were missing.

"My turn," said Charlotte, who pulled off one of her arms and threw it in the fire in a crackle of flames.

A black snake slipped out of Charlotte's anus. It wormed into Alice's and I tried to catch it, but I failed. The snake's head appeared in Alice's mouth, flicking its tongue, dot-eyes fixed on mine. I opened my mouth and the snake wriggled slowly in. I put Mr Browning's muzzle in after the snake and pulled the trigger.

*

"Gar. Gar!" A dull, distant voice.

My eyes hurt. There was grit in them. Dirt in my mouth. Rays of light flickered from behind my right ear. Thirsty. So thirsty. Cramp knifed my right thigh, a sadist stabbing me and twisting the blade. I howled.

Something had me by the ankles and was tugging. More light came from behind me. My legs straightened and the cramp cleared. I expanded my chest, sucking in air, blinking into sunlight. Dogs' faces came at mine. Big, hot tongues licked me. Hughie's dogs, Spike and Clive.

"What the fuck are you doing in a wombat hole?" Hughie looked down at me. I rolled on the grass away from the dogs. He was leaning on a long-handled shovel. He held out a leathery-skinned hand. I grabbed it and he pulled me to my feet, steadying me with his arm around my waist.

"Here," he said, handing me a water bottle. He scraped Mr Browning and my flashlight out of the hole with his shovel.

"You go hunting in there?" he said, scraping dirt from the gun with his fingernails, then a twig, before blowing on it.

"Rough night," I said, gulping the water. "Sleep walking."

"You ought-a chain ya-self to ya bed at night."

I checked my flashlight. The batteries were dead.

"Do you want a beer?" I said.

"Na, mate. How 'bout you have a wash and we both have a nice cuppa tea?"

I followed Hughie up the steps to the deck. He put the kettle on. I had a cold water bucket-bath on the deck and dressed in fresh clothes.

I found my phone in my jeans pocket, still dead, but the black circle was no longer a snake. It was a painted ring. The pine tree looked like a pine tree.

"What the fuck has she just dragged out of your wombat hole?" said Hughie, standing from his seat in a folding camp chair.

I looked at the hillside. Spike had something in her mouth that she was snapping from side-to-side. It looked like floppy liquorice rope. It took me a few seconds to register the dead snake. An inspection revealed its head had been shot off.

"What the hell is that?" Hughie eyeballed the wall as we walked into the kitchen to examine the contents of the fridge for possible breakfast. He lifted my Buck-mask off a hook and gave it a close inspection. I explained its origins

"You and your friends get up to some weird shit, Garsy," he said, putting it back on the hook.

I needed to talk to Tania about what was in her bottle of *Angel Tears* tequila which sat on the bench by the sink. I'd phone her from the city when I had it re-charged. If that conversation didn't throw a light on the events of last night, I figured I might need a doctor of some sort again.

After several cups of tea, a plate of bacon and eggs, and a discussion about how long it would take for the council inspector's broken shinbone to heal, Hughie washed the dishes and left me to pack up to go home.

XIX

IN MY HOME office in Darlinghurst, I plugged my phone into the charger and called Steele.

"Was Hills a regular heroin user?"

Steele replied: "That's what I'm told by the investigators."

"He didn't look it to me."

"It takes all types."

"Any sign of Bruce Tyson?"

"One of my copper mates has done some background work as a favour. Big Brucie cleared out his bank accounts and took it all in cash. We visited his flat. No sign of forced entry. But his phone hasn't answered for nearly three days and we can't get a trace on it either - looks like he's pulled the battery out, or someone has. His psych unit boss says Bruce hasn't had a sickie in ten years and he has just missed a weekend shift with penalty rates."

"Theories?"

"Someone's put the frighteners on him, or buried him."

"No kidding. Was he a gambler?"

"Na. That money you gave him was to sponsor some kids in Africa he looks after. They're on his Facebook page."

"Got time for a beer?" I wanted to tell Steele about my night in the bush.

"Sorry, mate, no can do. Karen's on the warpath. Her parents are here, brothers and sisters: the whole catastrophe. Carnival Day at the Steele's."

It was Saturday afternoon and warm. I could almost smell Steele's sizzling barbecue sausages and tiger prawns, and see his well-upholstered clansmen belly-flopping into the pool under the palm trees to the delight of his nieces and nephews.

Steele said: "Lunch. Monday. You book."

*

I phoned Tania Watson but the mobile reception at her property next to Moon Hill was worse than mine. I left a message asking her to call me. I hoped it would land, but I couldn't be sure when. She hated technology. Sometimes she didn't reply for weeks.

I had a hot bath and dressed in a tee-shirt and pyjamas. Fish and I settled down in the lounge to watch a football game. It was a recording of the previous day's Sydney Swans vs Collingwood Magpies in the AFL. I fast-forwarded to the start of the last quarter, knowing my Swans come-from-behind victory was on its way. I figured I had a crystal ball, a bit like Henry East had when he placed his bets on his inside share trades.

As the game came to a close, I flicked through the contact list on my phone. All Charles East could do was tell me to fuck off. I dialled him using my new spare phone with a new number to sneak up on him.

"Yes?" said Charles.

"Mr East. It's Gar Hart here. From *The Citizen*."

"Oh … look, I'm sorry, Edgar. I can't speak. I'm expecting a call."

"I wondered if we might meet."

"It's done, Edgar. It's over. We have nothing more to say."

"I'm sorry, Charles. But I've heard someone might have attacked Henry. That he didn't hurt himself. And now his best friend Bart Hills is dead."

Seconds passed.

"Charles?"

"Who told you that? About my son."

"I can't say who. I'm sorry if I shocked you," I lied.

"I'm horrified."

"Can we meet? I am happy to discuss what I know with you face-to-face. If you can answer some of my questions."

East took a few seconds. "When?"

"How about now? I can come to you."

"Yes. I suppose here at Tamerlane would be best. I'll let security know."

Tamerlane was a ten minute taxi ride from my place and as distant as Mars.

The Easts two-man-high, sandstone front wall was topped with wrought iron spearheads, giving the impression there was a legion of Roman soldiers marshalled behind it. The fuck-off wall stretched along one hundred metres of Old South Head Road. It was interrupted by double wrought-iron gates for vehicle entrance and a solid steel security door that was cut into the stone for pedestrian-only access. I walked to the door under the gaze of a swivelling CCTV camera mounted on a metal post inside the wall. I pressed the buzzer. The door opened on hydraulic hinges. I stepped inside and it clunked behind me like a bank vault.

Tamerlane's main residential building looked even more like a stone church than I remembered. It had twin, timber, gothic-arch entrance doors, tall and wide enough to accommodate an African elephant, if one should chance by. I got that idea because there was a small stone elephant standing beside a garden wall with some petunias growing out of a chair on its back. I crossed a circular, white-gravel driveway, in the middle of which stood a naked boy made of marble who was pissing into a pond. A showroom-shiny, royal blue Bentley sat smugly on the driveway.

Tamerlane had over a dozen intersecting roofs, by my quick count, with gargoyles on every corner, mostly goblins and dragons. At least one of the ancestral Easts had a sense of humour; some wit had added a local touch by commissioning a couple of gargoyles with kangaroos' bodies upon which sat the heads of eagles.

One of the twin entrance doors opened. Charles' lanky frame was dressed in a buttoned-up, single-breasted navy blue suit with an open-necked white shirt, a pair of bifocal reading glasses hanging by a gold chain from his neck. His black shoes reflected light. It was Saturday afternoon. I was wearing navy corduroy jeans, copper-coloured, elastic-sided boots and a black sports jacket over my black t-shirt. I resisted the urge to quickly polish my boots against my jeans. At least I'd brushed my teeth, had a shave, and cleaned Moon Hill's dirt from under my fingernails and out of my ears. I had my phone in my jeans and a notebook and pen inside my jacket.

"Please. Come in, Edgar," he said.

As I closed in on him, he extended a hand, giving me more fingers than palm. He winced, so I eased the pressure. His knuckle joints were swollen. I guessed arthritis. The old king was weakening, at least physically.

I stepped through the entrance hall onto a chessboard-tiled floor, each tile big enough to accommodate two feet. Human chess seemed an option. The hall had high-vaulted ceilings and multi-coloured, leadlight windows that were doing pretty things with the afternoon sun. The tiles led to a staircase that went up a dozen or so steps before curling both left and right to the upper storeys. Charles ushered me at ground level to the right side of the stairs into a hallway past several large rooms behind floor-to-ceiling, glass-panelled doors. One had a long dining table and chairs for about twenty people; the next had puckered leather sofas arranged in a four-piece pod, with floor-to-ceiling bookcases. Glancing inside the reading room, I was impressed by a globe of the world that was too big for any man to stretch his arms around. Now maybe if Charles and Henry held hands...

"First of all, Edgar," he said as we walked, "we're off the record. Agreed?"

"Yes." I knew I'd be bounced if I objected.

"And two: in the past, you and I have misunderstood each other. Let's put away the hatchet, as they say."

Charles made it sound like he was putting the weapon in a drawer for later, rather than burying it in the earth for good, as was the practice of the native Americans who gave birth to the expression.

"Consider it buried," I lied.

On my only previous visit to Tamerlane, about ten years ago, Charlotte and I had dinner with just Charles and his wife, Victoria, on a clear-skied, summer Saturday evening. After a waiter served us rock oysters and crayfish salad on the upper terrace, followed in the dining room by roast beef and vegetables, Victoria sponge cake and a cheese platter, Charles and I sat alone in cane armchairs on cream cushions on the garden-level veranda at the back of the main building. The sweet perfume of jasmine vines had mingled with salty harbour air and the smoke of Cuban cigars the size of baby cucumbers that we puffed on. We sipped old Scotch whisky, with no adulterating ice, from crystal tumblers while he pointed across his lawns through old trees to his twinkling new yacht in the bay, prattling on about its Italian makers and talking about visiting cities I'd only read about. "Welcome to my Garden of Eden," he'd proclaimed. Then he'd tried to bribe me with that job as his PR man at double my reporter's salary. I didn't dismiss the offer out of hand. With a young family, I was looking for a step up society's ladder - more money, a better chance at financial independence one distant day - but he gave his real game away that night by instructing the waiter with snaps of his fingers and flicks of his hands, like he was shooing around a fly wearing a bow tie.

"I'll think about it," I said. At my baulk, his smile vanished and he appeared puzzled, studying me like a specimen in a jar. He'd already grilled Charlotte and me over dinner, very politely, of course, about our family background, schooling, what suburb we lived in, what type of house we lived, and most importantly of all, whether or not we owned it. Before dinner started, I had sipped champagne and watched the teenage Henry doing wild, somersaulting bombies into the swimming pool by bouncing off a trampoline beside the pool. He was playing with another skinny boy. There was something soft about the other kid, who hopped off the trampoline into the pool, rather than bounced, and pinched his nose as he slipped into the water.

This afternoon, I wondered what had happened to that soft kid as Charles led me back to the garden-level veranda and directed me to sit in similar outdoor furniture to that which we shared years ago. Beyond the tiered acres of trees, flowering shrubs and fresh-cut lawns, sailboats drifted on the green water off Tamerlane's white beach under blue sky. It was some showroom.

East put his knobbly hands together, like he was praying, and bounced his index fingers on his chin: "What you told me about Henry being attacked. Are you sure?"

"It's what I've heard."

"We need to know who told you, Edgar. So we can take it to the police."

"We?"

"Our legal team."

"I can't tell you who told me, Charles. But you can ask the police to investigate the claim. I'm told he was attacked by his cellmate."

"If someone tried to kill or harm my son, and you are withholding evidence, it's a crime."

"It's speculation, Charles. I'm not a witness. Frankly, I still don't know why he did the insider trading in the first place. Why would he ruin his life like that?"

"Have you ever mucked up, Edgar?"

East fixed his eyes on me and waited. I wondered if he had found my old court records. I wasn't giving him easy points, so I said nothing.

He said: "Yes. We all have. Now, I'm asking you to leave Henry alone. He is a sick young man. You pursuing him is simply cruel. I know you've been bombarding him with interview requests."

"Do you believe he acted alone?"

"Of course I do."

"It's all very neat, isn't it?"

"You are very cynical, Edgar. Sometimes things are exactly as they seem."

"Why didn't you appeal his jail sentence?"

"There was no point. Henry made choices and now he is paying the price."

"What about Bart Hills? Did you know he was a heroin user?"

"Of course not. I know Bart's parents. They are shattered, like I am."

"Can I talk to Henry?"

"Edgar, I am asking you. Please leave us alone so we can make our son healthy again. You have children, don't you?"

"I do."

"A boy and a girl, isn't it? How old are they now?"

I didn't like his tangent but I figured he could get the basic information easily enough if he wanted to. He probably had it, and more, on my file already.

"They are young adults," I said.

There was a jug of water spiked with sliced lemon and ice on a side table. East poured two glasses. He spent a few moments focussing on the glasses.

"Please, help yourself," he said.

As I picked up a glass and took a sip, he smiled. There was a weird sense of satisfaction on his face like he'd made a smart chess move.

He said: "The choices you make will affect your children's wellbeing, Edgar. Sometimes in ways you can't imagine. You need to be wise on their behalf."

"Are you threatening us?"

East looked hurt. "Please. You misunderstand me. Your children need you. My son needs me. We can waste a lot of time chasing things that turn out to be wrong for our children."

East stood up. He looked away from me, across his garden towards the harbour, and dabbed an eye. Maybe I'd misjudged him.

"Do you know where your son and daughter are right now, what they are doing? Their state of mind?"

I thought of Hugo in Brighton, the internet porn, the old scars on Alice's wrists.

I said: "It's the examples we set as parents that matter, that guide them in adulthood."

"Yes," he said. "Monkey see, monkey do. Do you believe, ergo, that I am to blame for Henry's situation?"

"You didn't have him on reins, Charles, did you? He had his own head at twenty-six years of age."

"You're right," he said. "I lost him some time ago."

East seemed very old. I felt sad for him, like I did for Henry when he entered the revolving courtroom doors for sentencing. I decided to leave. Then East turned back towards me and tugged an eyelid like he just had a piece of grit in there he'd been trying to wash out. He'd almost got me.

I said: "What is the nature of your relationship with the Cavalcade Investment Group and its chairman, John Baker?"

He tugged an ear lobe as he turned to face me. A lie was coming, or pretty good chance of one.

"We gave them some advice once," he said, bending down to pick up his glass of water and moisten the slits of his lips.

"Gave?" I said. "As in the past tense?"

"That's right."

"Your China subsidiary, Trust8, lists Cavalcade as a current client."

"That is outdated."

"It was on a press release Trust8 put out a few days ago."

"There must have been an error in our China office," he said. "Translation can be a major problem. Look, I have some business to do. If there's nothing more you can tell me in relation to Henry, I must go."

"Who are *They*? The people Henry was worried would chase him down in prison. The ones he talked about the day he was sentenced."

"You must have misheard, Edgar. There were no such people. If, on the other hand, someone has subsequently decided to attack Henry in prison, as you say, then we can press the police to follow your line. So I thank you. But please, don't inflame things by pursuing Henry. I'm asking you, as a father to a father."

I heard a splash of water beside the veranda, then another as water drops spattered the chessboard tiles. I walked to the edge of the veranda and looked into a pond. It teemed with fat, orange and white speckled carp.

The words just shot from my mouth. "Did your goons hang a dead fish on my door?"

"I beg your pardon?"

"Those fish of yours," I said, nodding at the pond. "They get around."

"I have no idea what you are talking about. You need to take a few breaths, Edgar. You are sounding mentally unhinged."

Mentally unhinged? The words hit me like a hammer.

"Is Sandy Wallace working for you?" I said. I had no doubt she would give him dirt on me if it would help her get ahead with the big end of town.

"Who?"

"She works for DankeBank. They're clients of yours in China."

"Never heard of her." He touched his ear lobe again.

"You've become very clumsy, Charles. Or your people have."

"You should go, Edgar, before you do something you regret."

"You're dead right," I said.

We walked in silence through his house towards the front door. Even though East was in front of me, I wanted a hard shell on my back. Tiny cameras, tucked in ceiling corners, blinked green lights and swivelled as we passed by. In the entrance hall, near the base of the staircase, I glanced down a corridor and saw a figure in a wheelchair. They rolled back into a room.

East held the front door open. "With your history of mental illness, I'd tread very carefully before making any more wild accusations about me," he said. "See yourself out."

Inside the stone wall, the pedestrian door to the street opened automatically, beckoning me. East stepped back inside Tamerlane house and closed his door.

As I stepped onto the gravel driveway heading for the open door, the whiff of cigar smoke stopped me. I turned and felt a chill when I saw the source.

Leaning inside the archway of a sandstone wall to an inner garden was silver-haired Mr Greyhound, sans his courtroom pinstripe suit. He looked even wirier clad in a white singlet tucked into black trousers, bare-footed, his hands inside his trouser pockets. I nodded at him; it was polite instinct, rather than intention. He stood still as a statue, eyeballing me with no expression, unblinking. The only thing moving was smoke wafting out of the cigarillo hanging from one side of his skinny lips.

I stepped happily out of the insane asylum and flagged a taxi on the street.

"Fly Half Hotel," I said to the driver.

I was pleased that Carol was behind the bar. She was wearing her wife-beater singlet but I was drawn again to her tattooed biceps. Blood seemed to pulse through the tatts when she flexed to pour beer. As she filled my schooner, I saw her photo featured on a stack of leaflets on the bar, headlined *Carol Cougar – Cage Fighter*. I folded one and put it in my pocket. It might be a fun night, though I wondered where she tucked those drooping ear lobes with the black corks in them when she was belting the hell out of someone.

After downing most of my glass and feeling feisty, inspired by visions of Carol confronting her challengers inside a cage, I pulled out my phone and eyed Charles East's number. I was ninety-nine per cent sure I'd just seen Bruce Tyson's "Zeff" inside that garden arch, and I was just as sure he had left the calling-card carp, but I wondered if Charles had ordered it, or even knew about it. If he was Charles's house dog, he didn't look like he'd been to obedience school. I keyed his numbers into my phone, but hesitated over the dial button because Jack Darling's voice started echoing inside my skull: *never dial in anger*. Instead, I sent texts to Alice and Hugo. Only Alice replied; she was shopping in Melbourne.

"Seen Bruce Tyson?" I asked Carol.

"Nup," she said. "But you're not the only bloke asking."

"Police?"

"Nup. No ID. Shifty as a rat, this bloke, with eyes to match, so I told him fuck all."

"When?"

"A few days ago."

"Physical description?"

Carol described a man who sounded remarkably like the saw-toothed string bean I'd just seen inside the arch at Tamerlane. My spine fizzed and I didn't like the feeling.

XX

THE WIRY MAN stepped along a gravel walkway through the flowering rose garden of Tamerlane. He flicked the smouldering butt of his cigarillo into a pond and snapped a white flower from its thorny stem, drawing sweet perfume from its petals through his long, narrow nostrils. The smell reminded him of his mother. He walked on, under an arch of pink rose vines, up to the front door of a sandstone cottage. He opened the door without knocking. The girl was sitting on the king-sized bed, her back propped on pillows piled against the bedhead which butted against a wall in the open kitchen, sitting, and sleeping room. Her slim, muscular figure was dressed in a white tee-shirt and underpants. There was a purple bruise around a vein weeping a little blood on the top of her right foot.

An empty syringe sat in a dish on the bedside table. He guessed she had mixed a cocktail again, probably a combo of cocaine and heroin, because she appeared alert and dopey at the same time, jigging her head to the sound of something, probably music, pumping through a wireless headset clamped over her ears. Her eyes were open. He signalled for her to lift off the headset. She hung it around her neck like a high-tech horseshoe.

"You've seen the movie *Scarface*," he said with his back to her, placing his fresh rose with a handful of others in a vase on the kitchen table. He turned to face her. "Now read my lips: 'never get high on your own supply'."

"Fuck you, Seth!"

"Do you mean it, girl?"

"Sure. Why not? That's all you men ever want to do, unless it's watch football. And I'm bored."

He stepped into the bathroom and returned carrying a black briefcase, which he put on the bed beside her. He began taking his clothes off, folding each item neatly and stacking them upon the seat of a chair with military precision.

"Aren't you going to close the shutters?" she said. "That old perv, Charlie, will be knocking on the door next, wanting his turn."

The naked man smiled and closed the window shutters.

She opened the case and extracted a strap-on black dildo, the size of a cucumber, rippled with veins. Thank God, she thought, it's just a one-way, not a two-way piece. She lifted a short-sleeved, camouflage-patterned army shirt from the case that she put on over her tee-shirt and buttoned up to just below the collar, then she removed her underpants.

The naked man reached for a small, pink-glass bottle that sat on the bedside table, sprayed some of the rose scent on his wrists and rubbed them together. Then he lay on his back on the bed in the female missionary position with his knees bent. The standing girl strapped the device around her waist, buckled its belt and reached for her phone to wirelessly turn up the volume on her headset, which she replaced over her ears, listening to the sound of surf at the beach. She did not like the sounds he made when she did what she was about to do - the pathetic moaning – although she did like the way it contorted his face.

He opened his legs and she climbed in between them, kneeling on her shins. The flat, hand-sized base of the black proboscis was pressing firmly over her pubic bone, transmitting a faint, not unpleasant sensation to her clitoris.

"Can I have oil?" he said.

"No," she replied.

He used a hand to position the knob of the proboscis upon the sweaty rim of his anus, then gripped her small, muscular buttocks with both his hands. She plunged into him as brutally as she could, looking into his eyes for the impact of every thrust.

XXI

FISH AND I strolled along the foreshore of Rushcutter's Bay Park on the edge of the harbour a short walk from home. We rested on a bench under a hazy, mid-morning sky.

A young woman in a motorised wheelchair pulled up alongside us. She controlled the chair with her bony hands from joysticks at the end of the armrests. Fish jumped off the bench and put his front paws in her lap. She patted him.

"Just say if he's annoying you," I said.

"Mr Hart," said the woman, removing her cat's-eye sunglasses, "my name is Ellen East. I am Henry East's sister. You were at my home yesterday."

I looked around the park for her sidekicks. No sign of the silver dog.

"I'm alone, Mr Hart."

I rolled my eyes, unable to prevent a snigger.

"You might be surprised at what you can do in my condition if you put your mind to it."

"And you found me how?"

"Your home address is on the electoral role: a public record."

"I meant how did you find me here."

"Your neighbour said you were walking your dog."

"How can I help?" I made a mental note to caution Sue about talking to strangers in these increasingly unusual times.

"You wish to talk to my brother?"

"Your father doesn't approve."

"I can help you."

"Why would you do that?"

"So that you can understand Henry's situation and we can all have some peace."

"Good by me."

"I can't get you into Henry's hospital, but I can do a video call. And it has to be off the record. Do you agree?"

"Yes."

Off the record, always off the record, but any contact with Henry was better than none. I could test the depth of his *injuries,* for a start. I gave Ellen my phone number. She was fair-haired, pale-skinned and round-faced. No trace of the equine profile of Charles and Henry, and she did not look like her mother either. I took her on her word that she was the East's daughter.

"Ellen," I said, "there was a man smoking a cigar in your garden yesterday."

"Mr Peterson? He just drives Dad around."

"Does he have a first name?"

"Oscar."

"Has he been working for your dad for long?"

"About a year."

"Where's he from?"

"I suggest you ask him."

*

119

When Ellen's video call came a few hours later, I was seated in my home office with recording software running on my laptop, and a notebook and pen at hand.

On screen, a poor quality colour picture of Henry East emerged. He was propped up in bed on a stack of pillows. Ellen held her camera phone so I could see the top half of his body and his head. His lips were bloated and criss-crossed with dark stitches; the rim of his mouth was stained yellow with what I assumed was antiseptic. His eye sockets were dark. Henry's hair was shorter than when he was in court, as if it was just growing back after a shave. I glimpsed a thick bandage on one of his wrists as he stroked an itchy stitch on his lip. It didn't look like fake theatre.

Henry's voice was groggy and the tone deep: "Mither Hart, I have chosen ... to speak. Please do not tell ... do not say to my father."

"I will not tell Charles we have spoken," I said. "Did you act alone, Henry, with the insider trading?'

"I confessed ... all that to the court."

"That's a lawyer's answer. I don't believe you did act alone."

"The court believed. Are you ... are you smarter than the court?"

"Were you inside trading with Bart Hills?"

"Bart is dead."

"That is not an answer, Henry."

"No is an answer," he said.

"Bart died a few days after I spoke with him. Did someone kill him because of that?"

"That's why, Mr Hart ... I am speaking with you, Mr Hart. You are hurting people ... I made some very bad mistakes. I am paying now ... Bart had an accident ... a terrible accident."

"Did someone attack you in your cell?"

"No. Why ... would someone do that?"

"Who hurt you, Henry?"

"Mither Hart! Don't put words in my mouth. Ellen and I are asking you ... asking you ... leave our family alone. There is none ... no mystery."

"Who is John K Baker? What is your father's relationship with the Cavalcade Investment Group?"

"I have ... no idea, no idea."

"You rode Mr Baker's polo ponies."

"He rode me, Mr Hart."

"What do you mean, Mr Baker 'rode you'?"

"You ... you are mad, Mr Hart. Give us some peace, please."

"Do you know Sandy Wallace? The woman from Danke-Bank?"

My phone screen went black. I phoned Ellen East back. The message said the phone number was not in service.

Bruce Tyson hadn't hammed things up for his $500. Henry was a mess. Did Ellen East want me to see he was a gibbering wreck? To persuade me to back off?

I spent the afternoon transcribing notes from my interview with Henry and drawing on a whiteboard the characters and their places in the picture puzzle that was emerging: Henry East, Charles East, Ellen East, Bart Hills, Oscar Peterson, Bruce Tyson, and Sandy Wallace.

In the early evening, Steele returned a call I had made to him earlier, and I recounted my interview with Henry.

Steele said: "If he was a threat to anyone, sounds like they've neutralised him now."

"He might be foxing."

"He's a pretty good fox then."

I told Steele I'd booked lunch at his favourite restaurant the next day. We hung up. I'd tell him about Oscar Petersen then. I reckoned the only real Oscar Peterson I knew of was a dead, black jazz pianist from America. I put one of his albums on the music player in my bedroom which helped to mask Fish's snoring. I wanted Mr Browning handy beside me when I climbed into bed beside Fish. I scoured the house but couldn't find him anywhere. I slept, tried to, with a hunting knife under my pillow.

XXII

I WOKE with daybreak and headed to the Pickled Pig dressed in a suit to have breakfast before work. As I walked, the image of Henry East's yellow-stained mouth and stitched lips flashed on and off in my skull. I phoned Hugo.

It was early evening in Brighton. He was going to the movies with a girl from his school. That was the first date that I'd ever been told about. He sounded happy so I felt almost serene as I sat in a booth at the Pig and watched Mick work his hissing coffee machine. My calm lasted about thirty seconds. Oscar Petersen appeared in front of me.

He unbuttoned his navy pinstripe suit jacket, fingered his blue tie and sat opposite me, sliding his lean frame deep into the booth so his back touched the café wall. Clearly he didn't want anyone stabbing him from behind, which was my first instinct.

The say-cheese smile didn't shift on his pointy, tanned face. Up this close I noticed his bony nose was buckled. Maybe he boxed; either too often, or not too well, although he didn't look like a man who lost many fights. He stroked what was available of his silver hair, dragging it forward across his temples.

"Mr Hart," he said in his Afrikaans twang, "do you want to tell me why you are harassing Mr East?"

"I'm not."

"Oh yes you are."

"I hear you're a chauffeur for Mr East. You've stepped out of your box, haven't you?"

"I am an adviser."

"To which Mr East?"

"To the whole family. I want you to show them some respect, my friend. They have had a family tragedy."

"Yes. I understand. I just want to know the facts."

"What right. Do you have. To know. Private facts?"

I started reaching for my mobile phone. I would take his photo, record the threats I knew were coming. "You don't mind if I check your bona fides with Mr East, do you?"

His eyes glanced left and right, checking for eavesdroppers. The other customers were engrossed in their own conversations. "Do you think I am an idiot, Mr Hart?"

"I can't tell."

He leaned over the table towards me and hissed: "You touch that phone and I will smash your face." He bared his teeth as if he was showing a dentist his bite.

I weighed up testing him. I kept my phone in my pocket.

"I have some advice for you, Edgar Albert Hart, otherwise known as Gar: forty five years old; father of a boy and girl with a dead mother; resident of Darlinghurst in some shitty terrace house; owner of a three-legged poodle; playschool farmer at Moon Hill. You stick your beak inside my wall again and I will cut it fucking off. Are we clear?"

"Is this coming from Charles East or you?"

"Listen carefully to what I say, kaffir. Go back to chasing fire engines, or whatever you people do."

"If I don't?"

Mick arrived with my coffee and looked at the silver dog.

"He's not staying," I said to Mick, who put my coffee down, acknowledged my nod, and returned to his other customers.

"Strange chap," said the silver dog, stroking his tie, sneering at Mick who was wearing a bowler hat and a white cricket outfit with the trousers held up by braces. With his trousers tucked into calf-high, black Doc Marten boots, Mick was looking very *Clockwork Orange* droog, and my world was feeling just as surreal.

The silver dog slid out from the booth, stood up and rested a hand lightly on my shoulder. He bent and put his mouth close to my ear. I felt his breath. He whispered: "I hear you are not the sharpest knife in the block. Or the most mentally stable. If you are going to play games with people's lives, get some life insurance. Do the right thing by your family. Insure the lot. Your poodle can spend the money, if he lives long enough."

He smiled and walked into the street, lit a cigarillo and winked at me through the window before strolling out of sight.

Mick studied me. "You don't look well, Gar. Who was that?"

"He was an errand boy - I think."

"See that ring on his finger? Engraved with crossed daggers," said Mick. "Military, by the look. And he had a knife strapped inside his jacket."

"What?"

"I saw it when he slid from the booth."

I phoned Alice. She was still in Melbourne with Fred. They were flying back to Sydney the next morning.

There was a poster tacked to one of Mick's walls; a matador with a cape was dodging a bull. Mick had been to bullfights in

Mexico where he purchased it. He had told me that in the first act of a bullfight, the *banderillos*, or flagmen, jab barbed sticks into the bull's back to set them up for the kill.

I massaged a pain in my knotted shoulder muscle and wondered when and how the matador might make his next move ...

UNDER EDEN

Part 2

XXIII

THE RED Emperor restaurant on the King Street Wharf corporate eating strip on the western edge of the Sydney CBD was a roaring waterfall of voices. The glass and steel box was chock full of men and women in suits, with bigger waistlines and blander faces than the younger, finely chiselled mob at Babel. Steele was already seated, with a bottle of white wine half consumed and heavily pecked starter dishes on the table.

"Nasty," I said. I couldn't miss the parallel red and yellow scratch marks on the skin near his left ear.

"It wasn't Karen," he said, stroking the scratches, sliding his wine glass over the tablecloth so the waiter could get an easy pour. "One of my nephews in the swimming pool."

I wasn't convinced. Karen Steele was, on balance, a tolerant wife: volcanic at times. Steele, on the other hand, cruised through life like a basking shark, feeding opportunistically on stray delights. I was waiting for the right moment to talk to Steele about Karen's appearance. The last time I saw her, her muscles were toned like she'd been going to the gym, she'd cut her hair shorter and dyed out the grey. She looked good and so did her clothes. My father displayed similar signs before he walked out on my mother.

"How's Beth?" I said. I'd not seen his teenage daughter since her birthday almost three months ago.

"Karen reckons she needs counselling."

He must have noticed the quizzical look on my face. "Beth," he clarified.

Steele gazed blankly from our balcony table over the flashy wharves stocked with charter sailing catamarans and multi-story fibreglass cruisers. He clearly found the seas of family rough going, so I changed course.

"So what do you know about Bart Hills death? True he was a regular heroin user?"

"Ah," he said, brightening. "The story's changing a little. His flatmate says no. Apparently he was with a stray woman that night; they were playing magic shit with a Ouija board in his room, but she's disappeared off the radar. She may have been the supplier. Cops say he got knocked by some extra pure. There were half a dozen other deaths around the city via the same gear. Of course none of the other corpses had a neon name like Hills and his old man, the celebrity face changer, so there hasn't been any publicity - yet. No-one at my paper gives a shit about Jack Nobody and his girlfriend. But I've written a comment piece for tomorrow. A community service announcement. Hopefully the weekend users will read it. 'A little dab'll do ya' - that's our message. Though the food chain should have twigged by now and cut it down for economic purposes."

"I tell you what," I said, "the Easts have thrown so much at me in the last couple of days, there's got to be a serious cover-up. Problem is I can't get a clean line on anything. Charles is kissing my arse one minute, then threatening me the next. His kids are working behind his back, or appear to be.

Then the old fucker's lunatic chauffeur turns up at the Pig this morning, dressed like a banker, with a stiletto in his jacket and tries to terrorise me."

I told him what I knew about Oscar 'Silver Dog' Petersen.

"Tricky," said Steele, swirling the dregs of pale wine in his glass, holding it up to the sunlight like he was trying to discern the future.

"What can you see?"

"Grief. Infinite grief."

"You're perking me up."

"Ah," he said, putting his glass back on the table and reaching across to pat the back of my hand. "He's probably just a run-of-the mill psychopath who'll self-destruct. Unlike you, mate."

I told Steele about the Easts' murky links to John K. Baker and Cavalcade, and that something smelled around the drowning of Baker's partner a few years ago that put Baker on top of the Cavalcade heap in London.

"That's great," he said. "But you're just telling me a story about some apex predators who like to share horses and yachts, and one fell in the water."

"What? You reckon I should call it quits and go back to chasing fire engines like the silver dog says?"

"Let's face it. You might be barking up a tree without a cat in it. And now you're just annoying the tree's owners."

Steele's phone rang. He walked outside to take it. Maybe Steele was right about the empty tree. I felt tired, flat as a dropped beer, as my father-in-law likes to say.

A whole roasted snapper was lying on a plate on the table of the diners beside us. I could swear it winked at me. I saw myself back in the bush with my head stuck in the wombat hole. I crossed my fingers that the fish wouldn't start talking.

Steele returned from his phone call, ruffled my hair and sat down. He bared his teeth and pretended he was curling an invisible moustache with his fingers. He'd either scored some drugs, some information, or he was on a promise with a stray feline. Maybe all three at once, he looked that pleased.

"Cheer up. Just got something for you, hand-delivered a moment ago." He pulled a white envelope out of his pocket. "I might have found the cat that's up your tree."

I took the blank-faced envelope. It was gummed and closed.

"Don't read it here," he said, pouring himself another glass. "We've knocked off for the day."

"I need a hint."

"It ties Henry East and Bart Hills together in a right nefarious little caper. But you'll need a clear head to decipher it."

We ate and drank, and in their absence, we verbally savaged most of the people we knew. It was a large list of names which took time to get through, so we were forced to consume several bottles of white then red.

"You know what I don't get?" said Steele, filling his glass. "Your mate Charles East owns a billion bucks, give or take a hundred mill. Why wouldn't he just put it all in the bank at five per cent interest per annum - I'm talking on average - and make what? Fifty million a year, like clockwork! He pays the same price for a coffee as you and me. How much does someone want, for fuck's sake?"

"Some people can never have enough," I said, waving my empty glass at him.

My phone pinged. It was a text from Tania Watson: *Just got your message. Angels Tears = my magic mushroom potion. Fell from my bag. Help yourself, but proceed with caution. I'm heading OS. Xx, T*

"Hallelujah," I blurted.

Steele grinned and waved like the queen at four fat man seated at the table beside us who appeared disapproving of my lowbrow religious outburst. "Pop your teeth back in," he advised them.

Tania's text had me feeling like I did when my parachute popped the only time I went skydiving. In a hushed voice, I told Steele about my night at Moon Hill. The punchline, just received, was that Tania's tequila was infused with hallucinogenic psilocybin from some Blue Mountain's toadstools, meaning my brain had not stuffed up of its own accord. Steele wanted to drive straight out to the bush for a swig.

I pointed out that neither of us was in the best shape for driving. Steele countered that we could give it damn good crack. But I came up with a better idea.

"Call the Drug Squad."

"Excellent thinking." Steele hit speed dial on his phone. Nancy Cross, the Personal Wealth Editor of *The Sydney Daily News,* otherwise known as the head of the in-house Drug Squad, could get the best cocaine in the city. He left a voice message.

We decided to proceed to a newly opened bar named The Present, mainly because it was a short walk and would limit the wasteful gap between drinks. Soon we were clumping down stairs into the underground venue, gripping the handrail, passing a neon sign that read: *Welcome to The Present. No Past. No Future.* Steele added bourbon shots to our opening order of red wine and cigars.

I remember clicking my jaw with the ambition of making a set of Olympic rings from the smoke. Through the resultant fog, I tried to explain to Steele the feeling I had about the East case, of sticking my hand through a hole in a wall into an invisible place and not being able to pull it back because something had grabbed me.

I believe Steele handed me fresh shots and said: "Let's smash the wall and see what's there."

XXIV

I WOKE on my bed, jacket on, shoes and all. The radioactive green digits on my alarm said 8:55. From the blaze of light through my window, I figured it was AM. I used my hands to turn my head to face the ceiling and wondered if someone had hit me with fists. I managed to prop myself up on the pillows. From a distance, my face looked okay in the wall mirror. At least I was home and conscious. I put a finger to my jugular to measure my heart rate and blood pressure, and weigh the odds of a brain bleed coming on. I was in the safety zone, I thought.

I put my hand in my jacket pocket, searching for the envelope that Steele had given me at lunch time yesterday. It was there. I tore the envelope in my rush to open it and extracted several sheets of A4 paper. They were printed copies of a chain of emails. I was too nauseous to read more than a sentence and dropped the papers on my bed.

I reached into the other pocket of my jacket for the memory that never lies: my phone. I checked for voice messages, text and email. I counted fifteen calls to the Drug Squad's Nancy

Cross from my phone alone, none of them answered. I gave up looking at my call register after the first page. The night had been all beer, wine and spirits – a terrible combination. Things got worse as I sifted through more embers.

I found a photo, taken at 3:21am. Steele was puffy-faced and slit-eyed holding a tumbler of tea-coloured fluid on ice. He had a young woman I recognised under his other arm. Vicky Gleason had been a cadet journalist under both Steele and I. Now she worked in PR somewhere.

There were other photos. Claire Styler and her husband were caught, in a red-eyed flash, seated on a purple sofa. There was another of me next to Claire. I didn't remember crossing paths with her until I saw that photo. What did I say, and to whom? Who else had we encountered?

"Good night?" asked Alice as I staggered naked, dragging a towel, past the kitchen on my way to the bathroom. I hadn't heard her come home from the airport.

"Excellent, thanks." I struggled to get the towel around my waist.

"What's that on your back?"

"What do you mean?"

"Scratch marks. On your back."

"I had a wrestle with Steele." I made that up. I hoped Alice was joking.

"It looks like the hug of the beast," she said.

I went to the bathroom and looked in the mirror. There *were* scratch marks on my back, on the skin just under my shoulder blades. I counted four each side. Fingernail marks?

The hot rain of the shower brought me back a bit. About fifteen minutes of it, plus several glasses of cold water to drink with a couple of codeine-based painkillers I kept for emergencies. Wrapped in a towel, I sat on the end of my bed holding a wodge of toilet paper over a bleeding razor chip on my Adam's apple. My phone started its police whistling. The name on the screen: *Karen Steele*. She'd be fact-checking Steele's story about last night, if he even went home. I let it ring out.

I managed to get dressed in a suit: stuff the tie. Fred arrived to pick Alice up and take her and some clothes back to his parents' house, which helped my headache. I padded down our front steps and drifted into the street where I flagged a taxi and headed to the office at Circular Quay. My phone whistled again. Jack Darling was calling. I licked my lips to muster my best diction.

"Gidday, mate".

"Gar, you have a problem. A serious problem."

"What is it?"

"Why the fuck would you make a death threat against Charles East?"

XXV

"A WHAT?"

"A death threat," said Jack. "His lawyers lodged a complaint this morning with the New South Wales Police. They've copied our head office in London and HQ has passed it to me. East wants you charged with making a threat to kill under the Crimes Act. It carries a penalty of up to ten years in prison."

"This is bullshit. How am I meant to have done this?"

"Did you phone East last night?"

"No … I don't think so."

"You don't *THINK* so? Fuck, mate. They also want the police to press another charge of using a telecommunications device in an offensive manner. That carries a prison term too. What the hell were you doing?"

I stopped the taxi, handed the driver some cash, and stepped on to the pavement. My legs were wobbly, my mouth dry, my eyes burning. I walked into a nearby park and fell to sitting with my back against a tree. I told Jack what had happened over the past week: about my encounter with Bart Hills before he OD'd; my suspicions about Sandy

Wallace scouting for East; my visit to Tamerlane and my video call with Henry, culminating in the threats from the silver dog yesterday.

"You've stuffed up big time, mate. You've given East the opening he wanted to shut you down."

I put my phone on open speaker while Jack read me the nauseating details of East's complaint. While Jack talked, it enabled me to scroll through my handset's call register. Charles East's number wasn't on the first page. It was on the second.

"I did make two calls," I said. "Or more accurately, the calls were made from my phone."

"Are you saying a third party used your phone?"

"Maybe."

"I've listened to the voice recording they attached to the complaint, Gar. The one East's lawyers have given to the police. It's you! Unless they've found a very good fucking actor."

"What next then?"

"London HQ says if you did it, we have to suspend you. You need to get a lawyer and get advice on dealing with the police. Don't go to the office. I'll talk to Claire. She'll be in charge for now. I don't know if I can save your job this time. I'm going to have to think this through. I've got to go."

Jack emailed me a copy of the complaint, and attached the audio file and a typed transcript. East was a fast mover, I had to give him that. I guessed that I must have ripped into him live on the first call, because there was no recording of it. But he cleverly rejected my second call and diverted me to recorded voice mail, where I came to grief. I listened to the file to check that it was my voice: *"Listen you thieving old fuck. You're the one who should be insuring your family. You're the fucking dead man. I know where you live. I know where you are. I know you. Bang, bang, horse-face. You and your silver dog.*"

Moments later I received a text from Jack: "Do you still have your father's gun?"

XXVI

STEELE helped me find a criminal lawyer that afternoon and in his office we scripted and rehearsed my story for police consumption.

Two days later – most of which I spent bingeing on TV crime series, movies and football replays – the lawyer and I went to the concrete and steel vault of the Sydney Police Centre in Goulburn Street in Surry Hills where, inside a room with carpet on the walls, I gave them my version of events. I'd been in a room like it years ago; the bad cop had said that if I screamed, no one would hear, before he smashed his fist into a phone book which I assumed was meant to mimic my head. The good cop said all I had to do was sign the statement they had helpfully typed to save me time and trouble.

This time I had a lawyer by my side and I was more than twenty years older. I used the drunk's defence, arguing I had been speaking metaphorically about killing Charles East.

During the interview, I told the detectives about the dead carp on my door and the life insurance and career advice I had received from the silver dog. I signed a statement that my lawyer checked. The detectives said they'd be in touch. We left.

Over a subsequent coffee with my lawyer, ironically in the same café where I had eavesdropped on Henry East and his lawyer, my man said that if the police proceeded with criminal charges - which was likely because of the pressure being applied by East - and the Director of Public Prosecutions agreed they had enough evidence and went forward, it could be four to six months before my day in court, maybe longer. Plenty of time for East to make me stew. My lawyer agreed that the police and complainants often got pleasure from dragging things out to make the accused sweat with anxiety.

Walking home alone, I had visions of Charles East and Silver Dog sitting on Tamerlane's back veranda clinking fine china tea cups in celebration over sponge cake, or something tastier. I'd knocked myself out with a superb own-punch. I figured they were now working on a plan to snap my mental hinges, holus-bolus.

It was a long walk, past pubs that called to me like sirens to ancient sailors, before I turned into my street, more sober than I'd been for years, and plodded up the front steps of Sue's. Fish bounced all over me with that strange thing called unconditional love.

My phone rang as I was opening our front door. I hated the little electronic bastard right then, the filthy snitch, but I couldn't ignore my mother-in-law, Kate Halliday. This might ice the day. Was Hugo in trouble?

"Malcolm has had a bad turn, Gar," Kate said. "The doctors are saying a couple of weeks at best."

"It will take me a day or two to organise," I said. "Tell him Alice and I are coming."

Kate sobbed. She put Hugo on the phone. He said little. I told him things were fine in Sydney and that we'd see him soon.

"Love you, mate," I said.

"Yep."

Malcolm's illness yawned before me like a serendipitous porthole I could dive through to escape from where I was, and I had an excuse to take Alice with me that didn't require me to frighten her, or disappoint her with my latest lapse, which I would keep under wraps. I phoned her and told her about Malcolm. After the call, I booked online flights for our departure in 48 hours. I would phone Jack in the morning and tell him my plans because right then I couldn't bear to hear any more of the disappointment in his voice. Jack had thrown me several lifebuoys over the years. I had been unemployed when he dragged me up onto the deck of *The Citizen* about a year ago.

I went next door to talk with Sue. She would look after Fish while Alice and I were in the UK.

I made a glass of soda water with ice and a slice of lime, and sat in the back garden with Fish under the frangipani tree. Then I remembered Jack's text message about my father's gun. After stating to the police that my threat to kill East was a hollow metaphor, what would happen if the police arrived with a search warrant and found the unlicensed, loaded Mr Browning in my house, or car? I re-trawled the house and searched the car to no avail. I concluded I'd left it somewhere at Moon Hill. I wished Hughie would put the phone on. Tania was god-knows-where overseas, so she couldn't scour the hill for me. I was in no state for a long drive to the bush tonight. I'd go in the morning, do a quick in-out day trip and hide the gun before Alice and I flew to London.

Steele's envelope with the printed emails between Henry East and Bart Hills sat on my office table. I read them again with a pleasingly clear mind. They related to the takeover bid by China's Double Happiness Co. for Australia's Austar Gold. Henry and Bart had used email pseudonyms - corny, uncreative ones.

There was advice written by hand in pencil on the first page of the emails: *check the dates against the court transcripts... look for the name 'Christ'.*

Someone was providing me with guidance, and it wasn't Steele's handwriting. His style was doctors' cursive: in other words unreadable, like mine. This writing was neat and careful. Feminine was my guess.

The emails said:

From: GMan
To: Lisa Simpson
Sent: Wednesday, 12 July 11:05AM.
Austar Gold. Pin your ears back and go in. Christ says the Chinese are coming.

From: Lisa Simpson
To: GMan
Sent: Wednesday, 12 July 12:16PM
Done.

From: GMan
To: Lisa Simpson
Sent: Wednesday, 12 July 1.00PM
Good girl. This will double happiness.

I figured *Lisa* was Bart Hills, *GMan* was Henry. The email exchange occurred on Wednesday 12 July. I wrote the date on my notebook.

I went to Henry's court transcripts that were saved on my laptop and opened the pages where Henry described the meeting he attended inside the offices of his employer, Hagerman Brothers, in which Henry told the court he discovered that a takeover bid was coming from Double Happiness for Austar Gold. He swore to the court he had placed his inside trades from home on the night of that meeting.

I wrote on my notepad: *Hagerman Bros meeting = Friday 14 July.*

Those dates sparked me up. So Henry East had advised Bart Hills by email that a bid for Austar Gold was on its way, two whole days before Henry participated in the Hagerman Brothers meeting.

I now had hard evidence, unless the emails were faked, that Henry had not been acting alone in doing the inside trades for which he was jailed. He had lied to the prosecutors and the court about the source and timing of his inside information.

Further, Henry had been advised by somebody named Christ that the Chinese bid was coming. Who the hell was Christ? I had a fresh trail, but then I remembered I was out of a job.

XXVII

A YOUNG WOMAN opened the door of a front-loading clothes washer in the basement laundry of her apartment building. She began pulling damp clothes out and placing them in a basket. She heard a click behind her; the ceiling light went out, plunging the room into darkness.

"Who's there?" she called, grasping for the side of the washing machine to get her bearings, her heart racing.

"Shhh …"

Hands grabbed her: big hands, strong hands. One of the hands grabbed her by the hair, hurting her scalp. She tried to grab the hands, but her wrists were dragged behind her back and pressed together by someone vastly more powerful. Her scream was stifled by cloth being stuffed into her mouth, causing a gagging reaction when it grated against the back of her throat. Something tight was being wound around her mouth, around her head. She smelled glue. Tape, masking tape? She couldn't get enough air. Slow, slow down, she told herself, use your nose, use your nose!

Her attackers – a wiry man, a girl, and a burly man – did not speak. The wiry man slipped a black velvet sack over the young woman's head. The burly man kept hold of his captive's wrists with one of his hands, forcing his other hand under her armpit to keep her standing upright on her wilting legs.

The girl took a torch from her bomber jacket pocket and switched it on. She ran the beam over the woman, starting on her bare feet, tracing her bare legs, moving across her short denim skirt and pausing upon her heaving breasts under a white tee-shirt. The girl put the torch between her teeth, picked up a damp tee-shirt from the washed clothes basket and wiped the insides of the woman's shuddering legs clean of the body fluids released by her shock.

The girl took a folded plastic carry-bag from her other jacket pocket and stuffed the tee-shirt inside the bag while the wiry man tied the woman's wrists together with a stocking. He worked carefully, determined not to break her skin or cause lasting ligature marks.

Placing her torch and the plastic bag in the same hand, the girl used her spare hand to lift a pistol from a shoulder holster inside her jacket. She released the safety catch and led them out of the laundry, pointing her barrel along a short, dark corridor. The men followed, one on each side of their captive with a hand under her armpits, letting the woman regain strength and carry her own weight forward as they headed toward the basement carpark.

The wiry man smiled; the woman he was gripping started to feel to him as light as a feather. It always amazed him how quickly captive people co-operate when in motion, even though they have no idea what lies ahead. It must be hope that carries them, he thought.

The girl made sure the carpark was empty of people, then hand-signalled for the men to follow her into it. She clicked the remote car-key and unlocked a large, black sedan with tinted windows. She opened a back door and the wiry man pushed the woman into the middle of the bench seat. The burly man entered the car from the other side and the two men wedged the woman between them. He put a lap belt on their captive.

The girl holstered her pistol, climbed behind the driver's wheel and began motoring slowly out of the carpark. Before entering the road, she paused and looked in the rear view mirror at the trio: in the angular beam of a streetlamp, the wiry man winked at her before making a show of sucking the tip of his middle finger and sniffing it.

The car cruised the street; the men snapped the wrists of the latex rubber gloves they were wearing loudly against their skin a few times, the wiry man doing it close to where the woman's ear would be inside the sack. He reached into the pocket of the seat-back in front of him and withdrew a long brown feather. He stroked the rooster's plume over the woman's bare outer thighs. She bucked and jostled. The burly man tightened her lap-belt. When the girl pressed her legs together, the wiry man traced the feather up and down the line where her flesh met. The burly man put a clamping arm around her shoulders and the wiry man lifted her tee-shirt above her bare breasts and applied his feather. After a few minutes, the wiry man returned the feather to the seat pocket.

The men nodded at each other and trailed their gloved fingers gently over her outer thighs. The woman crossed her ankles and squeezed her legs together, trying to shrink herself. The wiry man grinned and wiggled a hand in behind her knees. The burly man forced his hand in, and both men slowly, and with great but gentle power, pulled her legs apart.

The girl drove, block-after-block and suburb-after-suburb, glancing occasionally into the rear-view mirror. She chewed on gum and remembered what the wiry man had told her: *Fear is a prison best built brick by brick.*

XXVIII

I LOOKED up from the emails between Henry East and Bart Hills and saw through my home office window that night had fallen. My joints ached but I couldn't drink the pain away, not tonight. A hot bath, that might work. As I stepped into the hallway, there was a knock at the front door. I looked through the peephole. Claire Styler buckled over and vomited into the planter box of bright red geraniums on the front porch.

I threw the door open. "What's wrong?" I said, going to her side, putting a hand on her shoulder. Claire wiped her glistening mouth on her tee-shirt sleeve. Her pupils were dark pools, her face was grey, her hair knotted, her body shaking. She clung to me.

I'd never seen her without trousers on. And bare feet? I thought she was bleeding down one outer thigh and calf. It looked like paint had spilled from under her short skirt. I realised it was a long, purple birthmark.

We shuffled through the door along the hallway and down to the kitchen-lounge where I sat her on the sofa. I fetched a glass of water that she sipped. Fish sat beside her while I found a couple of blankets.

"Do you have something stronger?" she said as I put the blanket around her shoulders and another over her legs. I poured a large glass of red wine. She gulped it.

"What's happened?"

She put her head in her shaking hands.

"I'll ring an ambulance."

"No!" She drank more wine.

I waited, sitting on a chair opposite her. It may have been a minute or two before her body stilled a little.

She said: "They were in the laundry under our flat."

"Who?"

"I didn't see. They switched the light off. Someone head-locked me."

She stroked her throat. I looked for bruises, couldn't see any from where I sat.

"They stuffed a sock in my mouth and taped it. Then put a bag over me, my head."

She started shaking again. She said she was put into a car, bodies smelling of sour sweat squeezed either side of her. She was held inside the moving car for about half an hour, maybe an hour, stopping, starting, accelerating, cornering. She was confused about time.

"I will take you to hospital, call the police."

"No, Gar. What am I going to say?"

"You've been abducted, assaulted."

"I need to use your bathroom."

"Claire, it's evidence."

"I just want to look.'

When she returned, she had some colour back in her face and had straightened her hair. She sat and reached for the wine.

"There's no evidence," she said. "Nothing to show."

She must have seen my puzzled look.

"They used gloves. They were very gentle. There *is* no evidence, for god's sake."

I wanted to say look in the mirror, there's the evidence, but I didn't.

"How do you know they used gloves?" I said.

"I could smell the latex. And they made sure I heard them putting them on."

"Did they …"

"No. Only their hands."

They had released her in an empty children's playground at the end of my street and told her not to look back or they would put a bullet in her head.

"What did their voices sound like?"

"There were no voices. They did everything in silence. Until the end, just at the end."

"What happened at the end?"

"I heard a voice. Not a real voice. Not a man or a woman. A robot. You know those machines, an electronic mask."

"Do you remember what it said?"

Claire looked into her wine as if she was reading the words on the purple surface: "You are at the crossroads, Claire. Choose wisely. Don't make us come back."

"They told me to tell *you* what happened," she said, helping herself to the wine. "And before you say you are sorry - don't!"

It had to be Silver Dog. He'd knocked me out of the ring. Now he was trying to knock out my replacement.

"We must be close to something big, Gar," Claire said.

"Do you want to pull out?"

"Have you ever been burgled, Gar. Do you know what it feels like?"

"Yes, I do."

"Then you'll know why I'm not backing off."

"Where's Carl?"

"Overseas. On business."

"You should call him."

"I will in the morning."

"You can stay here, in Alice's room."

I explained that Alice and I were flying to England to see a dying Malcolm Halliday. Claire and I agreed we would phone Jack Darling together in the morning and brief him. One regurgitation of events was enough for her tonight.

We also agreed Claire would need special protection from *The Citizen* - if we were to keep probing East's affairs.

"What about you?" said Claire. "They might come for you again too."

"I've lost my job, I'm facing criminal charges. I'm a laughing stock. And I'm leaving the country. You're the boss of *The Citizen* in Australia now, so your head's the one above the trench."

"There was one other thing," said Claire, as I gave her a towel for the shower and some of Alice's pyjamas. "I couldn't see them, and they didn't show their voices - but I could smell something else in that car."

"Such as?"

"Perfume. A woman's perfume. Roses."

XXIX

CLAIRE AND Fish were in the kitchen when I came down-stairs the next morning. She was wearing Alice's long-john pyjamas and making a pot of tea. I resisted the urge to comfort her with touch. She suggested we call Jack and get it over with. I dialled him on my house phone on open speaker on the kitchen table and Claire retold the events of last night in abridged form.

He urged her to go to the police. She refused until Jack argued that for him to put the case to our London HQ for a budget for 24-hour private security for Claire, he first needed Claire to make a police report to cover the internal paperwork. Jack added that without such security in place, he could not allow Claire to keep working on the East-Baker story. She agreed to file a report when I volunteered my lawyer to accompany her to the police station.

I told Claire I wanted a word with Jack in private about *my* police charges. She took her tea into the back garden with Fish.

"Help me here," said Jack. "My Australian bureau chief has self-destructed, his replacement has been assaulted and terrorised by invisible people - and we've not got one line of copy we can publish. My practical side says we are pulling a whole lot of grief upon ourselves for no good purpose. What do you suggest we do?"

I explained to Jack my 'discovery' of the emails between Henry East and Bart Hills proving that Henry had lied to the court about acting alone, and that his inside information had come from a third party codenamed Christ.

"That's not a story," he said. "That's an opening paragraph."

I said: "Some people are going to a lot of trouble, and doing some very nasty things, to stop us digging around in their dung heap. There must be something in there."

"You are off the case. Remember?" said Jack. "There are people in our London office who want you fired because you are a liability. A loose cannon were the words they used."

"I can work through Claire," I said.

"You remember when we climbed that glacier in New Zealand?" said Jack.

"Pure instinct," I said.

We had been roped together when he slipped. I smashed an ice pick into the outer lip of a crevasse as he pulled me in after him and I dislocated a shoulder hanging on. But we got out.

"I'm using *my* instinct now," said Jack. "Can you get Claire?"

I opened the door to the garden and called her in. The phone was still on open speaker.

Jack said: "Gar, I want your fingerprints on nothing more to do with East inside our database. You work through Claire. Be aware - both of you be aware - his lawyers, or the prosecutor's office, will likely subpoena our emails, phone logs, all sorts of internal shit if these charges against Gar proceed. So let's keep our noses clean - on our records at least. Let's not let them see what we have."

Claire asked: "Do you think that's what East is after now, Jack? To get a look inside our database?"

"That would be my strategy if I was him," said Jack.

My mobile phone pinged. A text message: *chase tigre.* "Interesting," I said as the name of the text sender flashed on my screen.

"Am I missing something?" said Jack.

"Just got a message from an old friend," I said.

I showed Claire my phone. She rolled her eyes. It was sent from the disappeared Bruce Tyson, and included a street address near Sydney Airport.

XXX

"BRUCE-EE. Oh, Bruce-ee. Are you in there?" the wiry man called through the locked bathroom door.

Bruce Tyson stayed silent, sitting on the toilet seat.

"You've been a naughty boy, Brucie. Ringing my boss. Trying to squeeze money out of him. You should have stuck to handing out the pills and washing prisoners' bottoms, shouldn't you? But oh, no. Brilliant Brucie starts putting his big ears to conversations that are none of his business."

A burly man stepped through a doorway into the cheaply furnished kitchen in which the wiry man was standing. He carried a dinner-plate-sized reel of raw copper wire. He nodded at the wiry man and said, "All set."

The wiry man nodded back. "Now, Brucie. Are you going to come out, or am I going to have to play the Big Bad Wolf?"

"Who *are* you?" Tyson groaned. He stayed seated on the toilet because the chemicals of fear kept flushing his insides out. His stomach cramped again.

Boom! The bathroom door smashed around the lock. Boom! The wiry man crashed through the door. "Oh, my.

God," he said, putting his jacket sleeve over his nose to mask the stench.

Tyson stood, pants around his ankles, and screamed, "Help! Help!"

The burly man dropped his reel of wire, stepped into the bathroom and clubbed Tyson in the face with a right-cross. The blow stunned the psychiatric nurse and stopped his cries. Tyson stumbled back and shattered the glass shower screen.

"Quick," said the wiry man. "Don't let him fall into that shit. He might cut an artery."

The burly man grabbed the staggering Tyson by his shirt, spun him around and locked his captive's neck into the crux of an elbow.

"Easy, easy," said the wiry man. "Let him breathe. Now," resumed the wiry man, "we need to have a chat, Brucie. But not in here. Phew!"

The burly man dragged Tyson into the kitchen and followed his leader through a door into a workshop with a concrete floor littered with cardboard boxes. In a corner there was a folding bed with a thin mattress on a metal frame.

"This will work best if you're relaxed, Brucie. So you lay down on the bed and we'll have a nice, friendly chat. Okay?"

Tyson gurgled. His captor dragged him to the edge of the bed and released his head-lock. Tyson quickly pulled up his pants and sat on the bed.

"No, no. Not sitting, Brucie. I want you to lie down, like you are going to sleep. And get those filthy clothes off."

Tyson's stomach cramped again. "Look. I'm sorry. You don't have to worry about me. I'll disappear. You won't hear from me again."

"Clothes off," insisted the wiry man. "And lie down."

Tyson complied. As he did so, the burly man stepped into the kitchen and returned with his reel of wire.

"Just for security purposes," said the wiry man as his companion pressed Tyson onto his back and wound copper strands around Tyson's wrists and ankles before starting to fix them to the corners of the bed.

"So, Brucie, who have you been speaking to, apart from young Mr East and his friend Mr Hills, sadly deceased?"

"Nobody."

"Is that so? A little birdie told me you had been speaking to a journalist. What have you told him?"

"Nothing, truly. I just scammed some money from him."

"Okay, Brucie. If that's how you want to play."

The wiry man nodded and his companion stood next to the head of the bed, hovering over Tyson's face. He began unwinding a long strand of copper.

The wiry man sat on an upturned crate next to the bed and pulled a crescent-shaped butcher's knife from the sheath that was strapped over his chest inside his suit jacket. He waved the knife at Tyson. "Brucie, I want you to stay very still while my friend does his work. He's a pro, so relax. If you fuck around, I'll have to poke this into you and extract a kidney. Now, that's a thought, isn't it? Organ donation. You could use a better brain, Brucie. Because if you had a good one, you wouldn't be here."

XXXI

AFTER THE CALL with Jack about Claire's assault, I phoned Alice and told her Claire was staying at our home until we left for London the following day.

"Stay with Fred today," I said. "Do not walk anywhere alone and do not come home until I contact you. There's been some trouble and we are sorting it out."

Alice must have been sensitive to the tone in my voice because she didn't question me.

I phoned my lawyer and arranged to meet him at his office in the city in two hours with Claire.

"You up for a drive first?" I said to Claire.

Tyson's text had directed me to an address in the industrial suburb of Mascot near the airport.

"It read like an invitation, didn't it?" I figured some diversion therapy would be good for us both. Fish bounced around. He was up for it too. I gave Claire some of Alice's clothes to wear.

"Did you call Carl?" I said, after she came downstairs dressed.

"I left a message."

It didn't take long to drive to Tyson's. It was a low-rise industrial park with a concrete driveway off the street that flowed into the middle of two matching strips of workshops and storage sheds with roller doors at their fronts. The place was busy with cars and trucks and utes backing in and out. I reversed into a parking bay on the opposite side and a few doors along from Tyson's shed. There was a panel-beater's shop on one side of Tyson's place and a surfboard maker on the other. All the shopfronts had a standard wood-panel-door entrance on the left side and a metal roller door in the middle. Both of Tyson's doors were closed. We sat in the car for a while and studied the scene. There were no CCTVs that we could see. Even so, I started the Defender and drove back into the street and around the corner, parking next to the curb in sight of a laneway behind the workshops. I phoned Tyson but it went straight to voice mail.

"Why don't you stay in the car with Fish while I see if we have the right address?" I said. "Tyson mightn't appreciate extra company - if he's even in there."

There was a woollen beanie on the back seat which I put on. I found a pair of sunglasses in the glove box.

As I stepped out, I said to Claire: "How about you jump behind the wheel and keep the key in the ignition, in case we need a fast getaway. The horn works a treat too."

"Yes, Dad," she said, shooing me away. Fish jumped in her lap and watched me walk.

I stepped into the laneway behind the sheds on Tyson's side. Each of the rear doors was numbered. I found Tyson's and knocked. Nothing. I put my hand inside my tee-shirt to keep my fingerprints off the door handle and tried it, but it was locked. So I walked into the street and turned into the main driveway towards the front of his shed.

A coffee van had arrived and parked a few doors from Tyson's. About a dozen workers were queued in a loose line, engrossed in the screens of their mobile phones. The electronic bastards were on my side for a change. There was no response to Tyson's front door buzzer. I tried the roller door with my boot and it came up. I ducked under quickly and closed it behind me with my foot. There was a stench of burnt meat, like an oily barbeque, and a pall of light smoke in the upper air of the workshop. I caught the unmistakable whiff of burnt hair and I dry-retched.

The workshop was dark, apart from a squeeze of light coming through a part-opened door to a backroom. I flicked on the light switches inside a fuse box attached to the workshop wall. Two big halogens in dome shades on the ceiling threw a harsh, white blaze on the scene.

The first thing I noticed were stacks of large cardboard cartons, the ones used for moving house. There were piles of folded clothes on the concrete floor, blankets sealed in plastic bags, boxes labelled as powdered milk and noodles. And there were stacks of books, mainly children's titles. I guessed Tyson used the shed to store and send stuff to his kids in Africa.

The smoke was nauseating. I walked past some cartons towards the rear of the shed, staying bent under the smoke layer to breathe the cleanest air. Bruce Tyson – I guessed it was him mainly from the Swans cap lying on the floor – was lying naked on his back on a folding bed. This time I vomited wet. His head was wrapped with what looked like copper wire, multiple strands of it. It made a rough X shape across his face, bound from the left side of his jaw to above his right ear and vice versa, squashing his nose. Someone had gone to a lot of trouble to wind that pattern. There was white electrical cord, heavy-duty, peeled back to expose its copper cores, trailing from the back of Tyson's head and plugged into a power board on the wall. His ankles, wrists and neck were secured to the frame of the stretcher with more copper wire. I saw from the wall switch that the killer, or killers, had turned off the power before they left the shed. Very thoughtful. Tyson's visible face was a hideous black and purple. Most of an ear had burned off and fallen as a scrap of charcoal on the floor. His fingers and toes were black, the rest of his body pink and purple. I wondered why the fire detectors hadn't gone off, until I saw a couple of them had been ripped out of the ceiling.

I wanted out, but not through the front door. With my foot, I pushed open a regular door that led to a separate back room. It was a kitchen. A near-empty plastic bag of bread sat on the bench. I shook out the left-over slices and used the bag as a glove. The air was clear and I could breathe okay. From the contents in the kitchen bin, it looked like he'd been hiding here for days. The bathroom door, on the right-side of the kitchen, was busted at the lock. Inside, underpants and socks were soaking in a bucket in the shower recess. I smelled shit. Brown was smeared on the floor.

Maybe Tyson had fired off the text to me before the killers trapped him in the bathroom. I couldn't see a phone anywhere. From the smoke and the stink in the main room, the killers hadn't been gone long. Why such a spectacular execution? Why didn't they take him away by pointing a gun in his back and dispose of him in secret? That could have been easily done.

There was banging on the roller door. Someone was trying to pull it up. Had I locked it down?

"For fuck's sake!" said an angry male voice. "What the fuck are you doin' in there? Fuckin' stinks."

I froze. The man outside kicked the door a couple of times, then it went quiet.

I picked a rag up off the floor and used it to rub all the light switches and door handles I'd touched. I slipped the bolt on the back door with my hand inside the bread bag and turned the handle. As I stepped into the laneway, I heard a crunch underfoot and looked down. I'd stepped on the shell of a mobile phone. The screen was cracked, like it had been dropped. Tyson's bathroom window opened onto the laneway. Had he fired off the text to me, then slipped his phone out of the window to cover his tracks as his killers kicked the door in? I put the phone in the plastic bag and walked fast down the laneway, resisting the urge to run.

I climbed into the Defender and Claire drove us several suburbs away while I explained what I had found. I asked her to park in a hotel carpark. I went inside and chanced upon one of the rarest creatures in the city – a working public phone.

I dialled Crime Stoppers and gave them an anonymous tip about a dead body in a Mascot shed.

*

Claire, Alice, Fred and I ate Thai take-away that night at our home and watched the TV news about the police finding a dead man in an industrial park. The circumstances were described by a police spokesman as suspicious. I scored them one-out-of-ten for deductive genius.

The TV reporter interviewed a glassy-eyed surfboard shaper from the shop next door who said he'd not seen movement at Tyson's place for days. Alice reckoned the shaper had the glazed look of someone who'd been on the bong. I hoped the other tenants of the business park were equally astute at the time we visited.

Steele phoned me just after the TV report with his professional analysis: "It's a display killing. Whoever did this wants to send a message far and wide. The audience is not just you, mate. They're warning other people not to fuck with them too."

"Really?" I said.

"Fuck you too," said Steele.

Claire made a phone call, then told me her concerned husband was finishing off an assignment in the Middle East: Saudi Arabia, to be precise. Carl would be back in town in a couple of days. He was advancing the human condition by issuing media releases about an Italian fashion company selling ten-thousand-dollar handbags to the womenfolk of oil sheiks. I offered Claire the use of Hugo's bedroom for the night which I had, by a stroke of luck, cleaned, and replaced the bedclothes, after he left for Brighton.

Claire phoned Jack on her work phone, given I was suspended, and briefed him on Tyson. Jack had obtained approval for Claire's private security.

*

A beefy, ex-armed robbery squad detective from Belfast named Billy Kelly arrived at our door as we were finishing dinner. "Call me Bat" Kelly was clearly uncomfortable in his suit and tie.

When I did the last rounds of the house about 11pm, Bat was reading a book about the Islamic States of Iraq and Syria on the sofa bed in my office. He'd rigged a mini-camera on the front porch and one in the back garden, all hooked up wirelessly to his laptop which was propped on a table by his bed, next to his Glock pistol.

Fish was in heaven bobbing from room to room, running the fences of his freshly populated estate. Alice and Fred eventually sent him up to me. I enjoyed the full house too, despite the circumstances, and looked forward to sleeping knowing our Irish guard was on watch. In bed, to the sound of Fish snoring, I recalled the afternoon's drive back to the city from Mascot for Claire's rendezvous with my lawyer to make her police statement. Claire had fiddled with the broken phone I found in the lane behind Tyson's shed.

"They're truly like hunting dogs, these people," said Claire. "Look what happened to Tyson. If you run from them, it just draws them to pounce."

"Are you saying we hold our ground? Stare them down."

"Yes. And Tyson was alone. We have a team."

I got her point, but as I drove I kept smelling Tyson's putrid, burnt skin - the smoke particles seemed embedded into my nostrils - and I kept seeing his copper-wired and incinerated face, the effort that had gone into it. It was a work of art in a Francis Bacon sort of way. There was no escaping the fact these people enjoyed their work; they liked to play before they killed. Psychopaths who'd studied the craft of bullfighting.

"What now?" she asked.

"Get the IT guy from the office to run Tyson's SIM card through a reader. If it is his handset, we need to know who his contacts are, who he talked to recently, and when. When we are finished, we can flick it anonymously to the cops."

"No need for the IT guy." Claire was triumphant. I heard the handset beep into life. "Tyson used the factory default as his PIN. 1-2-3-4."

I had pulled over to the kerb. We scrolled through his most recent dialled numbers. One stood out. The +44 20 prefix was a London UK number. I nodded. Claire hit redial and put the handset on open speaker. We heard three rings, a click, and the call diverted to a pre-recorded message:

"You have reached the office of the Cavalcade Investment Group. Our opening hours are 8am to 6pm. If your enquiry is urgent, please call our toll free 24-hour investor line on...."

XXXII

I WISHED I could sleep like Fish. I picked up my phone and checked its world clock. It was early morning in Sydney, but just after midday in London. Tyson's handset was recharged and sitting on my bedside table. I hit redial on the London number. This time there was no out-of-hours call diversion.

"Good afternoon. Cavalcade Investment Group. Mr Baker's office."

"Hello," I said. "Could I speak to Mr Baker, please?"

"Who can I say is calling?"

"It's Mr Tyson - from Australia."

"Mr Tyson, as I explained to you, Mr Baker is not available to take your call. I have passed on your message and contact details. There is nothing we can do to assist you. I'm sorry."

"Okay. Thanks for nothing," I said and hung up.

I gulped down the last of a glass of red that was on my bedside table and stared at the ceiling for a few seconds. "Oh, for fuck's sake," I muttered. I used my own phone to take photos of the contact list from the screen of Tyson's phone and then pulled his battery and SIM card out. I took off my pyjamas and dressed for the street, stuffing the pieces of Tyson's handset in one of my jeans' pockets. I put my own phone in the other.

"Quick trip to the shop," I said to Bat as I left the house. He was not impressed.

I walked for about fifteen minutes and stopped near a public rubbish bin. When I was sure no-one was watching, I threw Tyson's battery in the bin. A block further on, I dropped the SIM down a drain. I dumped the handset in a rubbish skip outside a building site.

How brilliant I was, I thought as I turned the key in my front door. Only half an hour ago, I was lying in my bed, phoning the Cavalcade head office in London on Tyson's phone from the inner sanctum of my own home. I didn't know how accurate the tracking systems of phone companies were at picking up the exact geographic coordinates of originating calls, but I'd just dialled out from my bedroom using a phone that belonged to a murdered man. If the homicide squad wasn't tracking his phone and phone records already, then they were as knuckleheaded as I was.

XXXIII

IN THE mid-morning, Claire and Bat drove me and Alice to the airport in Bat's car.

After checking in and moving through passport control, I went to a newsagency inside the retail hall and purchased the biggest folding map of the world I could find, and a packet of felt-tipped pens. We found a bar while we waited for boarding and I spread the map on a table and circled Sydney and London. I added Shanghai, where Double Happiness Trading Co. was based. Then there was the spot in the Atlantic Ocean about 200 miles off the coast of Portsmouth, south of England, where John K. Baker's business partner, Jean-Paul Marais, had fallen off a yacht and drowned.

Alice leaned over. "Is this to do with the trouble you told me about, why you didn't want me coming home the other night or walking alone?"

"We're getting on top of it," I said.

"Then why does Claire need a bodyguard?"

"It's temporary."

"You just tugged your ear," she said, smiling. "You told me what that means."

It was a relief to board the plane with Alice and switch off my phone. No-one could get between us for at least the twelve hours of the first leg between Sydney and Abu Dhabi Airport in the United Arab Emirates, but I didn't count on Vladimir Nabokov.

When the jet reached cruising altitude, Alice plugged her earphones in for a musical backdrop and opened a paperback of Nabokov's *Lolita*. What happened to *Alice in Wonderland*?

I dozed. Alice tapped my arm as the crew started serving meals.

"I have news," she said as we unwrapped the airline caterer's imagining of butter chicken with saffron rice. "Fred asked me to marry him."

"You're twenty years old."

"So?"

"It's a big call," I said.

Alice smiled. "He's too clingy. I said no."

"How's he taking it?"

"He's offended. He wants to end it."

"*C'est la vie*. There's plenty of fish in the sea."

"So why are you still alone?"

"Too scaly, I guess."

Alice lowered her brow and looked at me like a schoolteacher addressing a student who'd lied about his homework. "Who was the woman I saw leaving our house a week ago?"

"What?"

"Afro hair. Tall. Pretty."

"That was a mistake."

"Yes," said Alice. "She got into a car with a man in it."

"What did he look like?"

"I couldn't see much. It had tinted windows. BMW. Four-wheel-drive."

"Plates?"

"Shot off before I got that close."

I took my notebook from my pocket and looked at the words of Tyson's text message: *chase tigre*.

Alice leaned across. "Bad speller?"

"I think the author was under time pressure."

"How many ways can you spell tiger Phonetically, you've got T-I-G-E-R, or T-I-G-R-E, or T-I-G-A. Or you can drop in a 'Y' instead of an 'I' in all those words."

I wrote the possibilities down in my notepad. Tyson had indisputably been under extreme pressure in his shed; the shit all over his bathroom floor attested to that. Maybe he didn't mean to send me a text about a tiger of any sort.

A dust storm shrouded Abu Dhabi Airport on the edge of a cream desert as our jetliner rolled across the tarmac for a two hour stopover. We could have landed on the surface of the moon. At least its communications satellites worked. I used the airport's Wi-Fi to Google each of Alice's 'tigre' possibilities. It only took five minutes to find TIGA on the register of the Australian Companies and Securities Commission. Tamerlane Investment Group Asia Pty Ltd was a subsidiary of the keystone company Tamerlane Investment Group, controlled by Mr Charles Arthur East.

TIGA, the records said, had an office on the 51st floor of the Jin Mao Tower in the financial district of Shanghai. I knew Jin Mao from visiting Jack Darling. It made the Gunnaroo Tower in Sydney look like a corner shop.

Abu Dhabi Airport erupted with shouting and running people.

Soldiers in camouflage uniforms waving snub-nosed machine guns charged up the escalators towards us in the small, upstairs food hall. They went from table to table demanding to see passports. There had been a bomb threat. The airport authorities instantly crashed the airport's Wi-Fi and telephone system. The chaos ended after fifteen minutes, during which Alice and I did crosswords together and I cracked under the pressure and drank a beer with her at a bar.

I unfolded my world map and added "TIGA" to Shanghai, adding a cross-line to Bruce Tyson's tombstone in Sydney.

On the last leg of the flight to London, when the cabin lights were dimmed and passengers had draped themselves in tiny blankets, I drifted into Bert Hart's world. His voice came after me: "Your grandfather was a split personality, Gar. Like me and you."

My grandfather, according to the legend Bert gave him, was a labourer on the Glasgow docks who was sullen and sober Monday to Friday, got drunk and boxed bare-knuckle in a hall on Saturday nights for cash before he got more drunk, then sang his hangover off the next day as a tenor in the church choir.

Bert had given me the drum on my grandfather after making one of his regular calls home just after I got my driver's licence at seventeen, and demanded that I collect him by car from the local Tattersalls Club where, he said, the big wheels of the city come to turn - which was why he was there. The chamber of truth was in that car, just him and me inside. I heard about his girlfriends and his clever business scams, like the time he and one of his mates, who managed a big hotel, poured an industrial drum of detergent down a drain at the back of the hotel so the owners would have to buy more from Bert's chemical company. The stuff foamed up as big as a car and took a day to clear. It was an accident, they told the fire brigade's hazardous chemicals team. They got away with it. Bert closed that ride home from the Tattersalls with the observation that my mother was insane. Nothing to do with him, he insisted. "Some people are just like that." He closed his eyes when we pulled into the driveway and said: "You're a weak cunt." I was still trying to like Bert then, so I put the remark down to him parroting my grandfather talking about *his* disappointing son.

XXXIV

DICK Callahan, a retired printer who once pressed the buttons on the presses that published Malcolm Halliday's *Morning Sun*, picked us up from London's Heathrow Airport just before dawn. Callahan should have been a reporter for the London tabloids because his home-based chauffeur service was an excellent source of juicy, mostly unreliable gossip.

On the run south with the motorway herd to Brighton, under a dirty pink and grey sky, we were reminded that Charlotte's younger brothers, Trevor and Ryan, were joint owners of Brighton's most successful real estate agency. Sales were improving and the lettings side was strong from commuters fed up with London rents. Neither Trevor nor Ryan drank alcohol, smoked cigarettes, gambled, used obscene language, or raised their voices in anger. The boys' marriages, which included three young children each, were 'substantially intact'. His breaking news was that one of the wives 'is struggling with her weight and some connected psychological disorder'. Callahan believed it was brought on by the boys' recent religious conversion. Trevor and Ryan had become Buddhists.

Not only that, they were now vegetarians 'who don't even eat eggs because they contain the young of other animals'. The egg thing, according to Callahan, was 'a descent into madness'. He couldn't imagine life without bacon, let alone eggs.

As we pulled off the A23 freeway under drizzling rain and cruised into the suburbs of Brighton, the footpaths began filling with head-down commuters in water-proof jackets marching to the trains and buses. I wound my window down a little and enjoyed a few spits of rain on my cheek. The air smelled of greasy salt, traffic fumes, and the chronic damp that lives in the walls and basements of the Regency and Victorian-era buildings that dominate the inner suburbs of the seaside city.

"Sodom and Gomorrah, this place," said Callahan as a handful of neo-punks littered with face-piercing, including a girl trying to rein in a pit bull terrier on a rope, stepped in front of his car at traffic lights, spilling beer from long cans. One character of indeterminate sex bongo-drummed a decent tune on his bonnet.

We eventually stopped outside a four-story Regency apartment building on Marine Parade overlooking the ruffled waters of the English Channel. Kate Halliday, thin and pony-tailed, was standing in the front bay window of the penthouse. Her canary-yellow cardigan stood out. She waved as we unloaded the bags from the boot.

The tough old building showed few scars from the regular fury unleashed by the sea upon its white masonry columns, curves and rectangles. At the top of the handful of steps that led to the front door, I paused and turned around. The air was hazy but I found the long neck of Brighton Pier about a kilometre away, propped on its spidery steel legs in brown water. A Ferris wheel stood rigid but sparkling with lights in the dull daylight at the pier's carnival ride end. Brighton is an old lady who never forgets to put her lippy on for the tourists.

Kate and Hugo opened the front door, and after a round of quick hugs, we lugged the bags into the cage lift and rose slowly to the top floor. In the lift I had a proper look at Hugo's new haircut. Razor short on one side, long on the other, with a fringe that hung over an eye.

"Nice look," said Alice. Hugo flushed red. I said nothing because I knew I'd be hammered by Hugo whichever way I went, but the half-masculine, half-feminine haircut triggered my recall of the dress I found in his wardrobe at home.

Inside her flat, Kate dragged Alice by the hand to the kitchen to put the kettle on for tea. "Tell me about Fred," she said. Alice rolled her eyes at me.

Hugo helped me put our bags in the bedrooms.

"How's school?"

"Boring."

I didn't have the stamina for further interrogation. Our reunion had that misty quality that comes with twenty-four hours of fitful dozing in a sealed can breathing bottled air. We drank hot, milky tea at the kitchen table and ate Kate's curried egg sandwiches on white bread rectangles denuded of their crusts. No-one mentioned Malcolm, but I felt his presence. Alice and I showered and dressed in fresh clothes.

Kate drove us to the hospital, and in the car, Alice told us a fine tale about the bomb threat at Abu Dhabi Airport. In her version, a black African man in a kaftan with a backpack was machine-gunned and fell backwards over the railing of an escalator into a duty-free perfume counter, causing an eruption of sickly fumes, shattered glass, and shredded flesh. Kate was horrified. Hugo was busy with his phone. I thought she had the makings of a thriller writer.

My imagining of Malcolm as a yellow Michelin Man was frighteningly true. Entering his private room, we were confronted by a small, bug-eyed barrel figure lying on a bed weeping black fluid in patches through his blue pyjamas. It was blood, the nurses said. There were no significant splits in his jaundiced outer dermis, but his cells were breaking down and large tracts of his skin were little more than blood-soaked sponges. The hospital disinfectant, and a vase of fragrant orange roses, made the setting more surreal.

"I'm not dressed for the races, I'm afraid," he said, his eyes flickering with the strain of conversation.

I did most of the talking. Alice held one of his hands. I held the other. He soon closed his eyes and fell asleep.

On the way back to Kate's, I sat in the back seat of the car with Hugo. His skin was paler than ever, his eyes more distant, though he looked well fed.

"I'm going to ask Malcolm if he wants to see a priest," said Kate.

"He's not religious," I said.

Kate glared at me through the rear-vision mirror. Charlotte hadn't wanted a priest. We held her funeral service in our garden at home under the frangipani tree at her written request – and to Kate's everlasting horror.

XXXV

KATE installed me in a double bedroom with French doors opening on to the roof-top terrace of their three-level flat. The Hallidays had purchased in the early 1980s during a recession, when it was part of a seedy boarding house. Over the ensuing years, a few licks of paint, a heritage listing, and some dedicated fellow owners lifted the tone and the value exponentially. The view from the tiled terrace at the south side of the building took in the coast and the roof tops of the city for miles. I tightened my coat, scarf and beanie and put my gloved hands on the terrace railing to look out to sea. Kate appeared, waving the wireless handset of her home phone at me. "Jack," she said, passing it to me.

"You're being careful," I said to him, stepping off the windy terrace into my room.

"Just in case East subpoenas our phone records," he said. "If anyone grills me, I called Kate to check on Malcolm. How is he?"

"His body's not much chop, but his sense of humour's alive and kicking."

"Give him my best."

"Will do."

Jack knew the elder Hallidays well because he and Charlotte were lovers when I met them on a beach in Thailand over twenty years ago. I was traveling with Sandy Wallace. One morning, while Jack, Charlotte and I swam in the surf, Sandy was in a beach hut, with a local man named Maday, inserting a dozen drinking straws filled with pink rocks of pure heroin into the covers of a photo album. Sandy didn't tell me about Maday, but did ask me to carry our precious memories back to Australia in my suitcase because her case was full. If I'd been caught at Bangkok Airport, I may have been hanged. Instead a handsome beagle at Sydney Airport sniffed my case on the baggage carousel and I served six months in prison. Sandy apologised and offered me a hand-job in the taxi on the way to court on sentencing day. Charlotte visited me in jail when she moved to Australia to work as an English teacher. Jack sent me weekly letters from Hong Kong.

"Now this shit with Charles East," said Jack, "I can't believe you've kicked an own goal there. You gave up the booze, you did all that counselling. We paid for some of it, for god's sake, and that's pissing off our top brass in London. I really believed you had your act together."

"I'm sorry. It was a lapse."

"Look," said Jack. "Fuck knows what drives us with the drink and whatever else. I'm sick of looking under my hood too. But these are dangerous people we are dealing with. So you need to get sharp and stay sharp."

"Are you saying I've ducked a bullet?"

"HQ would have fired you from here to Mars if those scum-bags in Sydney hadn't monstered Claire and given your version of events some cred. So the deal is this; you are on three months' probation. One stuff-up and you are gone. And it's not just you, mate. I brought you in the first time and I've hauled you back again. You and I are roped. I have that in writing."

"What now?" "I'm not interested in East: not on his own. We want the whale. There has been a smell around Baker and Cavalcade for years. They almost go bust during the Global Financial Crisis, his partner, Marais, dies, and then Baker's back on top of the world. The miracle man."

I told Jack about the call register on Bruce Tyson's phone taking me straight into Baker's Cavalcade head office in London, and about Tyson's text tip to *chase the tigre* that lead me to East's Tamerlane Investment Group Asia office in Shanghai.

"Number one," he said. "Neither you, nor I, nor Claire know anything about the murdered man's phone. Number two. We have a lot of pieces, but I can't see a decent picture, not one we can publish."

"Let's step through what we have." I said.

I walked off the terrace, sat at the dressing table in my room and put my phone on open speaker. I opened a writing pad. Jack and I talked while I made notes:

- *Emails between Henry East and Bart Hills point to Christ. Christ gives tip-off to Henry about the Double Happiness takeover bid = proof Henry lied to the court about acting alone. Who/ where is Christ?*
- *The Easts don't appeal Henry's sentence. Aim = avoid further scrutiny? Did Henry buck against that deal? Did someone attack Henry in jail to shut him up?*
- *Bart Hills death - self-inflicted? Or arranged to shut him up?*
- *Bruce Tyson, Henry's nurse, is murdered. Did THEY discover he was talking to* The Citizen? *Did Tyson overhear things in*

the prison psych hospital we don't know about? Why was he trying to talk to Cavalcade's chairman, John K. Baker? Was Tyson a blackmailer?

- *Charles East and Baker/Cavalcade linked in China – and via the polo in London. But East denies/plays down links. Why? What is their history? Current status? TIGA?*
- *Who is Oscar Peterson? Did he kill Tyson for East? Who abducted Claire?*

"You know how many question marks I just counted?" I asked.

"Look," he said, "take a trip to the London office. You know Cliff McDonald. I've had a chat to him. You two have a sniff around Baker and see what you can find. Claire's following the Tyson murder in Sydney. My guys in Shanghai are having a look at the connection between Cavalcade and East here. And now we'll look at your tiger."

"Oh, last thing," said Jack. "Your threat to kill charges; we've had some legal advice."

Jack's words sparked a recall that I kept to myself: Mr Browning must be lying somewhere at Moon Hill, carelessly abandoned after my mushroom trip. What if the coppers drop in to the Hill and find the gun while I'm over here?

"What sort of advice?" I said.

"Do you think East really wants a court case, a public shit fight with a global media company, albeit small, shining lights up his arse so the world can see what's up there? His clients would hate it. Our advice is that he'll back off before any trial. And if he does, the police will drop the charges. So he'll try to string this out, and we need to be patient. And you need to count to ten whenever you feel like throwing wild punches."

XXXVI

THE NEXT morning, Hugo went to school, and Alice and Kate caught the train to London to visit Alice's godmother, an astronomer who worked at the planetarium near the home of Greenwich Mean Time. Alice once believed her godmother was a fairy who set the world's clocks from a magic cupboard in her office. I walked to the hospital to visit Malcolm.

I spoke to the nurse before I went in.

"He's just had a bath. He's bright, but a little delirious: a lot of morphine for the pain," she said.

When I entered the room, a brown stain was slowly expanding through a bandage around Malcolm's torso.

I sat beside his bed. "How are you doing?"

"Been on a trip."

"Where to?"

"The Apollo Club in Harlem. Listened to Miles Davis going solo. Then I ate spare ribs and collard greens with mashed potato, washed down with an icy cold Rolling Rock."

"Nice," I said. "When did you get back?"

"Just opened my eyes."

"Been anywhere else you want to talk about?"

"Morocco last night, playing a flute with some snake charmers."

"I'd join you for the next ride but I don't have any of that fine morphine they're feeding you."

"There's a few barriers to leap before you can get on board," said Malcolm. "I wouldn't recommend the crossing."

I felt a faint squeeze from his hand.

"What are you working on?" he said

"Just some global conspiracy."

"Cracking it?"

"Got some interesting emails, some death threats, a couple of bodies. Plenty of Qs and no As. I'm on probation for insulting a captain of industry. I made a death threat, if you really want to know."

Malcolm smiled: "I'd take you to The Rock for a pint and some expert counsel, but I'm a bit tied up."

The Rock Hotel in Kemp Town, East Brighton, was a regular hideout for me and Malcolm on our family holidays over the years. "Only exercise I get these days," Malcolm used to say with a boyish grin, flexing a chicken egg-sized bicep as he touched a pint glass to his lips.

"Now," he said, "this conspiracy. Anyone I'd know involved?"

"There is one shifty Pom."

"Always is. Name?"

"A big investment banking kahuna in London named John K. Baker."

"More a name you would associate with donuts," said Malcolm. "Got a company name?"

"Cavalcade."

"Cavalcade ... sounds like a merry-go-round. Do they do property?"

"It's in their repertoire, I believe. Why?"

"Never met him, but I did put his picture in my newspaper."

"On a polo pony?"

"We never did toffs' sports. It was a marina. Big deal for Brighton. Five hundred million quid's worth. That's what they promised the city."

"Promised?"

"They were going to build a five-star resort, super yacht marina. The visionary Mr Baker wanted to connect Brighton into the Eurostar line to Paris too. Big story for us at *The Morning Sun*. Then it all went as flat as a dropped beer."

"What happened?"

"You did hear about the Global Financial Crisis?" said Malcolm, who had perked up with the smelling salts of a yarn in his nostrils. "Almost sunk him. But he bounced back and dumped Brighton in the process. He chased fatter fish in foreign seas. Tell you what; you ought to talk to my old business editor, Bill Crewes. Kate knows where is. Runs a vintage bookshop in Lewes."

"What's he know?"

"Bill followed that Baker development like a dog with a bone. He owned a chunk of land where Baker said he was going to build. Bill got cranky as a bull with cut balls when it fell over."

Malcolm's eyes started to flicker. He reached for a kidney dish on the bedside cabinet. I helped him spit some dark fluid into it and gave him a handful of tissues.

"I'll let you have a rest," I said.

He nodded.

I stopped at the door on the way out of the room. "Where are you going tonight?"

"Don't know. Ideas?"

"Try that Christmas. Remember the family photo we took on your stairs? Charlotte arranged us like a tree and you sat on top like the bloody star."

"Cheers, son." Malcolm closed his eyes. "Gar," he called, eyes still shut.

"Yes, mate?"

"Stay in touch with Kate and the boys when I go."

I went back and sat with him until he fell asleep.

Back at the Halliday's, I sat on my bed and read new emails on my laptop.

Steele had sent me a scanned document with a cover note: *FYI, this is a letter from Henry East to Bart Hills sent from Silverwater Prison before he was cut/cut himself. Handwritten. I have the original. Best, T.*"

Henry wrote:

I can feel Charles crawling inside me. He will never let me go. Millions of him are coming out of my pores, I can see them now. Charles is an infection. Now I know what to do. If I chop off my hands, I chop off his. When are you and Christ coming to visit?

XXXVII

ALICE DROVE me to the town of Lewes in Kate's car to visit Malcolm's old business editor. She steered us into a pretty village tucked into a cold slope behind some evergreen hills off the coast, about thirty minutes' drive east of Brighton. We parked near the drawbridge entrance to a little grey-stone castle off the main street. Alice and I agreed to meet later in the pub next to the carpark and she went off to browse the clothes shops. I liked the place for about five minutes, until I walked into one of the countless antiquarian bookshops that populate the town.

The address for Bill Crewes that Kate gave me took me to a grocery store, so I thought I'd seek Crewes through one of his fellow book sellers. A pinched-face woman behind the counter could have been the twin sister of the lemon-sucking Justice Tobias Tanner who sent Henry East to prison. When I asked if she knew of *Bill Crewes Rare Books*, she bared her teeth and said, "Out there," pointing to her front door. I tried a few other shops and discovered the fine burghers of Lewes had a common taste for bitter fruit, or a distaste for foreign accents such as mine.

I eventually found Crewes's name printed in gilt lettering above the glass-panelled entrance to a Tudor-era building. A life-sized human skeleton stood just inside the door. On the black-painted shop counter there was a large quill pen with a matching inkpot. Three cobwebbed, stuffed ravens were suspended in flying formation on chains from the low ceiling. A handsome woman behind the counter unbalanced me with, what I read as a genuine smile. She was tall and wore no make-up. Her long hair was streaked with grey and tied in a ponytail. She wore a dark, clingy, full-length dress. Mid-forties, I guessed. She was busy with a customer.

"I'll be with you shortly," she told me.

I strayed to the back of the shop and walked down a handful of steps into a musty room filled with faded hardback books stacked into floor-to-ceiling shelves. A man was sitting in the middle of the room on a church pew at a long oak table.

He had a big head and curly, white, shoulder-length hair roughly parted in the middle. Rosy-faced, he was clean-shaven with lots of spare skin hanging under his jaw. He wore a three-piece, moss-coloured tweed suit, a cream shirt, brown tartan-check tie and peered through a magnifying glass at the spine of a large book opened cover-side-up.

"Bill Crewes?"

"I think that's me," he said, looking up and putting me in his magnifying glass.

I explained to Crewes my referral from Malcolm. Crewes was strangely vague on the existence, let alone progress of Malcolm's illness.

"Mal just needs some piss and vinegar in his veins," said Crewes. "This is the stuff."

He walked over to a small, wooden barrel of cider resting on its side in a cradle on a bench against a wall. He collected two pint glasses from the shelf above and filled them with cloudy fluid.

"Mal says you know about the Cavalcade company and a Mr John K. Baker," I said.

"He's a treacherous bastard," said Crewes, handing me a pint and beckoning me to sit on a wooden chair that wobbled.

"How so?"

"Know much about yachting, young man?"

"Not much."

"I'll give you a tip. It's dangerous if you walk around on deck in your underwear in the middle of the night."

"Not sure I'm with you, Bill."

"John Baker's partner, Jean-Paul Marais, was an experienced yachtsman. What's he doing falling into the Atlantic at midnight while Baker is on watch?"

"So Baker pushed him overboard?"

"Not what the investigators found."

"What do you think, Bill?"

"He should be doing porridge for life."

Crewes was clearly thirsty. He poured himself another pint. Mine was half empty. He topped it up.

"Why would he kill Marais?" I said.

"Cavalcade was in debt; the whole thing was about to go under. I heard they had an offer to bail them out and Marais didn't like the people who were offering."

"And who were they, Bill?"

Crewes's eyes widened. He looked full of fear. "Keep your voice down, son; these walls have ears."

Crewes grabbed my right hand, pulled me close to him, and whispered in my ear. He had terrible breath.

"Who is that woman in the front of my shop?" Crewes was bug-eyed. He had a powerful grip on my hand.

"I don't know, Bill"

"Get her out of here," he said. "She's a spy! She's Baker's spy!"

The woman emerged from the front of the shop and stood in the doorway at the top of the steps.

"Dad, it's me, Joanne. Everything is okay."

"Who's this?" said Crewes, pointing at me.

"He's a friend of mine," she said. "Now can you please repair that book?"

Crewes went back to examining the spine of the tome on his table. Joanne nodded for me to join her in the front of the shop.

"I apologise for Dad. He has Alzheimer's. Early stages but accelerating."

"Sorry to hear that. My father had something similar."

I explained my relationship with Malcolm and his suggestion that Bill may have been able to help me with background on the old marina project. Joanne broke the news that Bill had destroyed all his old work files from *The Morning Sun* by burning them with petrol in the back garden in a fit of paranoia that nearly destroyed the bookshop.

"I don't think Malcolm knows how bad Dad is. The drink sets him off sometimes, but if we don't have it here, he wanders the pubs and all hell breaks loose in the town."

"You can't chain him up, can you?"

"I've had advice on that. It's against the law unfortunately."

I gave Joanne my business card in case she found anything of Bill's that mentioned Cavalcade, Baker, or the Brighton marina project, or if she had any afterthoughts.

Darkness was falling and sleeting rain whipping in from the coast as Alice and I climbed into the car to drive back to Brighton. She plunged us into a blurry stream of cars and trucks, diamond-white headlamps and red tail lights. I dozed, warm and dry, feeling safe in Alice's hands. My phone startled us both with its whistle. I didn't recognise the incoming number, but the caller wasn't hiding behind a blocked ID, so I answered.

Joanne Crewes said: "Dad worked with a woman named Sarah Kerr at the *Morning Sun*. I think she helped him on the marina thing. Sarah sent dad a birthday card recently."

Joanne had thrown away the envelope with Sarah Kerr's name and address on the back flap. "She told Dad that she is now a lecturer at Bath University."

XXXVIII

SITTING in the lounge room at Kate's flat, with my laptop on my thighs, I searched for a Sarah Kerr on the Bath University website. There was a lecturer of that name in politics and international studies. I dug through some university press releases and found her mobile phone number. It was about 8pm when I stepped into the kitchen and dialled. Wherever Sarah Kerr was, it was rowdy and she was friendly.

She found a quiet place and told me she'd met Malcolm Halliday and Bill Crewes around the year 2000 when she was teaching at the University of Brighton. She started working with them by writing an occasional newspaper column about Brighton's history and architecture. She was interested in town planning, and working alongside Bill, crossed paths with Cavalcade's marina proposal.

"Let's meet," she said in a husky voice. "This conversation could get interesting."

"How's that?"

"Not over the phone, my love."

She had me hooked. We agreed to have lunch in two days' time at a pub in Bath called the Crystal Palace on Abby Green near the Roman Baths. I liked that she'd chosen a pub. We might get along.

*

The next morning I dressed in a suit and caught a train in the dark to central London and *The Citizen*'s headquarters at Covent Garden to meet Cliff McDonald.

On the train, I received a text sent from Claire in Sydney: *Call me. Don't email.*

Claire was agitated when I phoned.

"I'm getting strange emails," she said. "Emails sent to me at *The Citizen* - from *my* work email address. And I didn't send them."

"What do they say?"

"Nothing. The subject line and text box is blank. I received one from you too," she said. "Yesterday."

I scanned my sent items box. I'd not sent an email to Claire since I left Sydney days ago.

Claire said: "It's like we are talking to each other, but we're not the ones doing the talking. If that makes any sense."

"May just be a glitch in the system," I said. "Get the tech guys to have a look. But let Jack know."

An hour later my train arrived at London Bridge station and I joined the stony-eyed legions descending into the city's underground where we packed ourselves into carriages and fumed against each other like half-cooked sausages.

The Citizen was HQ'd a few hundred metres from the Covent Garden tube station in a modest 1970s brick building on cobblestoned Floral Street. My reflection in the windows of the high street clothes shops, pitched against the mannequins and the natty workers inside, made me think I needed a new suit and haircut, a view that was reinforced when I entered *The Citizen's* open plan office.

Jack had told me our London staff had an average age of 25. He didn't mention the IQ. I reckoned he'd seriously overshot the runway on age. Cliff McDonald, one of the senior hands, didn't have a decent facial furrow in sight. As he ushered me past quad-pods of desks peppered with unmistakably creative people, I calculated he was in his early thirties and trying to hide a silver spoon up his skinny backside. At least he was losing his hair early; his beard reminded me of the downy underbelly of a female crab.

Cliff took me into his glass-walled office and sat at a desk behind a computer screen that was only a tad smaller than my Defender's front window. I figured he had eyesight issues, or did a lot of video work, because was wearing thick-framed reading glasses, though they may have been props. I sat in a Scandinavian-style 1950s chair next to a matching coffee table.

Cliff opened: "So you're working under Claire Styler in Sydney?"

Not bad, I thought. His first ball was a bumper bowled at my head. I ducked and let it go through to the keeper. "You know her well?" I said.

"She's a smart operator. I went to university with her."

"What about her husband. Do you know Carl?"

"A chameleon."

"In what way?"

"Doesn't matter."

Cliff was either a master of intrigue or a petulant duffer. I decided we should play more before I made up my mind.

Cliff studied his fingernails as I gave him the background we'd gathered on the Easts, Baker and Cavalcade. So I made sure to include enough detail in my description of the electrocution of Bruce Tyson to make Cliff's chinless jaw drop a little. He brightened at my telling of the drowning of Baker's partner, Jean-Paul Marais.

"Do you know that in French, *marais* means swamp, or bog?" he said.

I counted to ten, as Jack had advised me to do before swinging punches, and then I went on to explain the media reports of trouble for Cavalcade during the Global Financial Crisis and Baker's subsequent solo navigation of the business into apparently rude financial health.

"And the point of all this?" Cliff said, turning his gaze back to his fingernails. He trimmed one with a small pair of scissors and looked pleased with the result.

"Listen, Clifford. At risk of interrupting your beauty treatment, your friend Claire Styler has been abducted and sexually assaulted, at least one man's been murdered, my family has been threatened, and a young man is sitting in a prison psych unit with a mutilated face and a fucked-up brain after lying about a crime he committed. All these events trace back to John Baker and Charles East. Do you think there might be something shifty going on that could make a decent yarn for *The Citizen*?'

Cliff sat up straight and put his scissors in his desk drawer.

I looked him in the eyes. "So, for a start, I want to know what makes Baker tick – and who pulled him out of the financial *marais*, as you call it."

"Sorry," he said. "I've had a bit of a tummy bug. It's affected my concentration."

"Do you want to go home?"

"Let's work."

Cliff rejuvenated himself with a fizzy vitamin pill in a glass of water. Over the course of the morning, he and I trawled *The Citizen*'s database and nosed around the internet. We learned Baker kept a low public profile, despite having some flashy pursuits like the polo ponies and yachts. Baker was single, and heterosexual as far as we could tell. Married once, then divorced. There was a twenty-eight-year old daughter, Anita Baker, from the short-lived marriage, drifting around somewhere.

Baker owned a house on the banks of The Thames in the Hammersmith bankers' belt that he purchased for 15 million British pounds in 2009. He also owned a farm in Surrey where he housed his polo ponies. Le Monde in France reported on a corporate party a few years ago when Baker purchased a US$50 million super yacht called *Electra2* that he kept anchored in Monaco Bay. Two French Government Ministers and a handful of banking chief executives from London and Paris had attended the Monaco soiree. One of the sons of the Libyan dictator Muammar Gaddafi was at the party too. Cliff thoughtfully reminded me, in case I didn't know it, that Muammar was killed in the Libyan wave of the Arab Spring.

We found press photos of John K. Baker with senior executives from Baker's former employer, the giant French bank BKB Nouveau, posing at the BKB Nouveau de L'Arc de Triomphe horse race in Paris. In one snap, Baker and his old BKB pals were standing with a former World Bank President, Rene Gasquet, and a dark-skinned man with hair styled in a classic 1970s coif, enhanced by a black moustache. The pic was taken in 2012.

"Is there a name in the photo caption for the guy wearing the caterpillar on his lip?" I said.

"Appears not," said Cliff.

"You reckon the real Saddam Hussein was hung from the gallows for war crimes in Baghdad in 2006, or is that him at the races with that lot?" I said.

"I see what you mean," said Cliff. "I'll ask the PR people at BKB if they can ID him. I have an in there."

"So you're close to BKB?"

"Gar, BKB is a bank with over 100,000 employees in more than 100 countries. They have more than a dozen PR people schmoozing and boozing every business journalist in the city of London. I'm not special."

"BKB may have been the ones who hauled Baker out of the shit of the GFC. We need to get inside their door and find out - without ringing their alarm bells. Stealth is our friend right now."

"So you're saying I shouldn't ask their PR people about the photo?"

"Let's hold fire for now."

"Okay. But I can tell you right now that Cavalcade and BKB are still close. I've got evidence."

"Such as?"

He shuffled papers on his desk and extracted a glossy brochure. "Baker's speaking at this BKB investment conference this week at the Dorchester Hotel."

Cliff's media invite to *The New Silk Roads* conference said the event was *by invitation only for a select group of global investment leaders*. BKB was courting executives who managed the world's major pension funds, both private and those controlled by governments and trade unions. They were after people who managed the retirement savings of hundreds of millions of workers.The brochure said: *Delegates will hear about opportunities to profit from projects to build roads, airports and new cities in South America, North Africa, India and China. Cavalcade's John K Baker will share his insights from more than three decades as an investment visionary growing his clients' wealth in an ever-changing world.*

"I want to attend," I said.

"I'll call BKB now and give them your name. I'm sure it'll be fine."

"Best not to do that, Cliff. I'll just turn up with you."

"Stealth?"

I nodded. The date was in two days' time. Tomorrow I was going to Bath to meet Sarah Kerr. I thanked Cliff for his help. He went to the staff room to make a coffee while I took photos on my phone of the photos we'd found of Baker and his friends.

I headed back to Brighton, wondering if I could trust Cliff McDonald because I had caught sight of another invitation on his desk while he was making coffee. One he clearly didn't want to talk about. It was in his drawer actually: a ticket to BKB's corporate suite at de L'Arc de Triomphe horse race in Paris in two weeks' time, return business class air tickets, and a booking confirmation for two nights stay at Le Meurice, one of the city's best hotels, free of charge. That little package could buy a lot of favours if handed to the right personality, and Cliff looked like he had it in spades.

XXXIX

THE HEAD OFFICE of the Cavalcade Investment Group was sparsely furnished. It's location on the 35th floor of the famed *Gherkin* building in the City of London's financial district was statement enough for its co-founder and chairman, John K Baker, who strode into the office and hugged and kissed the standing girl who had been waiting for him.

They sat opposite each other in orange-coloured leather armchairs beside a window, a glass-topped coffee table in the shape of a teardrop separating them.

"You look well," he said. The girl replied by sucking an ice cube from a glass of water and crunching it with her molars. He persisted, "A business suit suits you, if you'll excuse the pun."

"So why can't I kill him?"

"*You* have been spending too much time with that lunatic in Sydney."

"He gets the job done."

"Oh, yes. A nice job he did on that psychiatric nurse. Do you know that man phoned my office? Several times. How he found my numbers, I do not know. What do you think is going to happen if the police investigators find that man's phone, or records, with my contact details in it, and the dates and call times?"

The girl crunched more ice, and ran her fingers nonchalantly through her short, platinum blond hair.

Baker sat forward in his seat, put his elbows on his knees, and zoomed his eyes in on hers. "You *do know* that he called my office – after he was meant to be dead!"

"What?"

"Yes, I had a ghost on the line, it seems. Or there's someone else who knows too much. My God, you've let things fall to pieces since you allowed Henry East to jump off the rails. And now you want to kill a journalist. As if that won't draw a crowd."

"You're the genius. What do you want me to do?"

"Be smarter. Come up with a better plan. You've tracked him to the UK, haven't you?"

"He's staying in Brighton with his mother-in-law and his children."

"Well, work on his family. He's a normal human being, isn't he, with all those parenting instincts coursing through his veins? We need to know what he has on us, and we need to pressure him to hit the delete button. Everyone has a price."

"Not everyone, John. You seem to forget what you did five years ago and why."

"Okay," he said, raising his eyebrows and massaging his forehead at the memory of his ex-business partner, and the night he was lost at sea. "If we need to delete Hart, we will delete him. But let's try a little more sophistication in the meantime. I mean, for Christ's sake, wrapping a man's head in wire and electrocuting him?"

"It's creative."

"It's psychopathic."

"Are you worried Seth might come after *you*, John?"

"Should I be?"

The girl smiled. "I have some tricks up my sleeve for Mr Hart and his loved ones." She stood up. "I will be in touch."

"Don't I get a kiss?" he said.

She approached the seated man, who for as long ago as she could remember had wanted her to call him *father*. She avoided his offered lips and dabbed her own dryly upon his right cheek.

XL

I CAUGHT a morning train from Brighton to London Bridge, but this time I rode the underground to Paddington Station where I boarded an overground carriage with a table upon which I put my iPad and take-away coffee. It was a ninety-minute ride north to Bath. For the first thirty minutes, a mob of well-upholstered tourists wearing matching parkas and track pants ensured everyone else on the carriage knew their names and what their itinerary was for the day. I was gutted that they didn't mention the Crystal Palace where I was meeting Sarah Kerr. Gutted.

I read on my iPad about John K. Baker's role in *The New Silk Roads* conference, drafting questions I might put to him, wondering when and if I should grill him about Bruce Tyson. The rhythm of the train put me into a trance and I dozed, opening my eyes now and then to peer outside upon south-west England flickering past against an endless grey sky: cottages with thatched roofs, brick-box council flats and bitumen car parks, grassy paddocks spotted with sheep and cows, patches of forest, motorways streaming with lorries and cars.

Around midday, I stepped from Bath railway station and started walking up a wide, cobblestoned corridor into the historic, Roman-built centre of the city. The offspring of globalisation, housed in grand Georgian sandstone buildings, soon flanked me on all sides: mostly shopfronts for banks, fast-food chains and pop fashion houses. Near the Roman Baths, a pretty female gladiator in a leather tunic and sandals waved a shield at me advertising American donuts.

Sarah Kerr was drawing smoke from a long, ebony cigarette holder when I arrived in the cobblestoned square of Abby Green that housed the Crystal Palace pub. I recognised her from the cigarette holder she said she'd be carrying. As I closed in, I guessed she was in her late fifties or early sixties. She wore a dark trouser suit and open-necked blue shirt with a voluminous, red-and-white polka-dot hanky tucked in the top pocket of her jacket.

I introduced myself and we took a window table inside the pub with a bottle of Bordeaux, a cheese platter with mixed olives and a crisp baguette to share. Closer up, Sarah had a lot of youth in her face, which surprised me because of her smoking, which appeared to be a serious relationship from the way she fondled her holder. She seemed to know this about her face, putting it on full display by pinning her hair into a high bun. She examined me with large, dark, almond-shaped eyes.

"I've studied you online," I said. "Want to know anything about me?"

"I phoned Kate Halliday this morning. I know you were married to Malcolm's daughter. You're a little volatile. You have children, a boy and a girl."

"And a three-legged dog," I said, wondering what other personality traits of mine Kate had volunteered.

Sarah raised her eyebrows.

"He lost it in a hunter's trap," I said.

She sipped her wine. "And now you are the hunter, Gar."

"More a fisherman right now. Bill Crewes told me someone offered to bail John Baker and Jean-Paul Marais out of trouble during the GFC. He didn't get around to telling me who. But he said Marais didn't like the deal, so Baker drowned him, or had him drowned."

"Bill has dementia, Gar. And that's a serious charge, murder. People have been sued for much smaller defamations."

"So Bill was dreaming it up?"

Sarah took a sip of wine. "Do you mind if I smoke?"

We stepped outside into the square. Sarah tucked a cigarette into her holder and lit up. Her fine-featured face was how I imagined Audrey Hepburn would look in *Breakfast at Tiffany's* with age on her clock.

"Okay. So who do you think saved Cavalcade?"

"The Egyptians." Sarah took a long drag on her cigarette, removed it from her holder and squashed it under the toe of her dagger-heeled black shoe. She'd wasted most it.

"I'm trying to give up," she said. "More wine?"

I purchased another bottle of Bordeaux at the bar and placed it on our table, opened my briefcase and put my notebook and my voice recorder next to it.

"We're off the record?" she asked quizzically.

"Of course. No attribution. I just have a shocking memory."

"That's handy sometimes," she said, winking. "Anyway, heard of the Arab Spring?"

"I don't have a degree in it."

She grinned. "Headline: 2011. The people revolt. It starts in Tunisia, spreads to Algeria, Oman, Jordan, then Egypt, where it really erupts. Next it rumbles across Libya and Syria. The people got sick of despots standing on their throats with designer boots. The mood spreads to Eastern Europe. The Ukrainians throw that Russian puppet Yanukovych out of his Kiev palace but he just scurries off to Moscow, with some gold in his pockets, into the embrace of Vladimir Putin. Putin rolls his tanks into Crimea to stop the rot. On it goes."

"Your point?" I said.

"The dictators see these breakdowns coming. You don't think they take out lifestyle insurance?"

"By that you mean they stash money, preferably where their enemies can't find it."

"Bingo," said Sarah. "On an industrial scale." She clinked her glass on mine.

This sort of caper was Charles East's act to a tee. It was no secret that, for a fee, he helped the Chinese elite move wealth, and a selection of their children, overseas in case they fell foul of the ruling regime at home. If the shit hits the fan and the parents are put in a box of some sort, dead or alive, having a child or two planted OS would keep their precious DNA flowering richly elsewhere.

"So when you say you suspect the Egyptians had a funding deal going on with Baker and Cavalcade, who do you mean exactly?"

"The big papers in London started reporting Cavalcade was set to go bust because of the GFC. Jean-Paul Marais dies. Cavalcade is flush with cash again a few months later, but it withdraws from the Brighton marina deal. So Bill Crewes and I decided to see what was going on. Bill found a trail. I was helping. We found hints of Arab oil money going into Cavalcade, some of it from Egypt before the Mubarak regime collapsed."

"What can you give me?" I said. "Any documents?"

"Nothing concrete; you know that Bill burnt his files and now his brain is broken."

"But you have the knowledge."

"Some of it."

Sarah's phone rang. As she spoke, her smile gave way to an expression of pain. "I'm coming, darling," she said and hung up. "I'm sorry, Gar. I have a friend. She's ill." Sarah handed me a sheet of folded paper from her handbag. "Homework," she said. She stopped to light a cigarette outside my window, waved, and tottered away like a long-legged waterbird, trailing smoke across the uneven paving stones.

I plugged the cork back in the half-finished bottle of wine, stuffed it in my briefcase and walked to the train station. As the train rolled off to London, I rummaged in my briefcase for the music player I'd loaded with Miles Davis tunes that I'd forgotten to give to Malcolm. I put the ear plugs in and selected a French film noir soundtrack. The wafting trumpet of the track *Generique* touched me where I reckoned the night sirens touch Fish and prompt his singing. I sensed Malcolm wanted to talk, so I phoned his hospital room. The nurse said he'd just fallen asleep.

I unfolded Sarah's homework. It was a copy of a newspaper clipping from *The Washington Observer*:

Egypt's top prosecutor has notified governments around the world that former Finance Minister Karim Iskandar and his family may be involved in the theft of hundreds of billions of dollars' worth of cash, gold and other state-owned valuables.

Prosecutor General Mahmoud Rasekh said that Iskandar and his sons, Anwar and Kafr, may have violated laws prohibiting the seizing of public funds and profiteering and abuse of power by using complex business schemes to divert the assets to offshore companies and personal accounts.

This was good reading and deserved an accompaniment. I extracted the wine bottle from my briefcase, unplugged the cork and had a swig. A few passengers shook their heads. "Cheers," I said to no-one in particular and had another swig, ignoring the little voice that was nagging inside my head for me to put the cork back in. I thought something about Arabs and genies and bottles.

Iskandar and his close friend, President Hosni Mubarak, were key strategic allies of the United States for decades until Mubarak was forced from power in the wake of national protests and international pressure. The sum of the assets alleged to be appropriated by the Iskandar family and others — more than $200 billion — far exceeds earlier estimates and might be wildly exaggerated. Previous figures for the amount allegedly stolen by the Iskandars range from $1 billion to $70 billion.

Accounts of the Iskandar's wrong-doing - collected by investigators from the StAR partnership between the World Bank Group and the United Nations Office on Drugs and Crime - are supported only by hearsay witness testimony, second-hand news accounts, and what have proved to be fraudulent bank documents.

Anwar Iskandar's role at one of the Arab world's largest investment funds, KLR Vulcan, has long fuelled suspicion.

As I neared London, a text arrived from Sarah:

Sorry about the ending at Abby Green today. I have my spade in hand. Just found a doco in my files confirming Cavalcade link to KLR Vulcan. I'll be in touch. x, SK.

XLI

THE FIRST words that came into my mind were 'funeral parlour'. The only thing that suggested Cliff McDonald and I were entering *The New Silk Roads* investment conference was a sign on a floor-stand.

The Park Suite Left meeting room at the Dorchester Hotel on Park Lane in Mayfair was draped from ceiling to floor with silver-coloured curtains. Huge bouquets of red and white flowers, mixes of roses and lilies, sat on pedestal tables arranged around the walls. I could smell no perfume from the flowers, but there was plenty of perfume in the room. The competing scents of a hundred, highly-polished men and a dozen women merged with the odours of fresh coffee and French pastry.

The people sipping, nibbling, nattering and swapping business cards talked for a trillion dollars.

Of course none of the real owners of the money were attending BKB Nouveau's conference. Those men and women were in their workshops and factories, offices, classrooms and hospitals, entrusting their retirement savings to the professionals. From my eavesdropping, the card-swappers' core interest was discussing the quality of their rooms at the Dorchester and where to drink tonight after the official dinner.

"Where did they check them in?" I said to Cliff, nodding at the throng of talking heads. His eyes were scouting the room for the registration desk.

"What?"

"Their eye-patches and cutlasses."

At my utterance, a young woman chatting to a portly fellow beside us glanced sharply our way. Her brilliant red hair was pulled into a pony tail that looked painfully tight; it had lifted her eyebrows so high it was a wonder that her eyeballs hadn't popped from their sockets.

"Cliff!" she said gleefully, proudly displaying her glow-in-the-dark teeth. She grasped him by the forearm. "We are so glad you could come."

A badge over her left breast said: *Sally Hawkins. Communications Director.* BKB's elephant-eared PR woman talked brightly to Cliff about chaperoning him at their big horse race in Paris in two weeks. Cliff looked sheepish. I raised my eyebrows at him as if it was news.

Cliff said: "Sally, this is my colleague, Gar Hart. I hoped you could fit him in today."

"I'll see. This way please".

We followed her towards the registration desk. Cliff's name tag was already printed. She had to handwrite my name on a label. Her face suggested I was as welcome as a bout of herpes. I had no doubt she'd Google, or probe Linked In, for my pedigree at her first private opportunity.

"Now, gentlemen," she said, "just a reminder that you are here today as observers. I can give you copies of the presentations on a memory stick, or email them to you later, if you prefer. But I'm afraid there will be no questions from the media."

Cliff lapped the invisible sugar cube from her palm and nodded assent.

"Are you kidding?" I said.

She reached for her whip. "I'm afraid they are our rules, Mr Hart. You don't have to stay if you don't like them."

"Let's see how we go."

She moved to the side of the room and talked animatedly to a tall, young man in a dark suit wearing an earpiece. He eyed me and Cliff without expression. I couldn't help myself; I waved to them and smiled.

The pension fund managers – to whom BKB, Cavalcade and a handful of other *investment advisors* were trying to sell their wares – were quite rightly given the prime seats in the front rows on either side of a middle aisle of the main conference room. They filed in from the outer reception area, some still clutching their cups and saucers. There was a raised platform, with blue velvet skirting, sitting front and centre of the room. The platform had a speaker's podium and a large projection screen behind it. A red-roped area at the back of the room housed about a dozen seats beside a floor stand that read: *Media*. Cliff and I sat with a handful of others in our holding pen.

The program said John K Baker would be the third speaker. We sat through the opening razzle-dazzle, but when some joker from BKB launched into a diatribe about his fabulous bank, I signalled to Cliff to follow me outside. Cliff spoke briefly with the PR woman on the way out and joined me in the funeral parlour where there was self-serve coffee and tea. Cliff and I were alone.

"Gar," he said, stirring sugar into a cup of milky tea, "if you don't abide by the rules, we won't be invited back to these events."

I baa-ed like a sheep.

"Ever heard of subtlety, Gar?"

"I've heard of it. I've just not seen it crack many nuts".

Cliff chuckled. Maybe I was being too hard on him. Maybe. My phone whistled.

It was Jack. "We've done some work on East's Trust8 business. They've wiped all mention of the Trust8 connection to Cavalcade off their website. Problem for them is Trust8 also has a Chinese language website, a shadow site, if you like. There is a press release on there, written in Mandarin, where Trust8 brags about having Cavalcade as a client. It quotes East and Baker slapping each other on the back, all very palsy-walsy."

I walked to a corner of the room for additional privacy and told Jack about my meeting with Sarah Kerr and her theory about Egypt's Iskandar family possibly bailing Cavalcade out after the Global Financial Crisis.

He said: "Let's tread carefully here. If that's true, or partly true, the stakes are going to get very high. Did you know the youngest son, Kafr Iskandar, was blown up in his car in Rome a few months ago? The killers escaped."

Cliff signalled to me. Baker was on stage. I told Jack I'd call him back. I found my seat in the conference room.

I expected to see the plump, business-suited Musketeer from the Ascot Polo Club photo with Henry and Charles East. The man on the stage was similar, but he was leaner, with close-cropped, dark hair and a neat, thin moustache on his top lip. His nose looked narrower. He had a military fitness to him and was a much more elegant man. Plastic surgery? And a personal trainer? Or maybe cancer was trimming his physique, early stages.

Baker urged delegates to think with an open mind about investing alongside Cavalcade in regions that may be difficult for Western corporations to understand, such as North

Africa, South America, India and China. His pitch was that Cavalcade had a track record of picking the right local partners – particularly in the construction of infrastructure such as roads, airports and housing – in high growth, but politically risky parts of the world.

During question time, a couple of fund managers took to a microphone. Baker's sidekicks sidled up to the managers like real estate agents' flunkies at house auctions tagging clients for follow-up, and exchanged handshakes and business cards. Baker grinned like he was spearing fish in a bucket. When he walked off the stage and down the aisle towards the back doors, I followed his entourage of two men and a woman.

The pug-dog-eyed PR woman blocked my way.

"Thanks," I said and handed her my name tag. She spluttered something, but her dagger-heeled wheels and stumpy legs made her too slow to keep pace with me. I caught Baker near the lifts.

"Mr Baker, I hoped we might have a word."

"And you are?"

"My name is Gar Hart. I'm from *The Citizen*."

"Advertising sales?"

"Reporter."

"You're off your patch. Is that Australian I can hear?"

"Yes."

"I know your boss," he said.

"Really."

"Both of them actually: Ailsa Dusseldorf and Zachary Werner."

Baker's technique was quaintly old school: impress and intimidate by claiming intimacy with those who pay your wages. I had to acknowledge I bounced a little. I wondered if he knew I was on probation at work and facing criminal charges.

"How well do you know Mr Charles East?" I said.

"His name rings a faint bell."

"His son rode your polo ponies. You do business with Charles East in China. They live in Sydney."

"Is that so? We do business with a lot of people. I can't recall them all."

The lift doors opened. I followed Baker and his people inside. His male sidekicks stood side-by-side between me and Baker, a suited female behind him. They formed a neat triangle with him in the middle.

I could put him on the spot: show him the polo photo I had in my jacket pocket of him and the Easts; press him on the Easts and Trust8; ask him why the murdered psych nurse Bruce Tyson had called him; grill him on the Egyptians and his dead business partner, Jean-Paul Marais. I may never get another chance to corner him in person, but to spit all that out here would just telegraph our half-thought-out punches and give him the chance to duck for deeper cover. He was already junking his links with Trust8.

As Baker stepped out of the lift, I said: "*The Citizen* is doing a series on the world's leading investment advisory businesses, Mr Baker. Cavalcade is one of the firms we're profiling. It's a great chance for you to tell your story to the market, expand on what you just said to this conference."

"What do you really want, Mr Hart?" said Baker.

"I've just transferred to London from the Sydney office. It seems I was misled about the depth of your relationship with the Easts. We can clear everything up with an interview."

"Look," he said, "give my colleagues your business card. I promise we'll come back to you. Very soon."

I handed my card to the woman in his entourage. I felt I'd lit a fuse.

XLII

CLIFF and I had lunch at a nearby pub. From our conversation, he'd definitely been born with a silver spoon in his mouth, but he was letting it dull with age. Even so, he wouldn't drink more than one pint of beer. He was very fond of Claire Styler. They were housemates once, he conceded. I began to suspect they were roommates too, but he didn't like that terrain and shot back to the office before I could grill him further.

Outside the pub, rain threatened, but it looked a way off, so I took a stroll around Hyde Park near the Dorchester Hotel. I phoned Malcolm as I walked and promised to visit him the next day. When the rain caught me, I realised I'd left my overcoat in the Dorchester cloakroom. By the time I got there, the official part of the conference was over, but a few of the delegates were sitting at the Promenade Bar off the marble-pillared lobby. I joined the throng. I thought I'd eavesdrop, maybe pick up some gossip on Baker, and I felt like a guiltless drink without Cliff propped beside me sipping like a sparrow.

I found a tall stool at the oval bar and ordered a Martini, which appeared to be the poison of choice. My phone pinged. It was a text from Cliff with a note: *Here's how you crack nuts*. It included a link to a YouTube video of a Labrador dog nosing almonds in their shells across a shed floor towards a horse that proceeded to smash the nuts with its hoof for the dog to eat the kernels. I laughed too loudly and ordered a second Martini.

"Good joke?" said a female voice at my back. She was part of a couple aged in their early thirties, I guessed. They could have been brother and sister. With her liquorice hair and cream complexion, she looked a little like Claire. Her partner was fair-skinned too: tall and lean with a long, black fringe he kept combing with his fingers. They were both dressed for the Dorchester and formed their vowels as well as anyone at Buckingham Palace. We chatted. I immediately forgot their names.

I stepped to the edge of the bar and made a phone call to inform Cliff I'd be going straight back to Brighton from London and that I'd see him in the office in the morning. I asked him to gather all he could about the Iskandar corruption allegations in Egypt, and Kafr Iskandar's car bomb murder in Rome.

I returned to the bar to collect my overcoat off my seat and finish my Martini. The young woman pleaded with me to play *her* favourite YouTube dog video. I opened my phone and she dictated her search words. A few seconds later we watched a dog dressed in a skirt stand on its hind legs and dance to mariachi music for minutes on end. I don't know what happened to time after that.

I remember the marbled walls of the Dorchester toilet, and standing at the basin, looking in the mirror, splashing my face with cold water, having trouble staying upright. The room blurred. The young man with the fringe was standing behind me. I had no resistance when he took me by the arm. He led me, bobbing like a string puppet, into a cubicle and pushed me to sitting on the toilet seat. He locked the door behind us. I tried to yell but no sound came out. I could only watch. He pulled off my suit jacket and hung it on the hook on the back of the door. Then he loosened my tie and unbuttoned my collar. He lifted my tie over my head, with the knot still fastened, and hung it on the door hook with my jacket. He unbuttoned my shirt cuff and rolled the sleeve to above my elbow. I tried to move, I tried to yell again: nothing. He looped my tie over my arm, slid it to just above my elbow and pulled it tight, very tight. I saw my blue veins bulge inside my elbow joint. He pulled from his inside jacket pocket a small black case, something you'd keep reading glasses in. He extracted a syringe, neat and small. Not fucking air, I thought, not fucking air. He tapped my vein with a finger, puffed it up. He stuck the needle in, tugged the plunger back a little, until my blood swam with the clear fluid already in the syringe, then he squeezed. The fog was quick, warm at first, and soft. Nice. The gaps between my heartbeats got wide and blackness swallowed me.

XLIII

I HEARD Fish howling, way out in space, his night voice singing with his choir of sirens.

I blinked. The light hurt my eyes.

"Edgar, can you hear me?" A mouth was opening and closing inside ginger fur on a ballooning bald head. The speaker tucked a penlight in his mouth and pulled my eyelid up to spear the light beams in. He slapped my face with his open hand.

"Now stay with me, Edgar. Keep your eyes open. Tell me your full name. Talk to me, Edgar."

"Gar," I said.

He showed me a photo driver's licence. "Is this you?"

"Yes."

"We are taking you to hospital now, Edgar. You're back with us. You're a lucky man. We thought we'd lost you there."

"Where is *he*?" I decoded my vision of the speaker. He was wearing a paramedic's uniform.

"Who?"

"The one, the one who did this."

"Here we go, Edgar," the mouth said. The paramedic and his partner lifted me off the floor and laid me on their trolley. I saw their medical case on the bathroom bench; I recognised the label Naloxone on the bottle beside it, a used syringe next to that. So their guess was a heroin overdose? They must have got it right because I was back from wherever I'd fallen. I gagged on the smell and taste of my vomit. The man wiped my nose and mouth with a wet tissue. Nausea twisted my gut. They rolled me on the trolley out of the toilet, through the main lobby of the Dorchester Hotel.

The glow-in-the-dark teeth and red hair of the BKB PR woman caught my eye as they wheeled me past a huddle of gawping conference delegates.

"God damn drug addicts," said a male voice with an American accent from inside the huddle. "They'll as hell do it anywhere."

*

A young, male police constable took a statement from me as I lay in a bed in the emergency department of St Thomas's Hospital on the banks of the Thames. It was clear he thought I was cooking up the angle that a mysterious couple had spiked my drink with a stupefying drug and then injected me with heroin. As far as he was concerned, I was lamely trying to cover my butt with my family; his eyes said so. My mother-in-law and my children were on their way from Brighton, the nursing staff interrupted us to say.

"Why would someone try to murder you in a toilet at the Dorchester Hotel, Mr Hart?"

I ran the next steps in the conversation through my head before speaking. Do you have a day, Constable? See, I have this global conspiracy theory ... it goes like this ... nothing proven, of course.

I said to him: "I have a vivid imagination, Constable. I'll leave my statement there, thanks."

As the constable completed his forms, I remembered Steele's line at our table at the Red Emperor when we talked about Bart Hill's OD: *A little dab'll do ya.* I'd just had a dab too much, that's what the constable had concluded. So had the hospital staff; they'd seen it all before. Mine was just a new name on the A&E admission sheet with an old story.

Time went somewhere. Kate, Alice and Hugo walked in. They had looks on their faces like someone had died. Only Alice gave me a hug.

The staff suggested counselling. Kate collected the information papers after I threw them on the floor in the curtained hospital cubicle.

I had to acknowledge that my adversaries' tactics were first class. The fringe-comber had left me inside the toilet cubicle with the syringe hanging out of my arm *and* a plastic packet of high-grade smack in my shirt pocket. I'd been found with my wallet intact and my phone working: nothing stolen. It added up to a reckless, middle-aged tourist on a binge who'd gone too far on a new supply in a big city he didn't understand.

The barman and other staff at the Dorchester confirmed that I did have a drink with a couple. Two drinks apparently. The couple had paid for their drinks by cash and left. I was the dodgy one, they said. I'd left an unpaid bar tab.

What had saved me, I learned from the medico's at the hospital, were relentless calls to my phone and Hugo's police-whistle ring-tone which had alerted another man who was using the hotel's toilet. He had pushed open my cubicle door and called the hotel staff.

The drive back to Brighton with Kate at the wheel started in silence. It was raining heavily, the wipers squeaking a surreal beat and the oncoming headlights hurting my eyes. I was in the front passenger seat. Tears trickled down Kate's cheeks, camouflaged by the shadows of raindrops through the windscreen. I rubbed a few tears from *my* eye sockets.

Malcolm had died as I sat unconscious on that toilet seat at the Dorchester.

The calls that saved me were made by Alice trying to give me the news.

XLIV

KATE WAS not one for holding the hands of corpses. She had chosen to drive to London to collect me after a quick viewing of Malcolm's body.

There had been a family dinner at Kate's earlier in the evening with uncles Trev and Ryan and their families, to which I had been invited and which I had forgotten. A call from Malcolm's doctor at the hospital had interrupted the dinner with the report of his death.

On the London to Brighton road, Kate kept the radio off until Alice could take the silence no longer and asked if she could turn it on. Coldplay's "Yellow" joined us together somehow. All except Hugo; he wore his earmuff headset plugged into his mobile phone, cocooning his mind in some other place. It was nearly midnight when we got back to Marine Parade.

Alice patted me on the arm as we entered the flat. "I believe you, Dad," she said, doing so deliberately in front of Kate and Hugo.

They didn't respond.

During the night, I dreamed someone had cut off my arms and legs and piled them next to my head and torso on the bed like bloody pick-up-sticks. Charlotte was sitting on the end of my bed. She was toying with one of my severed legs, examining it like a puzzle piece. She lifted my head gently like a mother with a sleepy child and placed the leg under my head as if it was a pillow. "You've fallen apart," she said.

*

"Gar!"

Kate's voice was outside my bedroom door. I could see it was morning from a patch of blue sky that was visible through the French doors to the rooftop terrace.

"Phone call for you downstairs. It's the policeman who was at St Thomas's."

The constable was on the fixed line phone that hung on the wall in the kitchen. Kate started making a pot of tea, her ears pricked up.

"Mr Hart, it's Constable Burchill here. I'm afraid I have some difficult news."

"What's that?"

"My gov'ner wants you charged for possession of narcotics. There were five grams of almost pure heroin in your possession. He doesn't believe your story. You will be receiving a summons to appear in court. You should get legal advice."

Kate was hovering.

I hung up. "They're trying to locate the couple," I said.

I went for a long walk on the windy beach under a dirty orange sky, thinking: it had to be Baker who sent the couple to the Dorchester. Was Cliff McDonald at risk now? I had survived. Would they be back? Would they use Alice and Hugo to break me completely if I pressed on?

I slept during the afternoon, assisted by one of Kate's poorly-hidden Valium tablets that she kept in her bathroom cabinet. Jack Darling's phone call woke me in the gloom of early evening. It knocked me for six.

"You're gone, mate," he said. "We have to let you go."

I swung my legs around, sat on the edge of the bed and switched on the bedside light. My head thumped, my tongue felt raw. I lapped a few drops of water from the all-but-empty glass on the bedside table.

"Why?" I said. "What's happened?"

I hadn't told Jack, nor Claire, nor Cliff about yesterday's events. That was my next job. Maybe the BKB PR woman had gleefully phoned Cliff, who'd gone to Jack. Had Kate phoned Jack?

"For fuck sake, Gar, you need that counselling now," said Jack.

"They tried to kill me," I said. "How is that a sacking offence?"

Jack wasn't listening.

"Why the hell have you threatened Baker's daughter? And to top it off, you go back at East's whole family. Now he's got an Apprehended Violence Order against you. His wife's a judge, for god's sake. And now I'm in this sea of shit with you."

"I've got no idea what you are talking about."

"I've had enough, Gar. When you want to sober up and tell me the truth, call me. I've got an editorial conference now. Don't go anywhere near *The Citizen's* office. Don't call anyone."

I lay on the bed. My head spun; ringing started in my ears. I rolled on my side and checked the outgoing call log on my phone. Gears clicked into place when I saw the numbers.

The fringe-comber had knocked me out, and for good measure he'd used my phone to text Charles East. For fuck's sake, his girlfriend had got me to open my phone in front of her so we could play her favourite dog video. She must have seen me key-in my password. The text read: "*You're dead, cunt. You, wife, kids. I'm closing your eyes.*" It was despatched around the time I was in the toilet cubicle at the Dorchester.

There was another number on my phone's outgoing call register that I didn't recognise. A voice call was made to the number. It had lasted 26 seconds. I hit redial. Luckily it went straight to voice mail before the owner answered: "*Hi. This is Anita Baker. Please leave a message and I will return your call.*"

You can download a lot of vitriol in 26 seconds. All the fringe-comber had to do was twist his voice a bit. It didn't have to sound exactly like me. It just had to sound like it could have been me in a manic, heroin-drenched froth. Mentally unhinged, as Charles East had called me.

I went back to Kate's bathroom cabinet. I washed down two Valium with a few swigs of the bottle of duty-free bourbon I had in the bedroom, then I swigged more. I might have had another Valium. A bit later I reeled and collapsed in bed.

XLV

IN A COUNCIL flat in a tower block on the outskirts of London, two men, dressed in grey track pants and hoodies, adjusted their cheap party masks inside. The masks depicted the faces of girls. Not very pretty: more Miss Piggy than Snow White. A phone trilled inside one man's pocket.

"I've got him," said the girl. "We'll be there in about five minutes."

The man did not reply. He hung up and gave a thumbs-up to his companion, who pulled his phone from his pants pocket and connected the handset by Bluetooth to a single speaker that sat on the grimy carpet in the sitting room. Techno music thumped from the black box, pulsing with an underlying beat that mimicked the rhythm of the human heart – one that was momentarily calm, then racing and irregular, as if it was being shot by bursts of excitement or fear.

The man who had taken the call from the girl stepped through a door into a filthy kitchen and needlessly rearranged a brown-glass bottle full of fluid and a hand-sized pad of medical gauze that sat on a bench. He stepped back into the sitting room: playing with his hands, pacing. His companion was propped on the only piece of furniture: a shabby sofa. He was playing with several black Velcro straps, re-sealing, then peeling them with a zipping noise that was barely audible against the relentless *doof-doof! da-doof!* from the speaker that vibrated their ribcages.

*

"Are you sure this is the place?" asked the teenage boy as the older girl led him up the windswept external stairs of the council flat. He guessed they had been walking for about fifteen minutes from the Three Bridges railway station on the line between London and Brighton.

"Yes," she said, failing to disguise mild annoyance. "Where do you *think* I'm taking you?"

"Sorry," said the boy. "It's just that I expected Ruby to meet me at the station."

"I told you. She's already at the party. Here. Chill." She thrust a large vodka bottle at him with her black-leather-gloved hands.

The boy fought two emotions: part of him wanted to run; part of him wanted to stay the course of the adventure he had embarked upon. The boy took the vodka, had a hefty swig, and handed the bottle back.

There was no way he wanted to come across as Mr Straighty-one-eighty in front of this lean, pretty, uber-cool girl he guessed was older than twenty, and was as hard to impress as she was to fathom. Despite the grey sky, she wore large sunglasses and a droopy-topped, rainbow-coloured beanie into which she had tucked all of her hair. He could tell she was a white woman only from the exposed skin of her cheeks and neck. Her accent suggested she was of Irish origin and he liked the mellow tone.

If he was going to a party on a school day, he was going to party. As the vodka warmed and emboldened him, he wondered what sort of drugs might be available inside the flat they were approaching. He had plenty of cash in his pocket. Most of all, he wanted to meet Ruby in the flesh. He hoped that she would match her online profile. Even if she was only half as pretty in reality, he'd still be happy.

On the fourth floor of the block of flats, the girl stopped outside a bruised blue door. The windows on either side of the door were boarded with raw plywood but the thumping beat of The Crank, the boy's favourite band, and Ruby's too, was humping inside.

"You take the bottle in," said the girl, handing the boy the vodka.

He was happy with that, being the booze carrier. With his fingers, he dragged the wavy, lop-sided fringe of his dark hair across his forehead and watched her knock on the door. It opened.

"You first." She shoved him inside.

It was dim in the hallway. The girl stayed outside on the landing and pulled the door shut. The smell made him dry-retch: urine and faeces. His heart galloped.

A masked face lunged sideways into the hallway through a doorframe. "Hello!" boomed a gritty male voice. "I'm Ruby."

The other man poked his matching masked face into the hallway, just below his companion's. "I'm Ruby too!"

The boy dropped the vodka bottle and backed against the front door. He grabbed at the handle but it was deadlocked. The men's hands were upon him. He faced them and threw his clenched fists, cracking into their arms and torsos, kicking and kneeing them. They absorbed his fury, draining his energy, then let him go. He fell back against the door. The boy crouched, panting, cornered. He plunged a hand into his jeans pocket, searching for his phone.

The men moved in and wrestled the boy; one slapped his face hard and snatched his phone. The other man head-locked the boy inside the elbow of an arm and dragged his captive into the sitting room. His sidekick stepped to the kitchen, took the stopper out of the brown bottle and carried it, with the wad of gauze, into the sitting room.

The chemical-carrier put his mouth close to the head-locked boy's ear and said, "Ruby and I are going to have some fun with you, my little man. But we are going to do you a big favour. When you have a sniff of this, you will go on a nice holiday. You might be a bit sore when you wake up, but hey, you'll get over it. Nothing a few stitches won't fix."

"Dad!" the boy screamed into the horrible drumbeats that shook the room, beats that blurred with the pounding inside his chest: racing, skipping, tripping. He smelt a bleach-and-vinegar-like stink as the soaked cloth was clamped over his nose and mouth, and he refused to breathe it. Nothing a few stiches won't fix! Are these men going to harvest my organs, he wondered. He was suffocating, his chest aching, burning, imploding. He gasped for air. He could not stop his eyes closing; inside his head, neon green and orange blobs barged into each other like globules in a lava lamp. They began tearing each other apart.

*

The sun was falling when the men, unmasked, but with their hoodie-tops pulled over their heads, ushered the unconscious boy out of the flat, carrying him between them, his arms spread over each of their shoulders. In the street, they opened the sliding doors of a parked tradesman's van and climbed in. The girl was sitting behind the steering wheel. She started the engine.

XLVI

I HEARD KNOCKING at my bedroom door. My veins and arteries felt filled with weed killer, and my head with hot lead, but I managed to pull it up off the pillow. The clock said it was early evening. The near-empty bottle of bourbon was an ugly sight. I was still dressed, if that's what you'd call a man who'd rolled around fully clothed on his bed in a sweaty heap for fourteen hours. Alice opened the door.

"Nanna had a call from the school. Hugo didn't arrive this morning. We've been calling him for hours. He's not answering his phone."

"Clancy," I said. "Is he with that kid?"

"Clancy is with his exchange family on a driving holiday in Scotland. He doesn't know where Hugo is."

The possibilities whirled inside my head. I sat on the side of my bed, approaching a standing position in increments. It took a few minutes to dress and shuffle downstairs.

Alice and Kate were sitting at the kitchen table. I drank a couple of glasses of water in quick succession and sat with them. No-one spoke. I phoned Hugo, got his voice mail, left a message.

"We should call the police and report him missing," said Kate.

"Did you ever skive off school?" I said, ducking from the nightmare possibilities.

"No."

I realised she and Alice had spent hours stewing before they woke me from my torpor. They were well ahead of me, emotionally and rationally.

Alice was pale. "He's been acting weird lately. I should have talked to him."

"Your father should have talked to him," said Kate. "Your father should have noticed."

The big clock on the kitchen wall ticked loudly. I kept phoning Hugo.

"Alice," I said. "Can we get into Hugo's laptop?"

Alice and I went to his room. His laptop was password protected. We tried a few guesses. Nothing worked.

Alice said: "Could Hugo be in trouble, Dad? Like Claire in Sydney?"

"I don't think so, sweetheart," I said, being careful not to tug my ear.

Kate was standing in the doorway listening.

"You're pathetic, Gar. I'm going to report him missing. If he was okay, he would call us or answer."

Kate and Alice found Hugo's passport in a dresser drawer, put on their coats and drove to the police station.

I needed to move. It was autumn and the days were shortening. The sun was down when I put my coat on and walked into the city. A mist was in. The shops were closing. It was cold and people wore hats and scarves. Lots of young men had their hoodies pulled over their heads. They scowled as I tried to see their faces. I trawled the narrow shopping lanes and side streets, peering into café windows. I prowled the pubs. I kept phoning Hugo, begging him to call me. I phoned the Halliday's home number a couple of times. Kate and Alice had returned but Hugo was still missing. It was about 9pm when I turned the corner back into Marine Parade. I saw Kate open the curtains onto the street and look out. As I approached the entrance to the Halliday's flat, I saw a curled figure lying on the footpath near the steps. I ran to it.

Hugo was unconscious but breathing. There was a type-written note pinned to the breast of his leather hoodie jacket: *Now you are hurting your children.*

I phoned an ambulance and then I phoned upstairs to Kate.

Hugo had bruises and scratches on his knuckles. There was dried blood on his top lip under his nose. I tore off the note before Kate and Alice reached us with blankets. The ambulance arrived.

XLVII

I RODE with Hugo in the ambulance. Kate and Alice followed by car. By the time the ambulance stopped under the covered entrance of the Accident and Emergency department, Hugo was conscious and holding my hand. He didn't speak but he locked his eyes on mine, though he seemed to be wondering if I was really there.

We sat in the waiting room while Hugo was attended by a medical team. A doctor emerged, a young Asian woman in a white coat with a gentle smile and delicate hands that she offered to each of us in turn.

"Hugo has suffered some trauma," she said. "We've given him sedation. He's resting but conscious. We need to do some tests. "

"What sort of trauma?" I said.

"A sexual assault."

"Oh, god," said Kate. "Can we see him now?"

"Yes, but he wants to see his father first," the doctor said. "Alone."

Hugo had a saline drip in his arm to combat dehydration from the shock, the doctor said. She left us. I sat in a chair close to the bedside and we stared at the cubicle's blue curtains for a while. It was like I'd gone back in time 48 hours to St Thomas's Hospital in London. Hugo's place was darker though. It was clear from his face.

"Do you want to tell me?" I said.

Hugo motioned for the plastic cup of water on his table and I handed it to him. It took a minute, maybe two, before he spoke.

"We met some girls," he said, "on Facebook. There's a band we've been following."

"You and Clancy? A fan club thing?"

"I guess so. They asked us for pictures."

"The girls?"

He nodded.

"What sort of pictures?"

"We did it live to my laptop camera."

"No clothes," I said.

Hugo closed his eyes. "We went first, me and Clancy."

"And then?"

"I went to meet one of them today."

Hugo sipped from the plastic cup. He pulled his hand away from mine.

"They weren't girls, Dad." Hugo started shaking.

I tightened my grip on his hand.

"I thought they were going to cut out my kidneys."

"What?"

It was a few moments before he started talking again, mostly whispering about what he remembered happening in the flat. He said he didn't wake at all, after they gassed him with some chemicals on a rag, not until he saw my face in the ambulance.

I wasn't convinced.

Later, while Kate and Alice sat with Hugo in the cubicle, I spoke with the doctor and a police officer in a private room. The doctor said preliminary blood tests, and Hugo's description, indicated it was chloroform, possibly home-made with bleach and ethanol, that had rendered him unconscious.

With my assistance, Hugo gave a statement to the police officer. The officer said it was not an unusual crime for young people to be lured by predators posing with disguises on the internet. The officer warned me that pictures of Hugo may end up on the internet, but more likely on a private, members-only network on the dark web where paedophiles cloaked themselves. We took Hugo home around midnight.

After everyone else was in their rooms, I lay on my bed and read the note that had been pinned to Hugo's jacket: *Now you are hurting your children*. They had me now. It was time to pack it in; the stakes were too high. I would take the note to the police in the morning. I'd try to explain what I thought it meant. I drifted into half-sleep thinking up my lines. I didn't get much time to work on them. My phone whistled. It was 1:12am.

The screen read: *No caller ID*, but I answered anyway. I was sick of fucking around.

"Mr Hart?" It was a female voice.

"Yes."

"Come out to your balcony," she said. "Stay on your phone." Her accent sounded transatlantic, an American-Irish salad.

The sky was clear on the roof terrace.

"I'm waving at you," she said. I saw a dark, slender figure, wearing a hooded top, leaning against the steel tube railing across the road on the beachside of Marine Parade. "Come down."

"Why?"

"We need to discuss something."

"Give me a couple of minutes."

I found a sock in my bedroom drawer, lifted my overcoat off a chair and walked downstairs to the kitchen. I used scissors to cut the toe-end away from the sock and pulled it over my left forearm, making it into a tight sleeve. I tucked a long-bladed butcher's knife into the sock, wedging it between the fabric and the skin on top of my forearm. I put my coat on and tested that I could reach inside to the knife's grip with my right hand. I shook my arm and the knife stayed in place. I stepped silently into the hallway and used the internal stairs to pad down to the street.

She was standing directly across the parade on the footpath at the top of a set of concrete stairs which I knew led down, about ten metres, to another road along the edge of the pebble stone beach. As I crossed the road under the yellow glare of the streetlights, she disappeared down the stairs. I stopped when I reached the spot where she had been. I looked back, up at the place where Alice and Hugo were sleeping. Had I been lured away to ease their abduction, or worse? My heart clattered like a boxer's smacked speed bag. When it settled a little, I followed her down the steps.

At the bottom, she was standing in shadow, her back against the high retaining wall, her hood on, her jacket zipped up to the throat. I scanned the roadway for others. No-one I could see. I wondered how quickly I could rip the knife from my sock and plunge it into her throat. I should have phoned the police but I wanted to hurt someone else for a change - badly.

I stood close by the wall, a few metres from her, and we faced each other. My eyes adjusted to the light. A dark roll-neck sweater inside her hoodie was unfurled so that it covered her mouth and nose to just below her eyes. She wore dark gloves; I guessed latex. I thought of Claire's attackers in Sydney, and the rose-scented perfume she'd detected in her abductors' car. All I smelled now was stale fish-and-chip grease and the sea.

"Your phone," she said. "Show it to me."

She had a similar frame to the young woman at the Dorchester.

"I didn't bring it," I said. My phone was in my coat pocket with its voice recorder running. I'd switched it on coming down the stairs.

"Dee-ya thank I'm a stoopid cont?"

She'd overcooked the Irish brogue. Her dialogue coach would not be impressed. How many tongues was she trained in, I wondered.

I reached into my sleeve with my right hand and locked my fingers on the knife's handle. I eyed the soft spot under her windpipe, just above the breastplate. How I wanted to stab in there.

She wheeled the brogue back. "Take the battery out and put the pieces on the footpath. I want a private conversation."

I did what she said. She shuffled close to me, only an arm's length away, looking down long enough to kick my battery and handset further apart. I squeezed my knife handle, sizing up the back of her neck and spine. She straightened and looked me in the eyes. Hers were elusive under the shadow of her hoodie.

"I have an offer to deliver," she said.

"From whom?"

"You are upsetting people, Mr Hart, but you can make your troubles go away."

"How is that?"

She pulled an A4 envelope from inside her jacket, opened the flap and extracted a sheet of paper. She approached me and shone a penlight on the page. She was vulnerable now; both her hands were full. Cocky bitch.

It took me a few seconds to focus. It was a property title: a black-and-white photocopy. It carried an address in a street behind the Halliday's flat. I read the owner's name: *Edgar Bertram Hart.*

"Can we cut the riddles?"

"If you leave well enough alone, Mr Hart, and you answer my calls and do what I say, this document will become real. Just a start. And you and your children will live long and prosperous lives."

"If not?"

"You've seen our capability statements, Mr Hart."

"So under your plan, I live the rest of my life drinking beer on this beach. Is that it?"

I fingered the knife handle. The beachfront was mostly dark. The only witnesses would be a handful of seagulls that were scrapping over something rotten on the shoreline.

"Oh no, Mr Hart, we want you to stay in your job. Contrary to what you've been telling people, we didn't try to kill you in the Dorchester. You're more use to us alive; though to be honest, we're not that fussed. We want you back in the good books with your employer so you can assist your colleagues with fresh logic."

"What sort of logic?"

"I believe the term red herring is derived from the practice of drawing a strongly scented fish across the trail of hunting dogs to confuse and prevent them from catching a fox. You can manage that, I'm sure. There are millions of other stories you can chase, aren't there? We can all win."

"How do I get my job back?"

"You're a smart man, and you might find that people withdraw complaints that are currently with the police, here and back in your homeland."

"I need to think this through. I have a funeral."

"You're clock is ticking. I'd say it's not far off midnight before your own funeral. Imagine the state of your children then. I'll be in touch."

She tucked the promissory property document under her jumper and jogged up the steps like she was weightless. I put my phone back together.

I was breathless by the time I reached the front door of the Halliday's apartment. I hurried upstairs and looked in on each of Hugo, Alice and Kate. I made sure I heard them breathing before I backed out of their rooms.

I shed my clothes like dead skin beside my bed, looked in the mirror and had a thought: how did she know I'd been telling people they tried to kill me? It wouldn't take a genius to guess I would say that, but she said it with such confidence, like she was a fly on my walls.

Exhaustion made me question whether I'd actually been across to the beach a few minutes ago, or dreamed it. I drank a glass of water, slipped naked under the doona and curled up with the blurred memories of days of madness, locking my hand on the knife handle under my pillow.

At about 5am my luck changed.

XLVIII

I RECOGNISED the +61 dial code from Australia and the phone number of the Tangleton Hotel flashing on my screen.

"Garsy, mate," said Hughie Jones. "There's been an accident at Moon Hill. Terrible accident. I'm sorry but you need to know. Cops'll be callin' ya. I've told 'em you're in Pommyland."

"What sort of accident?"

Hughie unloaded, sounding like he'd put a few beers under his belt: "Some stupid prick's been shot. Dozy bugger was walkin' round wearin' your kangaroo mask. Can you fuckin' believe it?"

My heart faltered. Not Tania and Steve Watson playing Buck and the Bird of Paradise?

"Who was it?" I said.

"Local boys. Lovely boys. They're in terrible shock. They've killed a bloke, fired a slug as big as my thumbnail from a .300 Magnum rifle. It landed smack between his eyes."

"I don't mean the shooters, mate. Who was the dead bloke?"

"No-one knew him here. Cops are investigatin'. They found a driver's licence in his wallet. Funny thing, mate, he was from South Africa; that's what the boys said. Address on his driver's licence was in Johannesburg. What the fuck's he doin' wanderin' around the bush at sundown with a kangaroo hat on his fuckin' head? That's askin' to get hit."

"Very strange," I said. I crossed my fingers. "Any other ID on him?"

"The mad prick had a knife strapped to his chest and Glock 23 tucked in his belt. It was like he'd turned up for a shootout."

I whistled down the phone.

"And it gets weirder," said Hughie. "They found some Australian bloke's passport in the dead feller's glove box. I heard the coppers talkin' on their car radio. The passport matched with another feller who was murdered out at Mascot a couple of weeks ago."

"Name?" I said.

"Dunno. All our heads were spinnin' so I didn't catch it."

"You're heaven sent, Hughie. Did you know that?"

"That's what me old mum used t' say, mate. But you got a funny idea of good news. Sounds like ya need some shut-eye."

It sounded like Oscar "Silver Dog" Peterson had collected the head shot. What had he been doing out there, and carrying Bruce Tyson's passport, by the sound of it? My best guess was that he was going to fit me up for Tyson's murder by planting evidence. That passport in one of my cabins would have been fun to explain to the cops. Peterson was an A-class weirdo, but why would he roam around the bush in my Buck mask? It didn't matter now. East would be under fresh and rare pressure, trying to explain the actions of his unorthodox chauffer to the homicide squad.

This development would also have to rattle John K Baker and Ms Hoodie from the beach, when they found out. I'd let the news filter through to them via their own network, although that network now appeared out of sync. What was the point of trying to turn me into one of them in the UK while Peterson was trying to nudge me of a cliff in Australia? The slick, professional circus act I'd experienced to date had dropped one of their simultaneously spinning plates.

I was so tired that the bedroom walls and ceiling seemed to be warping when I lay down, like I was trapped in a living Salvador Dali painting. But no more Valium, nor booze; I needed to consider my response to Ms Hoodie's recruitment offer with a clear head. I took Hughie Jones' advice for moments like this and headed for the kitchen to make a cup of hot, milky tea.

XLIX

I WAS making vegemite toast and my third cup of tea when Kate stepped through the kitchen door and handed me a long, thin, brown-paper-wrapped parcel that simply had 'Gar' handwritten on it in black felt pen. Kate had found it on the street-side doorstep when she went out for her morning walk. I opened it. It had to be Ms Hoodie who had sent me the backscratcher. It had a telescoping handle and a small, metal chook's foot on the end of it. A note inside read: "You scratch mine and I'll…"

After my breakfast, and checking that Hugo and Alice were still asleep, I went for a stroll past some flats in St George's Street behind the Halliday's flat and browsed the real estate agents' windows. I calculated that the pile of bricks and mortar Ms Hoodie said could be mine was worth about three hundred thousand pounds sterling, or about double that in Australian dollars at current exchange rates.

I carried in my pocket the note that was pinned to Hugo's jacket last night and I weighed the merit of taking it to the police station and explaining how I believed it was linked to my own assault in London. But then, I figured, the Brighton coppers would have to call their London colleagues and Brighton would discover I wasn't believed about the Dorchester Hotel, and that I was facing narcotics possession charges to boot. My legal troubles in Sydney may also arise. None of that would help Hugo. Jack was sick of me. I needed Tom Steele's counsel.

I found a café, and seated with a bucket-sized cup of the milky brew the English call a latte, I dialled Australia. Steele's voice was barely audible inside a cocktail of chatter and thumping music. He walked outside wherever he was. I briefed him on my Dorchester disaster, Hugo's abduction, and the 1am job and property offer from Ms Hoodie.

"I would have disembowelled her," he said.

"It crossed my mind."

"Then again," he said. "I could use a holiday flat."

Someone brought Steele's drink to him in the street, a woman by the sound of it.

"Mm," he said, running on silent for a few seconds. I guessed he was enjoying the beer or the woman's lips, maybe both at once. "I've now heard," he resumed, "that Bart Hills was with a woman the night he OD'd. Pretty face, sporty type. Not dark haired though like your little beauty at the Dorch. A blond. People use dye of course, or wigs."

I told Steele about the hunting accident at Moon Hill. He laughed and it was infectious. When we stopped, he promised to make inquiries of his police sources for more details about Moon Hill.

"Nature abhors a vacuum," he said. "You get rid of one piece of shit, like at Moon Hill, and another just fills your empty rectum."

"I love the way you cheer me up," I said.

"Picking all the hairs off your predicament," said Steele, "there's a central conclusion, isn't there? You need to persuade Jack to give you your job back and turn serious lights on this cockroach nest. You can't sit out there alone, and if you try to walk away now, they'll fuck you anyway because you have special knowledge, my friend. You may have heard of the practice of tidying up loose ends. You are, of course, a loose end. As well as a loose cannon. But I rave on - what's your plan?"

"Malcolm's funeral first."

"Video-call me into the wake. I'll pass on the church service," said Steele. "In the meantime, I shall toast the budgie where I stand."

Steele only met Malcolm once. It was love at first sight on a party session that lasted until dawn. Steele immediately nicknamed Malcolm 'the budgie' after the small, colourful and excitable Australian bush parrot.

I walked back to Kate's. There wasn't much I could do for Malcolm today, apart from take my only suit to the dry cleaner for a super-fast clean to remove the scars of my OD so I could wear it to the big show tomorrow. Trevor, Ryan and Kate were buzzing around the flat organising things when I got back. There would be a wake on the rooftop terrace. Kate had tucked Alice under her wing to help.

I weighed up phoning Jack, to brief him on Ms Hoodie's job offer and Silver Dog's seeming demise, but deferred those plans when Hugo emerged from his room. I didn't have any better ideas for him than a walk along the beach. Hugo threw me off balance by agreeing. We threw pebbles into the sea instead of talking. For the first time in a long while he didn't have those earphones clamped to his head. He let me put my arm around his shoulder for a bit of the walk home. In the afternoon, Alice, Hugo and I went to the offices of *The Morning Sun,* where Malcolm's old colleagues helped us make a DVD of home movies, photos, and a selection of his best page one stories to play at the next day's church service. We left out John K Baker's failed Brighton Marina project, but my delving unearthed a photo of him standing on the seashore, beside Sarah Kerr. They looked very chummy. Very.

*

Malcolm Halliday could draw a crowd. As the hearse rolled away to the crematorium after the Anglican service, Kate said that more than three hundred people had signed the Condolence Book. He was farewelled by a priest who answered my prayers and kept it short.

Sarah Kerr came back to the Halliday's apartment with about a hundred others for the wake. It was a rainless day and most of the crowd milled on the rooftop terrace.

Joanne Crewes arrived with Bill. When he loudly accused Kate Halliday of being a Nazi spy and a Brighton prostitute during World War 2, I helped Joanne escort Bill to their car. Joanne was tender and calm with her raving father. She managed him like I'd once seen Hughie Jones lead a massive bull with a ring in its nose around an agricultural show.

"Want him in the boot?" I said to Joanne when we got to the street.

"I wish," she said.

As they drove away, I remembered my father's last days. Good old Bert chose my birthday to pop a bullet in his head. It was instant relief from the monster that was chewing his brain away. Pick's Disease causes progressive destruction of neurological pathways, the doctors said. It also leads to what they called impaired regulation of social conduct. Sufferers can forget to wash, take their clothes off in public, explode with rage: in short, act like complete pricks. It only helped explain Bert's last few years. At least he didn't blow other peoples' brains out before his own. His neurosurgeon's voice went all reedy and shaky over the phone when I told him that Bert had a gun and what he'd done with it, particularly when I described what Dad said in his farewell note about what he'd like to do to the neurosurgeon with a knife. I still don't know how he got hold of his guns - buried one in my garden at home - and made his way to my underground car park for his swan song against my front wheel. I put it down to tenacity and ingenuity, characteristics I hoped I'd inherited but could manage better. Pick's Disease can be passed on in the genes.

After a couple of hours at the wake, Sarah said she had to return to Bath. I volunteered to accompany her to the train. Of course we had a detour planned.

The Sidewinder pub on Upper James Street in the Kemp Town area of Brighton was a few minutes' walk from the Halliday's apartment. Sarah and I found a corner and a sofa next to a low table on which to perch our first bottle of Bordeaux. We toasted Malcolm.

"Did you ever hear him say he hated anyone?"

"I've never thought about it," she said.

"I say hate all the time. One night I was out with Malcolm and I realised he never used that word."

"To Saint Malcolm," she said, and we clinked glasses again. Sarah went outside for a cigarette.

Sitting alone, my thoughts buzzed like disturbed insects without a place to land. I conjured a montage of images: Silver Dog's shot head wearing my Buck mask; Henry East's stitched lips painted in yellow antiseptic; Bryan Tyson's burnt visage;

the fringe-comber's grin as he pressed the needle in my vein; and my imagining of Hugo being chloroformed in a filthy council flat.

Sarah returned. She ruffled my hair. "You're not here," she said.

"Sorry. I've lost my job."

I told her about the Dorchester and the consequences. When I told her about Hugo, she put a hand on my arm and kept it there.

"The truth will out," she said. "And your boss is under a lot of pressure."

She was right. I couldn't see what was happening to Jack.

"Don't lose heart, Edgar Hart. I gave up the chase when I moved to Bath, but now you've cracked the whip on me, I'm enjoying it. I need you."

"It might be a short ride," I said.

She ignored me. "I've been back to one of my contacts. She worked in the Cavalcade finance department. It appears I made a mistake about the Egyptians."

I put my head in my hands. I had wanted something fresh to take to Jack, to plead my case for reinstatement, and Sarah and the Egyptian money-connection to Baker were my best bet.

"Cheer up," she said. "You might want to take notes. I just had the wrong Arabs."

I topped up our glasses, took a digital voice recorder from my pocket and switched it on. The pub was noisy, so I pulled out my notepad and pen too.

Sarah drank and talked. I drank and scribbled, tossing in the odd question. Sarah's theory, supported by her friend who had worked at Cavalcade, was this; the Cavalcade founders, Baker and Marais, had personally borrowed hundreds of millions of dollars to invest in the surging global stock markets through the early to mid-2000s. It made each of them billionaires on paper. But when the global financial system collapsed during 2008, Baker and Marais were too slow to sell out. By early 2009, their personal debts far outweighed the value of their assets, and their lenders - global banks and wealthy private investors - wanted their money back. Baker and Marais couldn't pay.

Then along came a white knight: an agent claiming to represent Arab oil money. The agent offered to rescue the Cavalcade partners if they would help place oil dollars around the world for safe keeping in the event that his Arab employer's enemies - such as internal political rivals or hostile external forces like the United States - tried to oust him.

"So who was Cavalcade's white knight?"

"Muammar Gaddafi."

"He's dead," I said.

"He wasn't dead when he bailed them out. He left an Aladdin's Cave behind, with some vicious people holding the keys."

Sarah's friend further claimed that when the Libyan dictator was still alive, he had a secret meeting in Paris and personally appointed Baker as his agent. Baker's brief was to invest funds on behalf of the Libyan people, but the money trail between Baker and the Gaddafi had to be fingerprint-free.

"What do you mean, fingerprint-free?"

"No documentation."

"So what happened to Marais?"

"He didn't want to deal with Gaddafi."

"So Baker had him killed?"

"Gaddafi's mercenaries did the deed. Two French nationals who were crewing the yacht the night Marais drowned."

I opened a photo on my phone. I showed Sarah the picture of her and Baker, him standing with his arm around her shoulder by the Brighton seaside.

"How well do you know Baker?"

"Don't you trust me?"

"I want to."

"Trust involves risk, Gar."

"I keep taking risks and I keep getting burned - and so are my kids now."

"You don't strike me as the type to take pictures at face value, so don't start now. It was during that event with Baker that I met my current contact inside Cavalcade."

"Who is?"

"Mine."

I grinned.

She reached for my phone and I handed it to her. "Though I did like that dress," she said, examining her portrait, apparently accidentally swiping to the next photo when she handed it back to me.

"Where did you get that one?" She was looking at the image of Baker with the former World Bank President, Rene Gasquet, at BKB Nouveau's Paris racecourse event.

"It was on our files in head office."

"Do you know who that is?"

"I've looked up Gasquet. When he retired, he did some consulting work for Petro Europa's operations in Libya. Do you think the World Bank was, or is tied up with Baker?"

"I don't know about Gasquet," said Sarah. "I mean him." She pointed at the third man in the photo with Baker and Gasquet, the one wearing the caterpillar moustache.

"And he is?"

"Who do you think Baker was working through? He couldn't have direct contact with Gaddafi on an ongoing basis. Baker went through his agent. Until a few years ago, Nasim Naama was the Director General of the Libyan Investment Authority."

Sarah spelt out Naama's name, which I wrote in my notebook, and she went outside to smoke another cigarette.

I Googled on my phone and found a paragraph on Naama in *The London Examiner* online from 2011: *The head of the Libyan Investment Authority, Nasim Naama, has resigned his post as the rebel forces fighting the dictator Mohammed Gaddafi gain ground. Naama said he could no longer perform his duties for Libya. Naama has sought refuge in Vienna, Austria, with members of his family.*

Then I searched for the Libyan Investment Authority. A BBC News story dated November 2014 read: *Some US$3bn (£1.8bn) is reported missing from the accounts of Libya's sovereign wealth fund, the Libyan Investment Authority (LIA).*

....investigators say they have found evidence of 'misappropriation, misuse and misconduct of funds' at the LIA headquarters in Tripoli.

The LIA has total funds worth about $70bn. It was set up in 2006 by Saif al-Islam, one of Muammar Gaddafi's sons, to manage Libya's oil revenues. The LIA has overseas investments such as stakes in the Italian bank UniCredit, the Italian football club Juventus, and Pearson group, the owner of the Financial Times.

I felt Sarah's hand on my shoulder. She looked at my screen.

"Do you believe $3 billion went missing?"

"What do you think?"

"A think it's a drop in the ocean. The United Nations Security Council had frozen a hundred and seventy billion

US dollars' of foreign Libyan assets by the time Gaddafi was killed. But the UN was talking about known assets. What I'm talking about with Baker is the other money, the deep, black stuff: the money with all fingerprints removed."

Sarah sat down, drank the last of her wine and ran an index finger around the rim of her glass, making it sing an eerie opera. "I think that three billion dollars was a smoke screen used by Gaddafi's surviving cronies to cover their tracks. It's nothing in the bigger scheme of things, is it? Someone might even hand a little back to the authorities in exchange for immunity from prosecution. Everyone's a winner. End of story."

I saw my Henry East theory crystallise. Charles East had pressed his son to admit to a smaller crime to close the official case and cover up a larger one lurking out the back. I saw a dotted line from Henry's Double Happiness inside share trade in Sydney connecting to Charles East's Trust8 operation in Shanghai, linking now to Cavalcade in London, and then Gaddafi in Tripoli, Libya.

"How did Baker get the fingerprints off the money?"

"That sounds like your job, Gar."

Sarah pecked me on the cheek and left me in the pub scratching notes about possibilities. I had my world map at the Halliday's flat. I now had Tripoli to add.

As I walked back, I felt like we'd harpooned a whale - with a sewing needle and some cotton thread. Captain Ahab went insane chasing the uncatchable whale, Moby Dick, of course, and I was out of a job. I could even go to jail.

"You were a long time with Sarah," Kate said when I got back.

Alice was standing beside her and raised her eyebrows at me. "There's lipstick on your cheek, Dad".

L

A DOCTOR from St Thomas's phoned me at Kate's the next morning while I was eating scrambled eggs at the kitchen table. Kate was faking reading a newspaper, her ears twitching. I took the wireless handset into the adjoining lounge room.

"Mr Hart," said the doctor, "we have the results of your blood tests. I know you were anxious. There was heroin in your system. No HIV, hepatitis, or other nasties, but your liver enzymes were raised. That's probably alcohol-related. We also found scopolamine."

"I'm sorry. Scopola-what?"

"Sco-pol-a-mine. It has several uses. Motion sickness. Scuba divers use it for nausea. Sometimes it's administered as a pre-medication for surgery. It's an uncommon drug, but it has been used for nightclub robberies around our hospital catchment in London from time-to-time. They spike drinks with it."

"Side effects?"

"A decent dose will give you loss of motor skills, blurred vision, drowsiness, hallucinations."

"So why would I overdose myself on that stuff so I can have waking nightmares, then put enough heroin in my veins to fell a horse?"

"You're right. It doesn't make much sense."

"Doctor, can I put you on speaker phone. I'd like my mother-in-law to hear what you have to say."

I took the handset into the kitchen and put it on the table beside Kate. Her face softened as the doctor supported my version of events at the Dorchester. I asked him to provide a copy of the test results and a summary of the hospital's experience with scopolamine so that I might use it to assist my pleading with the police.

About an hour later, the doctor emailed my blood analysis to me, and a paragraph confirming the presence of scopolamine. I pulled some research on scopolamine off the internet and forwarded the lot to Jack with a detailed defence. I included a summary of Hugo's internet luring and assault. I didn't mention Ms Hoodie's bribe offer; it was too hard to explain in writing.

I brewed a pot of tea and waited. Oddly, when Jack's call arrived, it was on Kate's fixed home line.

He said: "Pull your battery out of your mobile phone - now."

"Why?"

"Just do it, mate, please."

I did as he asked. I knew Jack used an encrypted Blackberry, changed his email addresses regularly, had his office swept for bugs at least twice a week, and switched phone handsets, laptops and SIM cards like he changed his clothes. He had done so ever since he received a visit from an official of the State Council Information Office of the People's Republic asking why he was writing a story on the financial affairs of a high-ranking Communist Party official, when the story was still only an idea he'd discussed with *The Citizen's* head office by a private conference call between London and Shanghai.

"Even this fixed line is risky," he said. "But we need to talk."

"You got my email about the Scopolamine?"

"Yes. I'll get to that in a second. Listen, our tech people have looked into the email glitches Claire reported. There's been a foreign body in our system. We've traced it to an internet service provider in Mumbai. The trail blurs from there, but that's spilt milk."

"So they could have seen what I just sent you?"

"There're a lot of footprints in yours and Claire's email boxes, and more recently, Cliff McDonald's. We've put some fresh security protocols in place at our end but we think they are still in your handset. A bug: tracking software of some sort. Do you have GPS location services switched on?"

"Sure. Compass, maps; I've got a jogging app."

"Anyone else have access to your phone recently?"

"Apart from the Dorchester?"

"We'll get to that. I'm talking from weeks ago. We've traced back that far."

Sandy Wallace. I was asleep when she climbed out of my bed; heavily asleep, now I thought of it. My phone was on my bedside table when I woke and she was gone. My birth-date password wasn't hard to guess: lazy, easy to remember - stupid. Charles East and Silver Dog could have eavesdropped on every email and conversation I'd had for weeks, maybe even turned on the microphone remotely and listened to me talk with Baker in the lift at the Dorchester. I told Jack.

Jack said: "Go to the nearest phone shop and buy a new one. Get a new SIM card and phone number, and buy a new laptop too. Don't use your name to buy them. Get Kate to do it. We'll reimburse her. Then phone me back on this number."

Jack gave me his latest dial code.

"I thought I was off the payroll," I said.

"Get the fresh phone and we'll talk."

"Can you speak with Kate," I said. "She'll need to hear this directly from you."

Kate and Jack chatted, hung up.

"You're lucky to have Jack," she said. Kate had always wanted Jack for Charlotte.

About an hour later, sipping a mug of tea while standing on the roof terrace on a clear, cool, windless morning, I called Jack with my new kit. I explained Sarah Kerr's Muammar Gaddafi theory. I thanked chance that I'd used a separate digital recorder and not my phone to note our conversation in the Sidewinder pub. I remembered it had been noisy, too noisy, I hoped, for a remote listener to hear the conversation via my phone through my jacket pocket. Then I told Jack about Ms Hoodie's job offer.

"I've put Alice in the crosshairs of these scumbags, and worse with Hugo," I said. "I don't know where to go next."

"Do you think you can stick Alice and Hugo on your back and run for the rest of your life?"

"Yeah, okay. I'm not that fit."

Jack had spoken to *The Citizen*'s key decision-maker, Zac Werner, after our IT people found the bugs in Claire's and my emails. Jack was confident that, armed with the hospital report on the scopolamine and Hugo's abduction, he could have me reinstated on new probation.

"Look, mate," he said. "The upside is they didn't really want to knock you off. Not right now."

"Cheers."

"Let's think this through. They're targeting you as a possible new recruit. Let's play along and waste some of their time while we work on what we have, but let's not give them any more easy opportunities to fuck us up, which means we need to take Alice and Hugo off the field."

Jack and I sketched a plan. We needed Kate to take Alice and Hugo to her sister's home in the south of Ireland. Jack would supply a bodyguard for them. He would speak to Zac Werner about the security expenditure, which he'd pitch as an investment, because a story like this, if we could crack it, would put *The Citizen*'s reputation on another dimension as a global news service. I didn't say it to Jack, but after this project, I was heading off to make gourmet bush sausages with Hughie Jones for a living, and maybe grow some sheep.

"They are primarily focused on you," said Jack. "So you draw them away and come to me in Shanghai while we nut out the big picture. You can help me probe what Baker and East are up to in China. Let's run the fuckers ragged."

"One other thing," he said. "Don't get rid of your old phone, or your old laptop. Let's give them some red herrings of our making to chase. We'll leave their bugs inside your old devices. You are going to have two phones, two email addresses: two characters from now on."

I called Kate into the kitchen and we put Jack on my new phone with open speaker. We gave her the facts about the Easts and Baker. I'd never seen Kate so feisty. She had little faith in the authorities, I learned over the kitchen table. Malcolm had been threatened a few times by angry readers of the *Sun*. She wasn't impressed by the police response. In fact, she believed they were behind one break-in and vandalism attack at the *Sun*'s offices after the paper reported that detectives in the armed robbery squad were sharing parties and women with the villains they were meant to catch.

Jack hung up. Kate and I called Alice and Hugo into the kitchen and I recapped the situation, no holds barred. After Hugo's experience, it took no time to persuade them that going into a communications lock-down while they were in Ireland was essential. That meant no mobile phones, no internet. Hugo's school would be advised he had to return to Australia at short notice for family reasons.

Around 3am the next morning, I drove Kate's car to the nearby city of Hove. Kate sat beside me; Alice and Hugo spotted for me out of the rear window as we cruised the backstreets until I was convinced we weren't being followed. Kate saw the silver Range Rover first, parked kerbside next to a long stone wall in a suburban street. I parked behind it. The waiting car's driver, wearing a baseball cap, dark clothes and boots, helped me load our baggage into the back of his car. Todd, as he called himself, was an ex-British Army Major who had returned a few years ago from Afghanistan and was now working for the same global personal security firm that was protecting Claire in Sydney. I guessed he was around my age. A good age for his sort of craft, I thought: a blend of experience, physical strength, and at least average brain power. I didn't have the luxury of pre-testing Todd's cocktail of attributes. He drove away with my family behind his tinted windows, heading for the Holyhead car ferry port on the west coast of Wales en route to Dublin, and then south by road to the village of Portroe in County Tipperary, and the cottage of Kate's sister.

Todd had a special phone in his possession and I had the number.

*

258

Back at the Halliday's flat, I sent an email just after sunrise, using my old telephone handset and email address:

Hi, Jack. Just put the kids and Kate on the flight back to Australia. No further progress on Baker. I fear the trail is going cold. I think I'll stopover in Delhi on my way home. Malcolm Halliday wanted some of his ashes splashed in the Ganges. I'll let you know when I'm booked. Cheers, Gar

I phoned Steele on my new phone and briefed him on my improved employment status and my two-faces protocol.

"Your life's starting to read like a cheap thriller," he said. "Let's get the ending right, hey."

About an hour later, my old phone rang. The screen showed *No caller ID*. I figured it was Ms Hoodie following up her job offer. I hoped she'd seen my latest email. I let it ring out.

I packed my bag and headed for Heathrow Airport with Dick Callahan as my chauffer. I knew I could trust him to keep a secret, especially if I told him I was flying to India.

After Dick dropped me outside the Air India gate, and I had watched his taillights disappear into the throng of traffic departing the airport – with him, I had no doubt, gossiping hands-free into his phone to anyone who would listen about where I was going and why – I strolled past the check-in queues until I got to the gate for China Southern. Once I'd cleared security, there was ninety minutes until my flight to Shanghai departed. I found a bar and a tall stool and sipped the first glass of plain coke and ice I'd imbibed in years.

UNDER EDEN

Part 3

LI

AS THE jet from Heathrow climbed to cruising altitude, I read an old letter from Nasim Naama, written on Libyan Investment Authority letterhead, to John K. Baker at Cavalcade. Sarah Kerr had sourced the letter, but from whom she still wouldn't say. Naama wrote that he looked forward to meeting Baker in Vienna, Austria, to *discuss the China investment proposal relating to Red Box Telecommunications that you described at our last meeting.*

It was late afternoon local time when I bumped down on the tarmac at Shanghai Pudong International Airport. I expected a long immigration check upon entering a nation of 1.3 billion people, and a city of twenty million plus, but the officials simply opened the airport flood gates and humanity poured in. Less than thirty minutes after landing, I was plucking my bag off the luggage carousel, and a few minutes later, I strolled through customs. The officials seemed to be picking off dodgy characters using their intuition, or tip-offs, pulling them into windowless rooms and shutting the doors. My heart skipped a beat when a smiling Asian man in a light blue safari suit, wearing a badge on a lanyard, waved at me and blocked my path. I'd been heading for the taxi rank. Secret police? Ms Hoodie's local man?

"Welcome, Mr Hart," he said, holding up a blown-up passport photo of me, cheaply printed on A4 paper. "Mr Jack sent me."

He tried to take my bag. I phoned Jack.

"Mr Sang is okay," Jack said. "He's our regular driver, and his English is good, but he may pretend otherwise."

Jack warned me to be careful what I said in front of Mr Sang, especially inside his car, because Mr Sang was regularly invited to drink tea with a local police chief. Drinking tea was code for being managed by the authorities. Jack suspected Mr Sang had been coerced to hide a recording device and radio transmitter in his car to eavesdrop on the conversations of his mostly foreign passengers, but there was little point switching drivers, Jack reasoned, because the next man or woman he hired would just get the same invite to tea with the police chief.

We sped out of the airport onto a flyover freeway thick with trucks, buses and cars, where no driver indicated to change lanes, a manoeuvre they practised with hair-raising frequency, working on instinct and anticipation, as far as I could tell.

We cruised past sky-scraping electricity towers that looked like they could walk. Cheek-by-jowl with these creatures of steel and wire stood endless lines of high-rise concrete boxes, their balconies aflutter with shirts and sheets, underwear and towels. About an hour later, we swept down a ramp into the streets of the central city teeming with people on bicycles and motor scooters that swept around us like schools of fish avoiding a bigger animal. Traffic lights seemed to be pure decoration because neither pedestrian nor vehicle obeyed them. I'm not a great fan of rules, but some are handy. Survival here was going to demand my rapid adaptation.

The Darling's rented house was in the leafy, low-rise French Concession district of old Shanghai that was popular with foreigners. The London plane trees that lined the streets were in heavy leaf. The driver stopped in front of a high masonry wall painted a sickly lemon colour, stained with grime, and topped with rusty barbed wire and sharpened steel stakes. A solid-panel, steel security gate built into the wall began rolling sideways. Mr Sang motored onto a circular, white gravel drive and parked in front of a terracotta-tiled path that led to the red, double front door. Within seconds of stepping from the air-conditioned car, my sunglasses had fogged and sweat trickled down my forehead, stinging my eyes.

"Enjoying our weather, Gar?"

Hitomi, Jack's Japanese wife, was standing in the open doorway, looking cool in all ways, as usual. Her cat-like physique was dressed in a loose, white t-shirt, cotton shorts, barefooted, her black hair bob-cut.

"Like a dose of scarlet fever," I called, collecting my bag from the boot. My shirt and jeans had stuck to my skin by the time I hit the doormat.

She led me into the air-conditioned cool down a tiled passage to the kitchen and gave me a cold, damp flannel she kept in a plastic box in the fridge. I draped it over my face. The humidity was normal for this time of year, she said. Jack was on his way home in a taxi. Hitomi showed me to their guest bedroom and left me to unpack, shower and change.

I found Hitomi again in the kitchen. She offered me green tea and condolences for the death of my father-in-law. We talked about Alice and Hugo. I just said they were holidaying with their grandmother. If Jack had told her about Hugo's assault, she didn't let on and I didn't raise it.

When Jack arrived, he didn't want tea. He pulled two cold bottles of Tsingtao beer from the fridge and three frosty glasses from the freezer. I had consumed only water and coffee all the way from Heathrow to Shanghai, my first alcohol-free trip in all the flights that I could remember.

"No, thanks," I said.

"Moderation and relaxation," said Jack, "not abstinence and fear."

I took the glass of beer and it tasted as good as it looked. The three of us sat on a sofa around a low table in the living room. Jack was in a strange pond for a pale fish born in chilly London. Hitomi skolled her beer and left for work. She owned and managed a Japanese restaurant located a few blocks away named the Blue Ring, which was popular with foreigners looking for a change from the local cuisine.

Jack sat beside me while my two phones picked up a local telco network. It was probably overkill, but I manually selected a different telco for each phone. Any communications that mentioned Baker or East, and that we wanted to keep private to *The Citizen*, we were confining to the new email addresses our tech's had assigned to Claire, Cliff, Jack and me. Steele had my new email address too, and I saw that while I had been in flight, he had sent me an audio file.

"Want to listen?" I said to Jack.

"Play away."

Voice 1: *Mate, he's got to stay cool.*

Voice 2: *He's losing it in that jail.*

Voice 1: *If he tells, were fucked. Dead fucked. Does he want to do a few more months or put us all in a coffin?*

Voice 2: *I think he needs help.*

Voice 1: *You've got to persuade him. He'll get bumped if he doesn't smarten up. They've told me they already have people in Sydney limbering up for the job.*

The recording ended. I phoned Steele. He answered. I put him on open speaker so Jack could listen.

"Who was it on the tape?"

"Bart Hills was taking the call. Don't know who the other voice is," said Steele.

"Could it be Christ?"

"Maybe."

"Date?"

"About two months ago."

"Cops have this?"

"Not that I know." Steele sounded flat.

"You all right?"

"Karen's left me. She's got a bloke."

"Who?"

"Some middle-aged prick she met at the gym. She's moved in with him and his brother: single blokes."

"Two of them?"

"Don't worry," said Steele. "I've got an imagination."

"Speaking of pricks, how'd you go chasing up my dead man at Moon Hill?"

That perked Steele up. It sounded like he was reading from the police incident report.

"The shot man wearing the kangaroo mask was Seth Vagner, 42, a South African citizen working in Australia as a security consultant to the businessman Charles East of Double Bay in Sydney. Vagner was a former South African Special Forces commando. He died when a single .300 Winchester Magnum bullet, fired from a rifle at a distance of 89 metres in twilight conditions, pierced his forehead just above the left eye. The shooter was George Arnold Williams, 19, of Tangleton. Vagner had been wearing a papier-mache mask of a kangaroo's head. Mr Williams, a licensed kangaroo hunter, believed he was shooting at a wild animal. According to Mr East, Vagner had taken a two-day vacation to whereabouts that were neither known, nor of interest to him. Police were now investigating possible links between Vagner and a murdered Sydney psychiatric nurse named Bruce Tyson whose passport was found in Vagner's car near the site of the shooting.

Steele had a final twist: post-mortem examinations revealed the chemical compound "psylocibin" in Vagner's blood. He had ingested alcohol and the extract of magic mushrooms before he was shot. Tests revealed traces of the cocktail in an empty tequila bottle found on the ground beside Vagner's body.

"Remember what I told you about Tania Watson's *Angels Tears* tequila?" I said to Steele. "If you're going to knock up a yarn about this, leave her out of it. That dopey prick must have swiped it off my kitchen bench."

An hour later, Steele emailed me a preview of his front page story in tomorrow's *The Sydney Daily News*. Most of the page was covered with an artist's impression of a standing man wearing a kangaroo mask on his face under the headline: *Kangaroo Man's Deadly Trip*.

There was no comment from Vagner's employer about his chauffer's lethal, hallucinogenic journey into the Australian bush. I was elated that Steele had named East in public though, and in the tabloid *Daily News* to boot. That would set his toffy-nosed friends whispering behind his back.

I phoned Ireland before I went to bed. They had arrived safely in Portroe. Todd, Kate informed me, appears capable. Hugo and Alice had re-discovered reading books made of paper, and board games also made of paper. Todd was taking them all trout fishing the next day. Hugo said their protector had a snub-nosed machine gun in his bedroom, following which I asked Todd if he could practice some discretion. I phoned Sue Sinclair in Sydney and checked on Fish. She was patting the hairy brothers who were eating peeled slices of fresh apple and watching Shrek2 on TV. When I went to bed, I battled the feeling that this was too good to last.

LII

THE NEXT day, Jack and I walked from *The Citizen's* office in the French Concession to Hitomi's restaurant for lunch. We trekked inside a haze of eye-burning steam and grit, me lugging my briefcase so I could show Jack some more research when we got there. I considered donning a paper mask like some of the locals, but I bought a handkerchief from a street market instead and tied it around my nose and mouth like a cowboy in a dust storm, and put my sunglasses on.

"Very stylish," said Jack, whose lanky frame was dressed in a straw-coloured linen suit and open-necked, powder-blue shirt, his crumpled jacket slung over a shoulder.

"At least I'm not impersonating William Boot," I said. Jack had always matched the image I carry in my mind of the protagonist in Evelyn Waugh's 1938 novel, *Scoop*, Boot being an English toff who's mistaken for a real foreign correspondent.

I knew little about where Jack's river started, but I did know his education was expensive and he grew up in the toff's borough of Hampstead in London. He has a great mind for maths and can understand the hieroglyphics of big business finance better than most journalists. He could have been a banker making huge money like his neurosurgeon father had wanted. Instead he attacked the establishment like a foamy-mouthed mongrel, digging into their shifty transactions and exposing them in the media for all to see. His mother was a university professor of classics, but Jack displayed little interest in the achievements of Ancient Greece and Rome about which his mother was an expert. He was inclined to the exotic East. Yin to his parents' Yang, I guessed.

Hitomi's Blue Ring was located on a street-level corner in a low-rise office building. Inside, cool air floated in a discernible layer above a polished concrete floor. The open space echoed with the chatter of men and women, mostly Westerners sitting at long tables made of blond timber carpentered at sharp angles. The bulk of the posteriors really didn't need the cushions on the bench seats.

Jack and I perched on high stools near the cashier's desk at one end of the bar counter, behind which we watched the chefs surgically slicing raw fish in the open kitchen.

"Let's roll the dice," said Jack, who ordered a starter dish of puffer fish, or fugu, as it was called on the menu.

"Dice?"

"If fugu is not prepared perfectly, you'll get a nice dose of tetrodotoxin from the fish's glands."

"Outcome?"

"It paralyses all the muscles except the heart. You stop breathing, so you die slowly, wide awake."

"Sounds worth bottling. You've got connections. Can we get some take-away?" I was thinking about Ms Hoodie and her boyfriends.

As Jack was considering my question, a serve of translucent flesh, arranged like the petals of a daisy, arrived on a round, black plate. Jack lifted a petal with his chopsticks and popped it in his mouth. I watched. His eyes bulged and he started gagging, reaching for his throat.

"Hilarious," I said.

He swallowed. "There is a trick with this stuff."

"Yeah?"

"Always watch the chef try a sample before you partake," he said, nodding at the sashimi master slicing away behind the counter.

As we picked through the gooey fugu, a young man stood next to us to pay his bill. His Australian accent prompted me to have a closer look at him. When he handed his credit card to Hitomi, I noticed his right hand was scarred, slightly melted at the webbing between his little finger and the next. He completed his transaction, crossed the room, and began talking to a man beside the front door. I nodded to Hitomi and she came over.

I whispered: "Can we see his credit card receipt?"

She slid it across. Card holder's name: *James Carter.*

My iPad was in my briefcase. I retrieved a photo of Henry East and the crew of Charles East's yacht after a Sydney to Hobart race a few years ago. Henry and another young man had their arms around each other. The photo caption identified the other man as *James Carter.* I showed Jack the photo. His eyes popped wide open: I was pretty sure that standing in the doorway of our restaurant was James Carter, the son of the Australian Foreign Minister, Alexander Carter MP, who was also in the photo, standing in his yachting clothes, sporting a few days beard stubble on Constitution Dock in Hobart Harbour.

More gears clicked inside my skull. It was the burn-scar on James Carter's hand that had moved the first cog. It took me back to Claire's revelation about the fire, years ago at the Red Leaf swimming pool next to the East's home, Tamerlane, and the report in the local newspaper about a boy's hand being scorched when Henry, Bart Hills, and another boy tried – so the boys claimed – to extinguish an act of vandalism. I studied Carter's face across the restaurant and reversed time as best I could. I saw a pudgy kid pinching his nose and hopping off a trampoline into the East's swimming pool the night that Charlotte and I had dinner at Tamerlane about ten years ago. That boy was now grown and escaping through Blue Ring's front door.

Jack and I tossed down our beers and followed him. We were soon escalating into the machine-cooled air of the Shanghai subway. I kept an eye on Carter while Jack collected tickets from a vending machine outside the turnstiles. I'd noted which platform he'd headed for. We caught up with him in time to follow him aboard a crowded, spotless carriage that shuttled us towards the city's financial district. Jack stood and studied the subway map on a carriage wall. Carter admired his reflection in a window, arranging his blond hair with his fingers. I found a discarded newspaper on a seat and pretended I could read Mandarin, glancing up now and then at a tourism advertisement on the carriage's wall showing the CBD district above us, a forest of steel and glass towering along the edges of the city's snaking brown spine, the Huangpu River.

We followed him out of the train and up escalators to the footpath alongside the bustling ten lanes of Century Avenue. He entered the main lobby of the Jin Mao Tower. Uniformed guards with guns on hip-holsters were peppered through the lobby.

"We're stuffed," I whispered to Jack. "No security pass."

"Here," said Jack, reaching into a jacket pocket. "I've only got one. People who work in here know me. Less chance you'll be recognised if you follow him up."

Jack put a plastic security card in my hand and I tailed Carter, who swiped his card over the turnstile scanner to enter the lift lobby amid a stream of others. I squeezed with Carter into a full lift and travelled with him to the 51st floor of the 80-storey building. Carter got out and I followed, mingling with a handful of suited workers in front of the lift before they broke left and right along the curved corridor. I fell back and watched Carter travel left past a few offices. He opened glass doors and disappeared inside. I wandered past, glancing at a sign written in gold letters on the door. I didn't need to go close to read the names of the two companies: Trust8, and Tamerlane Investment Group Asia Pty Ltd. I was outside the cage of Bruce Tyson's TIGA.

I kept moving, strolling around the public corridor, checking the other company offices, looking for company names of interest. Three doors around from the TIGA office, there was a lifeless room behind a clear glass wall with a ghost mark on the front door where, I guessed, a nameplate had been. Inside there were low partition walls and empty desks and cardboard boxes stacked on the floor. The office door was locked. It smacked of hasty evacuation. I put my eyes close to the glass and peered inside. On the floor, there was a certificate in a picture frame leaning against a wall. The certificate's print was too small to read, so I took a photo of it with my phone. I caught the lift downstairs and found Jack in the lobby.

Over passable lattes at a nearby outlet of a global American coffee chain, we mulled over what we had: the son of the Australian Foreign Minister, and one of Henry East's best friends, is attending the Shanghai offices of the East family's TIGA company and its related Trust8. Did he work there?

"You thinking what I'm thinking?" said Jack.

"James Carter. JC. Jesus Christ!"

Did we have Christ in our crosshairs, the mystery figure mentioned in the emails between Henry and Bart, the character who advised Henry and Bart to buy the Double Happiness shares?

"He doesn't look like a mastermind, does he?" said Jack.

"Agreed, but Henry is in jail, Bart is dead, and this guy is swanning around Shanghai wearing a hundred thousand dollar watch. Did you see that thing he flashed at the restaurant?"

"Might be a fake; this is China."

I pulled out my phone and pinched and zoomed on the photo I'd taken of the empty office. It looked like a business registration certificate sitting in the picture frame leaning against the wall. My zoom showed a word beginning with the letter 'C' near the top of the certificate, but neither Jack nor I could make out the rest of the letters.

"It might be Cavalcade," said Jack.

"Where did you get that swipe card?"

"I employ a very good security firm."

As I moved to close my photo app, my finger pushed the zoomed picture of the office off-centre. There was a stick leaning against the wall, a metre of so from the framed certificate. I pinched and zoomed again. It looked like a polo mallet.

"We've got to get into that office," I said.

Jack and I took separate routes back to his office. In a taxi, using my new phone, I called Portroe in Ireland. Trout fishing had been a success. They were eating the pan-fried fish with oven-roasted potatoes and steamed cabbage while they watched Ireland's X Factor on TV.

I alighted from the taxi at the Huangpu River embankment in the Bund area of the city where the world's great trading houses had resided in grand style before Chairman Mao's communists established the People's Republic in 1949. They seemed to have left the buildings in reasonable nick, if not the capitalist owners of the day. I sat on a granite bench in front of the Waldorf-Astoria and inserted the battery into my old handset, intending to send a message to Ms Hoodie. The device flickered into life. A text was waiting for me: *You didn't tell us where you were going, Gar. We're not happy. Where RU?*

I replied: *I'm on your side. I'll be in touch.* I pulled the battery out again and headed back to the French Concession.

LIII

HOLDING his hands behind his back, John Baker paced back and forth alongside the main window of his office in the Gherkin tower. His mood was as filthy as the brown fog embracing the city of London outside. "So where is he?"

"We are working on it," said the seated girl, looking down at the shiny, black toes of dagger-heeled shoes that were hurting her feet. She much preferred lace-up army boots.

"And where are his children?"

"We are working on that too."

"Working, always working: how very blue-collar of you. The truth is you've lost control of this."

The girl silently fumed. She had been dragged into this project *ex post facto,* as her old Latin teacher might have said. She was trying to fix Baker's past choices: his mistakes. She had been a teenager when he made the first of the ones that were now coming home to roost. Some of the roosters were ghosts, like his old business partner, Jean-Paul Marais.

He stepped to her side and put the fingers of his right hand on her neck, stroking her throat, and pressing two middle fingers to her jugular vein to feel her pulse. She squirmed.

"Time to hit some delete buttons," he said, slipping his hand inside her shirt collar, fingering the roundness of her bare shoulder before sliding his fingertips down and stroking the skin above her nipple.

"Please," she said, gripping him by the wrist and dragging his hand out of her shirt, thinking how delightful it would be to break the bones in his fingers with her teeth. But she didn't plan to bite the hand that fed her. Not yet.

Baker sniffed the fingers that had touched her skin and said, "At least we know where the madman is. Shut him down - now - and get your other Australian friend to clean out his office. You have a team under your command. Manage them, or I will hand the reins to someone who can."

*

A few hours later, on the other side of the world, in a cheaply furnished recreation room with a table tennis table in the middle of it, a young man was sitting alone at a dining table reading a newspaper. A thick-set man approached the reader from behind. He was carrying a pillowslip half-filled with cans of tinned food. In his other hand he was carrying the wire triangle of a coat hanger stretched into a diamond shape.

He swung the sack into the sitting man's head, knocking him to the floor. The hit man lay on his back on the concrete floor, staring at the ceiling, his eyes rolling in their sockets. The attacker swung the sack in a tight circle, as if he was wielding a polo mallet at a stationary ball, and clubbed the man's head again. The victim's head slid in an arc across the floor, his body pivoting on his buttocks. The attacker knelt beside the man's head, lifted it by the hair and slipped the coat hanger over the man's skull, sliding it down to his throat. Using both his hands, the attacker twisted the wire around the man's neck. The attacker reached into his pants back pocket and extracted a toothbrush, the handle of which he inserted in a gap between the victim's neck and the wire. He screwed the wire tight, as if he was working a can opener. The victim's upper body bucked, his legs thrashed. The assailant was heavy and put his knee on his victim's chest, holding the toothbrush one-handed like a rein on a bucking horse. Blood oozed from the victim's neck and pooled on the floor. The attacker bent over the man's face and opened his mouth with his fingers. The attacker went mouth-to-mouth, whipping his head from side to side, like a dog wrestling a piece of rope.

LIV

JACK told me that Cai Zi – his Buddha-bellied, gun local reporter – spoke English with a Manhattan accent because he had been educated at Columbia University in New York City after a childhood in Shanghai. Zi's father worked for the Chinese Government-controlled China Central Television service. CCTV pushed English language programming that supported Beijing's political agenda to the rest of the world.

While I trusted my old friend's judgment about his man's integrity and reporting skills, I was sceptical about Zi's ability to deliver on his latest assignment: to get us into the empty office in the Jin Mao Tower, and get us out again without detection.

At least when Zi stepped from *The Citizen*'s office bathroom wearing a business suit, he extinguished my doubts that he would pass as a bright and shiny real estate agent if anyone inside the tower questioned our reasons for being there.

We rehearsed our cover in front of Jack: I was looking for office space for my employer's international law firm; Zi was a local letting agent showing me around. The act required me to suit up with tie too, and shave, straighten my hair, and shine my lace-up shoes.

Overnight, I had discovered that Zi had relatives with near-magical powers. A sister had our business cards printed, which was a snack in 24-hour-a-day Shanghai. His brother-in-law had relatives who owned a technology business that supplied the Jin Mao's main security firm, along with other security firms that serviced large tracts of Shanghai's CBD buildings. As well as creating fresh copies of Jack's security card, the brother-in-law supplied us with an electronic key to our targeted empty office: all for a fee, of course.

Over dinner last night, Jack, Zi and I had explored the pros and cons of an after-hours entry to the office, but we concluded that if unfriendly security guards, or other tenants, found us wandering around at night, it would be hard to explain. So a daylight break-and-enter it was.

Zi and I entered Jin Mao about 10am, after the first commuter rush, and at a respectable time for a junketeering Western tyre-kicker to be looking for office digs. Zi and I were quickly through the lobby turnstiles into the lifts. We stepped out with a few others onto the 51st floor and strode around the curved corridor. Zi waved his card over the scanner beside the door to the empty office. It clicked open and we walked in as if we owned the place. Zi watched the outside corridor through the glass wall while I went straight to the certificate in the picture frame leaning against the wall. The "C" that I had captured on my camera was simply a capital letter in a black square. No mention of Cavalcade. The rest of the text was written in Chinese. The polo mallet was gone. I had a feeling our horse had bolted. I started rifling through the boxes on the floor.

"Why don't you do that in the boardroom?" said Zi. "You're in the open if someone comes past."

I took a few boxes into the frosted-glass-wall boardroom and put them on a long table. Every document was written in Chinese and impenetrable to me.

"Zi," I called, "you need to do this."

I stood watch in the boardroom doorway, in sight of the corridor and with a glimpse of the lift doors. Zi got stuck into the boxes. About a minute later, a handful of people filed out of the lifts and walked directly into the TIGA office. James Carter trailed them and closed the TIGA door.

"We better get out of here," I said. "Anything useful?"

"Give me a minute," said Zi, shuffling paper.

"Too late," I said, nodding back at the corridor. Carter was leading a posse of people out of TIGA's office.

I stepped backwards into the boardroom and pushed the door to almost closed, peering through the gap between door edge and doorframe. Carter was in the company of three women pushing empty trolleys for moving boxes or the like, and two uniformed security men wearing pistols in hip-holsters. I pulled the boardroom door shut. There was another internal door. I looked inside: a bathroom, with another door to a toilet. We stuffed the document files back in their boxes on the boardroom table and slipped into the bathroom, gently pulling the door shut. Moments later there were voices in the boardroom. The bathroom door was thin, probably made from cardboard; at least it was good for listening through.

They were talking in Chinese. Zi straightened his tie in the bathroom mirror and cleaned his teeth with a finger. He checked that a crisp business card was in his jacket pocket and practised a salesman's smile, like he intended to stroll out and play the innocent, lost man. Fucking madman. I tapped Zi's shoulder as the voices became louder and we backed into the toilet cubicle itself. Zi's Buddha-like frame was tight against mine, his breath on my face. He needed to visit the dentist. He shuffled around and closed the door gently. At least there wasn't a gap between the floor and the bottom edge of the door. Zi locked it.

"No," I whispered. "They'll see the occupied sign." He re-opened the lock, keeping the door shut with his body.

Minutes passed. The bathroom door crashed open. Someone farted. Zi opened his mouth like a fairground clown waiting for a ball to be popped inside, circling his eyeballs around their sockets. I put a hand over my mouth to smother a laugh. Our only weapon was a spare roll of toilet paper. A phone started ringing. My heart galloped. It took me a moment to realise it wasn't a police whistle and it was ringing outside our cubicle. Zi shook his head slowly. I got his point; what if *our* phones start ringing.

"I'm doing it, okay. I'm doing it!" It was Carter's voice in the bathroom; I recognised it from the Blue Ring restaurant yesterday. "I've incinerated the lot. We're clean here."

I heard shuffling, sniffing. Hefty snorts, then a muttered, "Ooh, yeah". Was Carter putting something feisty up his nose? The cocky bugger turned on a tap and hummed as the water flowed. It sounded like he was sniffing a bit of water. At the sound of an air hand dryer, Zi's grin nearly split his face. It might have been ten minutes before all the rooms fell silent and we could break from the bathroom. The boardroom table had been cleared of all the boxes: so had the main room.

We exited into the outer corridor and walked to the lifts.

As a lift door opened, Carter stepped out from the TIGA office. "Hold that, will you, mate?" he called to me.

Inside the lift on the way down, I avoided eye contact with Carter, but I glimpsed in a lift mirror that he was studying me. He might have recognised me from the Blue Ring, or from the train, or from when I followed him into the Jin Mao. I was a few steps out of the lift into the main lobby when Carter called me from behind.

"Excuse me," he scuttled up to my side, "have we met?"

"I don't think so." I couldn't decide if his manic look was the result of the stuff he'd just put up his nose, prescribed medication, or genetics. Maybe it was all three. They gave me something to play with.

"I'm sure we've met," he said, putting his head at a forty-five degree angle, like an owl might study a worm, his pupils expanding and contracting with each blink.

"My name's Chas Tegan." I said, attempting an American accent. I handed him the business card for my New York law firm. "If you ever need some legal advice."

"Never heard of your crowd," he said, studying my card at arm's length before pulling it in close enough to almost touch his nose.

"We're up-and-comers: looking for office space here."

He tucked my card in his shirt pocket.

"I'll call you. I'll definitely call you," he said.

I turned quickly and left him standing still, pondering the various life-forms in the lobby.

Zi was waiting for me on the street. He flagged a taxi.

"That was fun,' I said, with the sincerity of a Charles East smile, closing the taxi door as it shot off into Century Avenue. "And what if that lunatic rings my so-called law firm?"

"Relax, Gar," said Zi. "The call will go to a virtual office my brother runs. If he leaves a message, we could even call him back, if we want to."

"And if he checks the website?"

"We've put a place holder up. You know, *Coming Soon* on a home page with some nice pictures."

Zi did his clown eyes and reached into his jacket pocket. He handed me a folded document. The cover of the A4, corner-stapled pages said *Cavalcade Sino*. I opened what was a legal agreement for a business partnership – under which Henry Charles East, Bartholomew Edmund Hills, and James Alexander Carter had each acquired 5% shareholdings in the *Cavalcade Sino* investment advisory business. I'd not seen John K. Baker's signature before, but his name was clearly printed underneath the hand-scrawled moniker on the legal agreement.

About thirty minutes later, Jack and I were seated in a sliding-doored, private booth at the Blue Ring chewing bar-bequed baby octopus with the contract document on the table in front of us.

Jack poked an octopus with his chopsticks and said: "So Baker decides to cut Henry and Co into his Chinese operation. When was that?"

"About eighteen months ago," I said, flipping pages. "There's no mention of Charles East, or TIGA, or any related company here. It's just Henry, Bart and Carter personally. It looks like Baker was cutting the young from their family herds."

"A secret deal to shaft the old man?"

"Could be."

"That sort of tension can work in our favour."

"It's odd though, because that little eel, Carter, is still swing-ing between East's premises and Baker's. And he doesn't look smart enough to play both of them."

Jack poked his octopus again. "Did you know that octopuses can perform autotomy when they're under attack," Jack said.

My expression said I didn't.

"They cut off their own arms, automatically. It's a bio-chemical reaction."

"Your point?"

"The severed limb keeps moving and distracts predators so the main body can escape. And even better, a new version of the discarded limb grows back after the danger has passed to make the main body whole again." Jack pincered his octopus and bit off several arms.

"Is this a metaphor of some sort?"

Jack separated the octopus's limbs with his chopsticks. "This arm is Charles East, this arm is his son, this arm is Carter, this arm is Baker, this arm is Hills."

"And that pretty face in the middle is Muammar Gaddafi, or what's left of his empire," I said, losing my appetite for scorched blubber.

"Something like that." He bit into an arm.

Jack's phone rang. He swallowed, answered, stood quickly and beckoned me to follow as he strode to the front counter of the restaurant where there was a TV hanging on the wall screening undersea pictures of a coral reef. He reached behind the counter for the remote and changed the channel to Sky News Australia.

A newsreader behind a studio desk said: *… was discovered in the recreation room of the prison's psychiatric ward.*

Police will not comment on the cause of death. Henry East was serving a twelve month term of imprisonment for insider share trading. He was twenty-six years old.

"It's Claire," said Jack, pointing to his phone. We quick-stepped through the streets back to his office while he briefed Claire about what we'd just discovered about Henry and Co's partnership with Baker in Cavalcade Sino.

In Jack's office, I phoned Steele and put the call on open speaker.

"It's very strange," said Steele. "The coppers are background-ing that it was suicide, but they won't go on the record. Their line is that he strangled himself. Finished the job he started weeks ago."

"You don't believe them?" I said.

"I believe he's dead. The rest sounds like bullshit."

I remembered the audio file Steele sent me a few days ago, with the two men talking about Henry's deteriorating mental health and the prospect that someone might put him in a coffin. I asked Steele what he made of it and where the recording came from.

"Still can't tell you who gave it to me, but my source is shitting bricks now that Henry is dead. They reckon he was bumped, to shut him up about that inside trading. They cut his lips as a first warning, but he just lost the plot. And now they're tidying up big time."

"Who are they?"

"Your dead mushroom man Seth Vagner was running it locally. But someone's picked up the slack. I reckon multiple contractors are at work here. There are layers. The orders could be coming from anywhere, like your latest friends in the UK."

When Steele hung up, I replayed the old audio file off my iPad to Jack: I could now recognise Voice 1: James Carter had sounded very cocky when he grilled me in the lobby of the Jin Mao Tower a few hours ago. I wondered how clever he felt now.

LV

JACK AND I entered *The Citizen*'s office around 7am the next morning. Zi had beaten us in. He handed me the large yellow envelope I'd been waiting for.

"Arrived in the overnight air bag," he said, "via the London office."

I flipped the envelope to check the name of the sender: Sarah Kerr, Bath University.

It contained a copy of a legal contract between two parties for the sale and purchase of a business named Red Box Telecommunications. The pages were printed on Cavalcade Investment Group head office letterhead. When I'd flicked through it, I explained to Jack that Cavalcade had sold a Chinese telephone company named Red Box to the Libyan Investment Authority. A letter signed by John K. Baker, sent to the chairman of the LIA, confirmed that US$700 million of Libyan cash had been received by electronic funds transfer into the account of Cavalcade at BKB Nouveau's London Wall corporate banking branch to complete the purchase of Red Box.

Jack said: "Okay, so we have Baker selling the Libyans a Chinese phone company. What's crook about that?"

"Can we have a look at Red Box?" I said. "What did Baker actually give the Libyans for seven hundred million US?"

Jack set his team to work. They did some quick internet searches. For such a valuable business, Red Box had no branding profile in the Chinese market.

"It's odd, I agree," Jack said, "but China is the world's second biggest economy behind the United States, so a US$700 million company could be swallowed here like a sardine by a shark."

"Let's knock on Red Box's door," I said. "We should have a look at what Baker actually sold them - physically."

The sales agreement said Red Box was headquartered in the southern Chinese capital of Guangzhou. The address wasn't available on Google Street View. Two hours later, Zi and I boarded a China Southern Airlines flight from Shanghai to Guangzhou Airport. I carried a copy of the Red Box contract document in my briefcase. A woman occupying the seat across the aisle from me adopted an interesting take-off posture: she sat sideways with her feet on her seat, facing the window, and adopted the balled crash position without using the seat belt. The air crew did not object. I sensed this was going to be a strange trip.

At the Guangzhou airport taxi rank, Zi showed a driver the Red Box HQ street address and we climbed into the back of his bruised, blue-and-white sedan. He drove up a ramp onto the concrete Jiebei Expressway, heading in the opposite direction to the city's office high-rise that we could see in the distance. We whizzed past countless medium-rise blocks of flats, all popped from the same mould. The flats gave way to patches of farmland scattered with fruit trees and cattle. The taxi meter was running hot.

I said to Zi. "Did you ask this guy for the scenic tour?"

Zi spoke to the driver, who spat back angrily. Moments later he veered off the expressway, took a hairpin bend onto a side road and pulled up at a grimy petrol station. I assumed we needed fuel. An old man wearing a filthy white singlet, grey shorts and rubber sandals, a cigarette hanging from the side of his mouth, was trying to fit a chain to a bicycle that was lying on the kerb. He took a swig from a large brown bottle of beer he was keeping close by his side.

"I think this is it," said Zi, pointing at the petrol station.

"You're kidding."

"No joke."

Zi got out of the taxi and approached the old man. There was a burst of talk and finger pointing. Zi walked across the driveway, past a couple of seriously unhealthy petrol bowsers, and entered the station's shopfront. In a covered garage by the shopfront, there was a truck on a hoist in one work bay, and a couple of motor scooters with their wheels missing in the next.

The taxi driver got out and sat on his bonnet to light a cigarette. I climbed out, clutching my briefcase because the driver looked as shifty to me as a car with ten gears. I walked towards the shopfront door, past the old man fixing the bicycle who was talking on his phone.

My jaw dropped when I read the business name on the shopfront window. There were a lot of Chinese characters but there were also three words painted in bold letters in English: Red Box Telecom. Sticky-taped to the inside of the window were advertising posters for phones with global brand names – Samsung, Nokia, Apple, Huawei – with prices listed in Chinese Renminbi. I took a photo of the window with my phone.

The nerve-jangling screech of stressed engines broke my focus. I turned to see three black-and-silver motorbikes flashing along the side road. The lean riders were covered, head to toe, in boots, gloves and body leathers, with full-faced helmets and tinted visors. They almost scraped their knees on the road as they whipped through the hairpin bend. They zipped onto the petrol station driveway and came straight at me. The middle rider's front tyre pinned me against the shopfront window, nudging against my groin. They throttled their engines in a nasty chorus. My man killed his engine, rolled his bike back a little, dismounted and put it on its stand. He unzipped his jacket and pulled a long-bladed knife from a sheath that was strapped over a tee-shirt, and pointed the tip at me.

"Engliss?" He flipped up his visor, revealing a pair of glazed, brown eyes.

"I speak it," I said.

"Give me bag." He nodded at my briefcase.

I handed it over. He looked inside, flicked through my papers, closed the case and threw it to one of his side-kicks.

"Money," he said.

"What money?"

He stepped up to me and put the tip of his blade under my chin. I felt a prick.

"Funny man," he said.

I reached into my trouser pocket. I had about US$300 in cash, and some Chinese Renminbi. I gave it to him.

"Not enough," he said, taking the cash in one hand, keeping his blade under my chin. He dug the tip in, close to my jawbone, and flicked.

I thrust a hand to the cut. Blood dripped down my wrist, onto my suit, spattering the driveway.

I heard Zi's voice. He was yelling at the biker in Chinese. The biker turned to him. Another rider dismounted. He pulled a handgun from inside his jacket and aimed at Zi.

An old Chinese man dressed in a yellow, open-necked business shirt and brown trousers shuffled from the shopfront door, smiling as serenely as a monk. He spoke to the riders. Zi ripped his shirt off, folded it and helped me hold it under my chin to plug the bleeding.

My briefcase was tossed at my feet. The riders kept my cash. They put their weapons back in their jackets, zipped up and remounted, firing their engines in a nerve-jangling sleet. They took turns to take-off, air-lifting their front wheels to ride to the side road, where they went flat and sped up the ramp to the expressway, disappearing in the direction of Guangzhou City.

Zi and the old man talked and shook hands. Zi said, "A misunderstanding, Gar. They thought we were wannabee rent collectors. This is their territory."

"They're quick," I said, watching blood drip over my shirtsleeves.

"This is Mr Tao," said Zi, introducing me to our saviour. "He is the managing director of Red Box Telecommunications - worldwide."

"Worldwide MD, hey. It's a pleasure," I said, bowing a little, offering Mr Tao my clean hand for a shake.

Mr Tao said something to Zi in Chinese.

"He's their spotter," Zi said, nodding at the old guy sitting on the kerb, tightening the nuts on his bicycle wheel, a phone beside his beer bottle. I resisted the urge to dent my shoe on his ribcage.

"Let me see," said Zi, who pulled his shirt and my hand away from my cut. He helped guide my hand back. "No vessels cut."

"Thank you, doctor."

Mr Tao found some butterfly band-aids in his first-aid kit in the garage and Zi stuck them over my cut, successfully closing the wound. We stood in front of the petrol station with Mr Tao, sipping tepid lemon soda from glass bottles. Zi took a selfie of the three of us next to the Red Box sign: me in my suit covered in bloodstains, him naked from the waist up, his shiny Buddha-belly hanging over his trouser waist, and the smiling, gap-toothed MD of Red Box.

We finished our sodas and turned to leave. The taxi driver was still sitting on his bonnet. As we approached him, he dropped a burning cigarette into a pile of butts at his feet and ground it out.

"Thanks for your help," I said. The driver didn't reply. When we climbed in, I saw his meter was still running.

On our way to the airport, Zi explained that Mr Tao had sold his petrol station's side-business, in telephone handset sales and call plans, to a Shanghai-based company named Cavalcade Sino about five years ago. Cavalcade gave him US$10,000 as a down payment, and promised to pay him another US$10,000 a year as long as he kept the business going at this address and paid the annual business registration fees to some government agency in Guangzhou City. The money stopped a few years ago.

Zi looked out the window and spotted a roadside shopping mall. We pulled in and purchased fresh clothes on my credit card. I felt better back in jeans and a tee-shirt. After checking in at the airport for the flight to Shanghai, I phoned Jack and gave him a quick heads up.

Jack said: "So the Libyans forked out seven hundred million US dollars for a ten grand company. What happened to the other six hundred and ninety nine million?"

*

By 9pm we were back in Jack's office, showing him our happy snaps of Red Box's HQ and talking him through the notes of our meeting with its MD.

Jack let Zi go home, and then shut his office door. "I'd like to meet her," he said.

"Who?"

"Your fabulous Ms Kerr at Bath University."

I pulled my new phone from my jeans and located Sarah's number.

"Use this," said Jack, opening a desk drawer. He inserted a fresh SIM card into another phone - he had plenty of both items in his drawer - and passed it to me. Jack and I sat opposite each other at his desk. I dialled on open speaker and introduced Sarah and Jack.

I said: "Sarah, can you tell us any more about the Red Box deal?"

"No, not right now; my friend is worried about Mr Baker."

Jack responded: "Then why would he, or she, give you these documents?"

"I think it's payback time for Mr Baker."

"Payback for what?" Jack kept pushing.

"Past sins. I think I can get more, but I have to tread gently. I'm dealing with a doe."

"Okay," I said. "Welcome to our team."

"Are you offering me a job, Gar?"

Jack glared at me. He silently mouthed, "What!?"

"Jack's nodding at me," I said. "You're freelance on this job, if you want it."

"How about that?" Sarah laughed. "I'll see what more I can get for you. We can talk about paid work if I come up trumps."

Jack was a little grumpy when Sarah hung up.

"She's on the inside here," I said. "Let's see what she can do."

Jack conceded with a nod. "Did you hear her say doe?"

"Yeah. So we probably have a woman leaking from inside Baker's tent, if Sarah didn't throw us a red herring, of course."

"Let's run through what we have," said Jack. "It's making my head spin."

I wrote notes on a pad.

- *Baker hides Libyan money. Proof = Red Box Telco scam.*
- *Baker puts Henry and Jamie Carter in his pocket via share stake in Cavalcade Sino. Deal secret from Charles East?*
- *Jamie Carter/ JC/ Christ gives Henry and Bart Hills illegal share-buying tips on a takeover deal directed by Baker and Cavalcade to buy Australian gold miner via Double Happiness, controlled out of Shanghai by Baker.*
- *Christ covers tracks after Henry jailed. Baker probably insisted on cover. Christ personally cleans out Cavalcade's Shanghai office.*
- *Henry threatens to talk. Henry dies by his own hand, or an assassin. Bart Hills dies of heroin overdose (Steele reckons set-up). Similar attempt on Gar Hart's life in London?*
- *Christ appears in employ of Charles in Shanghai. Is he playing both East and Baker?*
- *Relationship between Charles and Seth Vagner, ex South African Army?*

"We have the beast by the tail," I said.

"Yes. We need the throat."

*

Lying awake in the early hours of the next morning, I checked the world clock on my phone. When I called Portroe, they were sitting down to dinner of roast lamb with mint sauce, vegetables and gravy.

"How long is this going to last, Gar?" complained Kate. "We're starting to climb the walls."

"I'm sorry, Kate, but when we take the lid off this thing, it has to blow so high they can't put it back on. We are making good progress."

"Hugo has become very quiet. He's gone deep inside his shell."

I asked her to put Todd on the phone. We had a chat, and then I asked for Hugo.

"Todd is going to teach you some self-defence," I said.

"Physical or mental?"

"Both."

"Great," said Hugo, sullenly, and hung up.

LVI

SARAH sent us fresh documents in the overnight airbag from London. She and her doe had unearthed three other Cavalcade deals with the Libyan Investment Authority, all signed off by Baker.

In Brazil, the LIA had purchased a commercial office property named Silver Eagle Tower from a Cavalcade subsidiary for US$498 million. Google Street View revealed a crumbling two-story restaurant in the suburb of Queimados. I zoomed in on the restaurant's name, *Águia de Prata* – or Silver Eagle in English. Another search informed me that Queimados was better known for drive-by shootings than prime office space.

"Baker's a magician," I said as we sipped green tea.

"More of an alchemist," said Jack putting his fist under his chin like Rodin's sculpture of The Thinker, "who turns shit into gold with a swish of his Mont Blanc pen."

The fraud technique was crude but effective: Baker would set up a Cavalcade shell company in London, Paris, New York, Rio de Janeiro, Shanghai, or anywhere else he liked. These shells then acquired assets - like a cow paddock or a corner shop. Then Cavalcade would dress up the asset on paper so it was described as a greenfield housing estate or a bustling retail shopping mall worth hundreds of millions of dollars. The dressing up was easily done with a few mocked up contract documents and some faked glossy brochures that were tucked into the LIA's files in Tripoli as part of an official record.

The LIA, funded by Libyan oil and gas revenues of US$70 billion plus a year, could comfortably afford hundred million dollar prices for assets like Red Box and the Águia de Prata. After a respectable time, the LIA would write-off these investments as failed ventures or sell the investments to third parties at a fraction of their purchase price for a massive loss. The original money outlaid would simply be lost under an avalanche of paperwork that was shuffled around the planet. As long as Gaddafi and his cronies were in on the deals, there would be no recriminations over poor investment decisions.

In the case of Red Box, Baker had pocketed US$700 million of LIA cash. The key question was who got a slice of the remaining US$699,990,000. How much did Baker get to keep for himself? What would happen when Gaddafi's mob wanted money back? What was the retrieval process?

"You know what I don't get?" Jack put his fist back under his chin. "Why would Baker muck around with micro stuff like the Double Happiness-Austar Gold takeover bid, the thing that brought Henry unstuck?"

I started sketching a flow diagram on a notepad page with a pencil. "Look, I reckon it worked like this. Let's say Austar was digging out of the ground about a hundred million dollars' worth of gold a year, and selling it into the legitimate world market. Cavalcade owned forty percent of Austar, so it was entitled to forty percent of that gold, minus company operating costs, but because Austar was listed on the stock market - in other words it was regulated - there were public records of everything the company did. After the takeover, the company is off the stock market, so now there is piss-weak corporate governance, or most likely none at all. That gives Baker access to forty million dollars a year in clean cash, or the equivalent in gold bars, if he literally wanted to take his share and put it under the floorboards of a Paris apartment or the deck of yacht. Then the Gaddafi gang could peck at it unseen."

Jack's office assistant called. He had to do an editorial conference call with London and New York.

"Get a coffee," he said. "There is an interesting place across the street. It has a tank full of sharks."

I followed his advice but the air-conditioning in the shark cafe was on the blink. The predators drifting in the room-length tank stewed in their own juices. It was an innovative way to make shark fin soup. I sat at a table, mopped sweat off my brow with a paper towel and ordered a cold, sparkling mineral water. As the waiter put the water on my table, I noticed one of the sharks was floating upside-down and motionless.

"I think it's dead," I said.

"Sleeping," said the waiter, showing no expression.

My new phone rang: Sarah Kerr.

"Gar, I have someone who wants to talk to you."

I brightened. "A doe, by any chance?"

"I've told her you won't quote her, not in any way."

"Okay. When can we talk?"

"I will put her on."

"Hello?" It was a female voice: mellow, not as deep as Sarah's.

"Hi, it's Gar Hart."

"Sarah says I can trust you." Her English had a slight French accent.

"Thank you. Do you work there? At Cavalcade?"

"In a way."

"In what way?"

"I can tell you how it worked: the method."

I took a notebook and a pen out of my jacket which was hanging on the back of my chair. "I think we've worked out how the money was moved and lost in the system, if you like. But how did the Libyans get hold of it if they wanted it?"

"Gaddafi had an army."

"A bit clumsy; you can't invade London to twist John Baker's arm."

"Think of a surgeon's knife, Gar."

"Agents?"

"Gaddafi had a special unit that wore suits, not army uniforms. What's the point of running a nation if you can't get some fake passports, call in favours from your friends: the Italians, the French, the British. Money buys almost anything. And with some people it buys everything."

"Including South African soldiers?" I said, thinking about Seth Vagner.

"I believe he employed some ex-army from there, yes."

"Tell me about Baker."

"Gaddafi called people like Baker, treasure keepers. And then for every treasure keeper, there was another keeper."

"You mean a keeper of the keeper?

"Yes, something like that."

"Where did he get these men from?"

"You're thinking like a man, Gar."

"Women too?"

"Look up the Amazonian Guard. Perfumed assassins, I think some media call them." She coughed a couple of times, a wheezy cough, then resumed. "Gaddafi and his inner circle gave a special job to Baker, and to others. They wanted a layer of assets hidden, with no paper trails back to Gaddafi. No records. They gave money to these people on trust."

I said: "I've seen Red Box. Seven hundred million dollars is a lot of trust."

"The trust was reinforced. Do you want your children to disappear? People can get shot, accidentally drown even."

"Are you talking about Baker's business partner, Mr Marais? He drowned."

"He was the start."

"How does it work with Baker? Say with Red Box? What's the big picture?"

"Baker had to wash the money clean, take the Libyan fingerprints off it, and keep it in his own name: Cavalcade's name. When Gaddafi wanted some money, or his favoured children or lieutenants some, they'd just call Baker and he'd place what they wanted in a bank account of their choice, sent from one of his legitimate businesses."

"Or buy them an apartment in New York?"

"Or buy them a football team, Gar. I know Gaddafi got Baker to buy a club in Hamburg so one of his bastard sons could play there."

"Gaddafi is long dead," I said.

"Makes the game interesting, doesn't it?" she said. "And Baker didn't just work for Gaddafi."

"Who else then?"

"Try the North Koreans."

"Same set-up?"

"I'm not as clear on that." She coughed again. "I believe, for example, Baker bought a controlling share in an Israeli tech company that sells ground-to-air missile guidance software to NATO countries. Baker gets access to the intellectual property and sells it through a chain of intermediaries to the North Koreans." More coughing. Gasping and wheezing.

"Gar?" It was Sarah's voice.

"Yes."

"Was that helpful?"

"Very. If it's true."

"A truth so big and crazy can sound like fiction. That's how people get away with mega-crimes, isn't it?"

"The Surely Not Syndrome: fair point. By the way, that's some doe you've got there. She sounds more like a lioness with a cold."

"Anonymity gives people confidence," said Sarah. "Talking to you over the phone, it's like wearing a mask for her. Sorry, but I need to go."

I noticed the café shark was belly-up at the bottom of the tank. The waiter grinned at me. "Deep sleep," I said, smiling as if we were on the same page. We weren't.

I was thinking about the deep sleep of Muammar Gaddafi, whose obituary I downloaded on my iPad. It didn't take a genius to figure out that when Gaddafi and his cronies controlled the Libyan army and could fund an undercover network of assassins and torturers who could travel the world to discipline transgressors, who would dare rob the master. But Gaddafi, as the obit reminded me in detail, was beaten and shot to death by rebels after being dragged, begging for mercy, from a drain pipe on the outskirts of his home city of Sirte. Now his children and key henchmen were either dead, imprisoned, in exile, in hiding, or otherwise restrained from global roaming by their enemies within and outside Libya.

If Baker was just one of many treasure keepers, was Charles East another? Had Seth Vagner been a keeper of the keeper?

With the ticking of time since Gaddafi's death and the disempowerment of his cronies, the keepers must have been licking their lips, silently counting their spoils, waiting for enough days, and months and years to pass to feel safe in their secret corner of Gaddafi's treasure cave, safe enough to sneak away with sacks full, calculating the risk of detection and retribution was dwindling, moving ever closer towards zero. Then Henry East had spoiled things and his mistake had rippled across the world, threatening the future of others. No wonder he'd been erased.

I went back to the office and briefed Jack on my telephone meeting with Sarah's *Voice* and explained her treasure-keeper theory. Then we phoned Claire in Sydney to bring her up to speed.

"You've saved me a call," said Claire. "I'm hearing the Easts' marriage has collapsed. He has another woman, one of his staff."

Jack: "Name?"

"Helen Yee: thirty-years-old Chief Executive Officer of the Tamerlane Investment Group Asia."

Me: "Divorcing?"

"East and his wife are negotiating," said Claire.

Me: "Is this public?"

"No."

Me: "So how do you know all this?"

"Do you think I've been hiding under my bed while you've been grand touring?"

"*Touche*," I said. "You can fill me in face-to-face. I'm flying home tonight."

LVII

THAT evening, while Hitomi was at work, Jack and I drank beer and I told him about my bush food business plan with Hughie Jones. It prompted Jack to confess that he was thinking about moving to Tokyo because Hitomi's mother was ill and she wanted to be closer to her parents. He said he might even quit journalism to join the tourism business that Hitomi's father operated.

"Speaking of parents," I said. "How are yours?"

"Wouldn't know."

"What is it with you and them? You never go home, not even for Christmas. But your wife's mother gets crook and you turn into Florence Nightingale."

Jack sipped, frowned: said nothing.

"Seriously, what's it been? Twenty years since you've been home?"

"Longer."

"Okay. Solve the mystery for me."

"You really want to know?"

"I really want to know."

"You may find it disturbing."

"Disturb away."

"A friend of my sister was staying with us for Christmas. I thought I was in love with Kristen Jones." Jack covered the mouth of his beer bottle with his thumb pad and flipped it up with a pop. "I was home from boarding school. Fourteen: in bed, eyes closed, imagining her ..."

I sipped my beer and waited for the storyteller to catch his breath.

"It was pitch-black in my room. Someone climbed into my bed - behind me. I smelled perfume and alcohol. They put a hand in my pyjamas."

Jack stopped talking and seized up like cold fat.

"Sounds like a Merry Christmas so far," I said.

"It wasn't Kristen ... or my sister."

"... your mother?"

Jack took a deep breath, cupped a hand over his mouth and let the air out slowly.

We sat in silence for quite a while, until the sound of an alarm began blaring on my phone.

"Shit," I said. "Someone's breaking into Kate's flat in Brighton."

On my phone, I opened a video surveillance app that Todd had helped me download before he took my family to Ireland. It was linked to micro-cameras hidden inside smoke detectors we'd attached to some of the ceilings in Kate's home. The cameras were fitted with motion-activated triggers, linked to my phone and Todd's. Todd was calling me from Portroe within seconds. We synced our phones and watched the video of the intruders.

Two figures, dressed in dark street clothes, padded across the living room floor and started opening and closing the drawers of a dresser against a wall. They'd been bold enough to turn on a ceiling light.

"It's her," I said. "The bitch who set up my OD at the Dorchester and pulled the strings on Hugo's abduction."

Her companion was wearing a baseball cap, so I couldn't see the face, but from the body shape, it could have been the fringe-comber that stuck the needle in my arm. They moved to a bedroom and started working over the wardrobes.

"We can bring them down," said Todd. "But we have to move fast."

He sketched a plan and we agreed. He hung up to execute it.

We watched Ms Hoodie in Kate's bedroom. She took a photo from a frame on a wall - one of me, Charlotte and the kids - and put it inside her backpack, along with some papers she found in a writing desk. Did we leave Kate's sister's Portroe address lying around? Minutes passed, too many minutes; they exited through the front door and pulled it shut. I dialled Todd but he didn't answer. I figured he was cracking on with his plan, but we'd been too slow.

I went to Jack's guestroom and packed my bags for the midnight flight from Shanghai to Sydney. About ninety minutes later, as I was hugging Jack goodbye on his driveway beside the car that was taking me to the airport, Todd called.

"Good news," he said. "They're in police custody."

Todd and his colleagues had immediately alerted the Brighton police to a break and enter. They assisted by emailing to the police the security camera video of the burglary but the breakthrough came from a police CCTV camera on a street pole positioned beside Kate's flat. It captured the couple coming down the front steps and climbing into their car. The camera recorded their car's number plate. The pair was arrested later as they fuelled up at a petrol station on the motorway to London.

Even better, the male driver produced a licence that proved to be a fake. A subsequent inspection of the car revealed an unlicensed handgun, a few grams of heroin – and a packet of plastic explosive in the boot.

"Todd," I said. "They sound like terrorists to me."

"It's an angle."

"Look," I said, "how about this? One of your colleagues calls the anti-terrorism hotline with an anonymous tip. Make it female, a mother. She's a Muslim parent worried about her teenage son who was picked up in front of their house today by a strange couple. The kid has started hanging around unsavoury characters from the local mosque. She's found large sums of cash in his bedroom and a hand-drawn map of Oxford Circus tube station with the exits marked. She fears the couple may have sold, or is about to sell her son weapons of some sort. She gives a quick description of the couple and their car – and parrots the number plate. Bang, she hangs up."

"It's a long shot," he said.

"Let's do anything we can to keep them locked up while we dig out this cockroach nest."

I farewelled Jack. As my driver swept up a ramp and entered the main freeway, I decided to do my civic duty by giving the British authorities every assistance with their homeland security.

"Mr Sang," I said. "Would you know where I can buy a cheap phone to send a text message? I'll pay cash."

About thirty minutes later, we were swinging back onto the freeway, accelerating hard to make my flight. I had a new phone in my hand. I copied some Arabic script off the internet and pasted it into a text to despatch to Ms Hoodie: الله يكون معكم

I reasoned that her phone would likely be inside a police station, probably inside a plastic evidence bag while she was being grilled by investigators. So along with an anonymous tip to the anti-terror hotline, the appearance on her screen of the words, *Allah be with you,* written in Arabic, should give the interrogation a bit of zip. I hit the send key and tossed the handset out the window.

*

The ten-hour flight from Shanghai landed me in Sydney as dawn broke. I phoned Portroe from the taxi on my way home to Darlinghurst. Todd was taking them all on a driving tour of County Kerry on the south-west coast, including a visit to Blarney Castle where Hugo wanted to kiss the eponymous stone to get "the gift of the gab". I sent myself a mental note to ask Todd for a copy of the blueprint of the teenage synaptic network that he appeared to possess.

In other news, Todd reported that the terror tip-off, and a strange text message from China, had caused Ms Hoodie and her friend considerable distress. They were being detained by various levels of law enforcement on suspicion of supporting a planned act of violence against the State. They could be held for a week, he said, and possibly longer, depending on the creativity of their explanations.

The knowledge that those two were locked away in London, and that Seth Vagner was dead, gave me the feeling of being midway through a deep tissue massage, which I planned to have in the flesh later in the day. My high didn't last long. My lawyer phoned as the taxi turned into our home street.

The homicide squad, he said, wanted to speak with me about Vagner's death at Moon Hill and take a formal statement about my encounters with him: dates, times, places, content. He added that, now I was home, he would contact the detectives on my behalf and come back to me with a meeting place and time. Get it over and done with ASAP was his advice.

Steele and I had lunch at the Dolphin Hotel in Surry Hills. Karen had returned home, but not for his benefit. She did so on the proviso that Steele moved in the opposite direction, a gearshift that landed him in a serviced apartment next to the Dolphin. Beth was still at high school and Steele accepted Karen's logic that she was best placed to care for their daughter. It just happened that his apartment in exile was handy to his work, pubs and restaurants.

After lunch, I had a massage at a parlour a few doors from home, kept my underpants on, then went home and climbed upstairs to bed to sleep off the jetlag. Fish curled up with me, after I promised him a walk the next morning.

We hit the footpath not long after sunrise. On the way home, we dropped in at the Pickled Pig for breakfast, taking a table on the street. Mick O'Hara had a Charlie Chaplin theme going on, but the more I looked at him, the more I saw Adolf Hitler. I put it down to jetlag. Mick put my latte on the table and gave Fish a beef sausage on a saucer. My phone rang: Steele.

"I've just emailed you a password to a video file I've put on Dropbox. It's titled *Silverwater Hannibal*. I managed to copy it before the police had it pulled off YouTube."

The video was a fish-eye view from the corner of a recreation room with a table-tennis table in the middle of it. Henry East was reading a newspaper. A chunky man approached him from behind, carrying a sack with something weighty inside it, and what looked like a wire coat-hanger. I watched a few minutes of vision. The attacker went mouth-to-mouth with Henry, then jerked his head up, his face smeared with blood.

"What did he do?" I said to Steele.

"He bit his fucking tongue off. People thought it was a joke when it appeared on YouTube: a Halloween masquerade."

"Who is Silverwater Hannibal?"

"Stanley Arthur Ellis, thirty-six, married, three children. He was Henry's former cellmate, doing two years for drug dealing. He was admitted to the psych ward after – you guessed it – a failed suicide attempt."

"He's a twenty-four-carat nutcase."

"He knotted a hanky around his neck and twisted it by hand. Hardly left a mark on him but the shrinks reckoned he needed a spell in the psych ward and some counselling."

"What do your snouts say?"

"The hanky act got Ellis to where he wanted to be. They reckon someone leaned on Ellis's wife and kids to put the hubby up to the job. But Silvia Ellis is saying nothing. She's under police surveillance, phone taps."

"Can we catch up?"

"How long will it take for you to get home?"

"Fifteen minutes."

"Give me thirty."

Steele arrived at my door carrying a cardboard box. Inside my office, he lifted the lid. The box contained printed transcripts, and audio files stored on a USB memory stick.

"Henry gave this stuff to a contact of mine a few days before he went to jail. Life insurance, you might call it."

"Didn't work, then."

"Have a read, then tell me what you think. Got to go."

I made a cup of tea and started reading. The transcripts were headlined, 'The Diary'. A handwritten explanatory note said the pages were created from voice memos that Henry had recorded on a phone.

LVIII

The Diary of Henry East

Shanghai. 10am. Meeting. TIGA office. John K Baker, me, BH, JC.

Baker wants a Mudaraba *- some bloody Arab banking term – one partner gives money to another to invest. The cash comes from the first partner -* Rabb-ul-mal *(Baker) - he directs where the money goes - management all ours -* Mudarib *(us).*

Parties agree upfront on profit share, losses assumed by Baker. Mudarib *loses time and effort only. Awesome! This could be "the" deal! Too good?*

US$20 mill to start - a private client of his. He wants us, not Dad. You boys will make this work - his exact words.

High quality real estate, shares in good companies - banks, mining companies – in Australia. And there's more to come.

We just set up a Trust and skim 20% share of any profits, plus "sign-on fee" $US200K cash.

24 hours to agree. What's the rush?

April 6 -

Meeting. Me, BH, JC (no Baker).

I don't trust Baker. It's too much for too little.

JC needled me about being a Daddy's boy. Something about eating crumbs off my father's table. He always tries this shit.

BH pointed out it's a big table with big crumbs.

It is still my father's table though. We signed with Baker.

April 20 -

Baker's money arrived via his lawyers in British Virgin Islands (BVI). We set up BVI bank account. Funds go from his BVI to our BVI, then to us in Sydney.

May 19 –

Contracts to buy properties in Sydney, Melbourne, Perth –$10 mill. Cattle station, Northern Territory –$5.5 mill. The rest, blue chips - Westpac, Comm Bank, NAB, ANZ, BHP, Rio Tinto. Baker's happy.

May 29 –

Meeting: Baker. Extend by US$100 mill!

JC said later we could fuck him completely. We're sole trustees; we own all the assets. Nothing in Baker's or Cavalcade's name.

June 29 -

Dad's got me a job with Hagerman Brothers in Sydney. Starts September. Says I need experience. Insists I come back to Sydney. He never leaves me alone. BH will go back with me.

I don't want war with Dad. We work via JC at TIGA in Shanghai.

Baker's $100 million roughly in four - property, agriculture, wine, bullion.

August 29 -

Bad day. Baker meeting. Me, BH, JC. Three associates goons really. One had tattoos all over his face, same on his hands and wrists.

Baker wanted further investment. Too risky; I told him we had done all we could.

He says it stops when I say.

JC laughed.

And Baker slapped him hard, a few times. JC shit himself. Really. Baker would not let him leave the room.

*

I plugged the USB stick into my laptop. It contained files of Henry's voice. I did several random checks, comparing his voice notes to the printed transcripts: a professional had clearly done the audio-to-text job. But there was one audio file for which I couldn't find a transcript, so I listened to it carefully; I recognised Baker's voice from the lift at the Dorchester, and someone was being slapped, and whimpering. I assumed it was James Carter ...

"*...I have three sets of balls in my hands. I will tear them off, one by one, if I have to, and feed them to my dogs.*

"*When I send you money, you will invest it where I tell you.*

"*When I want my money back, I will instruct you. You will sell asset and bring the cash back to me along the routes that I tell you.*

"When I want to use the assets – because I may want a nice holiday in a big house in Sydney – I will tell you. You will fix it for me.

"If you talk to anyone about me, mention my name just once outside these walls, we will kill you: your families too.

"*Tu es mon falcons et maintenant, les garcons.*"

I knew that much French: "You are my falcons now, boys."

I went back to Henry's transcripts:

August 29 –

Invited alone to dinner, Baker's hotel room to "clear up loose ends". His goons pulled battery out my phone.

Says I'm number one man now. Some shit about one animal, and I'm the head. If the beast displeases me, I will cut off its head." He actually said that. Who does he think he is, Al Pacino?

More threats. He's been to Tamerlane. Well, out front in his yacht. Says he has an army, snipers: one in Bondi right now. Is he insane? I think so.

Went on about shooting Dad and Mum while they had breakfast on the balcony. He knows that much. Asked if I wanted a speedier inheritance. We can help you, as well as kill you. His actual words.

Said he would show me a capability *statement. I can't believe I'm actually writing this stuff down. How did this happen?*

His goon with the tattoos dragged in a naked local teen. He made the boy stand with his hands on the back of the sofa and kicked the boy's legs apart. The boy wet himself. Baker raped him. I tried not to watch but Baker's thug slapped my face. He held my head. When I closed my eyes, he punched my head until I opened my eyes. He said he'd put a cigarette in them if I closed them again. Then the goon did it to the boy while Baker watched and drank wine and smoked.

I thought they were going to do it to me. What can I do? How can I tell Dad about Baker?

*

I phoned Jack and briefed him about the diary.

"That's all the pieces we need," said Jack. "You need to start writing. Get me a draft story framework and we'll feed the others in to it."

I hung up. I stood up. I sipped water from a glass - and threw it with all my might against a wall. The shattering glass didn't stop the images I saw of Hugo, trapped and drugged in that filthy council flat. I took a deep breath and visualised rogering Baker with the long blade of a butcher's knife.

A text from Steele snapped me out of it: *There's someone you should meet. 7am tomorrow at the Pig.*

LIX

SOON after sunrise, I was seated in a booth at the Pig, back to the wall, reading on my iPad the scans I'd taken of Henry's diary. The original documents and the USB I had hidden in the roof of our terrace. I'd also emailed the scans to Jack: additional insurance.

Mick, dressed like a 1920s gangster in a three-piece suit with wide lapels and a smoky grey fedora on his skull, delivered a bacon and egg roll with my latte. I'd declined his offer of a bourbon shot. I wanted to be sharp for whatever was coming.

Steele arrived clean-shaven, not even a bristle showing on his lightly tanned skull. He was wearing a snug-fitting, silver-coloured, long-sleeved shirt, open at the neck and tucked into black trousers. It was a bigger shock to see that his chest was now bigger than his belly. I'd have raised the shape-change with him, but he was accompanied by a young man, a sleek character with curly, dark hair, full lips, and bright eyes set off by a slim-fit, sky blue suit and white shirt buttoned at the collar – no tie. He looked like a wanker.

"Gar Hart, this is Max Gleason," said Steele. "Vicky Gleason's brother."

As I looked at Max, fresh pieces of an old puzzle slotted into place. Vicky Gleason had been a cadet journalist under the tutelage of Steele and me years ago. The mention of her name flicked my recall of the photo I'd taken of Steele with his amorous arm around Vicky in that Darlinghurst night club weeks ago. "What's Vicky doing these days?"

Steele hesitated, then volunteered: "She's the PR person at Greenhill Partners, Bart Hill's law firm."

So there it was. Vicky had been Steele's key source for weeks. I wondered if she was also the reason he'd been working out so hard at the gym, or in the surf, or doing something else strenuous with his body.

Steele said: "Henry East, Bart Hills and Max were close friends."

"Since high school," said Gleason. "I know Jamie Carter too."

"Not friends with Jamie?"

"Not close," said Gleason.

I said: "Did Henry give you his diary?"

Gleason surveyed his surroundings. There was just a man wearing a business suit, sitting half a dozen booths away. He was drinking coffee, reading a newspaper.

Gleason said: "Henry first met John Baker through Charles at Baker's polo club in London. Henry was studying at Oxford then, before Charles sent him to work in China. Then Baker arrived in Shanghai a few years later and contacted Henry, behind Charles' back."

"I know most of that," I said.

Steele gave me the stink-eye.

Gleason continued: "Henry saw his chance to get away from Charles. The old man controlled everything Henry did.

Charles had a plan for him from the day he was born. He even had a wife lined up for him."

"Who?"

"Baker's daughter, Anita."

I pulled a pen and notebook from my inside jacket pocket.

"Max is off the record," said Steele.

"Of course," I said. I guessed Gleason's sister must be stroking Steele with great skill, training him up as a PR man.

Gleason pulled his phone from his jacket pocket. He had a photo on it. Baker's daughter had a big mane of black hair, caterpillar eyebrows, big eyes, big nose, big lips, big teeth.

"OK," I said. "I've got Henry's diary and the audio of the meeting where Baker threatens Henry, Bart and Jamie with a hit squad if they don't do what he wants. But why would Henry then come back to Sydney and dig himself deeper in the shit by insider trading on Baker's business deals?"

"He was going to leave Australia," said Gleason.

"So he wanted money," I said. "But didn't Henry make a pile in commissions by investing all that cash for Baker. He must have had millions?"

"Baker blocked the commissions. He ripped them off."

"Can you help me pick up where the diary left off?"

"Fire away."

"Henry says in his diary that he decided to tell Charles about his secret deals with Baker, after Baker dubbed Henry the "head of the beast" and threatened to cut his head off if Henry failed him."

Gleason said, "Henry told his dad everything – about Baker, about the insider trading with Bart and Jamie. You know what Charles said?"

"Save me guessing."

"*You've made your bed, now you've got to lie in it*. When the market police came after Henry, Charles told him to confess to the insider trading, to say it was an error of judgement due to depression. He'd get a doctor to sign off on that assessment. Henry would get nothing more than a rap over the knuckles from the law. And good old dad would get Baker off his back. Charles warned Henry that if the spotlight went on the big picture, though, everyone would be destroyed."

"What about Baker's relationship with Charles East?"

"They've been doing business for years. Henry told me that Baker bailed Charles out during the Global Financial Crisis. Secretly. Then he put Charles in his pocket. Baker sent a minder to Australia."

"A keeper of the keeper," I said.

"A what?" said Gleason.

"Seth Vagner. Oscar Peterson, as they called him. The chauffer's real job was to mind Charles East for Baker, right?"

"Yes."

"How did Baker actually get his claws into Charles?"

"Charles borrowed money from Baker to build some huge real estate project in Ireland. Charles also partnered with Baker to build a casino in Macau. A couple of hundred million pounds worth, so Henry said. Then everything collapsed after the GFC. Henry never worked out exactly how Charles survived financially, but Baker got him off the hook with the banks."

Max's phone was on the café table. He glanced over his shoulders. The other customer had gone. He hit the button on its media player.

Charles East's voice said: "*You're not worth tuppence of goat shit. You're my fucking greatest disappointment ... You're weak, Henry, weak of character ... listen to me, don't go crying like you're ten years old ... If your friends breathe any of this, it will be their last. You can tell them that for a fucking certainty."*

"Henry make that recording?" I said.

"In the car on the way home with Charles after visiting his lawyers when he was hauled in by the regulators on the insider trading."

"How come you know so much about the Easts?"

Gleason held up his left hand and flashed a gold band on a finger. "Henry and I were married in Germany on a holiday just over a year ago."

"He kept you well hidden. How come you're still alive?"

"I went back to Germany, worked as a tutor. Henry insisted I stay well clear until he'd served his prison sentence. He thought Vagner would come after me too. I think the kangaroo hat on your farm saved me too."

Gleason's phone rang. "Excuse me, I have to take this call." He stepped to the footpath outside to talk.

"This is rolled gold," I said to Steele. He winked.

Gleason came back into the café and said he had an appointment. He stirred the remains of his coffee with a spoon, looked me in the eye: "Listen, Mr Hart. You think this is just about greedy people who are insane about money. That wasn't Henry. He wanted to stop being his father's slave."

"What, Henry was the Nelson Mandela of Double Bay? Tamerlane was his Robben Island?"

Steele shook his head at me, clearly disappointed.

"Sorry," I said. "My father was a prick too."

Gleason got lyrical: "Charles treated him like one of those cormorants on a leg rope with a neck ring. He let the bird catch the fish, but he never let him swallow it. Charles was just going to use Henry to catch more money for himself."

"So you were going to remove the neck ring and the rope?"

"We had plans, Mr Hart. It required money and we couldn't stay in Australia. I'm a school teacher. Do the maths."

"So you make some quick cash on the side, break the chains of Charles and Baker, head to Brazil, or whatever? And what, buy new faces?"

"Something like that." Gleason stood up to leave

"I'm sorry for your loss," I said. Gleason and I shook hands. Gleason walked out to the footpath and loitered.

"I've got to look after him," said Steele, rising from the table, "until you get the genie well and truly out of the bottle."

"That's a wrap, I think. One thing though, why aren't you writing any of this stuff?"

"You think those drongo's I work with at the *Daily News* wouldn't stuff this up? All they give a shit about are the horse races, the footy scores, and who's fucking who when they shouldn't be."

"What makes you think *we* won't stuff this up?"

"Blind faith."

LX

I VISITED an art supplies shop and bought half-a-dozen of the biggest sheets of white paper they had. At home, Fish bounced around my legs while I cleared my office table and spread a sheet out, sticky-taping its corners to the tabletop. It occupied about half the table's surface. I pulled the map of the world from my briefcase and taped it over the other half.

On the white paper, I listed in black pen a column of the dead: Henry East; Bruce Tyson; Bart Hills; Seth Vagner; Jean-Paul Marais; Muammar Gaddafi. I used green to list the living; it included Charles East; John K Baker; Anita Baker; Ms Hoodie; Sandy Wallace; James Carter, and now Max Gleason. Where I had photos of them, I taped headshots of the players beside their names. In red pen on the white paper, I listed the major business transactions such as Red Box.

On the map, I used red to mark the locations of the transactions, and green and black to mark the people, using their initials.

The emerging monster needed a name. I wrote *GaBE* in blue block letters on top of the white page, an acronym of

Gaddafi-Baker-East. On saying it out loud, it sounded like a kid's toy. I dug around my skull. I found *Ebola* somewhere. I put a line through *GaBE* and wrote in the name of the flesh-eating bacteria.

As I went to close my briefcase, I saw the pieces of my old phone inside. Curiosity chewed at me. I put the battery in. Ms Hoodie's fresh text was waiting: *"You've broken my heart, Gar. Now I'm going to break yours."* My heart sprinted left and right, trying to break out of my chest as a tried to work out exactly when it was sent.

On working through the date and time zones, I calculated it was despatched several hours before she broke into Kate's flat. I phoned Portroe anyway. Alice said she was dismembering insects with a scalpel and tweezers to stop herself digging her own eyeballs out from boredom. Kate had the flu, which kept her quiet. Hugo told me Todd had taught him how to disarm a person who was wielding a knife. Todd was in the shower. Hugo would get him to call me back.

I spent the afternoon writing on my laptop, shuffling my notebooks and documents around the tabletop, building the skeletons of the key stories about *Ebola*. The sun was going down when I unscrewed the cap on a bottle of red; its contents, and part of a second, combined with jetlag to transport me through a flickering twilight into sunup the next morning.

The dong of the brass ship's bell on my front door, and Fish's yapping, woke me. Claire, dressed in blue jeans, a green t-shirt and red leather sandals, was standing on the front step when I opened up.

"Come to the beach," she said. "There's something I want to show you. Bring your sunglasses and a hat."

Claire's bodyguard, Bat, drove us on to Old South Head Road towards the harbour side suburb of Double Bay. We were soon cruising by the long sandstone wall in front of the East's mansion, Tamerlane. As we passed the front gates, Bat flicked the car's indicators and pulled over, parking a hundred metres from Tamerlane beside another stately home.

"Do I get any hints?" I said to Claire.

"I've given you a clue already," she said, nodding back towards Tamerlane. "Follow me. We're incognito, by the way."

I followed her lead to don my hat and sunglasses inside the car. We climbed out and stood on the footpath in bright sunlight. Claire carried a shoulder bag. Bat killed the engine and stayed in the car. I followed Claire down a narrow stone path between blocks of flats – art deco low-rises on one side, hulking steel and glass modern on the other – to Seven Shillings Beach. The emerald water was striking, lapping the brilliant white beach.

We took our shoes off, rolled up our jeans, and walked upon squeaking sand to the water's edge, wading up to our ankles in the shallows in the direction of Tamerlane. Claire took my hand. Hers felt good.

"We're a couple," she said: "for the optics."

Ahead of us, a lean, cream-skinned woman wearing a black bikini, her long, dark hair tied into a ponytail, emerged glistening from the water. She stepped towards a towel that was lying on the sand.

"Don't stare," said Claire.

It was hard *not* to stare at the young Asian woman. She had a bit of a tummy, which seemed incongruous with the rest of her body. She dried herself and walked to the security gate that led from the beach through the high, back wall into Tamerlane. She entered and the gate closed.

"Who the hell was that?" I said to Claire as we continued wading past Tamerlane.

"Let's sit under that tree," said Claire. "I don't want sunburn."

We perched on a sandy mound at the base of a flowering flame tree. The first-floor back balcony of Tamerlane's main building was visible.

"That," said Claire, "was Helen Yee."

My gears clicked: Charles East's girlfriend, the trigger for the divorce that Claire informed me and Jack about on my last night in Shanghai.

"She moves quickly," I said.

"Not as quickly as the old man."

"What do you mean?"

"Look," said Claire, pointing towards the main building of Tamerlane. She handed me a small pair of binoculars from her shoulder bag. Two people were moving on the upper balcony, shuffling around a table and chairs. Helen Yee was wearing sunglasses and a loose white robe.

"You're kidding," I said as my eyes adjusted. Yee sat in a chair and let her robe spill open, exposing ample breasts and swollen nipples. She massaged them. The young woman beside her reached down and lifted a baby from a cot. Yee attached the squirming child to a nipple and it settled in. The woman reached down again. Yee attached a second baby to her spare breast.

"Twins," said Claire. "Charles East's twins."

"I'm all ears," I said.

"Charles ditched Henry the moment he went to prison, probably sooner. He gave him up to Baker. But he was still going to have a direct male heir, by hook or by crook."

"How very old-fashioned. Daughter not good enough?"

"You've met Henry's sister, Ellen. Charles blamed his wife for that: nothing to do with *his* mighty seed, of course."

"So you know Ellen?"

"I met her, and her mother, while you were away: a fundraiser for women's education in India."

"Why are they talking to you?" As I spoke, I recalled Claire's revelation, weeks ago at Babel, about having a younger sister with autism. No doubt Claire had empathy for others with a disability.

"They've lost a son and brother to this madness," she said. "They were terrified of Vagner. And Ellen liked you, for some reason."

"Tell me about Yee."

"Her father owned a steel mill in China - in the Hebei province in the north-east. She went to Stanford University in the States, earned an economics degree, and met Charles when she was working at a bank in Hong Kong. He gave her a job at TIGA in China and eventually made her the boss. Now she's given him sons."

"Is Yee connected to Baker?"

"Ellen says that Yee's father was in jail in Beijing for corruption. So Baker gave the right people the money to get him out. And he keeps giving to keep him out."

"So Yee is Baker's new *keeper of the keeper* for Charles, now that Seth Vagner is dead?"

"It's a complex web. She gave birth to the twins here, by the way. They're little Aussie citizens. All part of the plan by Charles, it appears."

I chuckled. "What a pit of vipers."

"That's very unfair on snakes," said Claire, grasping a handful of beach sand and letting the grains fall. "You know, just a year ago, I was writing about the price of mortgages and the rising cost of household grocery bills."

"And now you are exposing theft, murder, infidelity, brutality and corruption on an industrial scale."

She laughed. The wind blew her hat off and she loped along the beach after it with the elegance of a cat. My phone whistled.

"Mr Hart, this is Detective Sergeant Warren Harper of the Homicide Squad. I'm calling to arrange a meeting."

"Yes, of course. My lawyer told me to expect a call. How do you want to proceed?"

"I hope it's not inconvenient, but we are actually close to your rural property today, working with the Tangleton Police to put this case to bed."

"So what are you thinking?" I said, thinking to myself about how badly I'd planned for this. Mr Browning was sitting somewhere at Moon Hill, mindlessly abandoned after my mushroom trip. I was thinking, too, that I still faced criminal charges of threatening to kill Charles East and his family, as well as Anita Baker in the UK. The discovery by DS Harper of a loaded, unlicensed, concealable firearm covered in my fingerprints would not help my case.

"Could we meet at Moon Hill? So we can have the benefit of your local knowledge," he said.

"Sure." I, aah…have plans for today. So why don't we meet on my property tomorrow, say mid-morning?"

My plan, cooked up mid-sentence, was to drive to Moon Hill this afternoon, find Mr Browning, bury him, and have everything nice and tidy for when DS Harper and his colleagues arrived tomorrow.

"It's great weather out here right now," he said. "If I was you, I'd be tempted to drive out tonight and enjoy a fire under the stars. I'm a big camper myself."

"I love the stars too," I said. "But I will see you tomorrow morning."

"I look forward to it."

Claire was standing in front of me wearing her freshly captured hat.

"Trouble?" she said.

"I need to go to my place in the mountains, for a day or so, to sort something out. It'll give me clear space to think and work on all this, so it's all good."

"When are you going to take me to this mysterious hideaway?"

"When this is over; that's a promise."

"I'll hold you to it," she said, offering me her hand to shake. It was a long shake and I liked it just as much as our walk along the beach.

As we stepped up the path away from the beach, Claire said: "Ellen told me something about your old school friend, Sandy Wallace. You were right about Sandy informing on you to Charles East."

Claire and Bat dropped me at home. I filled a cooler box with food and alcohol, and tossed in a steak from the freezer for tonight's dinner. Hughie Jones and I could catch and boil some freshwater yabbies from the dam tomorrow, hunt a pig maybe. I could work on *Ebola* by day and we could sit under the stars by a fire at night. DS Harper was on the money there. I made a call to my lawyer to let him know my plan; I left him a voice message.

I packed another box with my laptop, made doubly sure I had device chargers, and added hard copy documents and memory sticks. I unstuck my map of the world and my key-points sheet from the office table, rolled them up and packed them in the Defender too. I palmed Fish back to Sue next door.

A few hours later, I parked at Moon Hill beside the deck under the branches of the old pine. I stepped out, sucked in some air and scanned the valley and mountains to the east under cloudless sky. I took out my binoculars and looked downhill; ragged strips of police crime scene tape flapped around the pegs where Vagner had fallen.

I climbed the steps onto the deck and looked into the branches of the pine. The treehouse looked secure; the folding ladder was locked in place in the cabin floor. I walked to the other side of the deck and checked the padlocked door on the ground cabin. A piece of paper was stuffed into the door frame, an invoice for a padlock, scrawled upon in black pen: *You owe me, Hughie.* He had repaired Vagner's break and enter.

My first job was to find Mr Browning. I opened the cabin and looked in every cupboard, under chairs, behind the armchair cushions, inside the fridge and freezer. Nothing. I dropped the ladder from the treehouse floor and climbed up. I flipped the mattresses, shook out the sheets and doonas, lay on the floor and crawled under the beds. Zilch. I crawled under the deck, scouting for slithering things as much as the shape of a gun, and zig-zagged across my settlement, scanning the grass like a bird looking for bugs. My thoughts started to kaleidoscope. Had the police already been here and found Mr Browning? Was the homicide squad coming tomorrow to trap me into lying about evidence they already had? Had they discovered, from telephone company records, that someone had used Bruce Tyson's phone from my home in Darlinghurst, the day he was electrocuted in his Sydney workshop? And, or, had they matched the prints from my gun with something in his shed? My head throbbed. I had painkillers in the Defender's glovebox.

The pill packet fell with an avalanche of rubbish from the glovebox to the floor, sliding under the passenger seat. I reached for the packet and felt something hard: Mr Browning was wrapped inside an old t-shirt, alongside a lost joint of marijuana which I tucked behind my ear *for Ron.*

I took the gun to the kitchen cabin and wrapped it in cling-film. I carried the food box from my car into the kitchen, where I lit the joint and left it smouldering between my lips for a walk. Outside, I collected a shovel from the car, along with a metal cake tin I'd brought from home to make a coffin - on optimism I'd find Mr Browning - and trekked downhill to the dam.

I dropped the wrapped gun at my feet and leaned with one hand on the shovel to finish the joint, keeping an eye peeled for a sneak attack from DS Harper – a possibility that was amplified with each drag and exhalation. My phone erupted with the toots of the police whistle!

"What's up?" I said to Jack, spitting out the joint, trying to sound sharp.

"Where are you?"

"Moon Hill."

"You alone?"

It wasn't his intention, but he reminded me I was missing Hugo and Alice - and Claire.

"I needed peace and quiet to work on the yarn."

"Listen to me, Gar, you ..."

"Jack? ... Jack?"

The phone signal was lost. I set to work digging a hole in the dam wall and buried Mr Browning inside the tin.

By the time I got back to the deck, the forest to the west was casting long shadows. I tried to phone Jack from inside the Black Circle on the deck, but that failed.

I set up a campfire in the ring of rocks beside the deck, ready for igniting, washed my face and hands, and climbed into the treehouse to remake the beds. When I climbed down, Moon Hill was silent. There was not the slightest breath of wind. Not a bird called. Not a creature was visible. An engine revved deep in the forest, followed by a hideous squeal. It sounded like a pig being tortured. It made me want Mr Browning which I felt for like an amputated limb. There was a hunting knife in a sheath in my food box. I attached it to my jeans belt. I started a steak sizzling in a frypan on the cooktop and opened a bottle of red.

About ten minutes later, I sat in a folding chair by the flames of the campfire, eating chunks of meat off a plate with the point of my knife, drinking wine, gazing at a slit-eyed moon beside the Milky Way. I decided to drive to town when I'd finished eating because there was always good phone reception and I could reconnect with Jack. I'd leave my *Ebola* goody box under the tarpaulin in the back of the Defender until the homicide squad had finished its visit in the morning. Torch lights strobed from inside the forest, criss-crossing my face.

"Hughie?" I called, squinting into the lights.

The torch-bearers approached under the cover of smoke windswept from my fire. I stood.

"DS Harper?" I said hopefully, instantly realising what a bonehead I'd been.

Three dark figures closed me inside a triangle. One tugged a chain, dragging Sandy Wallace, scratched and filthy, out of the shadows …

A few minutes later, Sandy lost most of her head to a swarm of shotgun pellets, and I conned my way into the treehouse cabin before scrambling onto the roof and launching from the canopy of the pine upon the wire of the flying fox …

LXI

Forty minutes later...

THE HOLES in my right thigh, from where I'd pulled out the crossbow arrow, throbbed and burned. I limped for minutes into the forest behind the dam, before I turned again to look for Ms Hoodie's flashlight. Nothing. She must have been trying to save her shot boyfriend from the two bullets I'd fired into his chest. The jumper-bandage around my thigh was holding. Mr Browning was locked in my right hand; he had a bullet left. The distant revving of a car engine pricked up my ears. Maybe she was four-wheel-driving off the track to attend to her shot man by the dam. I sped up, picking my way over fallen branches on the moonlit forest floor, glad for once that there was no obvious track to Hughie's shack.

His tin and timber cottage was lightless when I spotted its silhouette. Even better: his white ute was parked out the front. Dogs barked from inside as I stepped onto the porch. I banged on the door.

"It's Gar Hart! Shut the dogs up, mate. Quick."

The porch light went on, creating a blazing beacon on the edge of the forest. The door opened. I pushed past Hughie and flicked the light switch off. Moonlight through the windows was enough.

"Ya fuckin' bleedin', mate!" said Hughie, tottering on skinny legs, dressed in his underpants.

"Madmen. Killers at Moon Hill. A woman's dead. We've got to get to the cops."

"Who's dead? What the fuck's happened?" The dogs licked my blood off the floor.

"They shot a woman. I dropped one with this." I waved Mr Browning.

"Cool down," said Hughie. "Ya like a headless chook."

He poured me a glass of water from the tap at his kitchen sink. "Sit," he said, tugging a chair from under the table in his all-purpose room, "drink this while I get me duds on."

Through his bedroom door off the kitchen, I watched him drag on trousers and boots and a baggy, black jumper.

"Show me that leg," he said.

"No time, mate. We have to get to town, get the coppers. I need to call people."

I checked my phone. The dam water had killed it. Hughie had no phone at his place. He grabbed his rifle from the corner of the room and a box of ammunition from a kitchen drawer. I was pleased the bullets were big.

After helping me into the passenger seat of his ute, he tucked his rifle behind the headrests of the seats, and sat behind the steering wheel. He clicked his fingers outside the open car window, at which the dogs bounded into the back tray, yapping with excitement. I stopped caring about the barking because we were quickly on the dirt road and moving at speed. Hughie fishtailed around a bend in the pale grit and speared through an ancient eucalypt forest that stood thick and dark on both sides of us. He was heading for the main bitumen road and the town of Tangleton.

"What the fuck have you done, Garsy?"

I gave him a potted version of *Ebola*, ending with Sandy Wallace bringing three raiders to ambush me at Moon Hill before they blew her head off with the shotgun and I escaped through my treehouse window into the pine tree and rode the flying fox.

"That Gaddafi prick's long dead, isn't he?" said Hughie, accelerating out of a bend, glancing in his rear-vision mirror, which prompted me to look behind too. "You're talkin' about that shifty Arab bloke who dyed his hair and raped schoolkids. Am I right?"

"This guy Baker has a big lump of Gaddafi's loot now," I said, "And he doesn't want to be outed. People will come after him then: governments, crooks. He may be tied up with those lunatics in North Korea too."

Hughie shook his head. "So your old girlfriend was a Judas, hey?"

"Don't know that she had much choice. They had her on a chain, bashed. Once they had my info, they were going to drop both of us in a very deep hole. No doubt about that."

"At least ya kids are safe."

"Yes," I said, now grasping why Jack was concerned about me being alone at Moon Hill. Ms Hoodie must have been re-leased from custody in London well over a day ago in order to get to me, probably within 24 hours of being busted – and we had missed her release. I guessed Jack had already warned Claire. I checked my phone again; it had as much life in it as Sandy.

"So the flying fox saved your arse," said Hughie, who had helped me build it. "I warned ya though, didn't I, not ta use that cheap-as-shit wire?"

I shook my head at how dim I had been. All Ms Hoodie needed to do right now was have a dig around in the back of my Defender and discover my box full of research, my map, my laptop, the copy of Henry's diary – she'd know everything I knew. And therefore what to erase.

Hughie was impressed when I told him how I clubbed the gorilla-man's skull with the pick handle that I kept under a bed in my treehouse. I clutched my leg with both hands, trying to massage away some pain.

Hughie wiped his nose with his jumper sleeve. "This is what happens when ya stick ya beak in other people's shit, Garsy."

"How long now?" I said.

"Turnoff's just up there." He nodded straight ahead. "The cop shop'll be closed, but the pub'll be full. Friday night darts. That's the spot: safety in numbers, son."

As Hughie turned left onto the main bitumen road and accelerated, a glint in the ute's wing mirror caught my eye.

"Lights!" I yelled.

"I see 'em," said Hughie, glancing in the rear-vision mirror.

"Go any faster?"

"Doin' one-twenty-kays an hour now. I don't fancy flippin' on a turn. Dogs are in the back too."

"They're gaining."

"Could be anyone."

"Could be the woman. She's got a shotgun. At least."

"Whoever it is," said Hughie, "they're fuckin' flyin'."

I gripped Mr Browning with both hands. "Wind your window down, mate."

"You can't pop some prick for speedin'," Hughie said as he reeled the handle and lowered the glass.

We entered a straight stretch of lumpy, two-lane highway. Hughie cranked the ute up to a hundred and forty kilometres an hour, at least that's what the speedo said. The wheels shuddered. The tyres seemed to lose touch with the road on the dips and humps. The approaching headlights ballooned in our back window and rear-view mirrors.

The other driver veered sideways into the passing lane and made a move. I pointed Mr Browning across Hughie's chest through his window, resting my finger on the trigger, aiming for where I guessed a head would appear. Hughie outguessed us all: he slipped his foot off the accelerator and braked. A huge, white four-wheel-drive whooshed past, two mad-eyed faces smiling through its open window. A blast of electronic dance music came and went.

"Fuckin' idiots!" roared Hughie.

Their red taillights faded into the distance on the road in front. Hughie accelerated up to cruising speed.

"Who were they?" I said.

"The Williams boys," said Hughie. "One of them shot that walloper who was wearin' your roo hat. Fuckin' kids: up to their gills on some chemical shit, by the look of it. Friday night madness."

The main street of Tangleton was lifeless as we raced down a hill and up the other side into the centre of town. Hughie angle-parked the ute near the front of the pub beside a cluster of four-wheel-drives bristling with spotlights and radio antennas that looked like giant insect feelers. Hughie came around to my side. I draped an arm around his shoulder and he helped me up the steps into the front bar. It was packed with ranting men, and fewer but no less rowdy women, clutching glasses, pool cues and darts. Heads turned towards us, eyes drawn to my blood-soaked leg.

"Gored by a pig," Hughie said to the gawkers. He wisely didn't want to create a fuss, though the idea of sending a drunken posse in pursuit of Ms Hoodie crossed my mind. I heard someone say "stupid cunt". The majority quickly turned back to the dart board on the wall, the pool table, and a footy game on the telly.

Hughie helped me through a side door to the dining room and sat me in a vinyl-covered chair. He propped my wounded leg in front of me on another chair. More thoughtfully, he bought us schooners of beer, then took his drink with him to the hotel's phone in the hallway to call the police and the ambulance service. On his return, he said the local ambulance had just been called to a car crash on the other side of town. A driver had missed a corner and thundered into a tree. I hoped it wasn't the Williams boys. For my benefit, the ambos adopted plan B and had contacted a district doctor who was dining at the Tangleton Bowling Club a few blocks from the pub. Duty police officers from the larger, nearby town of Canterwell were on their way. Hughie then cadged a mobile phone from the publican and brought it to me.

Because my phone was stuffed, and because I never bother to remember numbers due to the fact they were always in my phone, I had to use directory assistance to connect to the switchboard of *The Sydney Daily News* and negotiate my way to Steele on his mobile. Steele helped me link to Claire and Jack, who hooked me into Todd in Ireland.

Of course, all of them knew by now that Ms Hoodie had been released from police custody in London, about twenty-four hours after she and her companion were arrested for breaking into Kate's flat. Her male sidekick had taken the rap for the plastic explosive, the unregistered gun, and the fake ID. He was still behind bars – and he backed her story that he'd threatened her life if she didn't do what he wanted. She was bailed on one charge only of break-and-enter. Before I could get her name from Todd, Hughie, clutching fresh beers, led into the dining room two police officers. I said I'd call back.

The officers were a male and a female, both in their late twenties by my calculation. The male carried a beer, the female a glass of white wine. It *was* Friday night. Hughie introduced Sue and Johnno, who pulled up chairs either side of my propped leg. Sue put her glass on the floor by her feet and took out a notebook and a pen. Johnno gulped beer; he wasn't letting go of his glass.

"The doctor's not far away," Sue said.

Hughie, while I had been on the phone, had given them a heads-up on events at Moon Hill.

"So you didn't actually see the faces of any of these people who ambushed you, apart from the murdered woman, who was known to you?" Sue said. "An ex-girlfriend, was she?"

"Correct on both counts," I said, swapping my empty glass for the full one Hughie proffered. It occurred to me I might be in strife – if the only body at Moon Hill right now was Sandy Wallace's. And where was my hunting knife? Of course; I'd dropped it with my dinner plate by the campfire when the raiders arrived. All they had to do was smear Sandy's blood on the blade of my knife, or better still: do a re-cut with it. I felt like I was falling into a Francis Bacon painting again.

"Mr Hart," the male officer said, "some of our colleagues should be at your property soon. While we wait, could you please step us through exactly what happened? Take your time." Johnno sipped his beer while Sue took notes.

I was up to the part where I flung the treehouse trapdoor shut on a raider's finger, when a man clomped into the dining room as gracefully as a Clydesdale horse with a middle-ear problem. He had lots of stringy grey hair and a bulbous, blue-veined nose. He carried a black case.

"We'll let the doctor do his work," said Sue, "then pick up where we left off." She pocketed her notebook and decamped with her wine glass and Johnno to the front bar.

"Ah," said the doctor, after introducing himself with a name I missed because I was too busy ducking his combustible breath, "there's an operating table." He pointed at a large dining table beside a wall.

Hughie cleared away the plates and cutlery. The linen tablecloth was clean enough, the doctor assured me. Hughie took his jumper off and rolled it into a pillow for me. They helped me onto the surface.

"Finish your drink," the doctor ordered, "while I get set up."

Hughie handed me my beer and I propped myself on an elbow to down it. Hughie dragged across a smaller table upon which the doctor put his medical bag. He extracted some items: tweezers, bandages, syringes in plastic wrappers, bottles of fluid, ampoules of liquid.

"Now let's have a look," he said, undoing my jumper-dressing with his nicotine-stained hands. He peeled it off with surprising gentleness. Hughie helped him slice my jeans open with scissors and they pulled off my boots. The doctor injected my wounds with local anaesthetic. The publican donated a round of Scotch for doctor, patient and nurse while the painkiller kicked in.

"You're a lucky man, Mr Hart," said the doctor, probing my wounds with his tweezers. "Just some muscle tearing from the arrow: missed your femoral artery by millimetres. You could have bled to death out there."

He cleaned, stitched and bandaged, icing his work with a stinging tetanus shot in my upper arm.

"How's the pain? On a scale of one to ten," he said.

"Terrible," I lied: "eight point five and rising."

"Marty Price died this arvo," said the doctor. "This was his, for the cancer. Don't mix it with alcohol … not while I'm looking."

He took an ampoule of morphine from his bag and injected the contents into my buttock.

It worked fast. "Got any take-away?" I said.

The doctor peered at me like I was Oliver Twist.

Minutes later, I was standing in front of a wall mirror in the dining room. I cut quite a figure barefoot in my underpants and tee-shirt, my thigh bandaged from groin to knee, hair tidy as a sheep's arse: face just as attractive. Hughie was grinning like a cartoon toad. The publican donated some stylish track pants and a jumper from the hotel's mothballed lost-property basket. I washed and changed in the bathroom. The morphine had me feeling as serene as a busload of Dalai Lamas.

I found Hughie at the bar. He handed me a beer. "Here's to Malcolm Halliday," I said, raising my glass.

"Who?" said Hughie, clinking glasses.

Two new policemen walked through the front door of the pub, sporting flour-sack bellies and expressions that said they wanted to hit things. Drinkers parted before them like the Red Sea for Moses.

The younger coppers abandoned their drinks as if they belonged to strangers and shot across the bar to shake the hands of their seniors. The quartet huddled for a while. Sue and Johnno brought the flour-sack men over to me and Hughie. They'd just been out to Moon Hill. The six of us went to the dining room and sat around a table.

"Now, Mr Hart," said the officer with the biggest head and greyest beard stubble, "you told my colleagues that a woman was murdered on your property earlier this evening. And that you shot a man, and killed a dog in your dam?"

"Yes."

"And you said you had a fight with another man in your treehouse. You clubbed him, and you think you seriously injured him too."

"Yes."

"And what were you doing at your property? Why did all this happen tonight?"

"There's no secret," I said. "A man was shot dead at my place a few weeks ago."

"Yes," the senior man said. "We were involved with that."

"Well. I made arrangements to meet your colleague, Detective Sergeant Warren Harper, at my property tomorrow morning to talk about my relationship with the dead man and do a walk around the site."

"DS who?"

"DS Harper. From the Homicide Squad in Sydney. He's working with the Tangleton Police on the Vagner case."

"I've no idea who you are talking about, Mr Hart. I've never heard of DS Harper. How about you, Frank?"

Frank wasn't a word waster. He shook his head in the negative.

It felt like my busload of Dalai Lamas was slamming, in slow motion, into a power pole.

Greybeard went back in: "Look, Mr Hart, I can see you're in some shock. I suggest you and Mr Jones stay here at the pub tonight. My colleagues, Sue and John, will stay with you. And we'll pick things up fresh in the morning."

"Fine by me," I said. "So what did you find at my property?"

"What did you expect us to find?"

"Sandy Wallace's body, for a start."

"There was no body, Mr Hart. There were no bodies at all. Not even a dead dog."

"You are fucking kidding."

"I don't kid about murder."

"Did you find anything?"

"Yes."

"What?"

"Are you insured, Mr Hart?"

"Why?"

"Just answer the question, please. House and contents? Car?"

"At my property? Well, my car was insured."

"There's not much of anything left out there, Mr Hart. There were fires burning when we arrived. Frank and I put an extinguisher on what we could. The car was a smoking heap. Most of your cabins are gone."

"Fucking bitch!" I barked.

"Do you mean the woman you say was murdered on your property?" said slit-eyed Frank, perking up.

"No, no – I mean one of the raiders. She stole my research, or destroyed it. For fuck's sake."

"Calm down, Mr Hart," said Greybeard.

"So what are you saying? That I stabbed myself in the leg with a crossbow arrow? Made up a story about a dead woman and torched the place for insurance?"

"Look," Greybeard said. "There was some muck in the dirt near your campfire and stains on the timber deck that could be human blood, as you say. The forensic team will go out tomorrow. You get some rest tonight and we'll come back in the morning and drive out there together."

The four coppers walked to one side of the dining room and formed a huddle.

"It was her sidekick," I said to Hughie. "One of Baker's foot soldiers pretending he was DS Harper to lure me to Moon Hill and knock me off."

"For a bright bloke, Garsy, you've got a few light bulbs blown." Hughie scratched his chin. "Tell you what. I'm knackered. Let's do what the big plod says and get some shut eye. Everything'll be clearer in daylight."

Hughie and I shared a twin room upstairs. Sue and Johnno took separate rooms either side of ours. They were protecting us and boxing us in at the same time, which was pretty clever.

Hughie helped set me up in my bed with my gammy leg elevated on some pillows, then went downstairs to his ute to check on his dogs. A few minutes later, he walked back through the bedroom door with something long and slim, wrapped in a blanket tucked under his arm.

"No fuckin' bodies, eh," he muttered, sitting on his bed. "Tricky fuckers you're dealin' with, Garsy. They're tryin' hard to make you look like a liar. Doin' a darn good job too."

Hughie unwrapped his rifle from the blanket. He loaded it with a handful of shells from his trouser pocket. I didn't see what use the telescopic laser-sight would be at close quarters, but Hughie fiddled with it anyway. He laid the rifle on the floor by his bed, locked our door, and turned out the light.

I woke, groggy, to the sight of a figure standing in front of the window. "Oy!" I yelled, reaching to hurl the bedside lamp. Before I unleashed, I saw it was Hughie pissing out. He patted me on the head and went back to bed. I listened to him snoring.

I tried to ignore thirst, tinnitus, a headache, and throbbing in my leg. I couldn't beat the thirst so I limped along the hallway to the communal bathroom a few doors down. I flicked the light switch, but no light came on. Moonlight through a window helped me find the basin under a wall mirror. I turned the tap on and put my head down to lap the flow. I lifted my head to see two faces in the mirror. Hers was still wearing the stocking mask, though the eye and mouth holes had widened.

She jabbed the nose of the shotgun into my spine and nodded at a paper towel dispenser on the wall. "Stuff your mouth."

I hesitated.

"Do it, or I'll remove a kidney."

She wasn't hiding her Afrikaans twang anymore: no sweet, young Lady Dorchester or streetwise, Irish-American Ms Hoodie on the Brighton Beach steps. I guessed Afrikaans was her native tongue. I inserted the paper gag.

"Hands behind your back," she said. She slipped something around my wrists. I heard zipping and felt the band tighten.

"Hallway," she hissed.

At the end of the hallway, the door to the rear fire escape was ajar: nothing as flash as a door alarm in this joint. She jabbed my spine with the barrel and followed me outside, where we descended the metal steps into the car park behind the hotel. A handful of cars were scattered on the gravel lot, including the blue-and-white police car whose owners were dozing upstairs next to Hughie. A wind gusted at our backs, fluttering the leaves of scraggly gum trees that edged the carpark. The sky was thick with stars, but they were as useful to me as the rest of the town, which was in a coma from Friday night's bingeing.

"The van," she said.

About thirty metres away, in the corner of the carpark beside a cone of yellow streetlight, there was a white tradesman's vehicle, no windows in the back section. When we got to a few metres from the van, an owl hooted. It was sitting on the carpark fence. Its goggle eyes winked like an adjusting camera lens on something behind us. I didn't turn. A spot of red light wobbled upon the van's white paintwork, then disappeared. Ka-thack! I heard her shocked moan behind me. I spun around. She was staggering; white bone jutted from the elbow of her black jumper. She'd dropped her shotgun. She squatted, grasped the gun's stock with the hand of her good arm, got a finger inside the trigger guard as she stood, and swang the barrel at me. I kicked the muzzle as flame barked from its nostril. The percussion hurt my ears. I glanced toward the hotel. Hughie was stomach down on the ground, his rifle barrel propped on a boulder. His muzzle flashed. Thack! Her head whiplashed and her skull burst, spattering me with dark jelly. She reeled and dropped like a KO'd boxer. When her different body parts finished landing, nothing twitched.

I fell back against the side of the van and slid down to sitting on the gravel. Hughie stood and marched towards me, barefoot in his underpants and singlet, his rifle tucked under his arm as if he'd done no more than ping a duck at a carnival shooting gallery.

"You alright, mate?" he called as he closed in.

"Top shelf." My right ear was still ringing.

Hughie cut my hands free of the zip locks with his pocket knife, and helped me stand. I bent over her body. I wanted to peel the leftovers of the stocking from her shattered face, to see if it really was the pretty young woman who had laughed alongside me at the bar of the Dorchester Hotel.

"Let's leave that for the pro's, mate" said Hughie. He flung open the side-door of the van, triggering the inside light.

"Fuck!" he yelled, flinging his rifle stock into his shoulder, his finger on the trigger. "Don't move, cunt."

He was aiming at a figure sitting on the floor, leaning against a sidewall of the van. Hughie's target stayed rock-still. Ms Hoodie had done her sidekick the favour of taking off his mask, presumably so he could breathe more easily. It was wasted effort. His chest and lap glistened with blood that had pooled on the floor around his arse.

Hughie lowered his gun. "Let's wake those dozy coppers."

"One sec," I said. The box with my laptop and *Ebola* documents was on the floor next to the dead man. I guessed they had wanted to "interview" me before they erased me and my jottings from the annals of human history.

"Let me pop this in your ute before we sound the alarm," I said, collecting the container in my arms.

"You right with that?"

"Right as rain." I hobbled along the footpath at the side of the hotel. I glanced back and saw Hughie standing over Ms Hoodie's body. He was going through her pockets.

LXII

HUGHIE and I did what a twelve-gauge shotgun blast and two cracks from a hunting rifle couldn't. We roused Sue and Johnno from under the blanket of the hotel bed they were sharing.

By 1am, the dynamic duo was dressed and phoning their seniors from Canterwell, who contacted some real homicide detectives from the city and informed them about the shootout at the Tangleton Hotel.

I phoned Jack, then Steele. After we'd briefed the sheepish police couple about what happened in the carpark, Hughie and I tried to get some kip. It was comforting, like being at home in Darlinghurst, drifting in and out of consciousness to the sound of sirens and blinking lights through the windows from the arriving police cars and ambulances. All I missed was Fish's alto voice.

About 7am, Hughie and I entered the dining room for breakfast.

"Good morning, love birds," called Steele, not bothering to stand. He was sharing a table with a handful of newspapers, a coffee cup, a plate of toast crumbs, and his laptop which was connected to a wall socket by a long cord that I nearly tripped over with my gammy leg.

He informed us that he had arrived soon after daybreak and had already learned some interesting stuff by milking the pub's big-eared staff, as well as weary coppers whose numbers were multiplying around town like flies on a dropped chop at a BBQ as "the body count grew".

"What body count?" I said.

"A crew took a cadaver dog out to your place at first light. There was blood on your deck, and down by the dam. But no bodies, mate."

"I know that."

"Well, the crew had the bright idea to follow some tyre tracks from your place that went into the forest. A German Shepherd named Ralph sniffed out a woman's body, a dead dog, and a fat man's corpse settling into a swamp about a kilometre from Moon Hill."

We made instant coffee at an urn that was sitting upon my reclaimed operating table. The tablecloth had a few suspicious dark stains underneath small boxes of rice bubbles and corn flakes and a couple of glass bowls of tinned prunes and apricots. Outside the window, television news helicopters fluttered in the sky.

"Stainless!" a male voice called from behind me.

I turned and recognised the TV reporter from the court-house lift the day Henry East was sentenced. He put his hand on Steele's shoulder.

"Help me with the lowdown here, mate," he said to Steele. "We need to interview someone. I want the bloke who shot that masked woman out the back of the pub. And the guy who was attacked at that farm last night. Know where they are?"

"Shit, Donny," said Steele, "I think the victim has gone into police protection. Hasn't he, Rosco?" Steele directed the question at me.

"Yeah," I said. "That's what I hear."

"So who are you, mate?" said Donny, glancing at me before adjusting his necktie using the wall mirror at my back.

"He's a local bush foods entrepreneur," said Steele. "Black Snake something. What is it, Rosco?"

"Black Snake Organic Bush Foods."

"You're a great help as always, Stainless," said Donny, scanning the room for more interesting people. "Look. We're choppering out to the other crime scene where the dog found those bodies. I'd give you a lift, but you know how it is. Insurance, and all that, these days."

"Sure," said Steele. "Love your work, by the way. Never miss it."

Donny dashed.

Steele said to me in a low voice: "You and Hughie ought to scarper or these clods are going to stuff up your yarn. What are you code-naming it? Revolver?"

"*Ebola,*" I said. He was right; it was time to get back to Sydney, gather *The Citizen*'s troops and pound the keyboards for publication ASAP. "Before I hit the bitumen, anything else you can enlighten me with?"

"I suggest we retire to your room," Steele whispered.

On the way upstairs, Steele winked at the publican's wife, who was exiting a door labelled *Private – Office.* I frowned at him.

"What?" Steele protested with the expression of the falsely accused.

In our room, Hughie boiled a kettle and made cups of tea while Steele and I sat on the bedsides and faced each other.

"That sumo wrestler you smacked over the head in the treehouse," said Steele. "You probably didn't kill him. He had two holes in his head this morning – made by bullets."

In other news, inside the spare-wheel housing of the stolen plumber's van at the back of the pub, the police found a backpack. Inside that they found a cigarette packet stuffed with a few baggies of crystal meth, a glass pipe, a handful of passports, and wads of cash in US dollars, Pounds Sterling, Euros, and Australian dollars.

"Cash must be king for the meth-flying international assassin," said Steele. "Credit cards leave such an unhelpful trail of evidence, don't they?"

Ms Hoodie's original ute, the one they drove to Moon Hill, was abandoned beside the local park a few blocks from the Tangleton pub. She and her friends had a radio scanner, tuned to the local police radio frequency. No wonder they knew exactly where I was at the hotel last night.

"The woman Hughie shot," said Steele, "she had a UK and an Italian passport, like her boyfriend. Your Kojo had an Indonesian passport, and get this – he had a photo of that whacko North Korean dictator tucked inside his wallet like a lover's portrait."

"What were her names?"

"The coppers are withholding the names while they continue their inquiries."

"Come on, mate."

Steele thumbed the pages of his notebook: "Anne Darcy … and … her Italian passport … Lucia Bresi."

"Him?"

"Mark Darcy … and Carlo. Carlo Bresi."

"How sweet. So they could have been brother and sister. Or husband and wife?"

"They're bullshit names," said Steele.

I didn't care. Anne Darcy would do.

Hughie drove us a few blocks to the Tangleton Police Station. A handful of reporters and cameramen were hanging around the front. Luckily I didn't recognise any of them. Hughie rolled down the driveway at the side and parked next to the coppers' town cars and two squad cars. He pulled a battered fedora from behind the headrest of his driver's seat and plonked it on his head, pulling it low at the front. He handed me a pair of ugly, wraparound sunglasses from his glovebox, a perfect match for my hand-me-down track pants. As we stepped out, a couple of reporters ambled down the driveway towards us. Hughie had a shovel and a rake on the back of his ute; he took the digger and handed me the rake. As the reporters approached, he called to them: "We've got work to do and we don't get Sunday penalty rates anymore. So if ya don't mind …."

We got stuck into the garden beside the back entrance to the station, turning over soil and raking leaves. When the reporters strayed back around the front, Hughie and I slipped inside and signed our statements about last night, after which we were given permission to leave town. Hughie volunteered to drive me back to Sydney.

We were soon cruising on a sealed road through hills of green pasture peppered with sheep and cattle, en route to the motorway. Hughie's dogs shot back and forth across the rear tray, biting the wind as if it was a juicy leg of lamb. Hughie lifted a hand off the steering wheel and cocked his hat. He reached into his door's side pocket.

"Got a present for you."

He passed me a sky blue telephone handset. "It's Anne Darcy's. It was tucked in her pants."

"You are a genius."

I still had the Tangleton publican's phone in my tracksuit's hip pocket. I'd post it back to him. I phoned Steele on it.

"Anne Darcy," I said. "Did you write down her date of birth from those passports you had a squiz at?"

"Why?"

"I'm trying to break a code."

Steele read me the DOB, the same for her British and Italian passports. I guessed that having the same birth dates would make it harder to be tripped up if you were ever grilled by the authorities. I just wanted the four digits of her birth year. It's amazing how unimaginative most people are. I keyed them into her phone. *Bong-bong!* No go.

"Fuck!"

"Reverse it," suggested Hughie.

Bong-bong!

It's a funny thing about persistence: after about five minutes of playing with her birth date combos, I struck gold. I phoned Steele back using the publican's loaner.

"I need your help on one other thing," I said. "You know all the background on Bart Hills' OD, right? You know what happened to Henry East in Silverwater Prison. You know about the Hannibal Ellis stuff when that psycho strangled Henry. I want you to write it up for us. For *The Citizen.*"

"Oh right, *The Daily News* will be very happy to see me moonlighting for your tin-pot online outfit."

"Use a pseudonym."

"What, like Anne Darcy?"

"Sure."

"You paying for this?"

"Mate's rates, of course."

As Hughie turned onto the motorway, I was deep into Anne Darcy's emails, call logs and contact lists. I called

Jack about an item and a name I found in her calendar. On the basis of that information, Jack moved forward his flight to Sydney.

LXIII

AROUND lunchtime the following day, I waved to Jack as he wheeled his bag out of the customs gate into the arrivals hall of Sydney International. He looked fresh and smug like the rest of the travellers who'd slept horizontal in the pointy end of the jet.

"So he's still on his way here?" he asked, throwing his bag into the boot of a taxi.

"No indication otherwise."

Seated beside Jack in the back seat, I opened Anne's phone, tapped on her text messages and handed it to Jack.

"Look at the message chain."

The handset held records of almost daily dialogue between Anne and a character named *Noah*, or *Noah X*. I had studied the prolix linguistic style of their exchanges; I wasn't sure if the X was amorous. Yesterday, as she laid dead in a hospital morgue in Canterwell, she had received a text that said: *Update?* After opening her phone in Hughie's car en route to Sydney, I had replied: *Contract signed off*. The response was immediate: "*Excellent. Arriving as planned. Noah X.*"

In the calendar on Darcy's phone, she had a meeting sched-
uled with Noah for 10pm on Tuesday. Today was Sunday.
The calendar entry listed an address: *Rozelle Bay Super Yacht
Marina, Sydney.*

"So you reckon Noah is John Baker?"

"That's my guess. Plan A is that she sneaks into Australia,
finds out everything we know, and takes me out - Claire too
- then she picks her way through anyone else who's a risk:
so *sayonara*, Sandy Wallace," I said. "And then, with our
knowledge in their bag, they can dust their tracks and build
the counter-PR to anything we might publish."

"What's his yacht called again?"

"Electra2. See those last two weeks of messages between
Anne and Noah? In one, he attached a picture of the Panama
Canal. Then there's a snap a few days ago of Papeete harbour
in Tahiti. He must be on his way here to pick her up."

"You sure he thinks she's still alive?"

"Who knows if he's reading any news from Australia, but
no names have been publicly released from the shootout.
Not yet. The police are withholding them while they make
their inquiries."

"But Steele has the names?" quizzed Jack.

"He didn't get that info from the police. He's playing his
public reveals by the rules because he'll be *persona non grata*
with his copper sources if he breaks from the barrier without
their green light."

Jack turned his palms up at me, as if he was waiting for me
to throw him a ball.

"The publican's wife slipped them to him. The silly plods
used the pub's digital photo copier. It has a memory,"
I added.

Jack shook his head in admiration of a master craftsman.

I said: "As long as Anne Darcy stays in touch with Noah, we can keep him on course."

The taxi took us to Jack's regular Sydney hotel in a converted Victorian terrace house in The Rocks district at the southern end of the metal coat hanger otherwise known as the Harbour Bridge. By nightfall, Jack, Claire and I were pushing four desks into a crescent shape in *The Citizen*'s office at Circular Quay: one desk each, for our laptops, and connected screens so we could sit side-by-side and share our work. The spare screen, the biggest, was for tele-conferencing, and watching online TV and broadcast news. We synced our war room with Sarah and Cliff in London, and Zi in Shanghai.

Anne's phone held a treasure trove of photos. My favourite was a happy snap; Baker, Charles and Henry East, the many-chinned former British Prime Minister, Tim Winter, and Muammar Gaddafi and his son, Nasser. The cheesy sextet was toasting a racehorse with a winner's garland around its neck at Tripoli's Abu Sittah racetrack.

My second favourite was a selfie of Anne and Baker, wet-haired in swimsuits on the tailboard of Electra2, their arms around each other's shoulders, set against coconut palms on a white beach.

Electra2 was an impressive beast. In one picture, Baker waved down at the photo's snapper from a helicopter on the landing deck of his multi-storey yacht on a sunny day. I recognised the backdrop of glitzy, cliff-side apartments of Monaco bay; I'd seen them in magazines.

*

Just after sunrise, Jack and I caught a water taxi from a jetty near his hotel and travelled for about twenty minutes along the western edge of the city to the Rozelle Super Yacht Marina. After getting our bearings on where Baker and his boat were due to dock tomorrow night, we returned to our war room and spent the rest of the day writing and conferring with London and Shanghai. Moby Dick was taking shape.

At dusk, Jack, Claire and I donned cloth bibs in a Rocks restaurant and attacked chilli crabs with tools fit for a dentist, drank beer, and dissected the contents of Henry's diary and his audio recordings. Jack had a problem.

"Henry East is really the only person talking to us on the record. And he's dead."

"It's pretty good talking," I said. "But I get your point. How about we call Sarah? If we ask nicely, we might get her friend on the record."

I dialled Sarah who promised to call us back in our office in an hour. She was good to her word. Jack and Claire sat beside me as I opened the batting over the speaker phone.

"*Bonsoir*, Gar."

There was no mistaking the voice of the woman I'd spoken to by phone from China inside the sleeping shark restaurant. "We need someone to say what you told me in Shanghai – on the record. Otherwise our story will fly like a lead balloon."

Seconds passed.

"You can use my words."

I inched further in. "Can we call you a former Cavalcade executive, if that is what you are? Is that okay with you?"

"Will that have impact?"

"Better if we had a name, a real name."

Jack said: "We understand you need to be protected."

Coughing. Small, weak hacks. Wheezing. "My past has caught up with me, I'm afraid."

"What's wrong?"

"I ran a hospital: near a mine in South Africa."

"What sort of mine?"

"Diamonds. But there was asbestos too. I have it in my lungs, Gar. It can't be fixed."

"Can you keep talking? Do you need a rest?"

"No."

"How did you get involved with Cavalcade?"

"They supported my medical charity. International aid."

"Are you a doctor?"

"Nothing as glamorous. I'm a nurse."

"You ran the charity?"

"I started it. Then years later, Cavalcade came in and supported it."

"Generous John Baker."

"Yes. That's him. John Kingsford Baker."

"What is the charity?"

"The Marais Foundation."

"As in Jean-Paul Marais? The man who drowned at sea?"

"Yes."

"And your name is?"

"Julianne. Julianne Marais."

"Jean-Paul was unmarried, no children."

"I'm his sister."

Jack, Claire and I exchanged glances, eyebrows lifted.

"So is the charity still running?"

"Yes. It says a great deal about Mr Baker's fine character to support a lasting tribute to his dead friend, doesn't it?"

"Do you run it?"

"Yes. But only on paper."

"So who does run it?"

"John Baker."

"So is he using it to wash money, to hide money?"

"He's been doing it for years."

"Did he kill your brother?"

"I believe so. He arranged it."

"Why didn't you tell anyone?"

"I had a daughter, Gar."

That silenced me.

"They took her once: only once. She was fifteen. They put a tattoo on her: a blue stick with a red notch, just the first notch. But they left room on the stick. Then they sent her home."

"Why are you talking to us now?"

"She is dead, Gar: a brain tumour. A few months ago."

"God. We're so sorry."

"What else can I tell you?"

"Do you know Charles East?"

"One of Baker's puppets."

"How did that start?"

"After the Global Financial Crisis, Baker stopped East from becoming bankrupt. He made me put Marais Foundation money into East's accounts."

"How did it work?"

"You mean the method?"

"Yes."

"There were many. But let's say we award one of East's international companies with a contract to provide water for a town in Somalia. In effect, he installs a rainwater tank with a tap in the town square and he bills us for building a dam and plumbing for several thousand homes. Multiply that project twenty or thirty times and you will see the picture."

"What are accountants like in Africa?"

"Oh, highly trained with impeccable ethics."

"Got any proof of the foreign aid scam?"

"The Marais Foundation records. And me."

"That's not good for you. Where are you now?"

"I believe it's called heaven's door."

"Can we quote you? As Julianne Marais, sister of Jean-Paul. Is it founder of the Marais Foundation?"

"Yes."

"Another thing. The people who just attacked me, one of them was carrying a photo of the North Korean leader. Any thoughts?"

"Baker loves being a hidden emperor. He's an expansionist. The North Koreans wanted to thumb their noses at the international sanctions. I believe Baker bought the Supreme Leader a Rolls Royce ... a Black Badge Ghost, or Phantom model, I recall. Something terribly apt like that, and had it shipped to Pyongyang from Shanghai in a container of Marais Foundation medical supplies. And he helped the regime get relatives into an elite boarding school in Switzerland under false names: The Rumsfeld Steiner School in Bern."

"How do you know this?"

"My foundation paid the fees. We enrolled the students with fake Chinese passports to get around the sanctions. The youngsters made connections with some powerful families: arms dealers, European Union politicians mainly. That is what the regime wanted: information about influential families."

"To blackmail them down the track?"

"Some people will do anything to protect their children."

"True," I said. "Fear of loss is a powerful weapon."

"So is love. Are you open to advice?"

"Fire away."

"You need to strike Baker very hard, and hit him now. Publish what you know to set other people chasing him. If you don't, he will send others after you. Don't think the Darcy's were the only ones he had."

"The North Koreans?" I said.

"He is very United Nations in his hiring policies."

"Anne Darcy. Do you know where he got her from?"

"Baker has sponsored an orphanage in South Africa for over two decades. She was his adopted daughter. He collected several children, though Anne was his favourite."

LXIV

UNDER a moonless sky, a matt-black jet ski went airborne over a white-capped swell on the western Pacific Ocean. The passenger hugged the driver's waist and the wetsuit-clad riders rode the bump. The driver flicked the headlight off. She sliced across the windswept chop and closed in on the cruising hulk of a five-storey motor yacht. The driver accelerated to the yacht's tailboard, manoeuvred alongside it and matched her quarry's speed.

Her passenger threw two black backpacks onto the tailboard, dismounted from the ski's saddle and stepped with the poise of a panther onto the board, her feet finding grip on its slip-proof surface. She took a rope from a pack, tied it to a bollard on the yacht and threw its looped end to the driver, who grasped it with one hand. The driver gave her hand-throttle a burst and the ski shot forward, slackening the rope which she now grasped with both hands.

As the rope tightened from the pull of the yacht, the driver slid from her craft into the sea, her body aquaplaning in the wake of the bigger vessel. Her companion hauled her out of the water. The bobbing jet-ski fell behind them. Another ski was strapped to a platform on the far side of the tailboard, its prow painted with the word, Electra2. A key was in the ignition. One woman stuffed it in her backpack.

The black-clad figures, wearing water-proof hip holsters and handguns, donned the backpacks and crab-walked along the outer deck, checking for human movement inside. A handful of crew were sitting on sofas in a stateroom, watching a movie on a large screen. The intruders dropped to their stomachs and crawled past the windows.

At the front of the main deck, they arrived at a large, opaque hatch-cover that was partially open. One of the women pulled the hatch up; it locked at a forty-five-degree angle. She put her head inside and scanned the room below. She gave her companion a thumbs-up, removed her pack, and descended feet first through the hatch. Her companion lowered the packs into the hole and followed her leader inside.

The spacious, unoccupied bathroom was walled and floored with white marble. Gold taps dressed the twin showers and a sunken spa bath. The women stepped into an adjoining dressing room and tucked their packs into a wardrobe, moving a stack of towels to make it harder to see the packs if the door was opened. They hung their guns side by side on wall hooks in the bathroom. The young white woman and the young black woman, who were of similar size and shape, peeled back the hoods of their rubber suits and washed the sea salt from their faces in the benchtop sinks.

"I am going to have someone's guts for garters," boomed a male voice from behind them.

In the wall mirror above the sinks, the women observed the white-towelling-robed figure of the master and commander of Electra2: John K. Baker.

Baker, framed in the bathroom's open doorway, sipped champagne from a flute, his robe loose, revealing glimpses of his naked, plump body.

"No alarms. Nothing," he growled. "Either you two are very good, or what I have on board right now is the most cretinous security team in the free world."

The white woman fluffed her finger-length, platinum blond hair: "That's why Anne ordered these test runs, John. You've got more holes to plug here than poor Seth's hair stitcher used to have." She waved a key at him. "One of your geniuses left this sitting in the ski."

Baker shook his head. He'd scorch his crew later. "Take those wetsuits off and I'll pour you girls a drink."

"Have you heard from her?" said the white woman, unzipping her wetsuit from neck to navel and peeling it from an arm like a layer of black skin from white underlay.

Baker studied her taut body like a farmer might review livestock. "Yes. I believe we are about to pull the curtain down on this most sordid fuck-up."

The black woman had a shower. The white woman dressed in a bathrobe and followed Baker through the bathroom door into the circle-shaped master bedroom of Electra2. Baker stepped to a wall-side bar, poured plenty of vodka into a glass and handed it to the woman, who gulped it down. It had been cold on the ocean, riding the ski from a fishing boat launch-ramp on the nearby coast to intercept Electra2. The white woman enjoyed the warm feeling the alcohol gave her. She would have a hot spa bath – after she had gleaned further news of Anne Darcy's mission from Baker, who was their mutual employer and lifelong guardian – the man who had trained all three young women to call him "father".

The black woman entered the bedroom wearing a towel around her waist. Baker handed her a glass of vodka which she grasped and tossed down her throat as eagerly as her companion had. Baker re-filled the women's glasses, trying to hide a growing smile.

He picked up a remote control from the bar counter and dialled a music station named Psychedelic Chill into the room's sound system, setting the volume to background. He glanced at his wristwatch and said: "We are going to have a party tonight. A pre-celebration."

At the word "pre-celebration" the women winced.

They looked up to the ceiling – into the fisheye lens of a micro-camera – then at the empty glasses in their hands. They shook their heads in synchronicity at their stupidity: the guards had dropped their guard.

They knew this room: the CCTV camera – *if* it was live and transmitting to the yacht's master control room and its duty security officer – would show a blinking pinprick of green light on its casement. It showed nothing. So unless it was broken, they knew Baker had one of his games in mind, and he didn't want to be observed.

The room in which they stood was large enough to hold twenty people or more, if they were standing, or sitting on the leather-upholstered bench seats that curled around the mirrored walls. The women knew the room was occasionally used as a theatre on that scale – where the intermingling of people and occasionally animals was amplified by the mirrors – but it was also used for more intimate gatherings. Its centrepiece was a massive, circular bed. Inserted into the mirrored ceiling above the bed were a handful of hooks from which chains and leather straps dangled, rigged to pulley systems.

The white woman's legs felt like jelly. She stumbled back and dropped on her bottom on a bench seat against a wall. The glass fell from her hand. She glimpsed Baker opening a cupboard in the adjoining kitchen, from which he extracted a wine-bottle-sized gas canister that was attached to a tube with a clear plastic face mask on the end of it.

LXV

AT MY desk in *The Citizen*'s office, I sipped from a cup of muddy coffee. Julianne Marais' revelations about Anne Darcy's childhood had left me in a rare mental state; the last thing I wanted was alcohol. I wanted to think with a clear head about the little bit of her life that I'd learned of.

I flicked through handwritten notes I'd made during Julianne's call. Anne had been taken from an orphanage in Johannesburg at the age of four to live with Baker and a nanny in London. At this time, Baker was still employed by the French bank BKP Nouveau, so it was many years before he set up his own international finance shop, and his own charitable institution. He was clearly a long-range planner. Anne had spent her teenage life swinging from country to country under many forms of tutelage, including boarding at the elite Rumsfeld Steiner School in Switzerland, followed by a stint at a military academy in South Africa, after which she joined Baker's personal security staff and teamed with Seth Vagner.

"That child was trained from birth to be a mercenary," Julianne had said. "And so were some other boys and girls. I will send you something."

"You are very brave," I had replied, referring to her agreement to be quoted by name.

"That part of my character has experienced a long and painful birth, sadly."

"I believe I know how you feel."

My note checking was interrupted by the *bing* of an arriving email. My extra-sensory-perception was in sparkling form; either that or it was a pure coincidence: the bing heralded a missive from Julianne which contained a link that connected me to a YouTube video: Muammar Gaddafi, wearing a shiny gold kaftan, swept through a girls' school in Libya. The voiceover said he was selecting girls to take to his Tripoli palace for "education". Seth Vagner trailed the entourage, dressed in a short-sleeved camouflage uniform with a pistol holstered on a hip. A pixie-faced Anne Darcy, wearing a matching uniform and sidearm, followed Vagner, as did a handful of other women.

These were Gaddafi's famed Perfumed Assassins, or Amazonian Guard, as some media outlets had dubbed them, the sisterhood of women Julianne had first told me about during our phone conversation in Shanghai. The dictator apparently deemed female bodyguards more trustworthy than men, more compliant, and some were well-trained and capable in war craft. They looked good in uniform and were trained in bed craft too. Ultimately, as Julianne told me, they were as disposable as paper plates.

A second email arrived from Julianne, an extract from a Gaddafi speech: *To the Women of Sabha, October 4, 2003: ... We must train women to place explosives in cars and blow them up in the midst of enemies, and blow up houses so that they can collapse on enemy soldiers. Traps must be prepared. You have seen how the enemy checks baggage. We must fix these suitcases in order for them to explode when they open them. Women must be taught to place mines in cupboards, bags, shoes, children's toys, so that they explode on enemy soldiers."*

*

Jack went to his hotel for the night. I set my phone alarm for 4am and Claire and I settled into folding beds side-by-side in the office. When the alarm rang, I opened the fridge in the kitchen. Anne's phone was stored on a shelf in a plastic food container. It was charged and switched on so it would appear active if someone phoned or messaged her. If the caller had the ability to remotely turn on the microphone, they could listen to the hum of an electric fridge motor. I typed a text into her phone - staying true to her verbose lyrical form: *Progress?* - and hit send.

The reply was almost instantaneous: *On schedule. Noah X*

I returned to my cot and fell asleep, wondering if Baker and his boat would turn up at the marina at eleven o'clock tomorrow night, and if they did arrive, what sort of welcoming party we might arrange that wouldn't get us killed.

*

When I woke in the morning, Claire was dressed and sitting at her desk watching the TV news.

"Did we get a run?" I was wondering how the shootout at Tangleton was being reported.

"Your treehouse did. What a shame about that fire."

"Anne Darcy. Did they name her?"

"No. The police are still withholding the victims' names."

"Excellent."

It was 6.19am in Sydney, according to the office wall clocks, which showed 8.19pm the previous day in London, and 3.19am today in Shanghai.

I walked, not limped, to the bathroom with little pain. Impressed with the surgical skills of Dr Clydesdale, I wrapped my bandaged leg in cling-film, had a shower, shaved and dressed in a suit that I kept in my office wardrobe.

Rain lashed the windows of Gunnaroo Tower. I used binoculars to scan the waterway under the harbour bridge that Baker's yacht would have to navigate to get to the marina. It didn't worry me that the rain blurred my vision. Bat Kelly was our eyes and ears, stationed at the marina carpark. I phoned him.

"A seagull just shit on my windscreen, like, but the rain washed it off. So I have a clear view: nothing to report."

At 7am, Jack, Claire and I video-linked with Sarah, Cliff and Zi.

I'd already penned on a whiteboard in our boardroom the headlines and summaries of the package of stories we would unleash soon on *The Citizen*'s website. I orally top-lined the content to the team:

Lords of Thieves – The Hidden Vaults of Muammar Gaddafi

Jack and I had written an overview of Gaddafi's money-hiding network to accompany the world map. We speculated that John K. Baker may be just one of a web of treasure keepers who, today, were running rogue, years after the dictator's death and the geographic splintering of his family and his cronies.

Birth of the Falcon Master

Sarah and Cliff profiled Baker and the history of the Cavalcade Group, including the probable murder at sea of his partner, Jean-Paul Marais, and the links to the Gaddafi regime starting amid the Global Financial Crisis in 2009. They referenced Baker's recorded death threats and assertion to Henry East, Bart Hills and Jamie Carter that he had made them his hunting falcons.

Born to Rule

Claire profiled the East family, including Charles' eugenicist father, Sir Arthur, and his view that criminals should be sterilised to prevent them from breeding. She also profiled Helen Yee, her family, and the secret birth of Charles' twin sons.

Inside the Insider

I detailed Henry East's insider trading conviction and his prior fall, with Carter and Hills, into the clutches of Baker. I quoted his diary, and his secret recording of his father in the car threatening to have Hills killed. I also quoted from my interview with Henry's husband, Max Gleason. I'd negotiated with Gleason to use his words, but not mention their marriage or Gleason's name. In my copy, Gleason became "a close friend of Henry East".

The Keepers of the Keepers

Steele chose a pseudonym named after a house paint he saw in a hardware store window: Sienna Blue. Sienna profiled Charles East's keeper, Seth Vagner, a former South African soldier and Gaddafi security consultant, and explored Bart Hills' suspicious heroin OD. Sienna also described Henry's original faked suicide attempt, where his lips were slashed by hired bikies, and his subsequent murder at the hands of Stanley "Silverwater Hannibal" Ellis in a prison psychiatric ward after Henry threatened to reveal his father's and Baker's secrets.

I borrowed Sienna's penname to describe the electrocution murder of Henry's psych nurse, Bruce Tyson, based on an anonymous, eyewitness account.

Under my own name, I'd written a firsthand account of Sandy Wallace's life leading to her slaughter at Moon Hill.

The Magic Red Box

Jack and I described how deals like the Red Box telco scam, and the Silver Eagle office fraud in Brazil, were the key to Baker's method for hiding money for Gaddafi.

The Mother

We quoted Julianne Marais extensively about her blackmail via the abduction of her daughter and the lifelong threat to her child's safety, orchestrated by Baker, and explained Baker's corruption of the Marais Foundation.

The Rolls Royce Ghost, the Swiss School and the Supreme Leader

I described the discovery of the North Korean leader's photo in the wallet of the dead man called Kojo, and the assertions by Julianne Marais about Baker's links to the regime's elites.

When we ended the conference call, I had one unfinished story. I had given it the draft title: **The Short Life of Anne Darcy.** I worked on it during the afternoon. I was rocked a little when Steele waved his wand and conjured up some police crime scene photographs from the various death sites in the mountains, including several from the carpark of the Tangleton Hotel, which he emailed to me and that I shared with Claire and Jack. Anne looked so small. I couldn't hit the last full-stop until I had spoken to her adoptive father. And he was close.

LXVI

INSIDE the master bedroom of Electra2, the black woman lay naked on her back, her legs spreadeagled, her wrists and ankles chained to the underside of the circular bed. Teeth marks on her skin were weeping. Love bites, Baker called them. Her eyes flickered; she was waking up.

Baker, unclothed, strolled around the bed, studying her, drinking champagne. He tapped on a small glass screen on the wall and the room-lights brightened. He put on a pair of eyeglasses that hung on a strap around his neck and leaned down to more closely observe her flesh. He sniffed her skin; *peppery* was the word he thought of.

The white woman was sitting on the wall seat and holding a plastic mask over her mouth and nose, breathing gas through a tube from a hand-held canister. She was glad of the euphoriant effect of the nitrous oxide, the way the laughing gas transported her from where she was, even for a short time, for she was sickened by the odour and touch of the man who wanted her to call him Daddy when he was in this mood, when he was fuelled by this gas and intermittent whiffs of amyl nitrate and pills of Viagra. She was thinking that Anne knew how to manage him, how to make him jump at times like a circus dog through rings. Anne had always taken the brunt of him, ever since they were saved, as Baker described it to them, from the orphanage. The three children were not blood-relatives, but they had always called each other sister. When Anne gets here, the woman thought, we will execute our plan: we will make the Suicide Bag that she taught us about. Soon, this humiliation and pain will end. She breathed more gas, put the kit on a wall-side table, and stepped to the bedside, putting a key in the handcuffs to unlock her sister's chains. It was time to swap places, to share the load.

The black woman locked her sister down, while Baker took his turn breathing gas.

With her chin on the mattress, the white woman looked through the bathroom door into the adjoining dressing room at the wardrobe, inside which her backpack sat. She visualised what was inside it: another canister marked with the symbol N2O for nitrous oxide, but that was the only way it resembled laughing gas. She groaned … Baker was exploring her with a hand, or "pleasuring" her as he insisted on calling it. Only a little longer, she consoled herself: Anne will be waiting for us when we dock.

The whinnying of an excited horse entered the room, followed by the blubbering of its lips, as if the animal was pausing for breath. Silence. The sound repeated. Again. And again.

"Shit," Baker snapped. He stepped to a wall seat and picked up his whinnying phone. The screen said: *Shanghai - James Carter.*

"This better be fucking important," Baker growled.

"She's dead," Carter screamed. "She's been murdered: Mark and Kojo too. They're all dead."

Baker felt like he'd been struck a physical blow to the head. "Say that again."

"Anne is dead!"

Baker reeled, his body jerked, he staggered backwards, the laughing gas cocktailing with bursts of adrenalin triggered by Carter's words. He plonked on his bare buttocks on the leather wall seat. "Anne is dead?" he parroted, the objects in the room contorting as if he was sliding into a surrealist painting.

"*Mort*," said Carter.

The chained woman began thrashing at her restraints. Her sister began unlocking her feet and hand cuffs.

Baker tapped his phone's screen to activate its open speaker, and placed the handset upon the bench so he could massage his temples with his fingers. "How do you know this?"

"The media is reporting that four people were killed near Hart's property in the mountains."

"When?"

"The news is breaking now."

"How do you know Anne was one of them? Have the police named the names?"

"No."

"Then let's not jump at shadows. She's been sending us messages."

"We have a mole planted inside *The Citizen*," said Carter. "Anne was shot in the head in the carpark of a country hotel. I've seen the crime scene photos. Have you wondered why she hasn't actually called us? She is gone. No question. Hart and his scumbag journalist friends have set a trap. If you dock at that marina tonight, the police will be waiting. Do you hear me?"

The women huddled inside the bathroom. The white woman donned a bathrobe and whispered, "Anne had a premonition about this. That she might not see us again." The whites of her eyes were pink, their tiny capillaries bursting from the inflaming chemistry of grief and rage, but she had not cried in front of Baker since she was ten years old and she would not do it now, especially not now.

"So we go ahead?" the black woman whispered, letting a tear run down her cheek.

"Yes." The white woman collected her backpack from the dressing room cupboard, checked that the gas canister inside it was still intact, and extracted a medicine bottle. From the other backpack, the black woman removed two pairs of surgeons' gloves.

Shaking from the medicine bottle a large capsule into her hand, the white woman twisted the capsule's halves open and stepped into the bedroom, glancing to the ceiling's corner to make sure the CCTV camera's lights were still off. She picked up an open bottle of champagne from the bar counter and poured the sedative powder in, keeping her back to Baker.

"Here, John," she said, swivelling, handing Baker the bottle, knowing his habits under stress, "looks like you could use this."

He took it and swigged. And swigged twice more, until it foamed and spilled from his lips. He wiped his mouth with the back of a hand and leaned down towards his phone. "This mole of yours, Carter. Who is it?"

The white woman snatched Baker's phone and turned its power button off. Wearing gloves, the black woman, dressed in her wetsuit, its hood crumpled upon her shoulders, stepped out of the bathroom and aimed a pistol, silencer screwed on, at Baker.

"What *the fuck* are you doing?" Baker stood up, gripping the champagne bottle by its throat.

"Sit on the bed, John," the black woman ordered.

"Fuck off, Katya!" growled Baker, his face contorting as if he was confronting a creature from another dimension, an apparition. "You don't treat me like this! Ever!"

Katya stepped closer to Baker, holding the gun with two hands, and aimed at his heart.

"Have you gone mad?" said Baker.

"Try the reverse," she said.

"Look," said Baker. "I know you girls are upset about Anne. This is a shock, a terrible shock for all of us. She was my daughter, for God's sake!"

"She was your slave," said the white woman. "We were all your trained dogs."

Katya said calmly and firmly, "The bed, John. On three. Or I am going to send you like lightning to meet your ancestors. One ..."

Baker swigged champagne then shuffled towards the bed, his eyes darting, looking for a way out. He turned to the white woman. "What is going on, Dasha?"

"A tide is turning in all our lives, John."

"Stop the riddles, Dasha. What do you want?"

"You wouldn't understand."

"Try me."

"Freedom."

"Oh, for fuck's sake," said Baker. "How pathetically romantic."

"I said you wouldn't understand. Now get on the bed,"

"Fuck you," roared Baker, "you don't order me around."

Katya pressed the cold silencer of her gun against Baker's breast. He backed up and sat on the edge of the bed, placing the champagne bottle on the floor at his feet, slowly switching his grip on its neck so that he held it like a club.

"I gave you fantastic lives," said Baker. "I lifted you all out of the gutter in Johannesburg. You owe me."

"What do we owe you?" said Dasha.

Baker swigged. "Loyalty at least."

Dasha scoffed, "You just swapped gutters on us, John. Yours are made of gold, but you still showered us with piss and shit. And you've never stopped putting your hideous hands all over us."

Baker eyed a red button on the wall, a couple of body lengths away. All he had to do was hit it, or just fall on it – and the yacht's security team would swarm into the room. He set himself for the lunge.

Katya blocked his path. She grinned at him, challenging him to make a move.

"So this freedom thing. What's the plan?" said Baker. "You're not stupid enough to kill me."

"No, we're not stupid, John. Remember all those IQ tests you had us do before you'd take us from the orphanage? And the genetic analysis? We might have been unloved, but we came from good seed, didn't we, John."

"Fuck you ungrateful bitches," he roared, foamy mouthed. "You're nothing without me. I made you for fuck's sake!"

"Yes, John. You're God. How could we forget?" Dasha was smiling, weeping, trying to repel her thoughts about Anne.

Baker gripped the neck of the champagne bottle and hurled it at Katya's gun-toting hand, but he was groggy, slow. She sidestepped the missile. Baker charged towards the red button, right hand outstretched.

Dasha kicked Baker's ankles; he crashed to the floor, dazed, staring up at the button, trying to slam it but he kept coming up short. Dasha put her foot on his throat to stop him rising. His hands wrestled with her ankle.

She paused. It would be best if Baker was not bruised. The sedative was a fast worker, and Baker felt quite weak under her foot, but another minute or two would be helpful for what they had in mind. The room was silent. The three occupants swapped glances, the women's faces were expressionless, their voices mute. But the women couldn't hide their tears for their missing sister.

Baker gave up slapping Dasha's leg and focused his eyes on hers. He gasped, "You will inherit this. The world I have built. But not if you do things this way."

Dasha wiped her eyes and smiled. "You have a blood daughter, John."

"So?" he said. "There's plenty for you all. For you, Katya – and Anita."

"We've seen your last will and testament, Daddy," said Dasha, releasing her foot from his throat. "Princess Anita gets the entire palace. Any more last lies you'd like to tell?"

"Whad do you mean *last*," mumbled Baker. His tongue felt thick. He tried to move his limbs but they were leaden, useless.

Dasha nodded at Katya who placed her gun on the bench seat. The women teamed to lift Baker by his hands and feet and plonked him on the bed.

Baker, his eyes glazed, forced words from his lips. "People will come for you ... your future is pain ... terror."

Dasha smiled. "Old news, Daddy. Old news." She stepped into the bathroom.

The black woman began positioning Baker's limbs as easily if he was a doll. Although she felt it was overkill, she wasn't taking chances: she cuffed his non-preferred left hand to the bed and hoped he was feeling as vulnerable as she had felt moments ago.

Dasha emerged wearing surgeons' gloves, carrying her wine-bottle-sized gas canister which was labelled N2O, and a packet of bleach-wetted wipes that were good for destroying DNA. She placed her things on a wall-side table, unhooked the mask and the feeder tube from the real N2O canister and attached them to hers. Using a wipe, she cleaned the mask and tube as best she could of her and her sister's saliva and prints. She tested it by releasing a hiss of clear, odourless helium into the room. Baker tried to lift his head.

"Whath that?" His head fell back.

"Ever heard of a Helium Hood, John?" Dasha carried the kit to the side of the bed.

"Whath?"

"There's no pain. It's quite popular with people wanting to put a full stop on their lives."

"Su ... cide?" Baker's face contorted.

"Well deduced."

"You flugging blitch."

Dasha said, "It's an interesting sensation, isn't it, John: paralysis without unconsciousness?" She turned to her sister. "Katya, what do you think the crew is going to find in here later tonight, or in the morning?"

Katya replied, "I believe it will be a mystery." She removed Baker's sparkling wristwatch and put it on her own wrist, tightening its strap over her wetsuit sleeve.

Dasha stood over Baker's face, observing that his eyes were still open and, concluding that his brain was switched on in one way or another, she spoke slowly and clearly, "You see, John. No-one saw us come on board. You didn't get a chance to tell Carter we are here. And no-one will see us leave, if all goes according to our plan. Of course, there is always a risk, just like you said about Anne's last mission ... oh, didn't she tell you? This was going to be her last for you, whatever happened."

Baker gurgled.

She resumed, "You see, John. We are being forced to ad-lib here. We had planned this parting gift for you from all three of us, to be delivered on the high seas on the way home. But seeing that Anne won't be joining us, we are bringing the party forward."

She opened the helium canister's valve and placed the mask over Baker's nose and mouth, stretching the mask's elastic strap behind his paralysed head. She took her hands away and left the hood hissing on auto-pilot.

She lifted Baker's right hand so that it appeared to be holding the mask over his face, and kept the left handcuff on. "Given this posture, and the fact the canister is labelled N2O, the investigating authorities will probably conclude you died through *misadventure*. Your wrist shows no sign of trauma, I mean you can hardly pull against it, but you don't mind self-bondage games, do you? And here's another sweet to suck on: it is highly likely that when the canister bleeds out, there will be no trace of helium detectable. Nor will it be in your lungs. Although, why you would want to lie alone and naked and partly-chained to a bed may be outside a normal person's comprehension. But as I said, you are an A-grade deviant, John. So the pattern fits."

Katya stroked her chin. "I believe we need some window dressing. Something tasteful, a little panache. Are they in their usual place, Daddy?"

She stepped behind Baker's bar counter and opened a drawer from which she removed two gold rings that were too big for fingers. Returning to Baker's bedside, she placed one ring over Baker's penis and slid it down to the base. Through the other ring, she squeezed his testicles, one at a time. She said, "What games have you been playing, Daddy?"

As Baker's chest rose and fell, less and less perceptibly, Dasha walked into the dressing room and pulled her wetsuit on. She collected their backpacks, inside which were street clothes, several passports each, matching credit cards and cash in watertight bags.

The women tidied the bedroom and bathroom, aware their efforts would be imperfect, but likely good enough for their purposes, and used the bleach-wipes on the flat surfaces, glassware, handles and taps. Baker's chest had stopped moving. They put the used wipes in a plastic bag and stuffed it into their backpacks, which they donned and tightened over their shoulders.

After pulling their wetsuit hoods over their heads and locking their pistols in their hip holsters, they took a last look at Baker's body which was pale and already waxy-looking. In the bathroom, Dasha stood on Katya's shoulders, using the uplift to grasp the rim of the ceiling hatch and haul herself onto the deck. Then she lifted up the backpacks – and Katya. They backtracked along the route they had used to enter Baker's inner sanctum.

Standing on the tailboard of the cruising Electra2, they observed, through falling rain, the blurred lights of the coastline and approaching heads of Sydney Harbour. Electra2's jet ski was still in place. For the first time, the women were grateful for Baker's, and Anne's insistence that they regularly practice entering and exiting watercraft and buildings without trace. With any luck, the yacht's crew, or the police, might conclude the jet ski had slipped its bindings. Regardless, they were now free to take their chances. Katya unbuckled Baker's watch from her wrist, and dropped it into the ocean. Dasha took the ski's key from her backpack, while her sister undid its bindings.

LXVII

"THE WORD I'm hearing from homicide," said Steele, "is that one, or more, of the crew knocked him off. There's a five million dollar Patek-Phillipe wristwatch missing from Baker's wrist. One of a kind, apparently. And cash has disappeared from a safe."

Sitting in *The Citizen*'s boardroom, partaking of breakfast - black coffee from a paper cup - and eyeing the apricot heart of a Danish pastry, Steele explained to Jack and me what he'd gleaned about events after Electra2's captain opened the yacht's master bedroom door to inform Baker that they had entered Sydney Harbour, and that he should prepare for the routine inspection at the Rozelle Marina by Immigration and Border Protection officers.

Steele reached over the pastry and took a red apple from a plate of fruit. He sunk his teeth in and said between chews: "Baker was wearing a pair of cock-and-ball rings, and he'd been guzzling laughing gas ... It seems he overdosed on a cocktail of drugs doing some weird auto-erotic shit. But someone might have slipped him some dodgy gas. They're doing forensics ... What's your timing?"

"We are going to conference that now," said Jack. "Our competitors are starting to swarm all over this sordid event like——"

"Investment bankers on a dropped wallet," I quipped.

"I was going to say like journo's at a free bar," said Jack.

"Keep me posted, poets," said Steele, heading towards the door.

"Tom," I called. "What sort of dodgy gas?"

He turned and winked. "Barbeque. I don't know. It's just speculation. And killing a bloke to steal a watch like that? It's a bit hard to sell … I favour the romantic ending: he wanked himself to death." He bit his apple. "Truth? It's shaping as a serious fucking mystery."

Claire knocked on the doorframe and leaned in: "The focus on Baker and Cavalcade is heating up. BBC Worldwide and CNN are running stories about the boat. So are *The Financial Times* and *The Wall Street Journal* online. Our own story could break like wildfire all around us."

"Too true," said Jack. "We need to hit the button. I'll call London now and work it through."

Our lawyers had already spent days scouring our copy for defamation. We had written, and re-written, and re-written. We were ready for take-off, though last night's event necessitated some narrative extension and renovation. Claire and I set to it side-by-side.

Jack emerged from my private office: "We go today at 4pm Sydney time. That will make it 2pm in Shanghai, and 7am the same-day in London. That should give the local media in each region a good chance to pick up our stuff and fan the fires for us."

There was one last big job to do before we published: seek the comment of the people we were going to accuse. We had pre-prepared questions for each of them. All we really needed was a "no comment". At least we would have asked.

Sarah would go to East's associate, the former British PM, Tim Winter, in his Knightsbridge townhouse in London. Cliff would go to Nasim Naama in his Vienna apartment. Gaddafi was dead so he had no comment, which was handy for us. Ditto for Baker.

Claire would go to Charles East in Sydney, not least because I was still the subject of a court-issued Apprehended Violence Order that outlawed me from making contact with him, apart from by eyesight at a distance of no less than one hundred metres.

Jack and I sat silently at the boardroom table with Claire. She hit open speaker and dialled East's office. I turned a digital tape recorder on. We expected his admin assistant to block us at the first hurdle. She put Claire straight through.

"This is Charles East."

"Mr East, this is Claire Styler from *The Citizen*."

"Yes, Claire."

"I'm working on a story that relates to your business interests. I'd like to put some questions to you."

"Really. What's your deadline?"

"Now."

"That's short notice."

"Yes. I'm sorry."

"So ask me a question."

"How well did you know the British businessman John K Baker?"

"A little. I've just been reading about the terrible tragedy that unfolded at the marina last night. Truly awful business."

"How much money did Mr Baker lend you, to save you from bankruptcy?"

"Oh, Claire. You are so predictable."

"Can you answer the question, please?"

"Here's a quote, my dear, just for you. Would you like to record this, for accuracy?"

"I'm ready."

Charles said: "*The Citizen*'s allegations about me and my family are lies. One of its employees, Edgar Hart, has threatened the lives of me and my family. Those threats are the subject of criminal proceedings against Mr Hart. The Citizen engaged in a long-running vendetta against my son, Henry. That vendetta led to his death."

East paused. "Did you get all that, Claire?"

"Yes."

"Can I give you some personal advice, my dear?"

"If you must."

"Many years ago, your colleague, Edgar, printed some lies about me after I rejected his request for a job. As a result, he lost his job and, quite rightly, had a very hard time finding another."

Jack put his hand firmly on my arm.

"So," Charles continued. "I advise you to carefully consider your own future."

Claire took a deep breath and exhaled: "Did you send Seth Vagner to sexually assault me?"

"Goodbye, Claire."

LXVIII

The Citizen's worldwide platform launched our stories under the banner *Lords of Thieves*.

There was a risk that our work would burst as brightly as New Year's Eve fireworks, dazzling the crowd for a few moments, before the smoke cleared and the onlookers walked away looking for their next thrill, or a good sleep.

We would achieve little without buy-in from other media outlets, the big global ones. We knew English-language news leaders like the BBC and CNN were interested in what happened on Electra2. But would they bite the hook on our bigger story about *Ebola*? The clock on the twenty-four-hour news cycle ticked. We sat in our offices and scanned the websites of our competitors, looking for our blips on their online news radars.

"Tick, tock, beer o'clock," I said to Jack.

"Just a heart-starter," Jack agreed.

Claire nodded. I collected three coldies from the fridge.

A few sips in, specks appeared on the BBC, CCN, Sky News, China's state-owned CCTV, and the Arab-owned Al

Jazeera. Online, *The New York Times, The Wall Street Journal* and all the big London newspapers started quoting *The Citizen*'s revelations. It was done through gritted teeth, but they couldn't ignore us.

North Korea's propaganda unit responded to "The Rolls Royce Ghost, the Swiss School and the Supreme Leader" by releasing a statement saying *The Citizen* was a filthy, lying serpent created by the Five Eyes spy alliance of the US, the UK, Canada, Australia and New Zealand. Our bemusement evaporated when the unit released a follow-up statement saying that five officials had been rounded up and executed by firing squad for spying on behalf of Five Eyes. They uploaded a video to YouTube of a group execution. Who knew who those people really were, or when, where, why – or even *if* – they were shot? The unpredictable ripple-effect of our revelations was only beginning.

Claire called our attention to her screen. "Have you seen this just in from Cliff? It's running on a newswire out of Vienna."

The body of the former chairman of the Libyan Investment Authority has been found in the River Danube, city police said.

Nasim Naama was a subject of a damning series of news reports released today by the online publisher, The Citizen, *claiming Naama worked in concert with corrupt businessmen in Britain and Australia to thieve billions of US dollars from Libya through a complex secret network.*

The former Muammar Gaddafi confidant was privy to potentially damaging information, including on oil and armaments deals with Western governments.

A Viennese friend of Naama's, who did not want to be named, said, "For the old guys from the Gaddafi regime, he was a defector, a rat. For the rebels, he was also a rat because he did not defect early enough".

I took a break to call Kate, Alice and Hugo. Todd and I started arrangements for them to travel to Sydney from Ireland. Claire and I slept on the folding beds in our office again.

Claire prodded me awake just after 6am. Her eyes were pink. She was suffering sudden-onset conjunctivitis or she'd been crying. I leaned towards the latter conclusion as my eyes gained focus. They were angry tears, not sad.

"You need to read this," she said, thrusting a folded copy of *The National* broadsheet newspaper into my hands.

I sat on the cot's side and unfolded the newspaper. Charles East stared back at me from the front page under a massive headline: *Exclusive: Gaddafi's Henchmen Threatened to Kill My Family.*

In the photo, that occupied half the page, Charles looked almost working class; his reading glasses were hanging on a chain around the collar of an open-necked, long-sleeved white shirt. No gold cuff links. Cute. He was sitting at a kitchen table – there were no signs of the magnificent trappings of Tamerlane – holding a photograph in a frame like it was a precious baby. I had to concede he was good, very good; it was a picture of him squatting next to Ellen in her wheelchair, alongside Henry and his mother. Ellen was wearing a university graduation cap.

The newspaper read: "*Mr East refuted allegations made about him yesterday by a small circulation, far-left agenda, online only news platform.*"

The National did not deign to print *The Citizen*'s brand name in its pages but it reported that, contrary to our claims about Charles being a willing accomplice, a corrupt British businessman named John K. Baker had threatened to murder the East family if Charles did not do what Baker wanted. Charles made an error, he admitted, when Baker loaned him money years ago. The arrangement went sour when Baker entrapped his son, Henry, in a business deal without Charles' knowledge. Charles' fear of Baker had been vindicated by the fact that Henry had been killed in prison by a man who had been hired by Baker's people, led by a mercenary named Seth Vagner, and Baker's adopted daughter, Anne Darcy. I had to admire Charles bravely putting the boots into the dead.

Charles countered our recording of his in-car conversation with Henry – in which he had threatened to have Bart Hills and James Carter killed if they breathed a word of his dealings with Baker – by trumpeting a modern US President: it was fake news made up by *The Citizen* using actors, based on the anonymous hearsay of a close friend of Henry East that *The Citizen* claimed to have found.

His explanations, I conceded as I read, were as clever as the photo; they were littered with half-truths being portrayed as whole-truths, making it difficult for a casual reader to discern fact from fiction if they were to place our stories side by side with *The National*.

"It was Carl," said Claire, who sat beside me on the cot and put her head in her hands. "My husband leaked our information to East and Baker: some of it, at least."

"How?"

"His PR firm is working for East. Wordsworth Communications' name is on East's media release this morning, denying virtually everything we say."

"How did Carl know what we had?"

"I should have told you. He moved out a week ago, but he must have hacked my emails; he knew my passwords for months. I didn't see it until now. Maybe I didn't want to see."

"I'm sorry," I said.

She looked me in the eye. "East and Carl, they were all set up and ready to go with this reactive story, weren't they? Just waiting for us to alert them to our timing. And that was my call to East yesterday."

Jack walked in with a bundle of newspapers under his arm and aimed a grin at us that was fit for a Muppet. "Cracking coverage this morning; every major international news organisation is quoting us. London is ecstatic. We are on the map bigtime."

I passed Jack *The National*.

"Seen that," Jack said. "Those churlish pricks were never going to back us. Having that mob of fascists going south, when a hundred others are marching north with us, is no big deal."

"My husband leaked our information, from me to East," said Claire. "He's doing East's PR."

"Well, that's a slight problem if you're sharing pillow talk."

"We're not. As of last week. Well, longer actually."

"Good, because we have follow-up to do. Someone needs to hunt down the Foreign Minister, for a start. Zi called me this morning. James Carter has disappeared from Shanghai, leaving a trail of gambling debts and some bad people sniffing his scent."

"Claire and I will do it together," I said to Jack. "We'll do it by hoof."

Claire smiled a little. She phoned Ellen East and obtained a street address.

The Foreign Minister's residence looked like a stainless steel fridge with delusions of grandeur. At least it had a few windows. It was only a few blocks from Tamerlane, though it wasn't water frontage. Claire pressed the buzzer on the gate. A voice, admitting to being Carter, spoke to us through the intercom. No, he didn't know John K. Baker. And no, he didn't know anything about his son's business dealings with Baker and the East family, or his gambling debts. And no, he didn't keep tabs on his son's movements; he was an adult who made his own decisions. What a public-relations-trained prick: he was neatly disowning the problem child just like Charles did with Henry.

"What if I told you he'd won the Nobel Prize," I said into Carter's intercom, "would you know where he was then?"

Carter hung up. The outing was a waste of time on the information front, but it served its main purpose: the fresh-air and locomotion had perked Claire up.

Back in the office, eating an egg sandwich at my desk and thinking about how to open a follow-on story about East's test-tube babies, an email arrived from Julianne Marais, via Sarah in London.

"Well, well, well," I said to Claire, who was seated at the desk beside me, "Mr Carter senior has a very poor memory, or he doesn't know his wife very well."

Claire rolled her chair next to mine. We opened Julianne's document. It was a property ownership title for a Swiss ski chalet in the name of June Nancy Carter. Accompanying it was a legal contract and a mortgage document showing the chalet was purchased with a loan to lucky June provided by the Cavalcade Investment Group at zero interest payments with a 100 year term.

Julianne had signed off: *Baker gave things away, but he never let them go.*

*

A few days later, Carter resigned as a Government Minister but followed the convention of disgraced politicians and refused to resign from his parliamentary seat. So from the comfort of the backbench, with his taxpayer-funded salary still flowing, he worked with his lawyers on a plan to spill the dirt on his former best friend, Charles, and obtain immunity from criminal prosecution for him and his son, who was missing and for whom he held grave fears. He said publicly that he was "determined to do the right thing". He did not say that a criminal conviction would see him lose his lifetime parliamentary pension and its privileges.

A few days after that, *The Citizen* was contacted by the Australian Taxation Office. They were launching a probe into Charles East's businesses and asked if we could assist with any records we might have. Our lawyers said we could be subpoenaed to provide our data, and would most likely be raided if we resisted, so we jumped on the front foot, boxed up a package - leaving out the juiciest pieces that we were still working on - and handed it over. It not only got the ATO off our back, but in return, they told us the UK tax authorities had joined them in the hunt and were digging into the records of all the Cavalcade and Tamerlane group companies, including Shanghai-based Trust8 from which the former British PM, Tim Winter, very publicly resigned in horror and surprise at recent events. Winter leaped to the active defence of justice - after a mystery fire in Cavalcade's data warehouse in Scotland destroyed much of the company's history. In a media statement issued by his lawyers, Winter said he was providing Interpol, and tax collectors flying various national flags, with his complete co-operation.

The Stolen Asset Recovery Initiative, or StAR partnership, between the World Bank and the United Nations Office on Drugs and Crime, joined the party and asked us for any information we could supply.

"Fuck those people," said Jack. "They're more Baker than Baker."

I wasn't sure we wanted to get the StARs offside, but he was the boss, and I had other things to attend to.

Claire had a girlfriend, Denise from London, visiting Sydney in the wake of her separation from Carl, who had scarpered to Dubai to work as in-house PR for a luxury goods brand.

Claire invited me to dinner on Denise Worthington's last night. The three of us ate at a Japanese restaurant, one of those barbeque places where the chef throws the food and you catch it with your plate if you can.

"Catch her if you can," Claire said to me when Denise went to the bathroom.

"I already have a fish," I said. I think she thought I meant our poodle.

Denise gave me one of her business cards before Claire drove her to the airport. I put the card for Dr Denise Worthington. R. Psych. in my wallet. For Ron, I told myself, or maybe Hugo; he wouldn't go back to school.

That night I dreamed about Dr Denise. I paced the floor of her art deco consulting room. She was reclining on a chaise lounge beside a burning log fire. She had wavy blond hair and milky skin, just as in real life, and wore a sheer, clingy, green dress that failed to hide bullet-headed nipples that made me think of Mr Browning.

"Tell me about the cot, Gar. When you were a baby."

"I smeared my shit on the fly-wire sides. My mother was out. My father left me in the filth for hours until my mother came home and cleaned it."

"Is that why you relate to Henry East? Because you both shit in your nests."

"We had shit fathers."

"What was shit about yours?"

"He was always jumping in the cot with other women. It killed my mother."

"That's shit husband, not shit father."

"I just told you. He left me in the shit."

"What about you and your kids?"

"I changed their nappies. I would never leave my kids in the shit."

"You put them in the shit though, didn't you? Look what happened to Hugo."

*

Alice, Hugo, Fish and I collected Claire from her apartment. We drove out of the city, drinking coffee with the windows down on my new, old Defender. Fish sat in Claire's lap and thrust his head out the window to bite the air.

Hughie and his dogs were waiting for us when we arrived at Moon Hill. Spike and Clive didn't seem to notice Fish was missing a leg.

Hughie had repaired most of the burnt deck. The part-roasted pine tree was a shock. The front-end of the treehouse cabin had burned away, exposing the insides, but as I climbed onto the deck, I saw plenty of green shoots on the blackened branches.

Hughie had rigged a walk-in tent on the grass next to the deck for us to sleep in. He had also trucked in fresh timber to rebuild the treehouse. This one, we decided, would have a stairway curling around the trunk.

"Our first job today," said Hughie, "is to fix that flying fox."

He pulled an extension ladder from his truck and Hugo helped him stand it on the deck and lay it into the branches. The two of them set to work repairing the take-off platform.

Alice and Fish showed Claire around. While they were checking the yabby traps in the dam, I tied a rope to the end of the huge reel of new wire that Hughie had transported on the back of his truck. I tossed the rope to Hugo and they hauled the wire up. It took a couple of hours to secure and tension the connection between the tree and downhill post.

Hughie and I took a break and drank mugs of tea, dangling our legs over the deck, looking to the mountains. He took a part-burned scrap of paper from his shirt pocket and handed it to me. I recognised my father's handwriting.

"Thanks," I said, not sure if I meant it. Before the fire, the letter had been in a suitcase of memorabilia under one of the beds. I read the scrap:

…can't see why it helps anyone to drag this out. There's a will with my lawyer, his details are on the back of this. You should know you almost had a brother. A twin. He died inside your mother. What did you do to him? I'll be meeting him in a minute, maybe. I'll get his POV. There's a gun for you buried in your garden under that frangipani if you want to join us. Love, Dad."

"Funny bugger," said Hughie, sipping tea with one hand, offering me a box of matches with the other. "What did he have again?"

"Prick's Disease."

Hughie chuckled. I put the note and matches in my jacket pocket. Fish nuzzled my leg and I patted him. There was laughter inside the tree canopy. Hugo and Alice were teaching Claire how to ride the flying fox.

*

Thank you for reading *UNDER EDEN (Complete Edition, Parts 1-3).*

Gar Hart, Claire Styler, Jack Darling and the investigative team from *The Citizen* will return soon in *FBEyes* (working title), when they uncover corruption at the high-tech frontier of the global arms industry. The British Crime Writers Association Debut Dagger competition long-listed *FBEyes*. The Debut Dagger recognises outstanding work in development.

Please visit Mark's website at www.markfurnesswriter.com to learn more about *UNDER EDEN, FBEyes* and Mark's other published works. On the website you can also join the **Mark Furness Readers Club** where you can get FREE books as well as occasional news about future book releases.

Acknowledgements

Under Eden had a long birth. It started with my collected observations of human behaviour in corporate and political life over decades. The honest journalists I've met – of whom there are a few – are outsiders, observers. Spin doctors and lobbyists (both groups are often ex-journalists) like to think they are insiders, players not watchers. I've played the trifecta of parts. Everywhere I've stepped in business, politics and the media, I've come across some terrific liars with tremendous smiles and mind-boggling egos. In other words, I found a massive mine for creating entertainment, and a rich landscape for gathering occasionally glittering insights into human nature. Hopefully readers will find *Under Eden* usefully illuminating and amusing, at least in some small measure.

So to specific acknowledgments: I'd like to thank every shady character I've ever met – some living, some now dead – for contributing to *Under Eden*. Then there are the good, of which my immediate family Sarah, Holly and Minta top the list: they have watched over my shoulder – mostly wearing wry smiles, and more than occasionally rolling their eyeballs at my madness – as I brought this monster into the world. There's more on the way. The seeds are sown. I can see their eyeballs rolling.

www.ingramcontent.com/pod-product-compliance
Lightning Source LLC
Chambersburg PA
CBHW020652110726
47901CB00001B/155